Goosebumps

THE GRAPHIC NOVEL

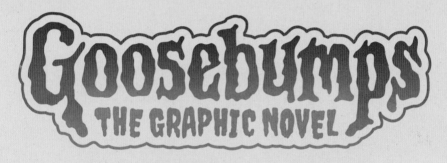

THE HAUNTED MASK

R.L. STINE

Goosebumps
THE GRAPHIC NOVEL

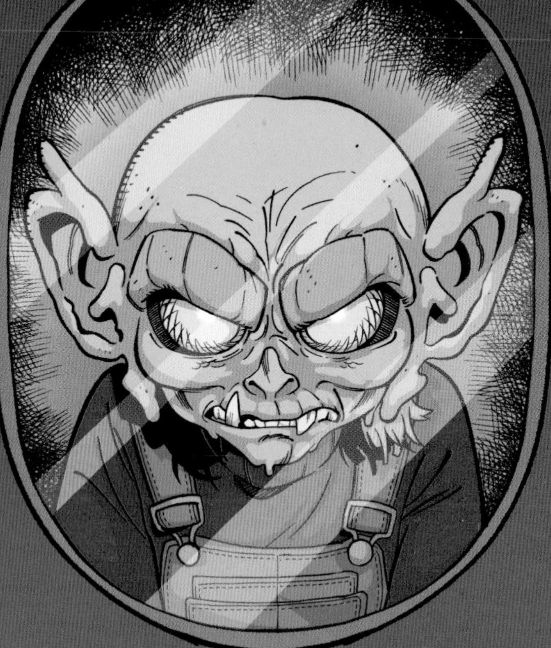

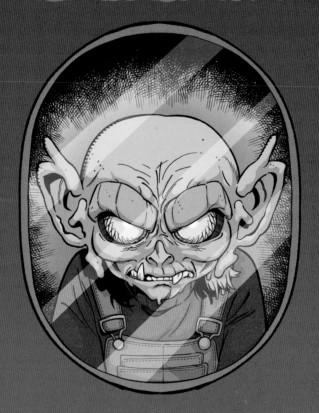

THE HAUNTED MASK

ADAPTED BY MADDI GONZALEZ
WITH COLOR BY COREY BARBA AND AMANDA BARBA

graphix
An Imprint of
SCHOLASTIC

Goosebumps book series created by Parachute Press
Text copyright © 1993 by Scholastic Inc.
Art copyright © 2024 by Maddi Gonzalez

ISBN 978-1-338-87940-7 (hardcover)
ISBN 978-1-338-87939-1 (paperback)

10 9 8 7 6 5 4 3 2 1   24 25 26 27 28

Printed in China 62
First edition, September 2024
Edited by Anna Bloom
Color by Corey Barba and Amanda Barba
Lettering by Jesse Post
Book design by Larsson McSwain
Creative Director: Phil Falco
Publisher: David Saylor

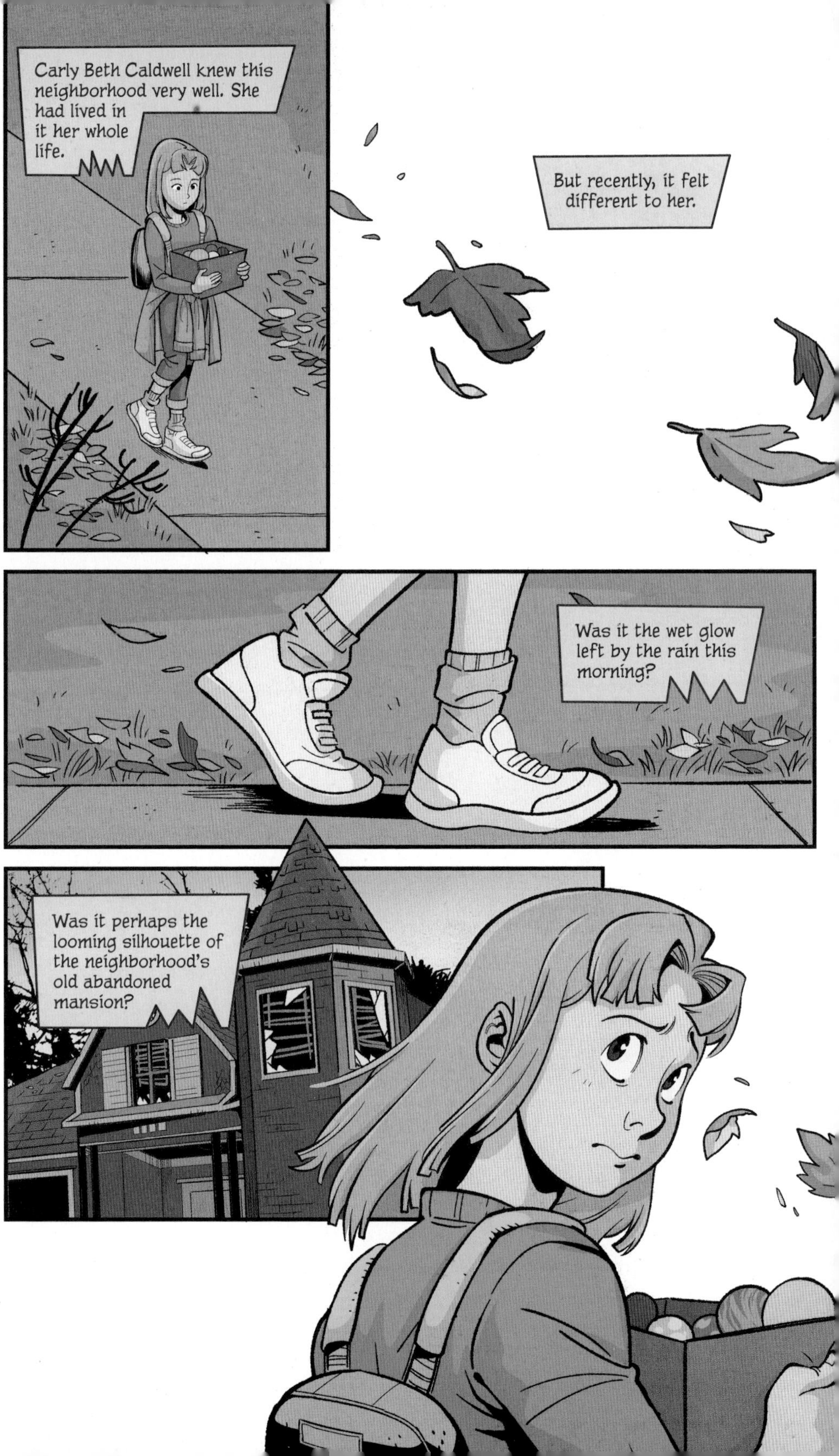
Carly Beth Caldwell knew this neighborhood very well. She had lived in it her whole life.
But recently, it felt different to her.
Was it the wet glow left by the rain this morning?
Was it perhaps the looming silhouette of the neighborhood's old abandoned mansion?

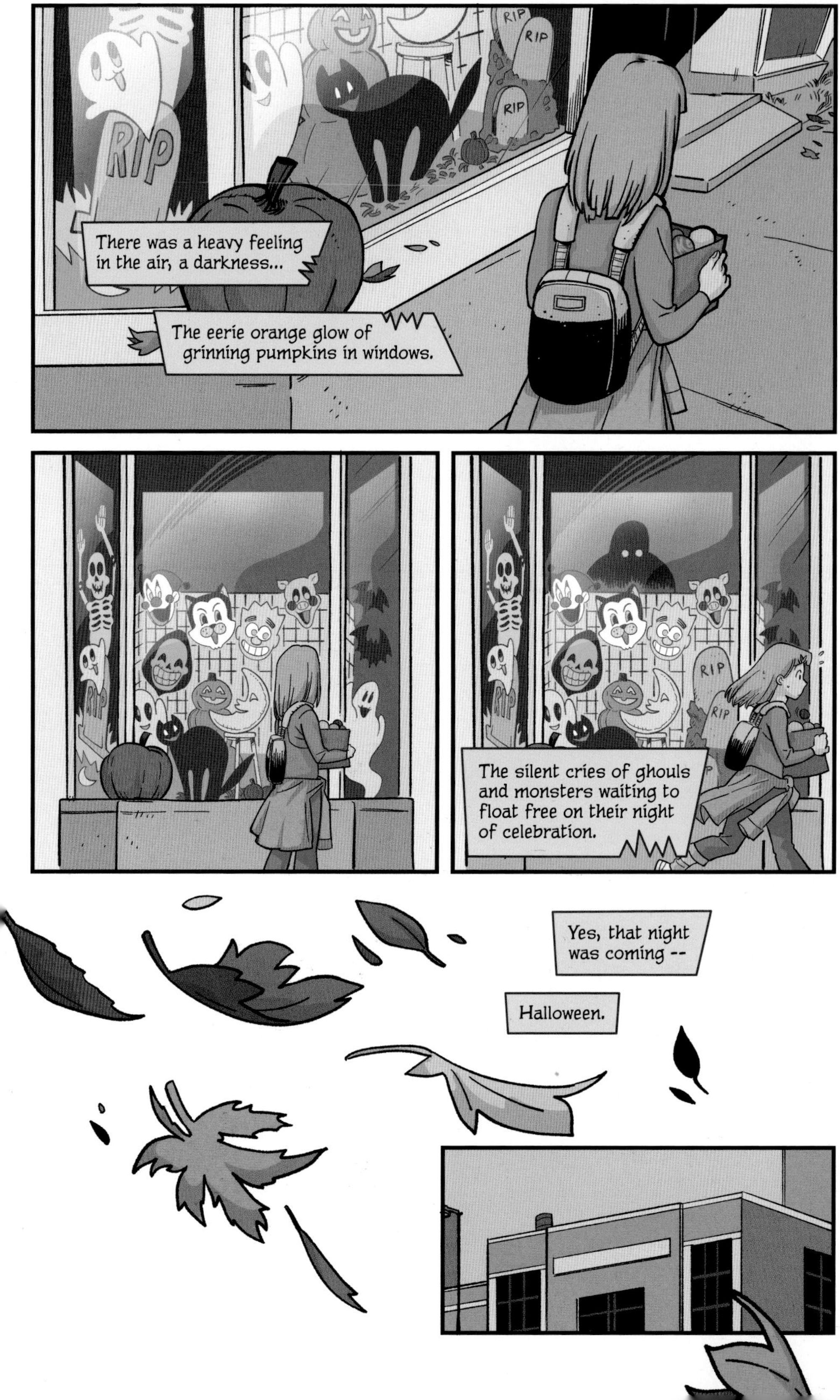

RIP
RIP
RIP
RIP
There was a heavy feeling in the air, a darkness...
The eerie orange glow of grinning pumpkins in windows.
RIP
RIP
The silent cries of ghouls and monsters waiting to float free on their night of celebration.
Yes, that night was coming --
Halloween.

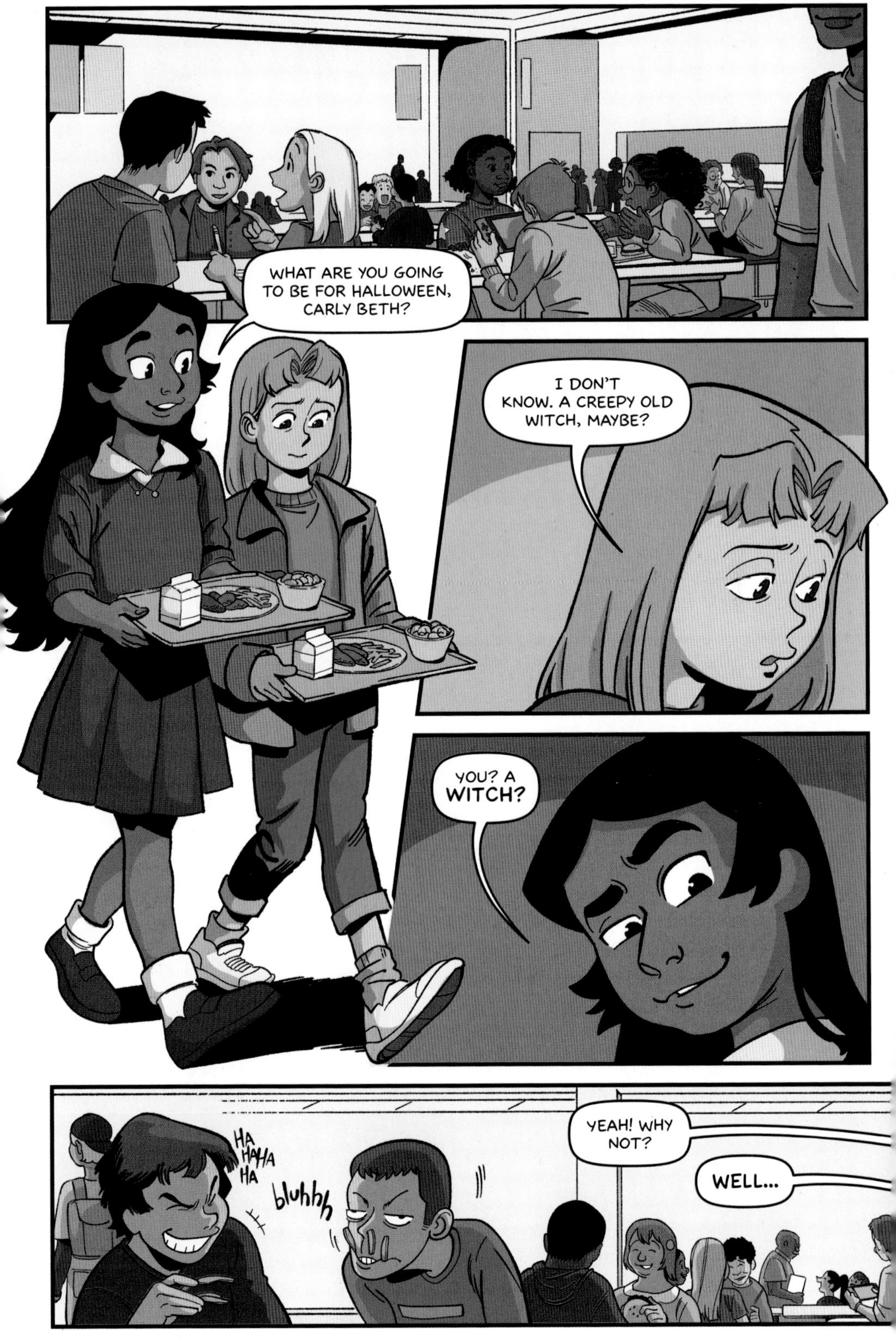
WHAT ARE YOU GOING TO BE FOR HALLOWEEN, CARLY BETH?
I DON'T KNOW. A CREEPY OLD WITCH, MAYBE?
YOU? A WITCH?
HA HAHA HA
bluhhh
YEAH! WHY NOT?
WELL...

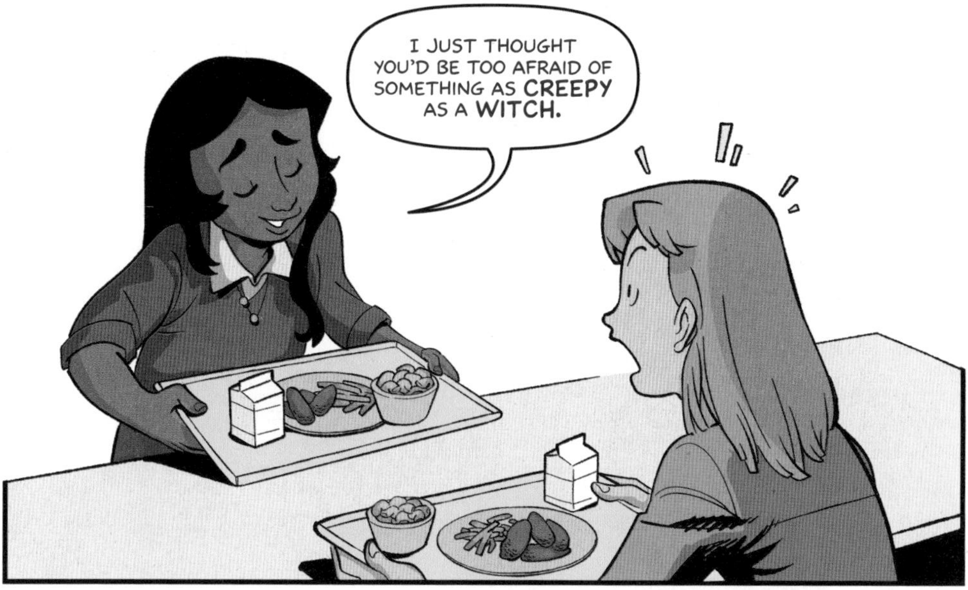
I JUST THOUGHT YOU'D BE TOO AFRAID OF SOMETHING AS CREEPY AS A WITCH.

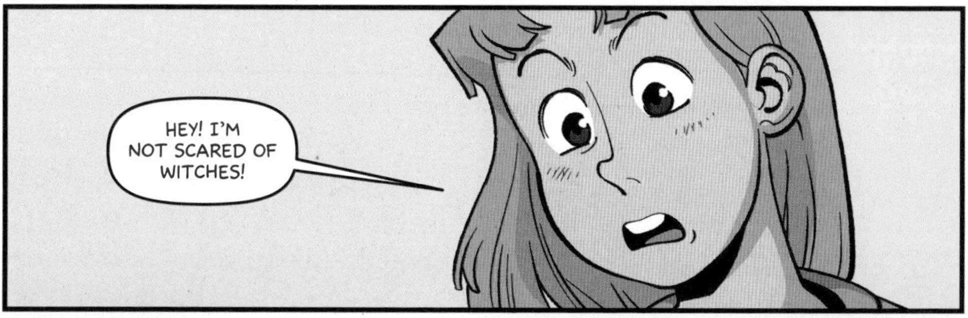
HEY! I'M NOT SCARED OF WITCHES!

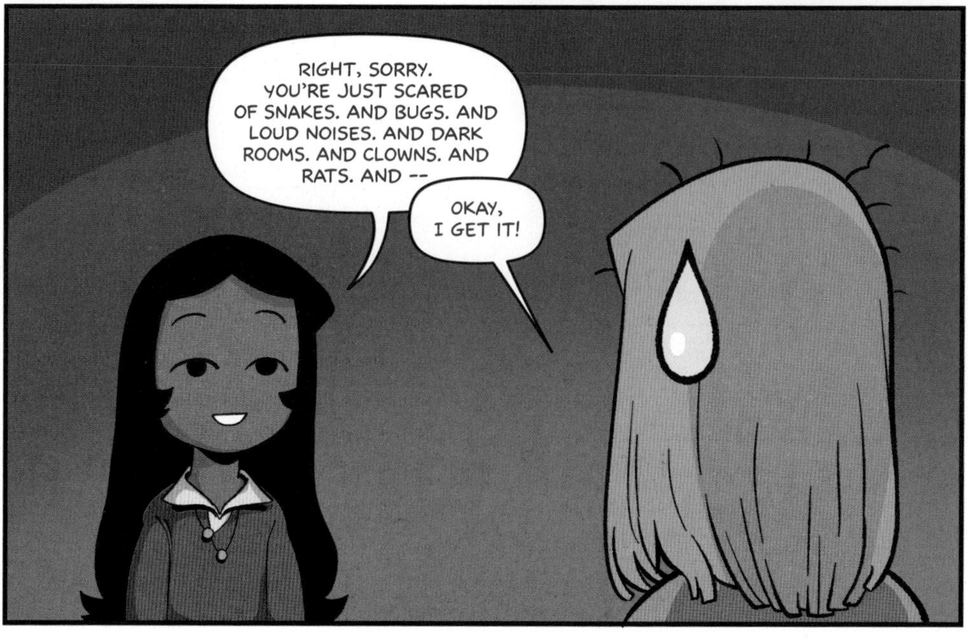
RIGHT, SORRY. YOU'RE JUST SCARED OF SNAKES. AND BUGS. AND LOUD NOISES. AND DARK ROOMS. AND CLOWNS. AND RATS. AND --
OKAY, I GET IT!

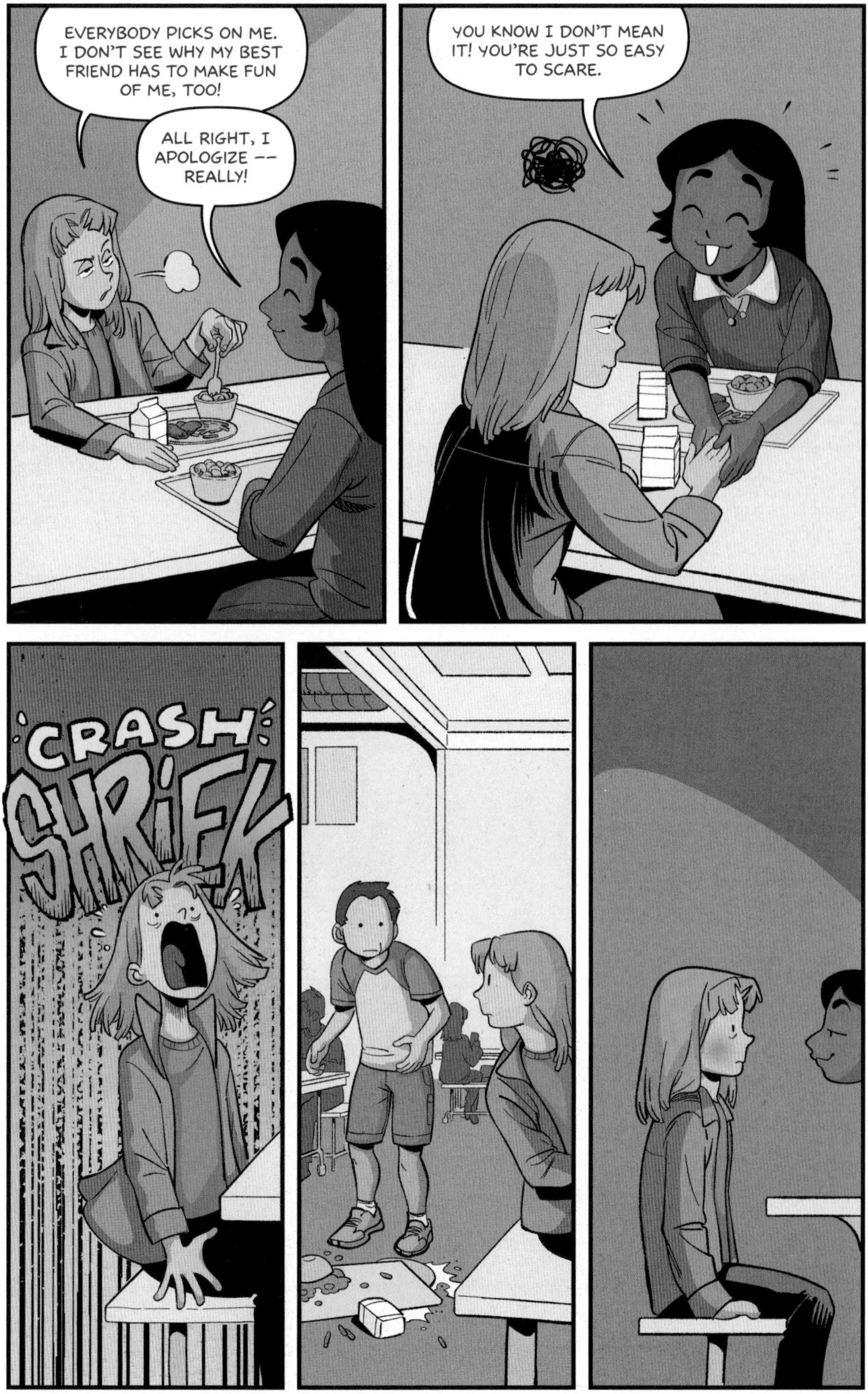
EVERYBODY PICKS ON ME. I DON'T SEE WHY MY BEST FRIEND HAS TO MAKE FUN OF ME, TOO!
ALL RIGHT, I APOLOGIZE -- REALLY!
YOU KNOW I DON'T MEAN IT! YOU'RE JUST SO EASY TO SCARE.
CRASH
SHRIEK

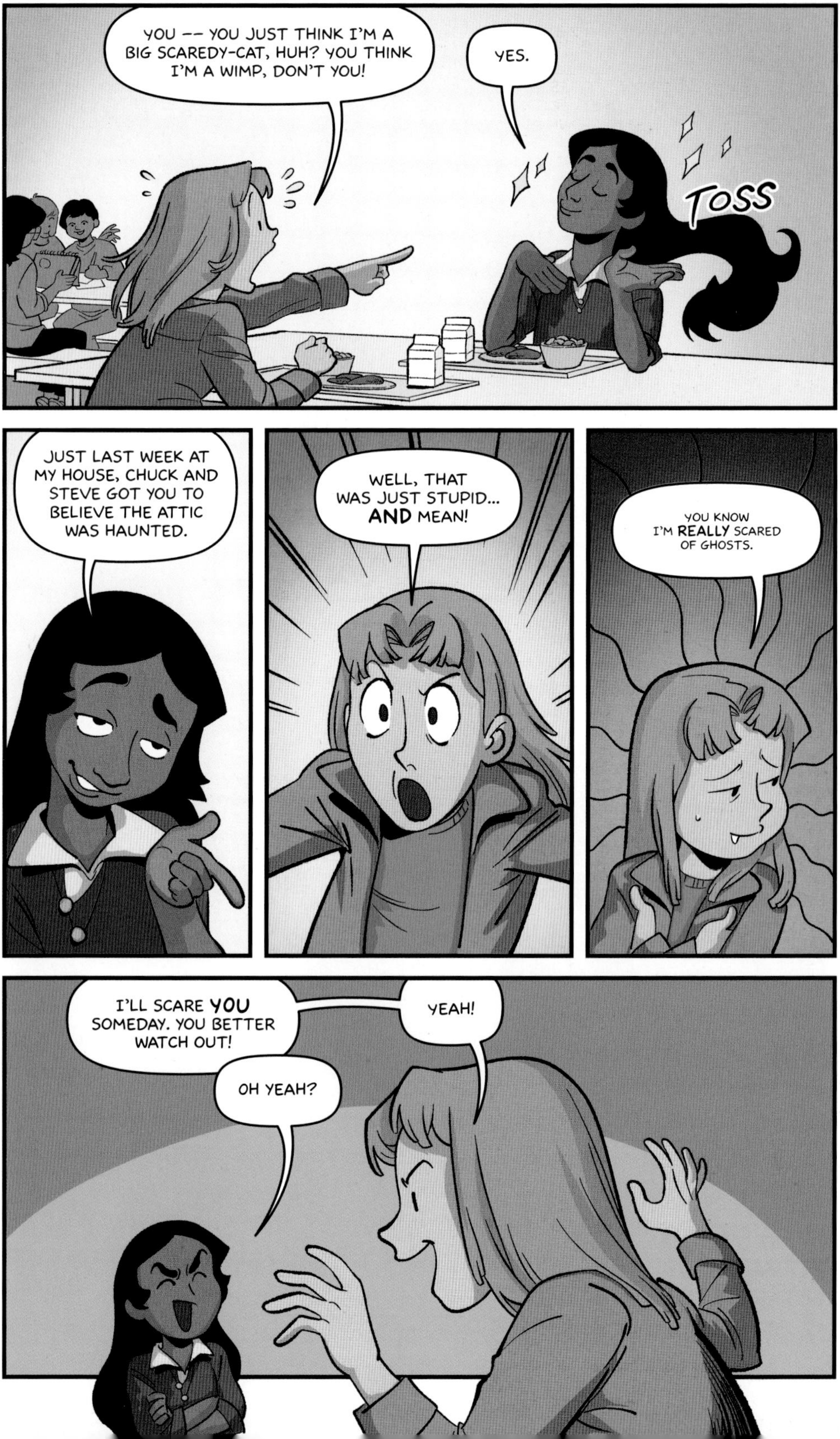
YOU -- YOU JUST THINK I'M A BIG SCAREDY-CAT, HUH? YOU THINK I'M A WIMP, DON'T YOU!
YES.
TOSS
JUST LAST WEEK AT MY HOUSE, CHUCK AND STEVE GOT YOU TO BELIEVE THE ATTIC WAS HAUNTED.
WELL, THAT WAS JUST STUPID... **AND** MEAN!
YOU KNOW I'M **REALLY** SCARED OF GHOSTS.
I'LL SCARE **YOU** SOMEDAY. YOU BETTER WATCH OUT!
OH YEAH?
YEAH!

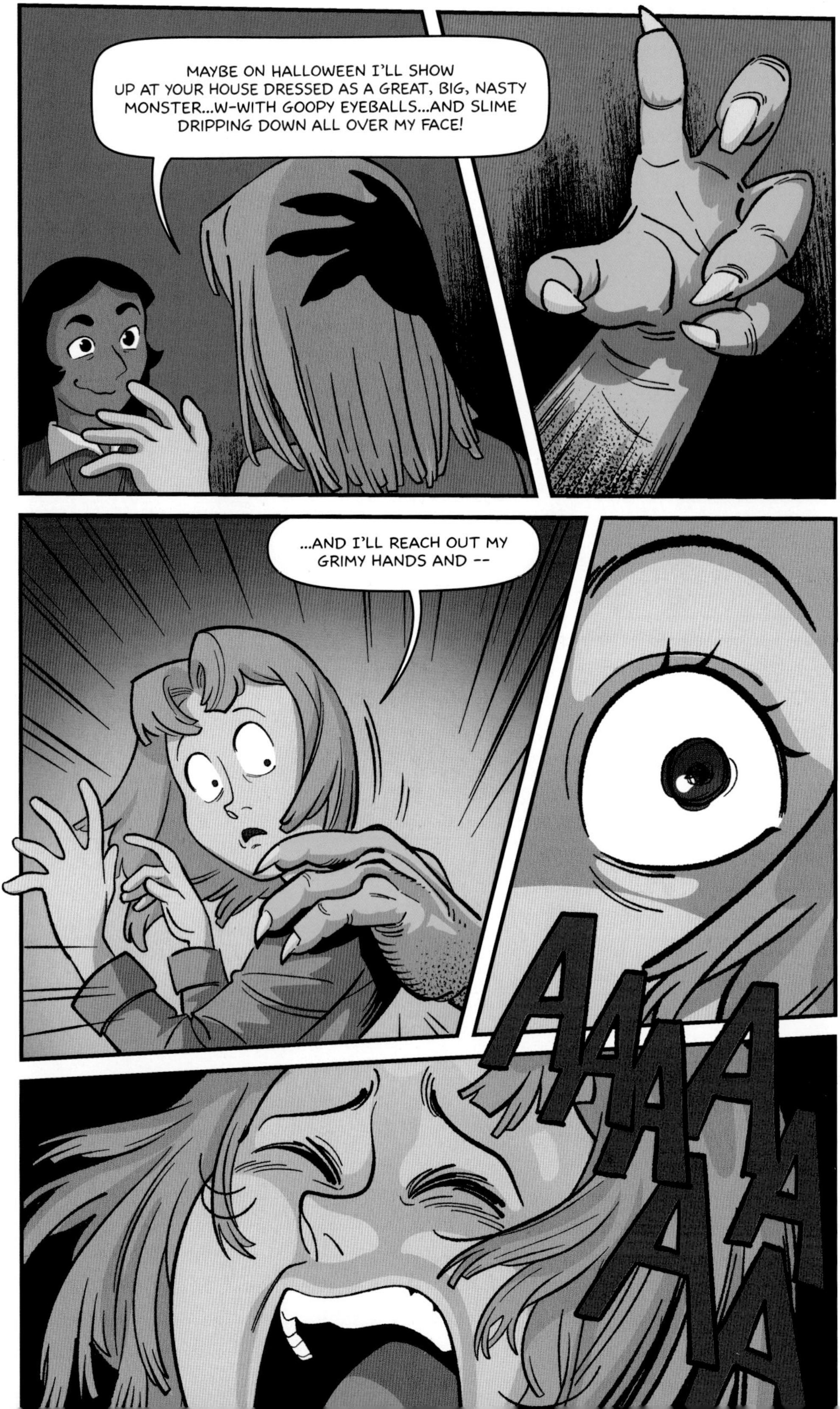
MAYBE ON HALLOWEEN I'LL SHOW UP AT YOUR HOUSE DRESSED AS A GREAT, BIG, NASTY MONSTER...W-WITH GOOPY EYEBALLS...AND SLIME DRIPPING DOWN ALL OVER MY FACE!
...AND I'LL REACH OUT MY GRIMY HANDS AND --
AAAAAAAAAA

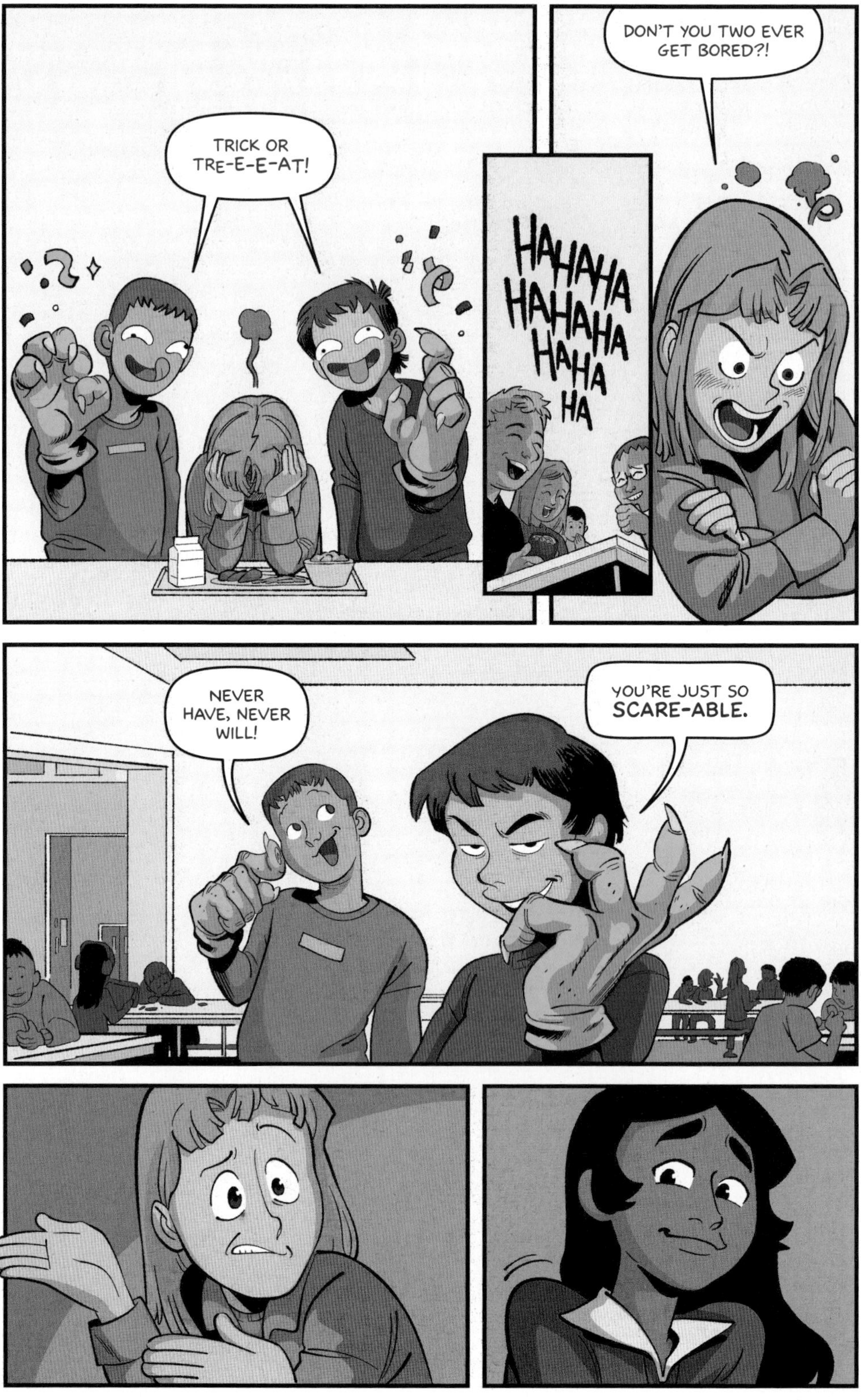
TRICK OR TRE-E-E-AT!
HAHAHA HAHAHA HAHA HA
DON'T YOU TWO EVER GET BORED?!
NEVER HAVE, NEVER WILL!
YOU'RE JUST SO SCARE-ABLE.

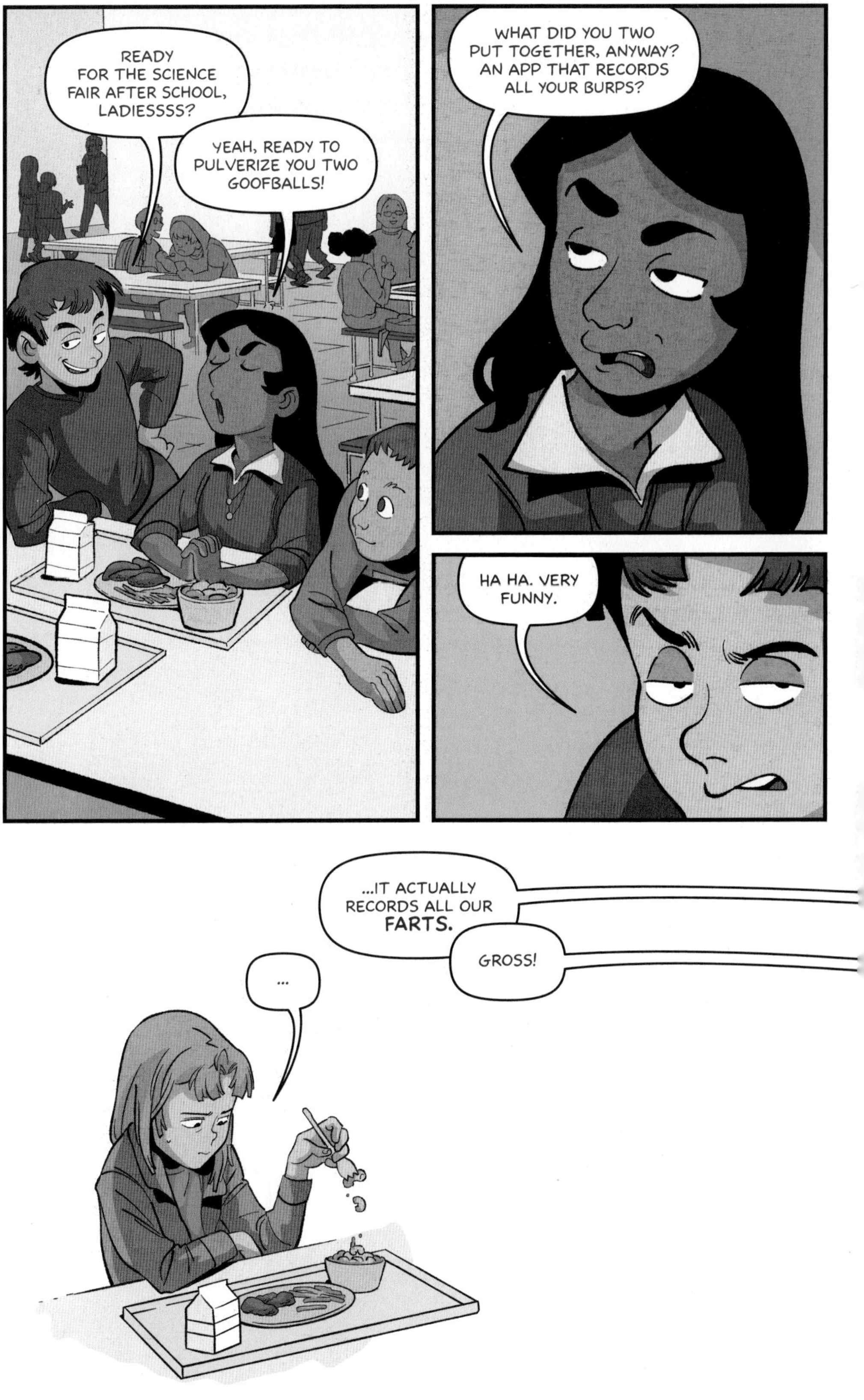
READY FOR THE SCIENCE FAIR AFTER SCHOOL, LADIESSSS?
YEAH, READY TO PULVERIZE YOU TWO GOOFBALLS!
WHAT DID YOU TWO PUT TOGETHER, ANYWAY? AN APP THAT RECORDS ALL YOUR BURPS?
HA HA. VERY FUNNY.
...IT ACTUALLY RECORDS ALL OUR FARTS.
GROSS!
...

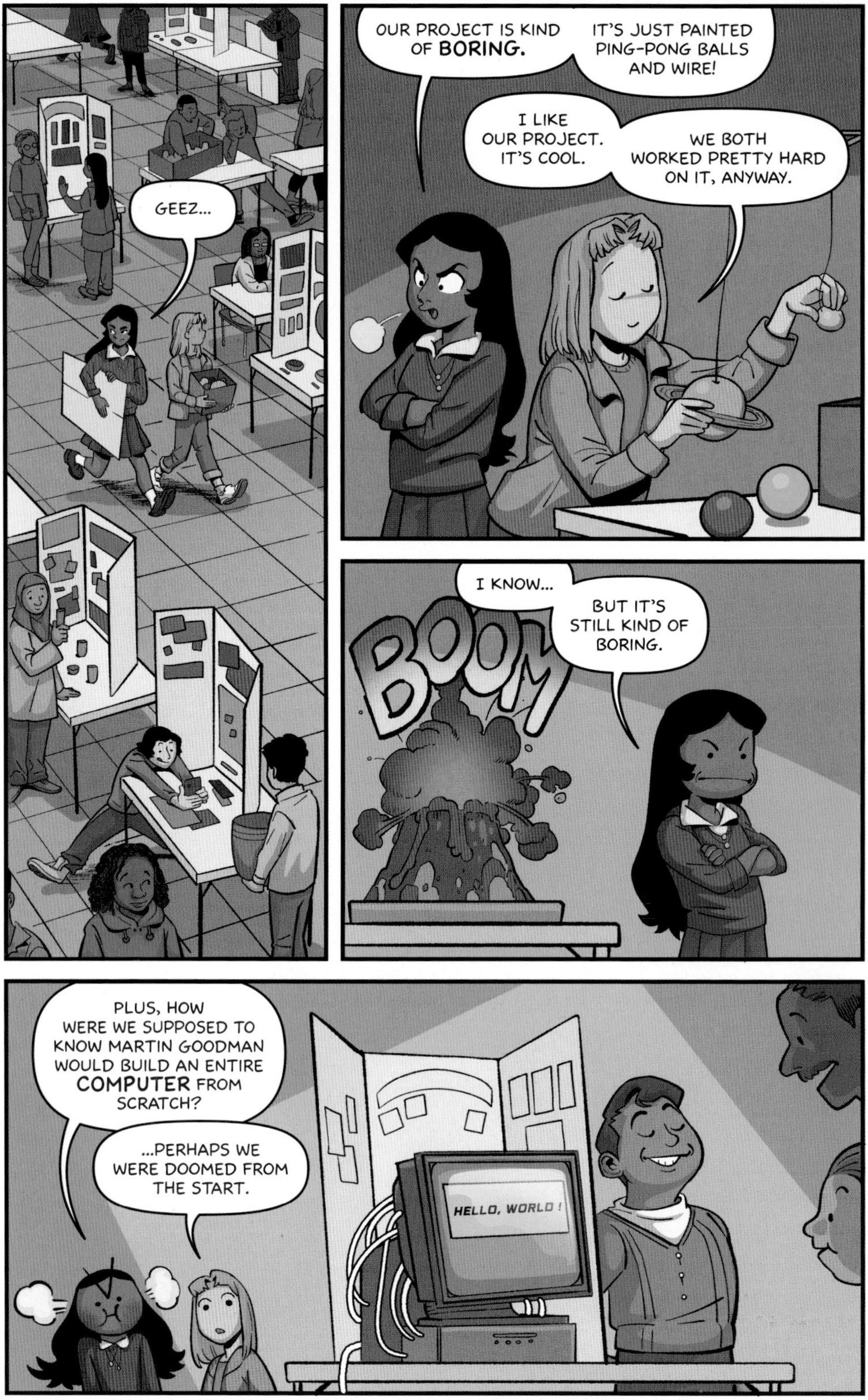
GEEZ...
OUR PROJECT IS KIND OF **BORING.**
IT'S JUST PAINTED PING-PONG BALLS AND WIRE!
I LIKE OUR PROJECT. IT'S COOL.
WE BOTH WORKED PRETTY HARD ON IT, ANYWAY.
I KNOW...
BOOM
BUT IT'S STILL KIND OF BORING.
PLUS, HOW WERE WE SUPPOSED TO KNOW MARTIN GOODMAN WOULD BUILD AN ENTIRE **COMPUTER** FROM SCRATCH?
...PERHAPS WE WERE DOOMED FROM THE START.
HELLO, WORLD!

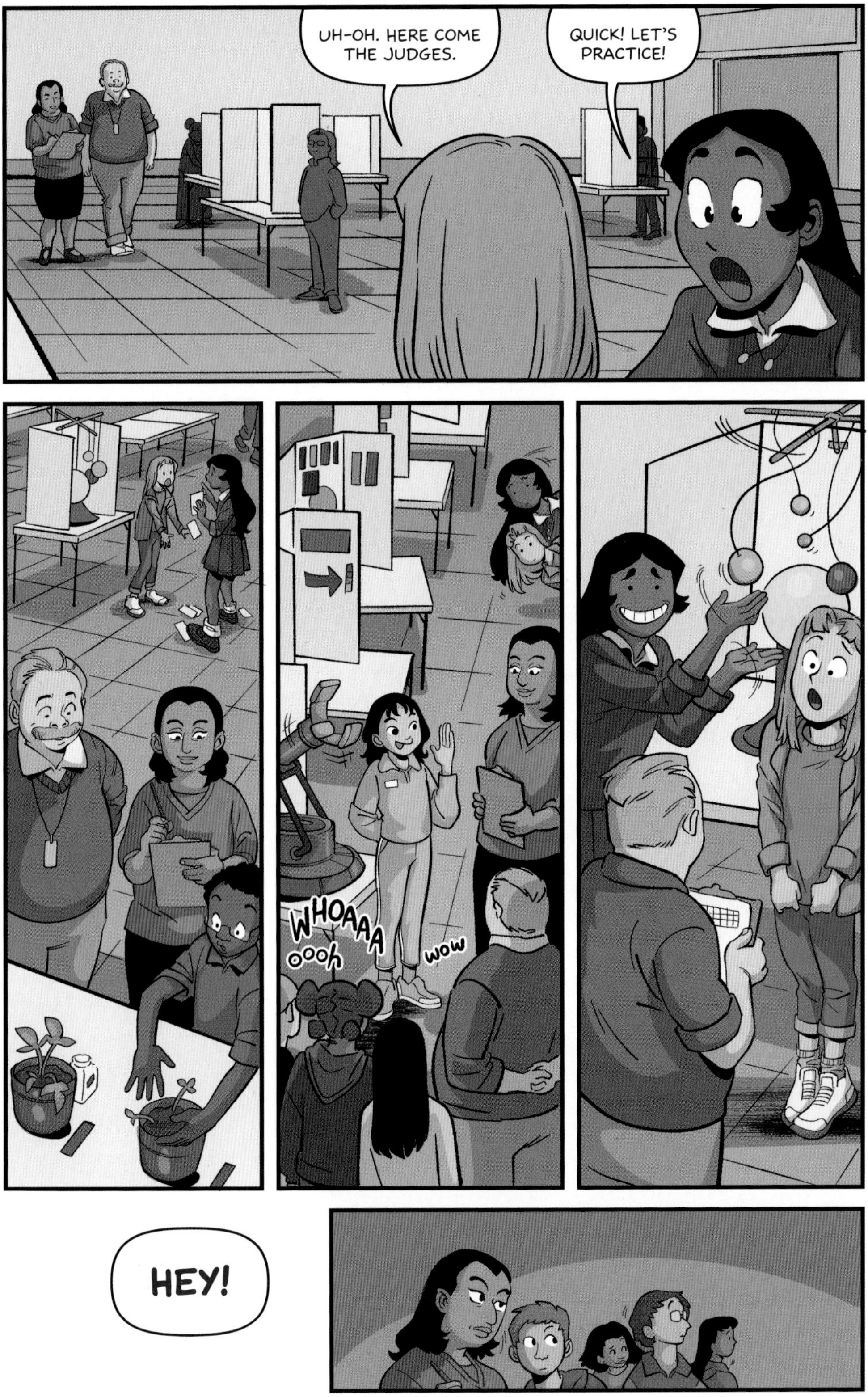

UH-OH. HERE COME THE JUDGES.
QUICK! LET'S PRACTICE!
WHOAAA
oooh
wow
HEY!

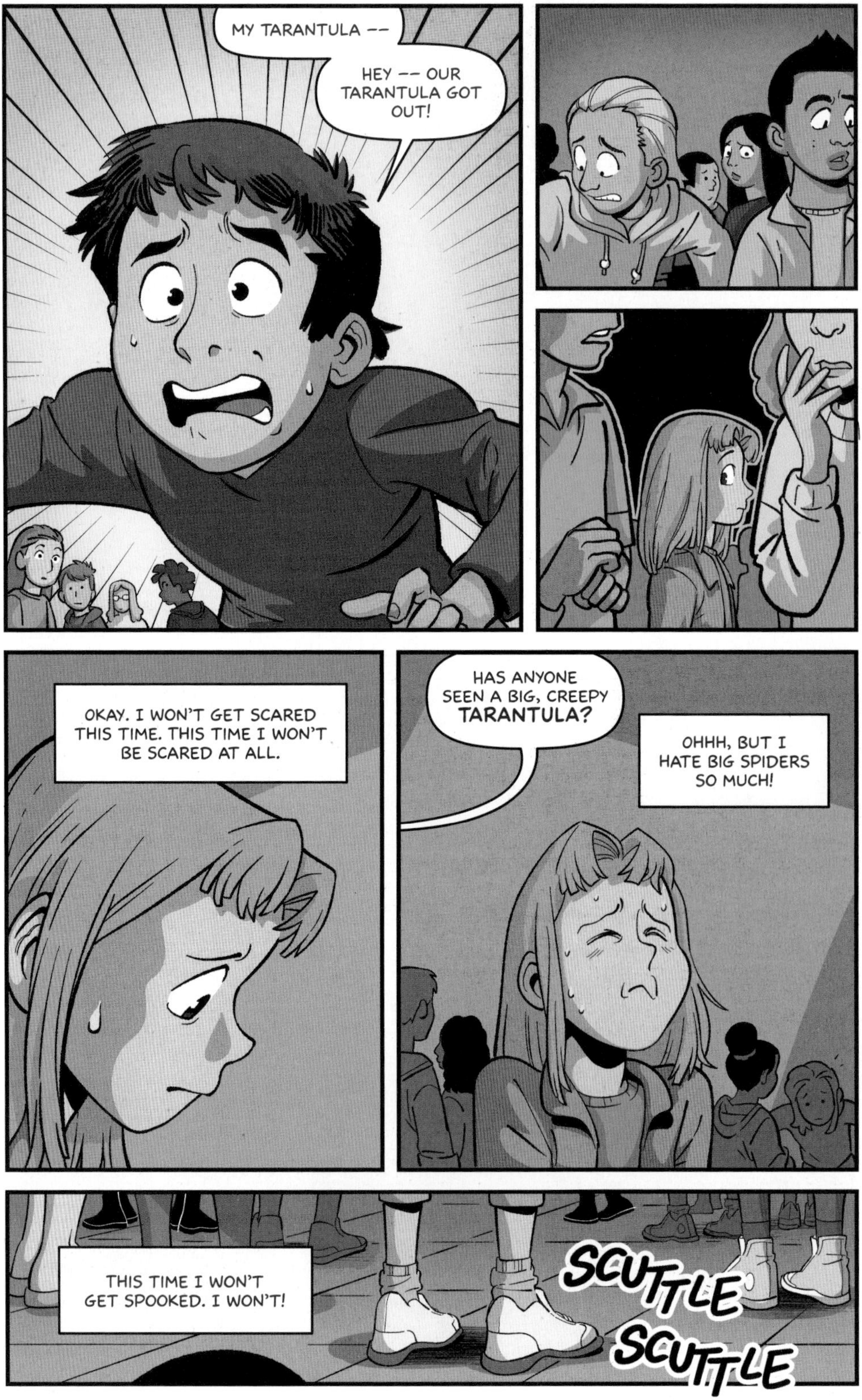
MY TARANTULA --
HEY -- OUR TARANTULA GOT OUT!
OKAY. I WON'T GET SCARED THIS TIME. THIS TIME I WON'T BE SCARED AT ALL.
HAS ANYONE SEEN A BIG, CREEPY **TARANTULA?**
OHHH, BUT I HATE BIG SPIDERS SO MUCH!
THIS TIME I WON'T GET SPOOKED. I WON'T!
SCUTTLE
SCUTTLE

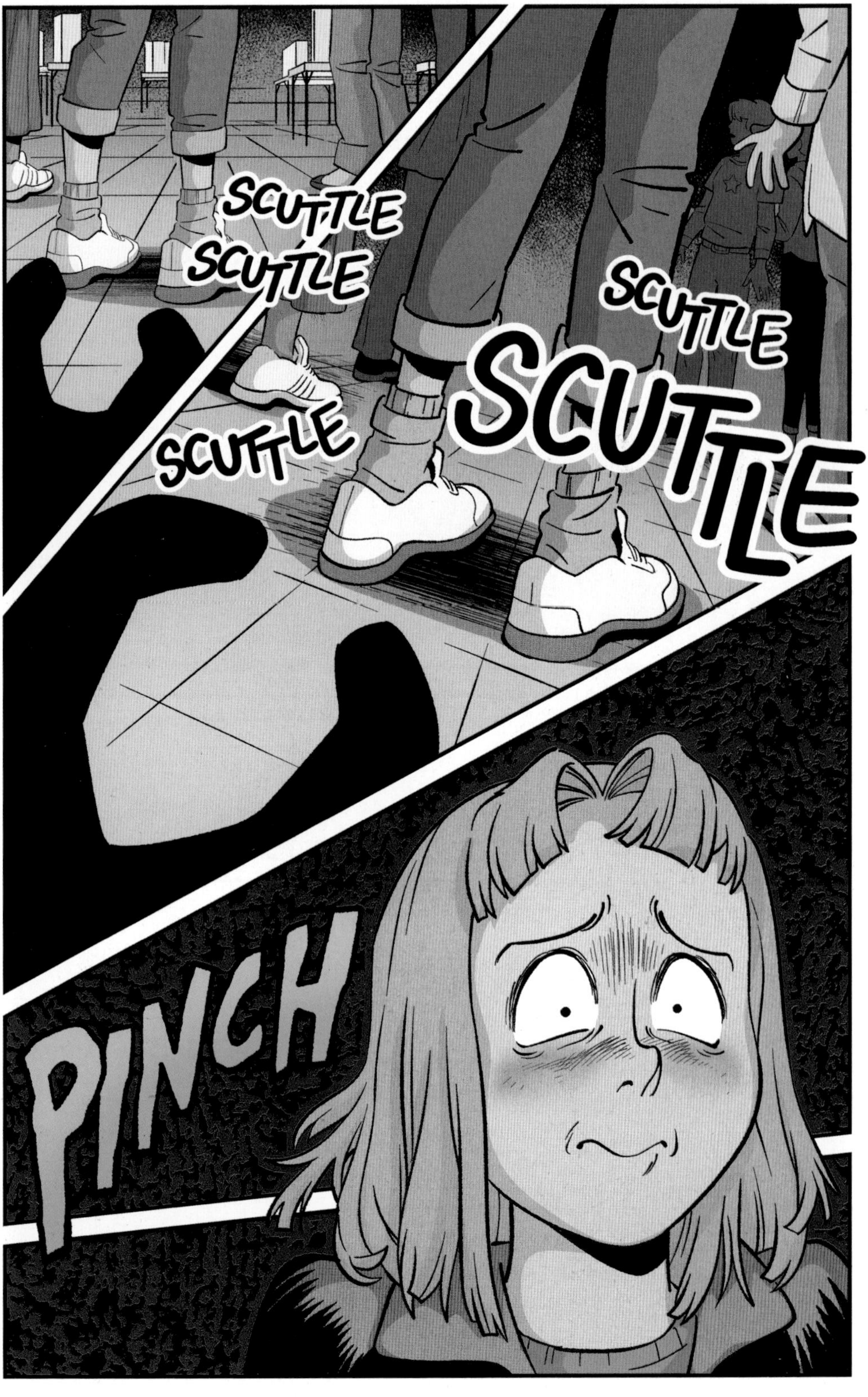
SCUTTLE
SCUTTLE
SCUTTLE
SCUTTLE
SCUTTLE
PINCH

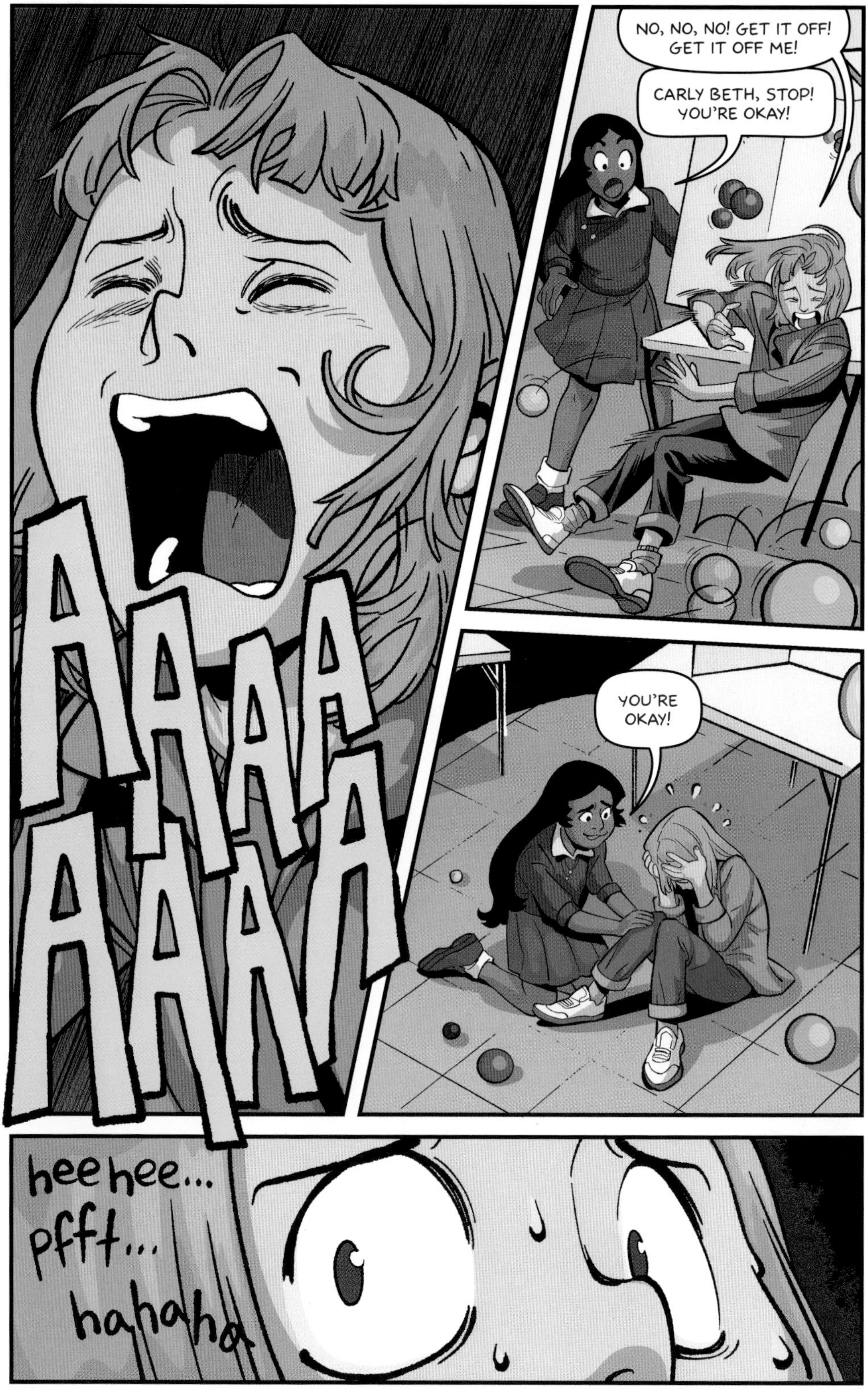
AAAA
AAAA
NO, NO, NO! GET IT OFF! GET IT OFF ME!
CARLY BETH, STOP! YOU'RE OKAY!
YOU'RE OKAY!
hee hee... pfft... hahaha

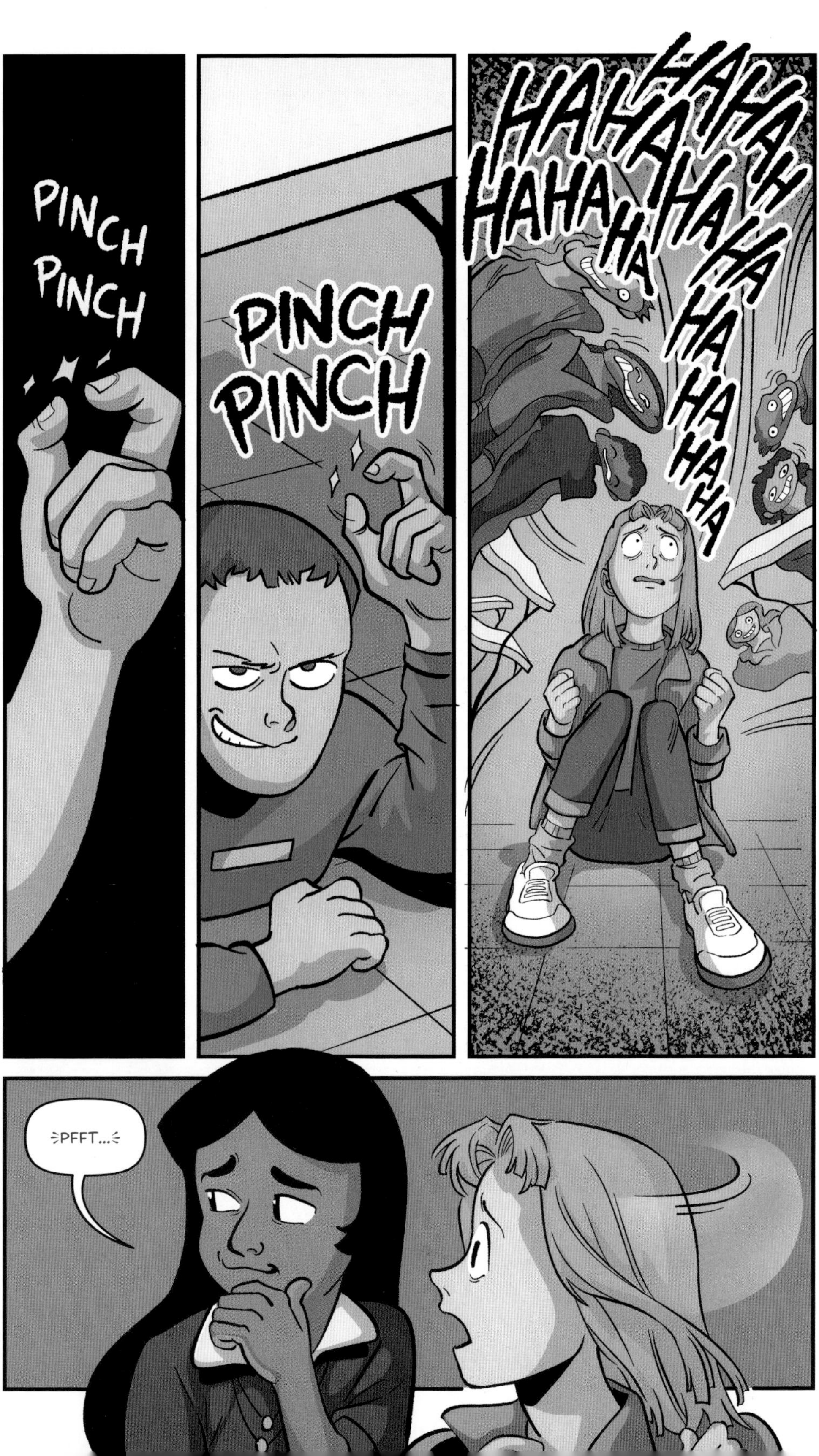
PINCH PINCH
PINCH PINCH
HAHAHAHA HAHAHA HAHAHAHAHAHAHAHAHAHAHA
PFFT...

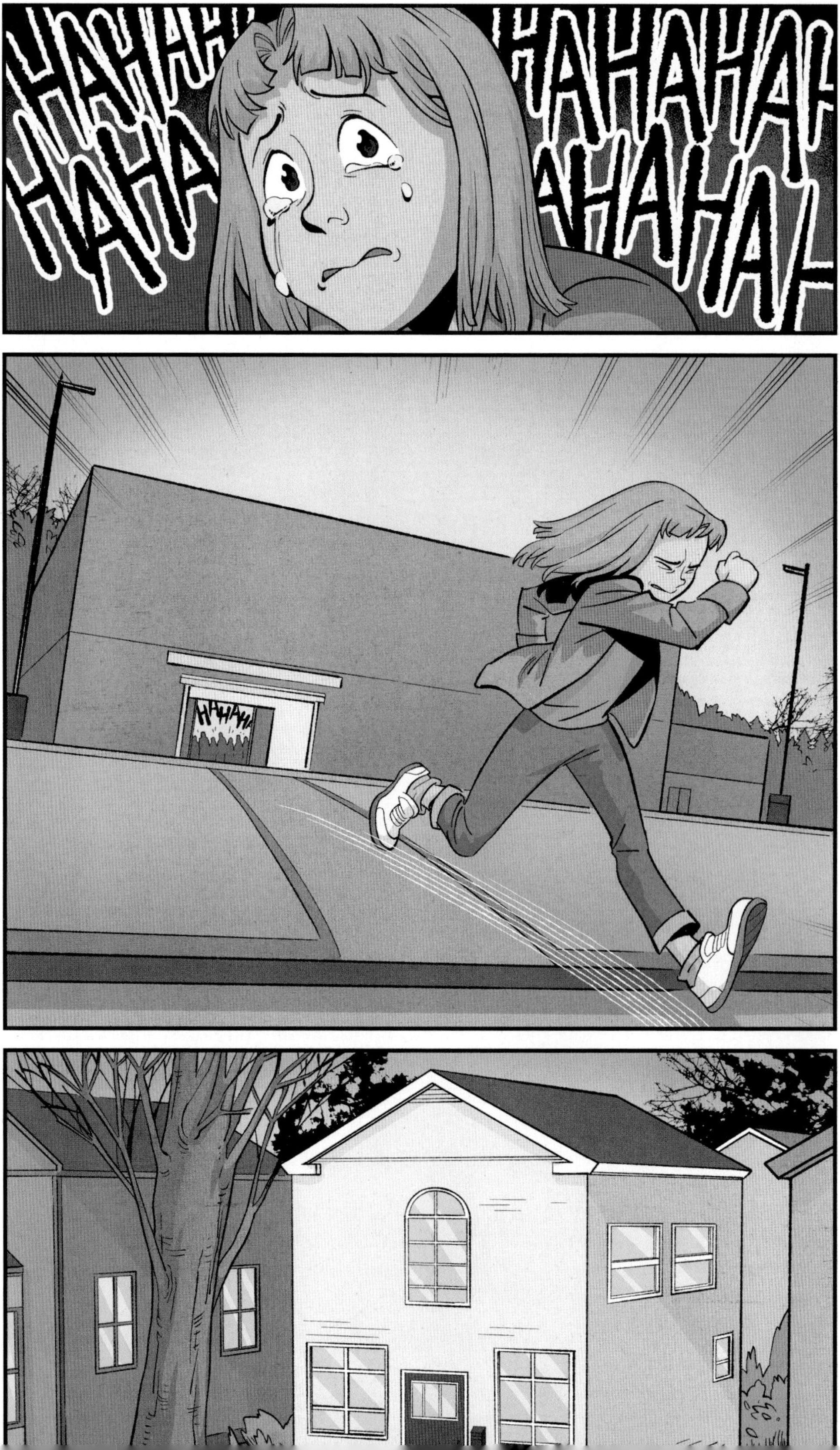
HAHAH
HAHA
HAHAHAH
HAHAHAH
HAHAHA

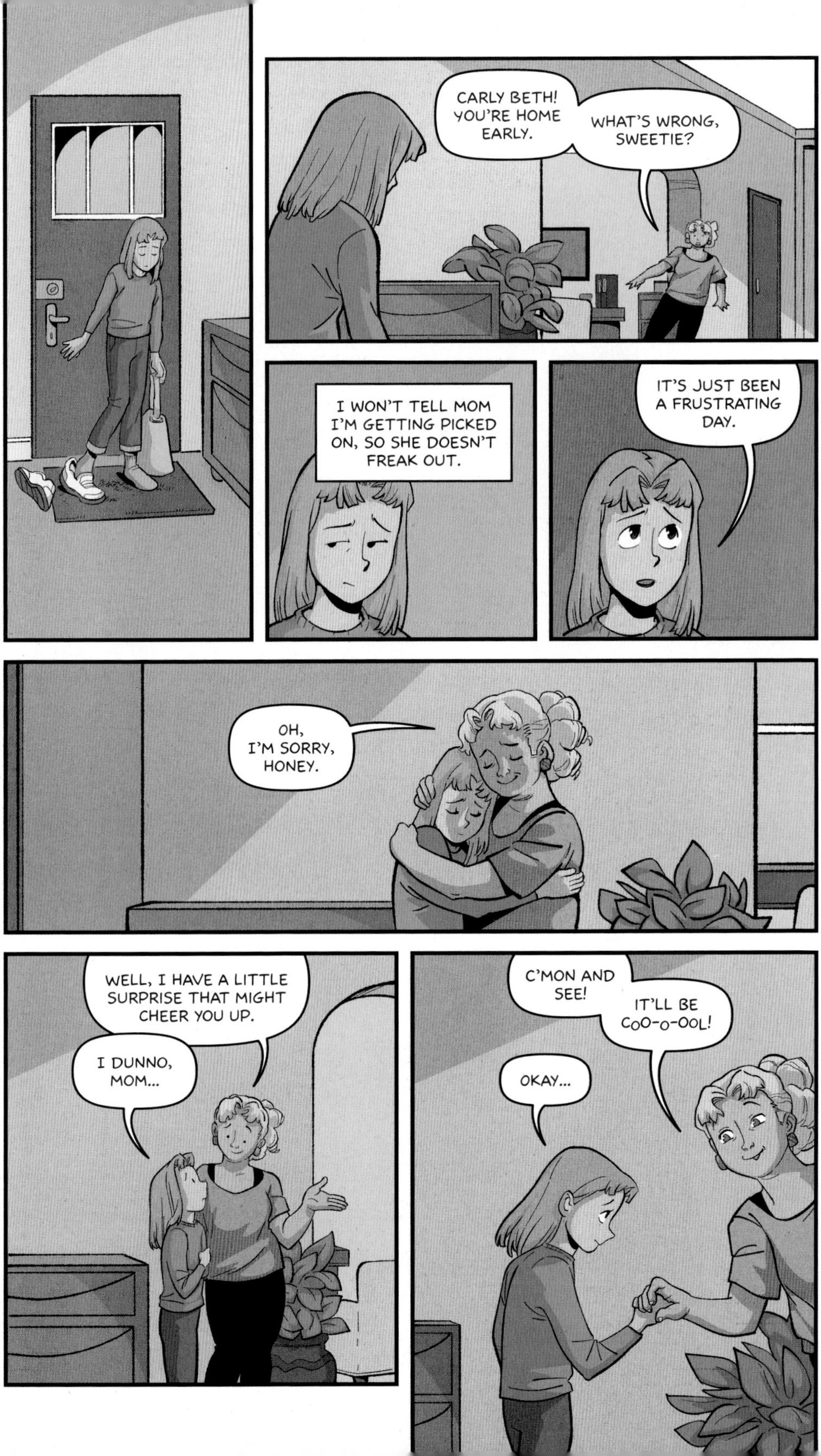
CARLY BETH! YOU'RE HOME EARLY.
WHAT'S WRONG, SWEETIE?
I WON'T TELL MOM I'M GETTING PICKED ON, SO SHE DOESN'T FREAK OUT.
IT'S JUST BEEN A FRUSTRATING DAY.
OH, I'M SORRY, HONEY.
WELL, I HAVE A LITTLE SURPRISE THAT MIGHT CHEER YOU UP.
I DUNNO, MOM...
C'MON AND SEE!
IT'LL BE COO-O-OOL!
OKAY...

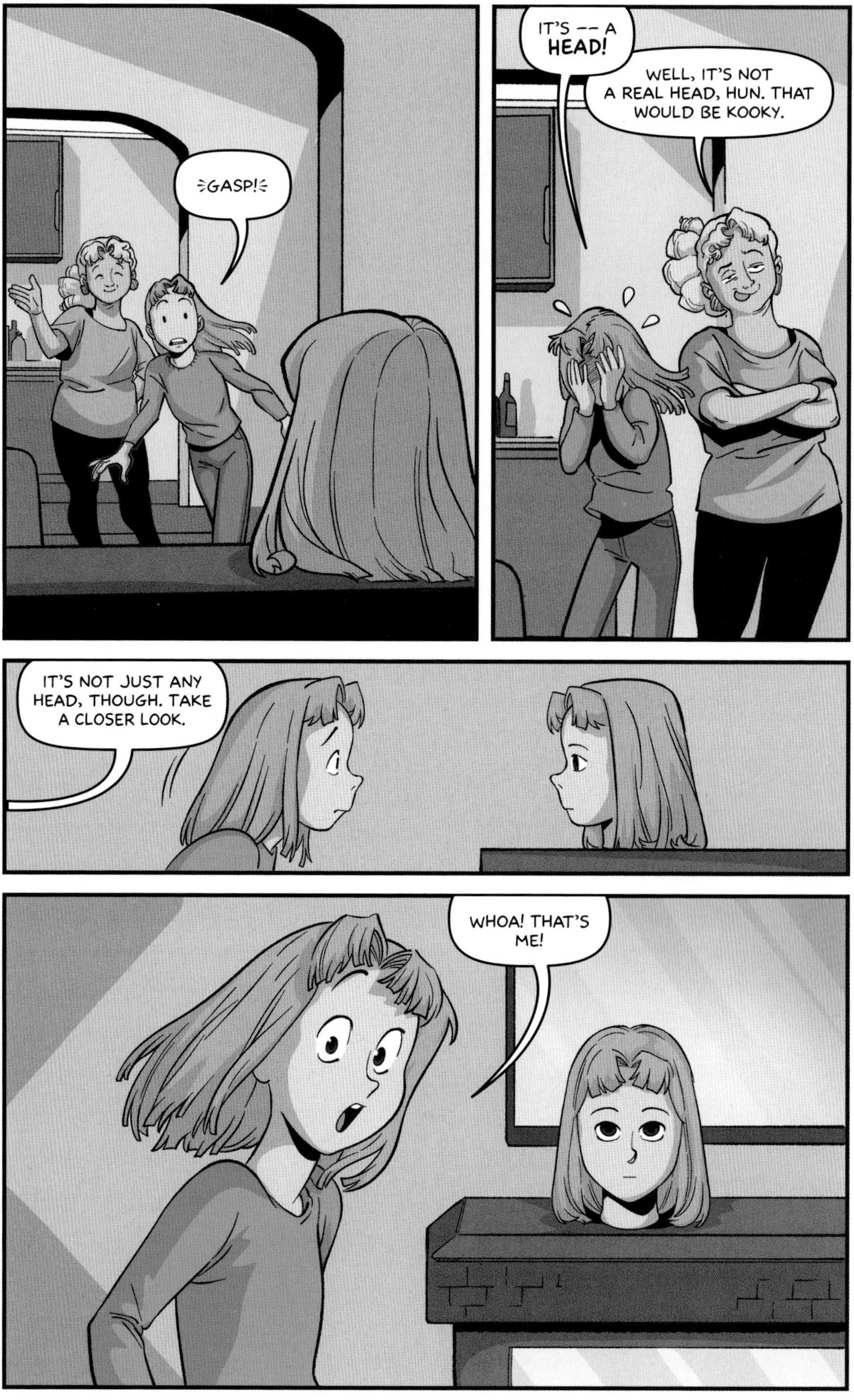
≈GASP!≈
IT'S -- A HEAD!
WELL, IT'S NOT A REAL HEAD, HUN. THAT WOULD BE KOOKY.
IT'S NOT JUST ANY HEAD, THOUGH. TAKE A CLOSER LOOK.
WHOA! THAT'S ME!

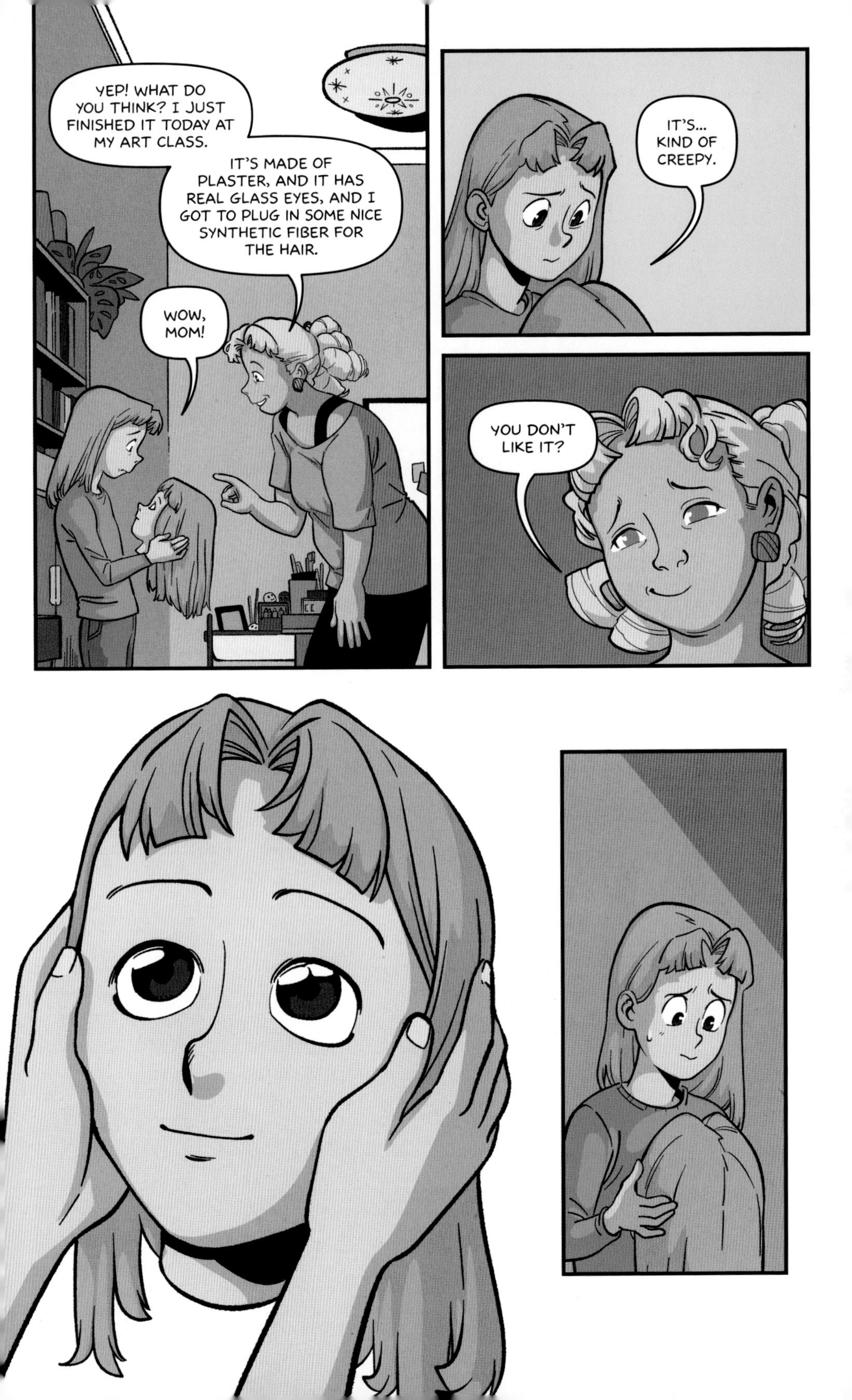
YEP! WHAT DO YOU THINK? I JUST FINISHED IT TODAY AT MY ART CLASS.
IT'S MADE OF PLASTER, AND IT HAS REAL GLASS EYES, AND I GOT TO PLUG IN SOME NICE SYNTHETIC FIBER FOR THE HAIR.
WOW, MOM!
IT'S... KIND OF CREEPY.
YOU DON'T LIKE IT?

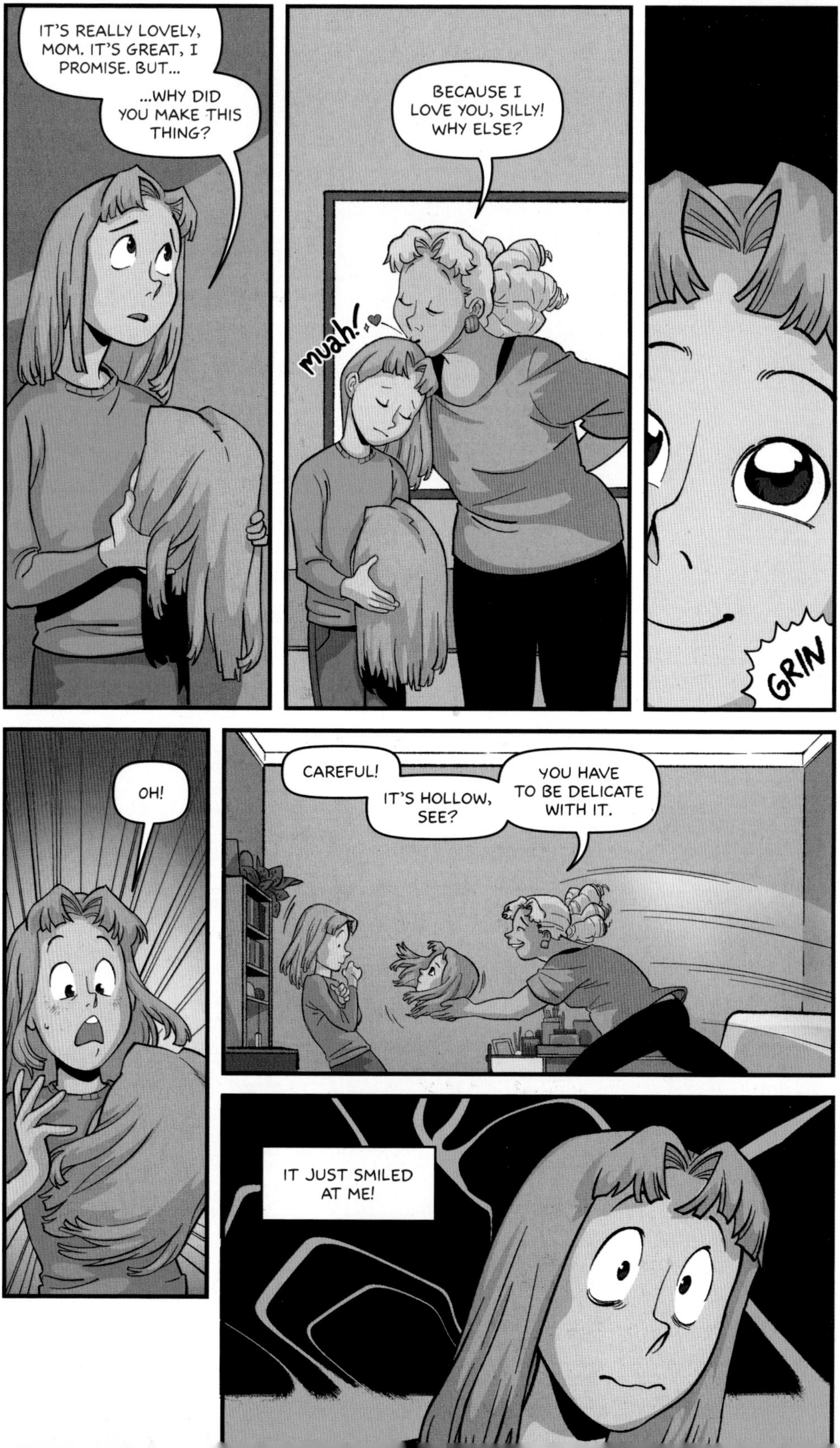
IT'S REALLY LOVELY, MOM. IT'S GREAT, I PROMISE. BUT...
...WHY DID YOU MAKE THIS THING?
BECAUSE I LOVE YOU, SILLY! WHY ELSE?
muah!
GRIN
OH!
CAREFUL!
IT'S HOLLOW, SEE?
YOU HAVE TO BE DELICATE WITH IT.
IT JUST SMILED AT ME!

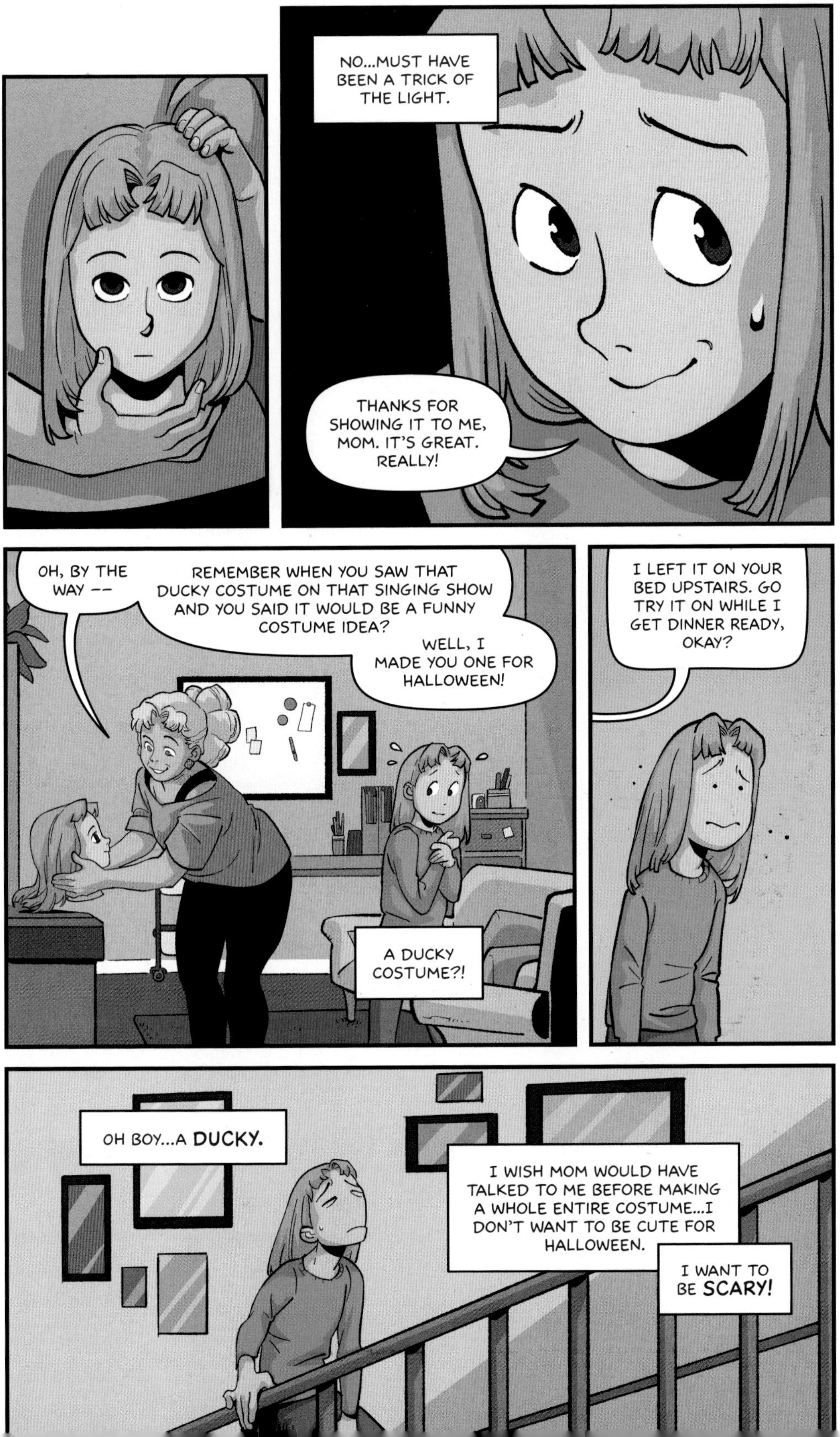
NO...MUST HAVE BEEN A TRICK OF THE LIGHT.
THANKS FOR SHOWING IT TO ME, MOM. IT'S GREAT. REALLY!
OH, BY THE WAY --
REMEMBER WHEN YOU SAW THAT DUCKY COSTUME ON THAT SINGING SHOW AND YOU SAID IT WOULD BE A FUNNY COSTUME IDEA?
WELL, I MADE YOU ONE FOR HALLOWEEN!
A DUCKY COSTUME?!
I LEFT IT ON YOUR BED UPSTAIRS. GO TRY IT ON WHILE I GET DINNER READY, OKAY?
OH BOY...A **DUCKY.**
I WISH MOM WOULD HAVE TALKED TO ME BEFORE MAKING A WHOLE ENTIRE COSTUME...I DON'T WANT TO BE CUTE FOR HALLOWEEN.
I WANT TO BE **SCARY!**

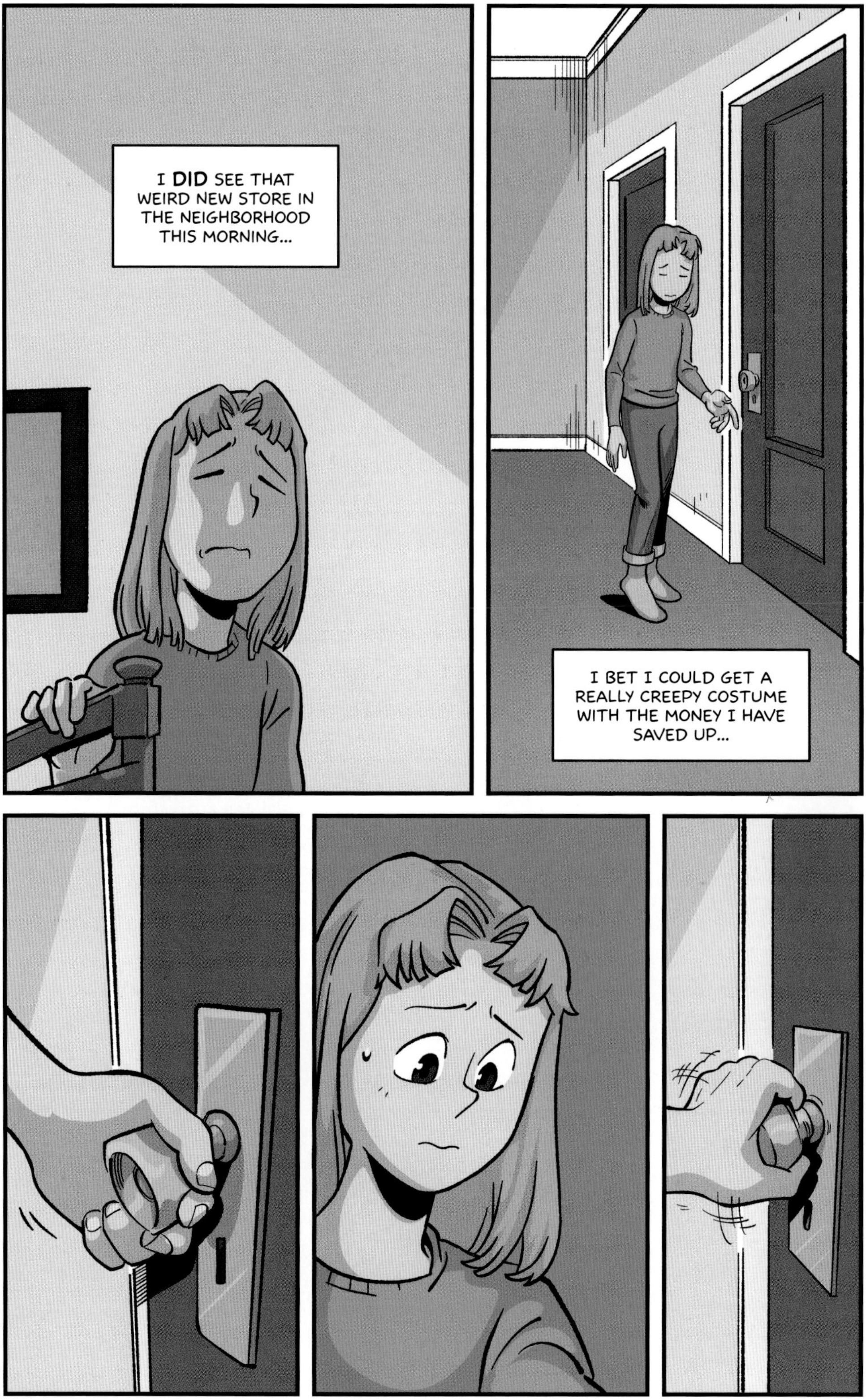
I DID SEE THAT WEIRD NEW STORE IN THE NEIGHBORHOOD THIS MORNING...
I BET I COULD GET A REALLY CREEPY COSTUME WITH THE MONEY I HAVE SAVED UP...

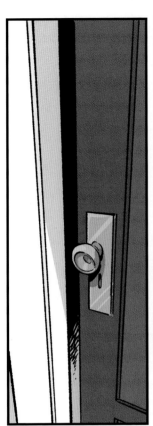

⋛SIGH⋚...A CUTE LITTLE DUCKY COSTUME.

WHO'D BE AFRAID OF THAT?

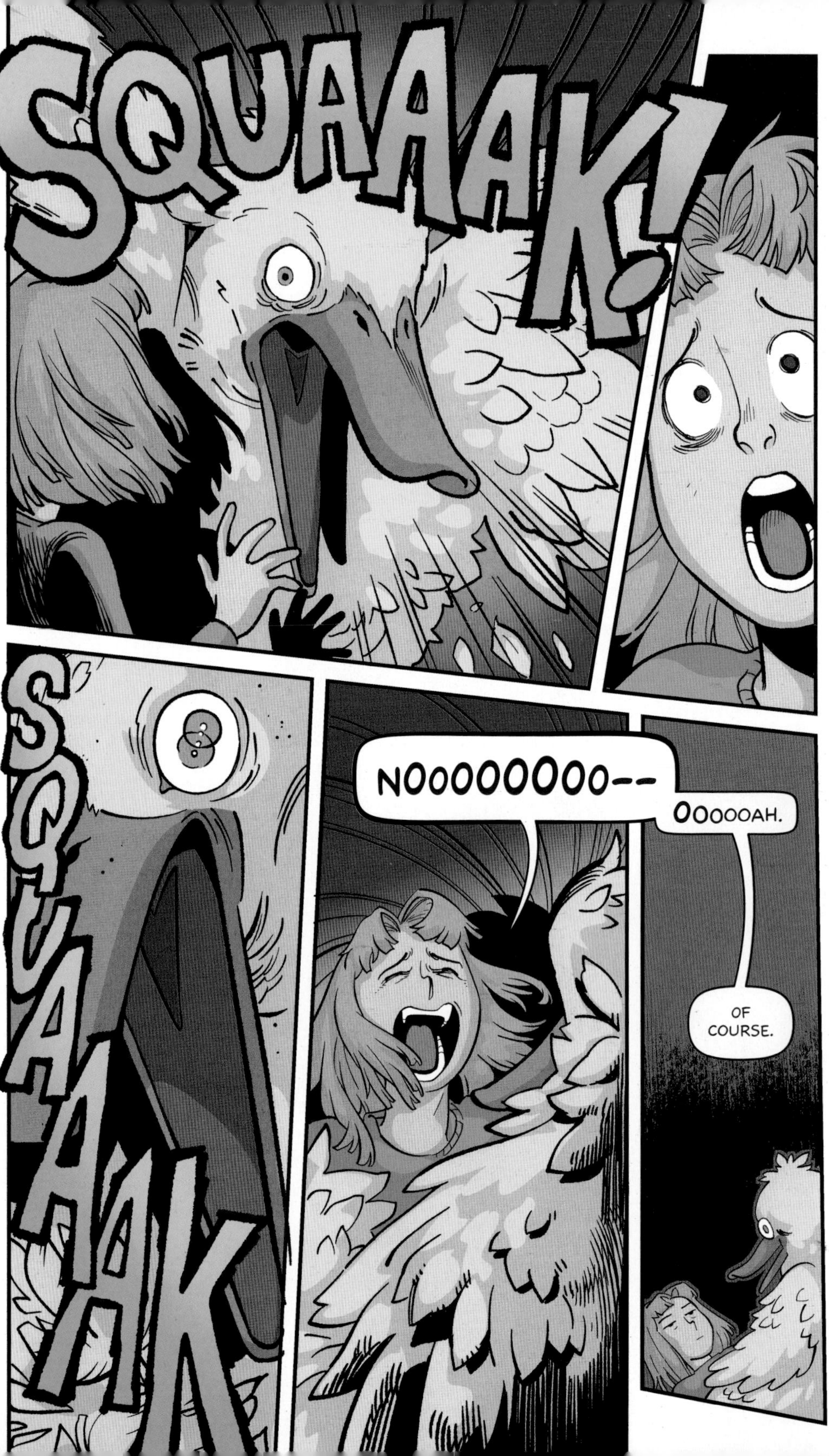
SQUAAAK!
SQUAAAAK
NOOOOOOOO--
OOOOOAH.
OF COURSE.

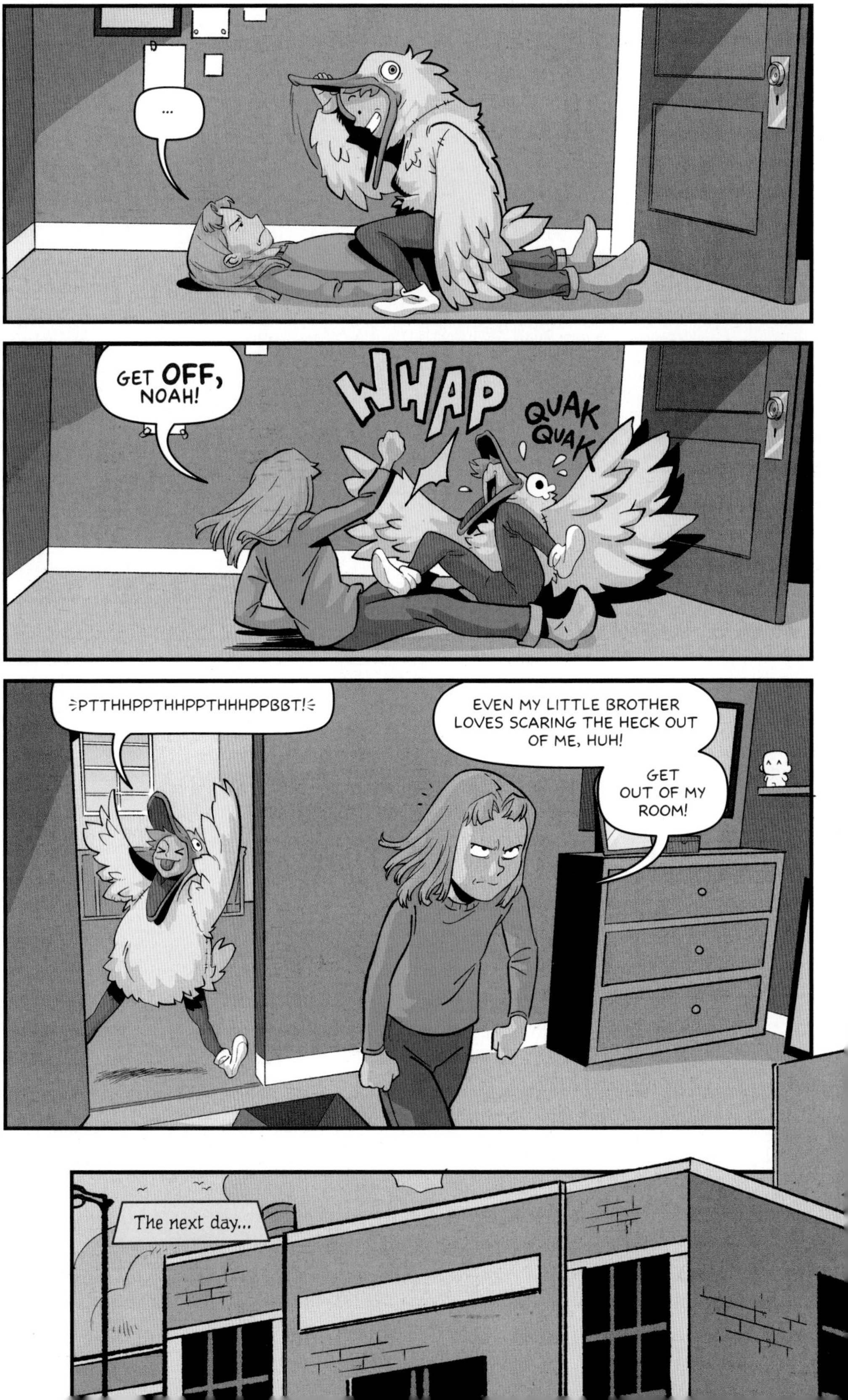
...
GET OFF, NOAH!
WHAP
QUAK QUAK
PTTHHPPTHHPPTHHHPPBBT!
EVEN MY LITTLE BROTHER LOVES SCARING THE HECK OUT OF ME, HUH!
GET OUT OF MY ROOM!
The next day...

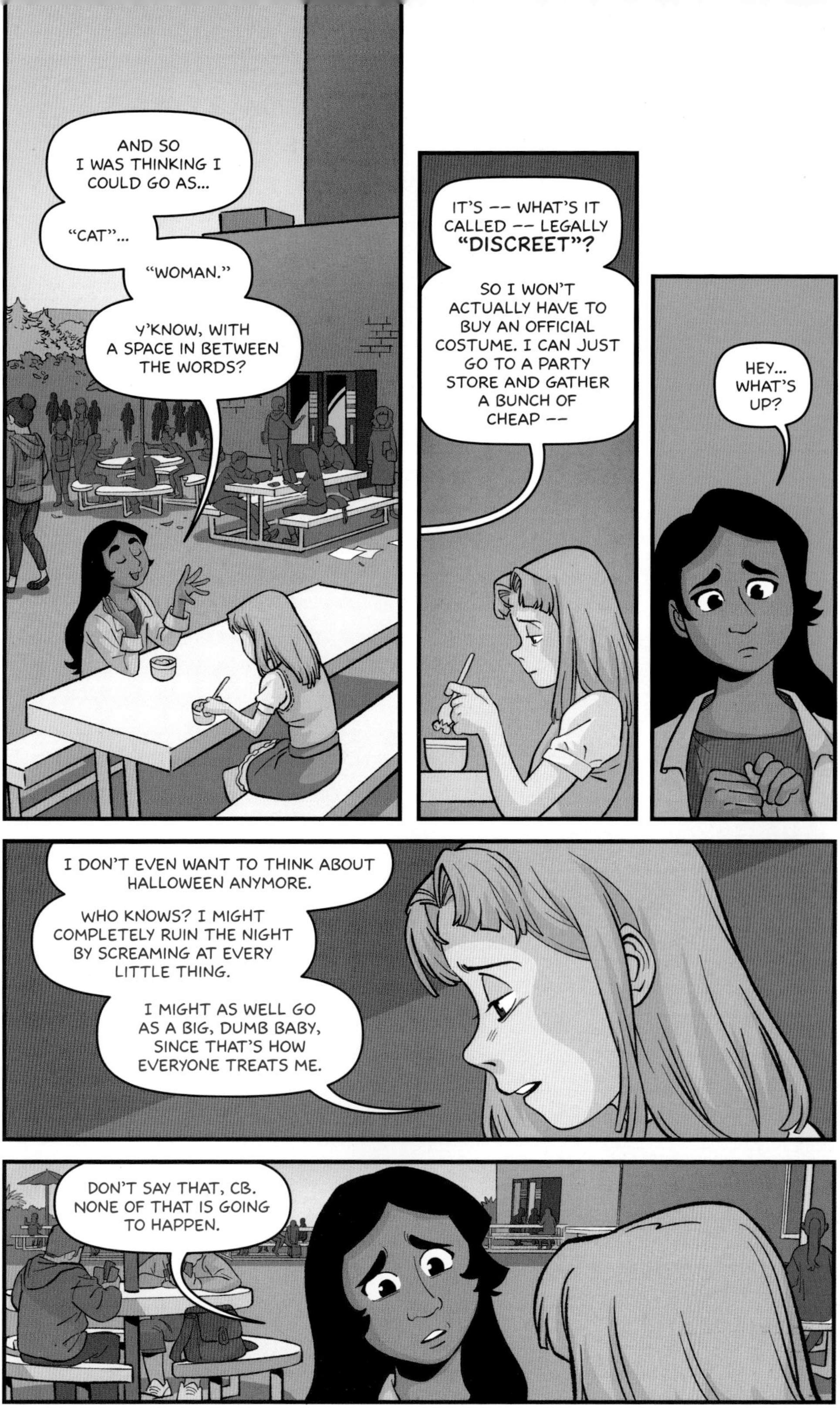
AND SO I WAS THINKING I COULD GO AS...
"CAT"...
"WOMAN."
Y'KNOW, WITH A SPACE IN BETWEEN THE WORDS?
IT'S -- WHAT'S IT CALLED -- LEGALLY "DISCREET"?
SO I WON'T ACTUALLY HAVE TO BUY AN OFFICIAL COSTUME. I CAN JUST GO TO A PARTY STORE AND GATHER A BUNCH OF CHEAP --
HEY... WHAT'S UP?
I DON'T EVEN WANT TO THINK ABOUT HALLOWEEN ANYMORE.
WHO KNOWS? I MIGHT COMPLETELY RUIN THE NIGHT BY SCREAMING AT EVERY LITTLE THING.
I MIGHT AS WELL GO AS A BIG, DUMB BABY, SINCE THAT'S HOW EVERYONE TREATS ME.
DON'T SAY THAT, CB. NONE OF THAT IS GOING TO HAPPEN.

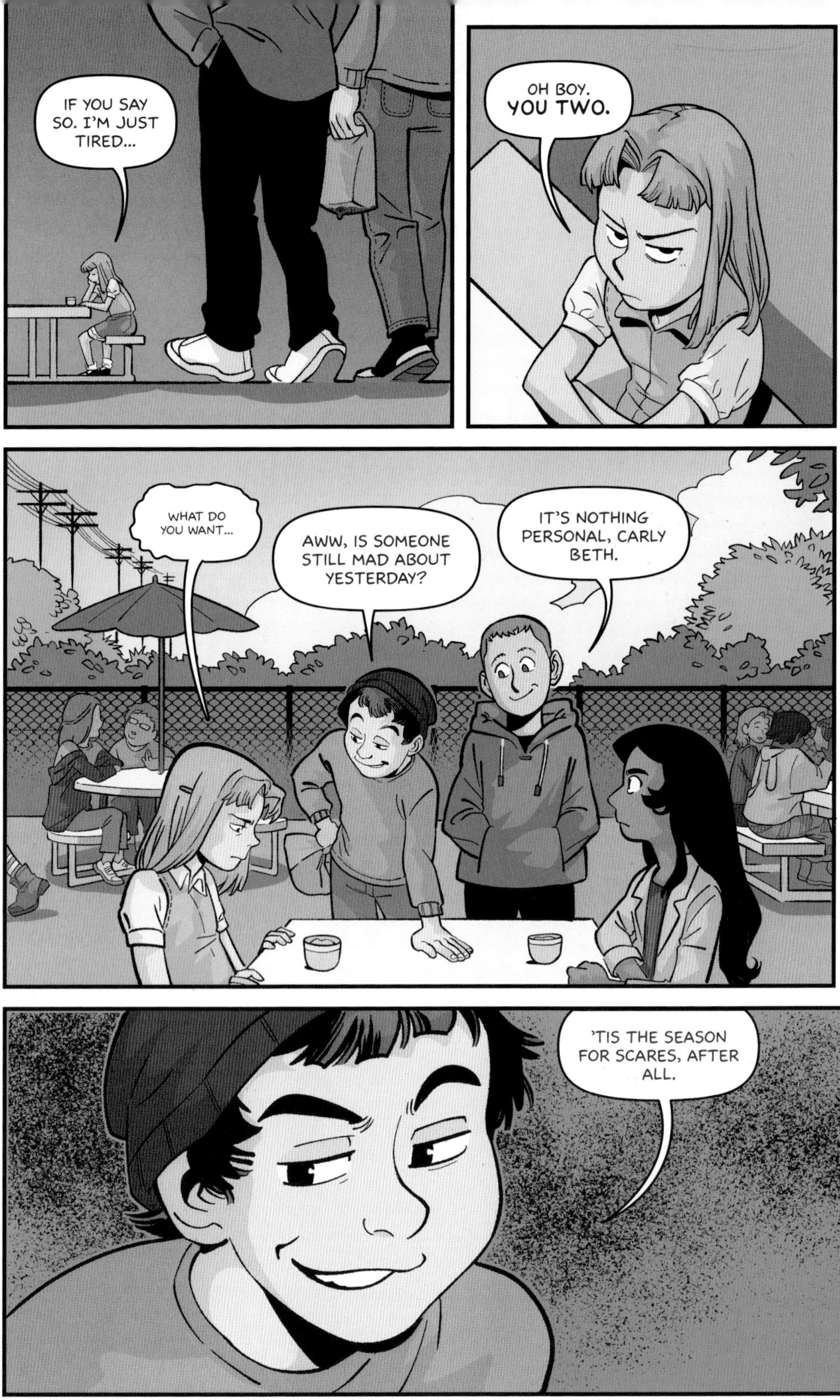
IF YOU SAY SO. I'M JUST TIRED...
OH BOY. **YOU TWO.**
WHAT DO YOU WANT...
AWW, IS SOMEONE STILL MAD ABOUT YESTERDAY?
IT'S NOTHING PERSONAL, CARLY BETH.
'TIS THE SEASON FOR SCARES, AFTER ALL.

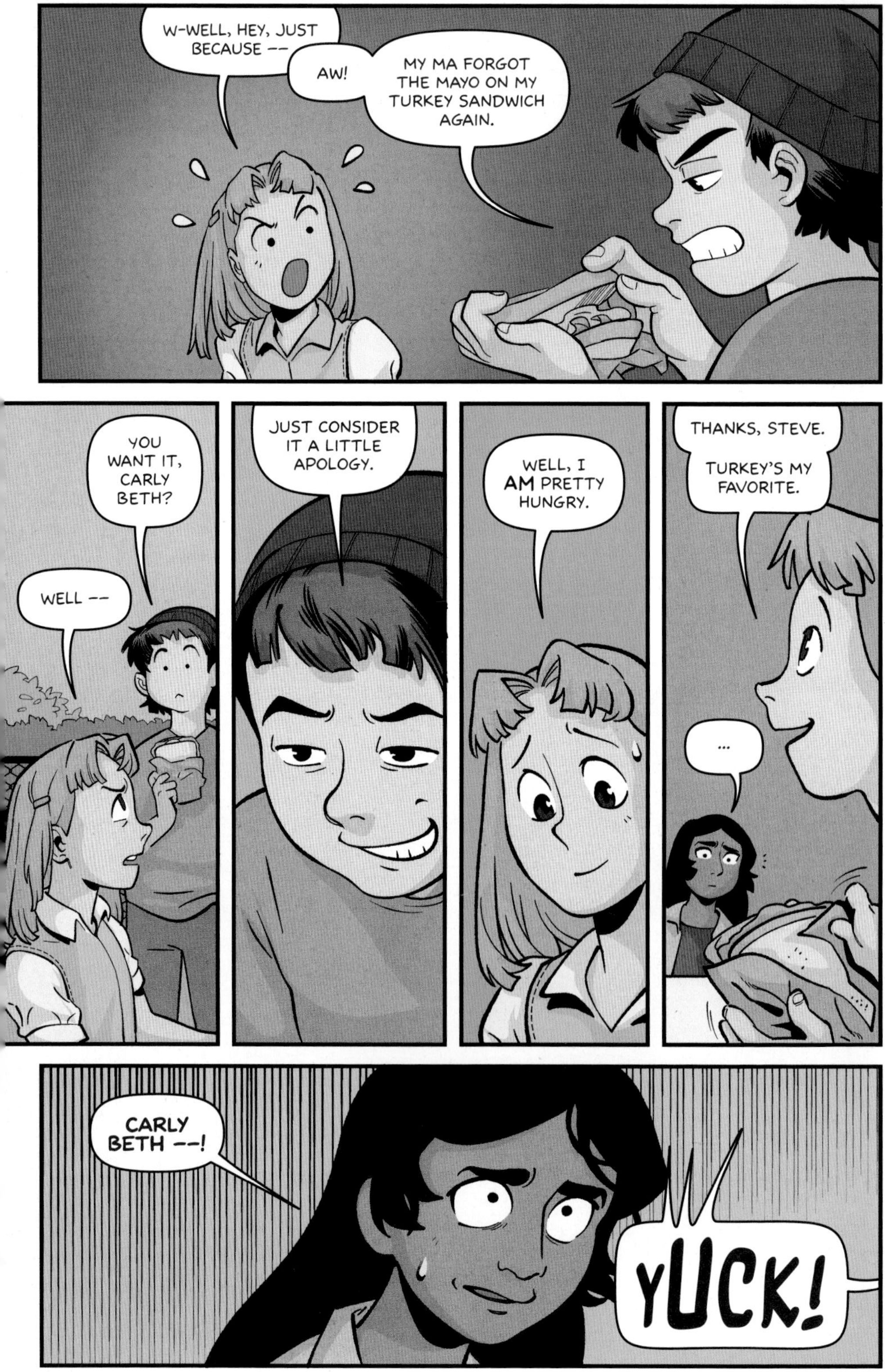
W-WELL, HEY, JUST BECAUSE --
AW!
MY MA FORGOT THE MAYO ON MY TURKEY SANDWICH AGAIN.
YOU WANT IT, CARLY BETH?
WELL --
JUST CONSIDER IT A LITTLE APOLOGY.
WELL, I AM PRETTY HUNGRY.
THANKS, STEVE.
TURKEY'S MY FAVORITE.
...
CARLY BETH --!
YUCK!

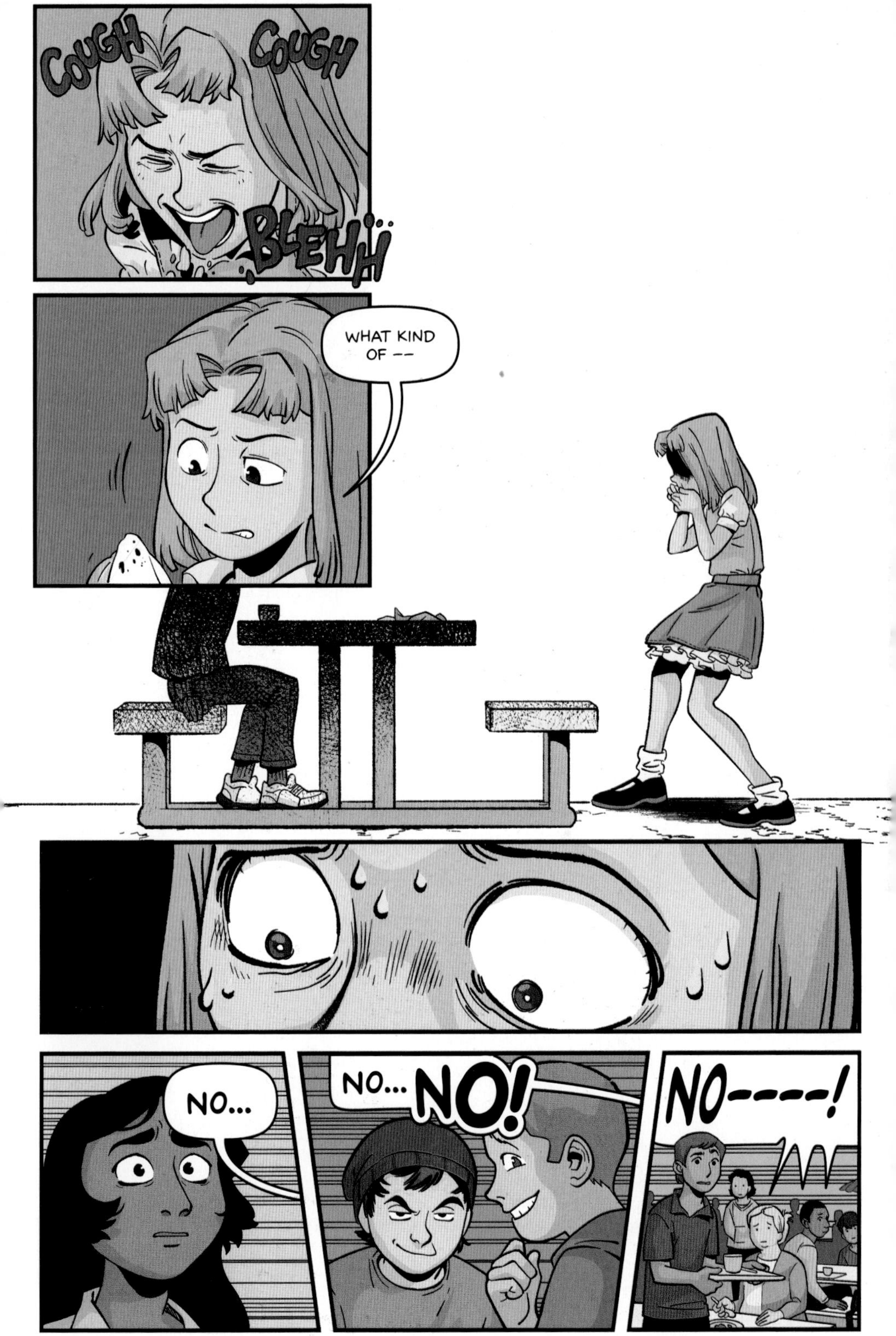
COUGH
COUGH
BLEHH...
WHAT KIND OF --
NO...
NO... NO!
NO----!

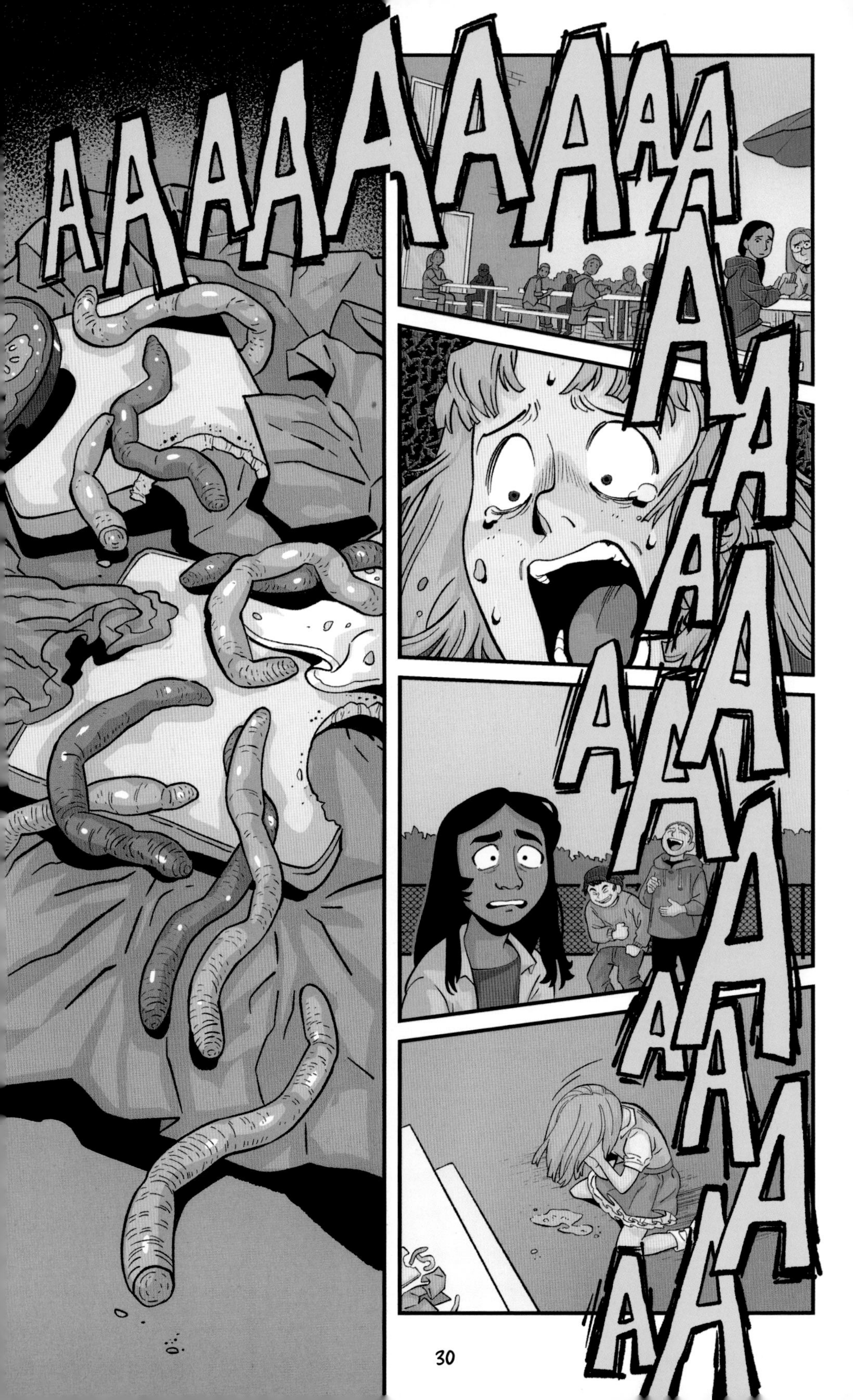
AAAAAAAAAAAAAAAAAAAAAAAAAAAA

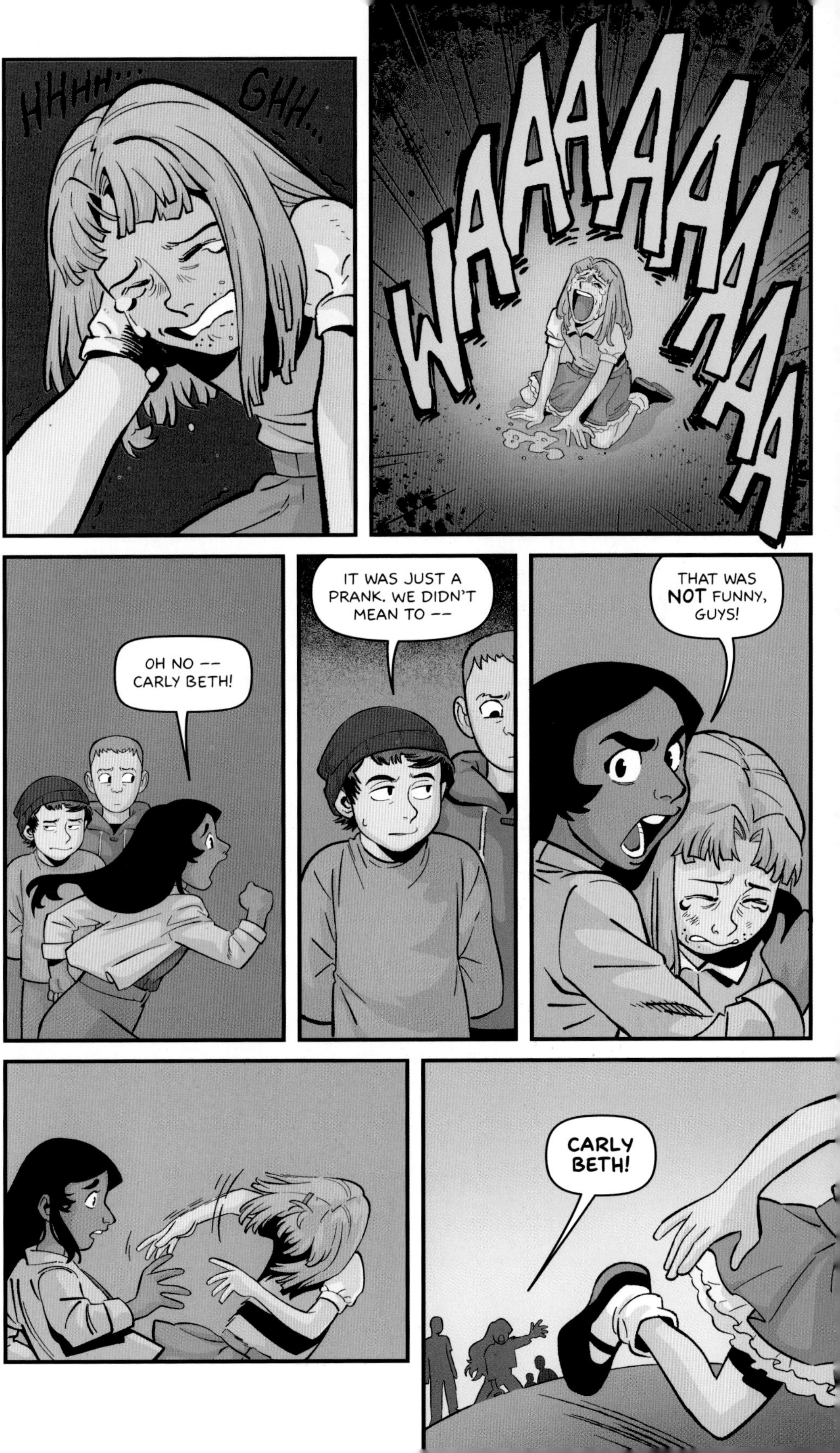
HHHH...
GHH...
WAAAAAAAAA
OH NO -- CARLY BETH!
IT WAS JUST A PRANK. WE DIDN'T MEAN TO --
THAT WAS **NOT** FUNNY, GUYS!
CARLY BETH!

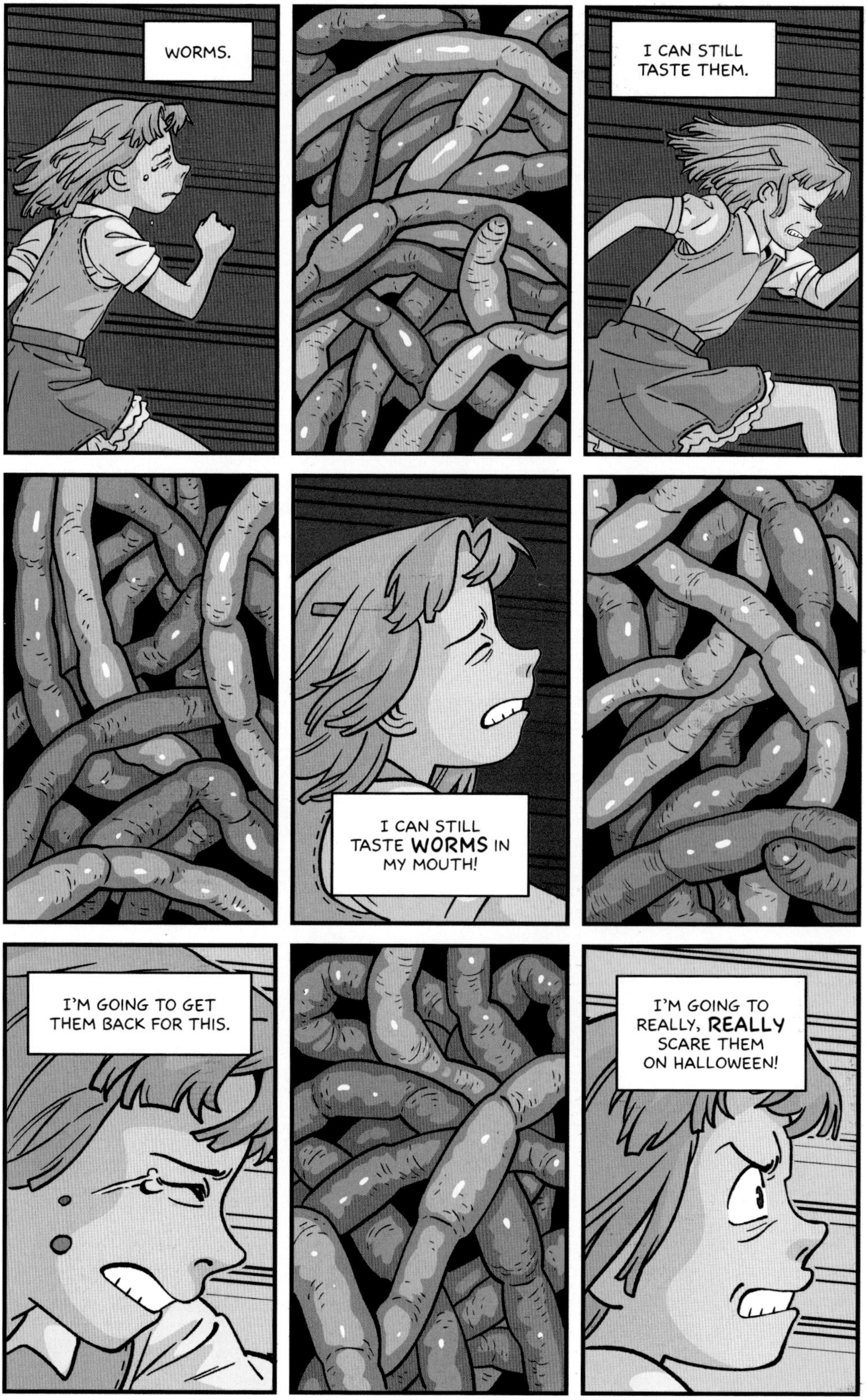
WORMS.
I CAN STILL TASTE THEM.
I CAN STILL TASTE WORMS IN MY MOUTH!
I'M GOING TO GET THEM BACK FOR THIS.
I'M GOING TO REALLY, REALLY SCARE THEM ON HALLOWEEN!

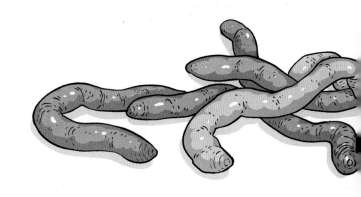

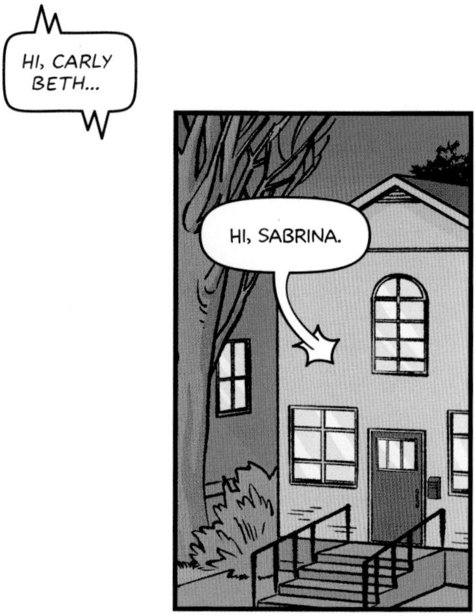
HI, CARLY BETH...
HI, SABRINA.

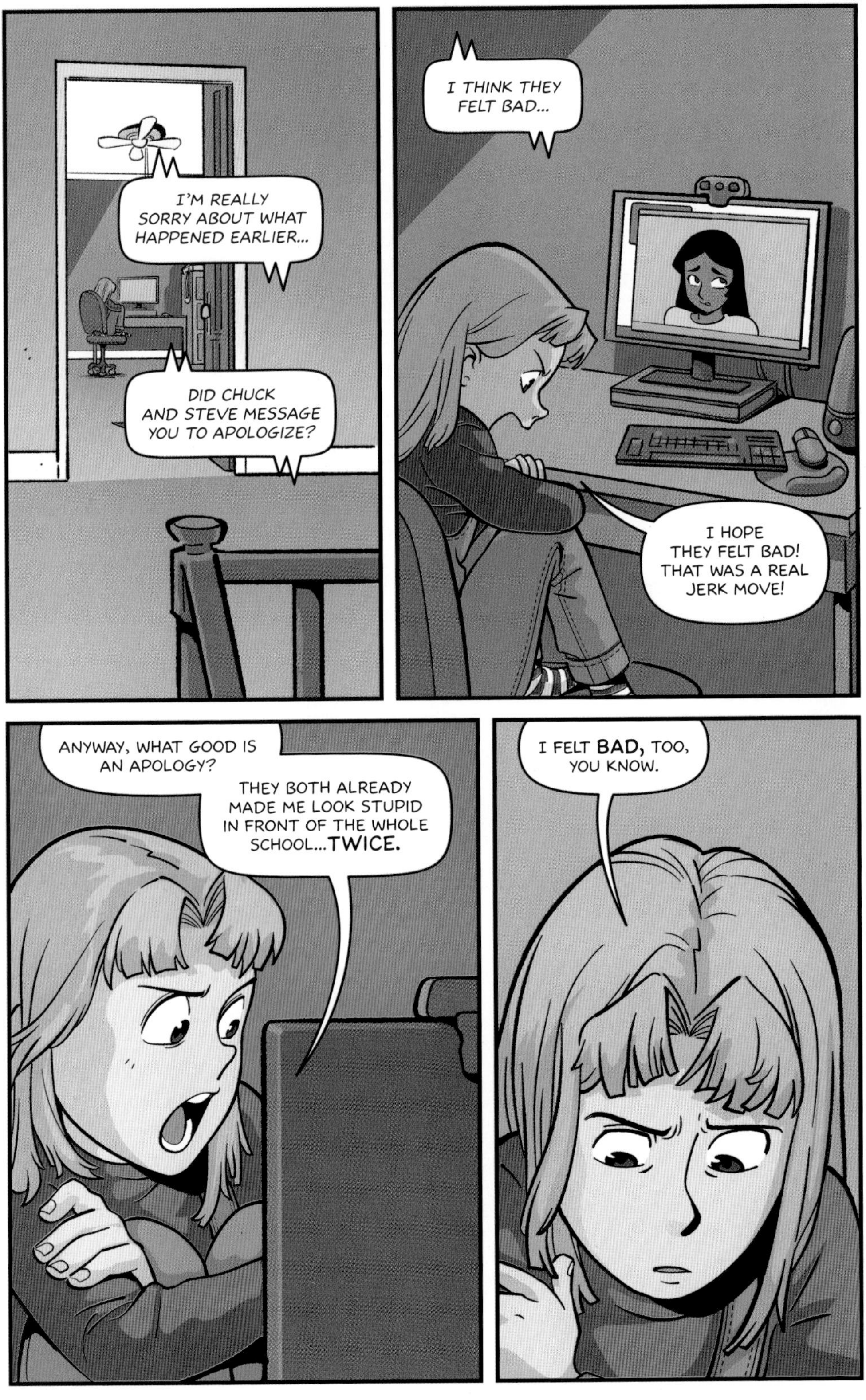
I'M REALLY SORRY ABOUT WHAT HAPPENED EARLIER...
DID CHUCK AND STEVE MESSAGE YOU TO APOLOGIZE?
I THINK THEY FELT BAD...
I HOPE THEY FELT BAD! THAT WAS A REAL JERK MOVE!
ANYWAY, WHAT GOOD IS AN APOLOGY?
THEY BOTH ALREADY MADE ME LOOK STUPID IN FRONT OF THE WHOLE SCHOOL...TWICE.
I FELT BAD, TOO, YOU KNOW.

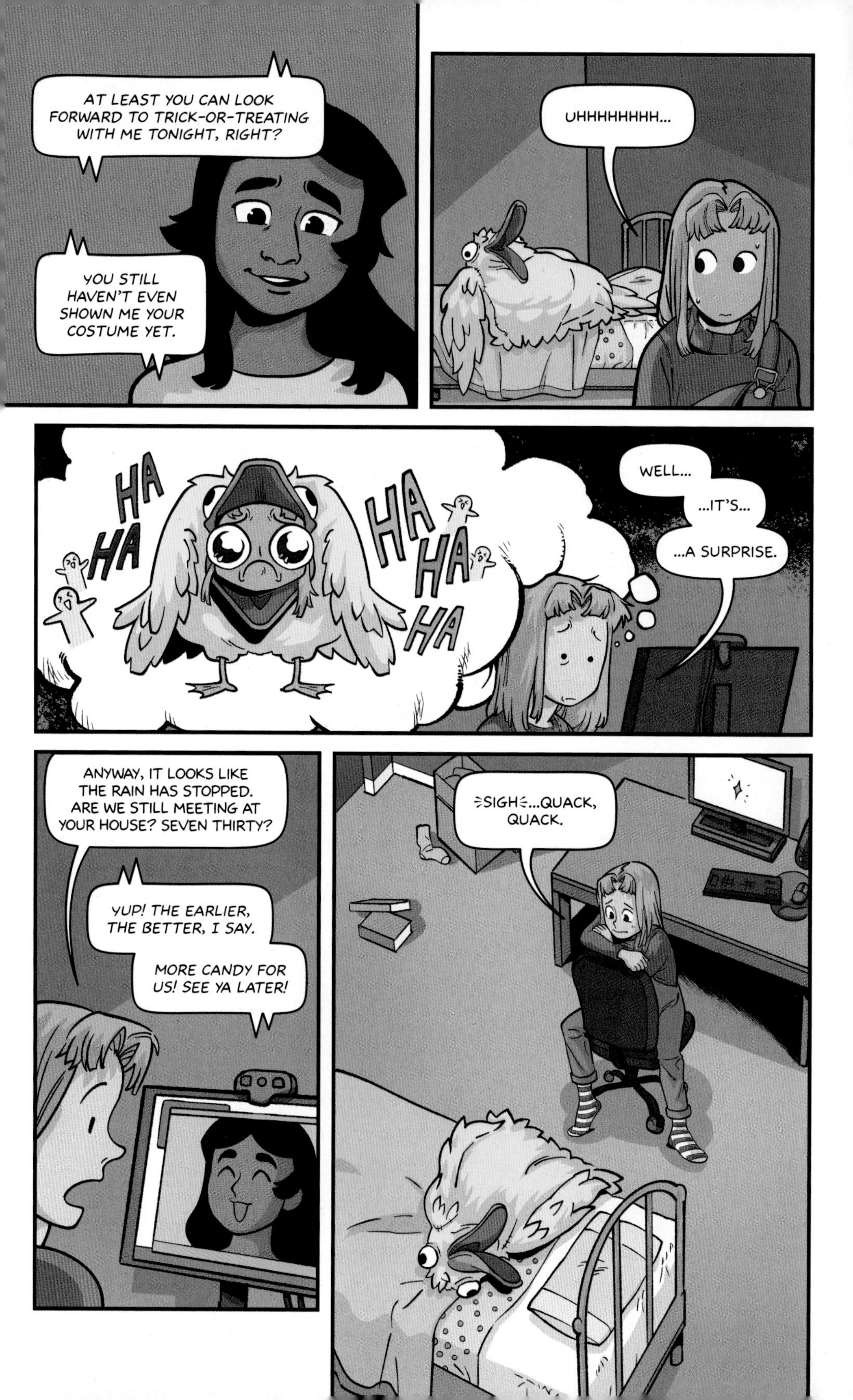
AT LEAST YOU CAN LOOK FORWARD TO TRICK-OR-TREATING WITH ME TONIGHT, RIGHT?
YOU STILL HAVEN'T EVEN SHOWN ME YOUR COSTUME YET.
UHHHHHHHH...
HA HA
HA HA HA HA
WELL...
...IT'S...
...A SURPRISE.
ANYWAY, IT LOOKS LIKE THE RAIN HAS STOPPED. ARE WE STILL MEETING AT YOUR HOUSE? SEVEN THIRTY?
YUP! THE EARLIER, THE BETTER, I SAY.
MORE CANDY FOR US! SEE YA LATER!
SIGH...QUACK, QUACK.

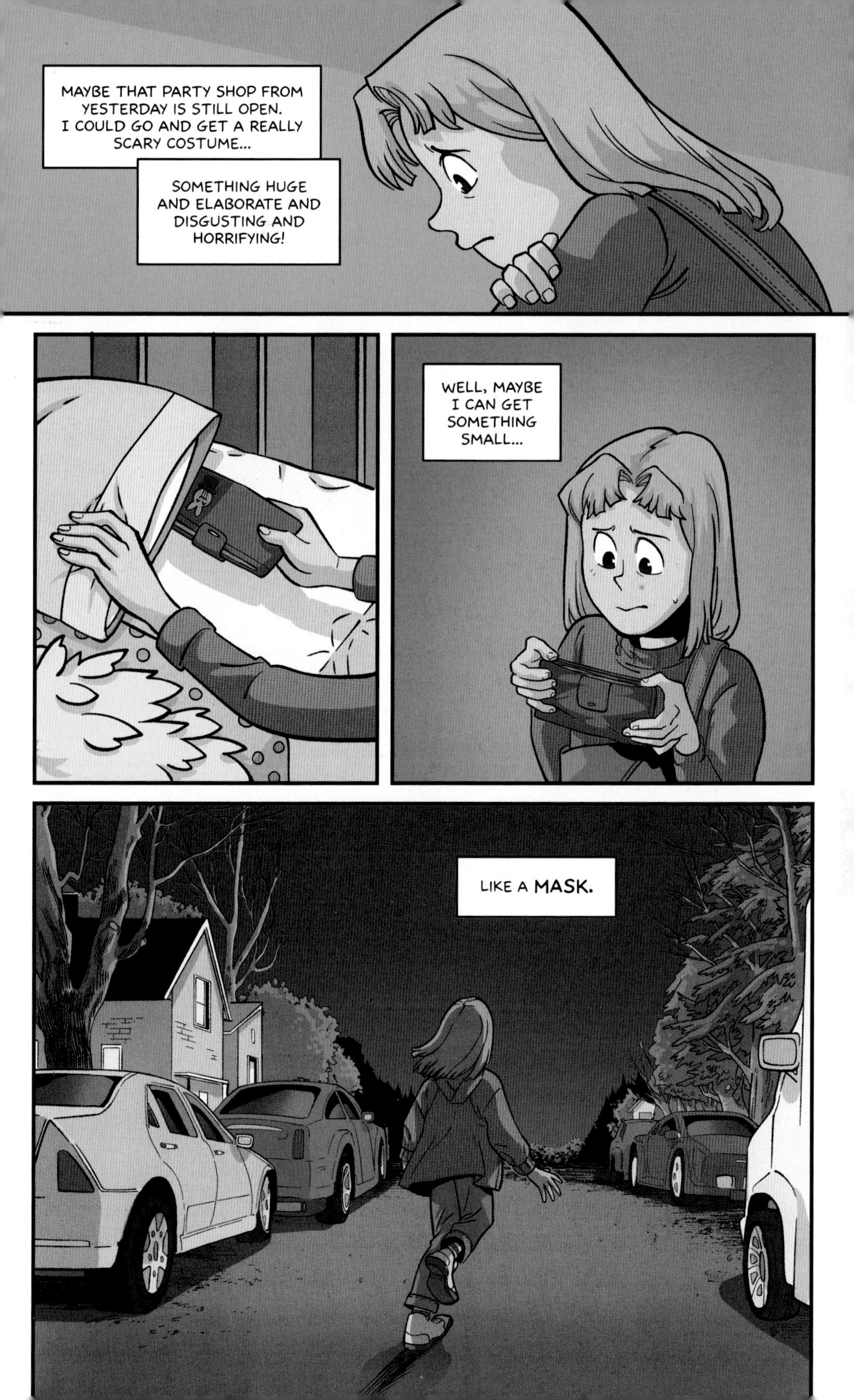
MAYBE THAT PARTY SHOP FROM YESTERDAY IS STILL OPEN. I COULD GO AND GET A REALLY SCARY COSTUME...
SOMETHING HUGE AND ELABORATE AND DISGUSTING AND HORRIFYING!
WELL, MAYBE I CAN GET SOMETHING SMALL...
LIKE A MASK.

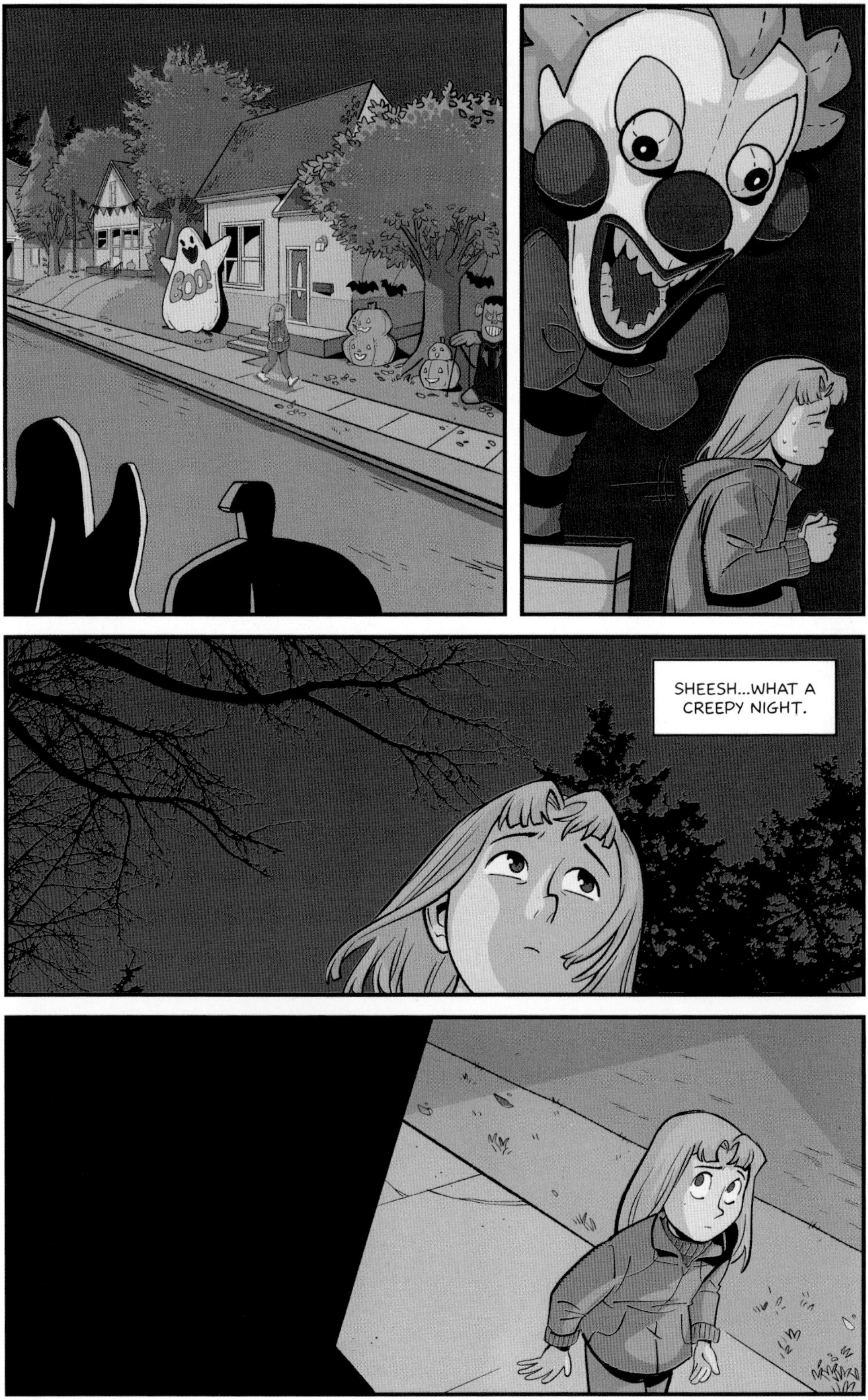
BOO!
SHEESH...WHAT A CREEPY NIGHT.

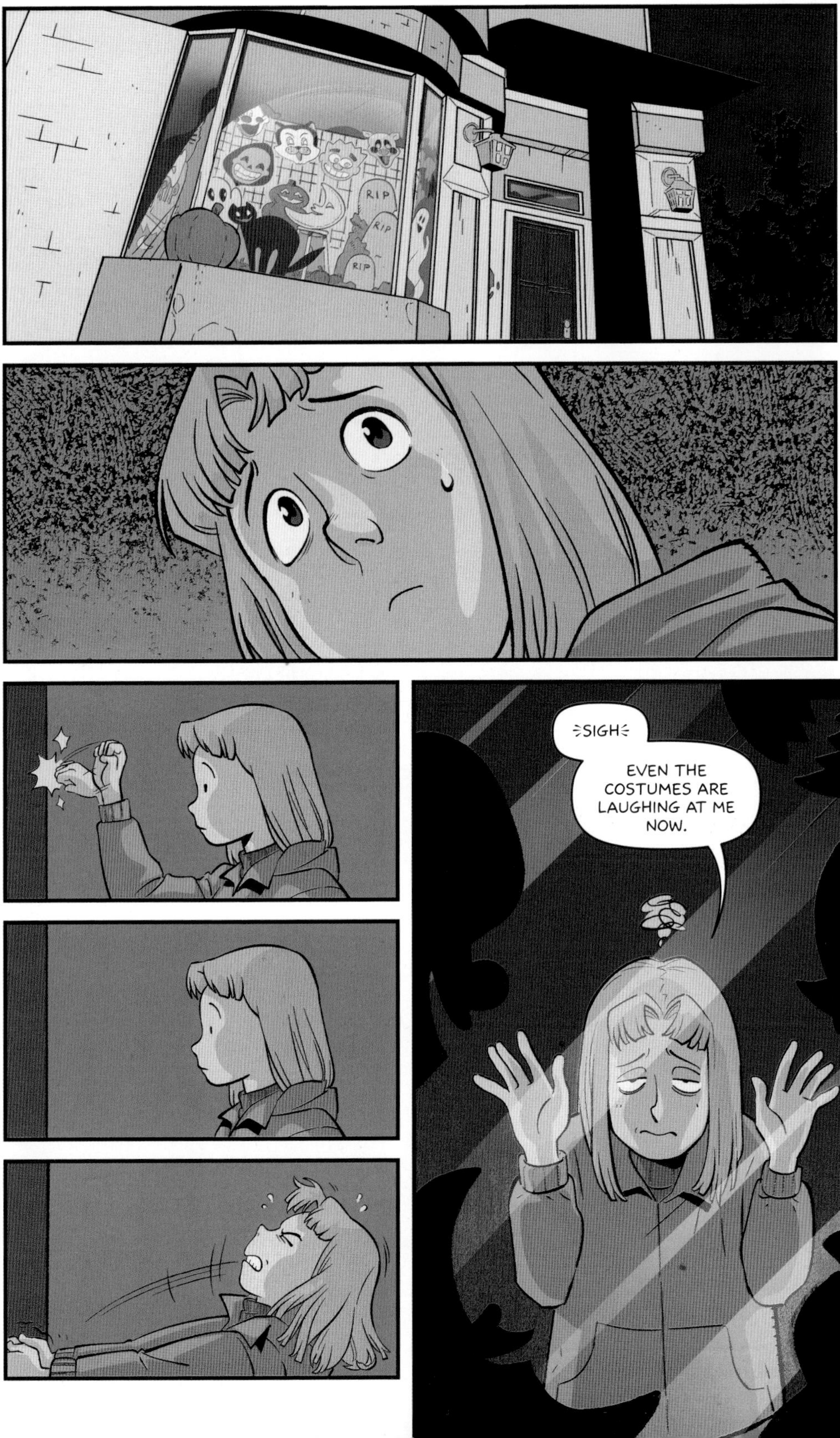

SIGH
EVEN THE COSTUMES ARE LAUGHING AT ME NOW.

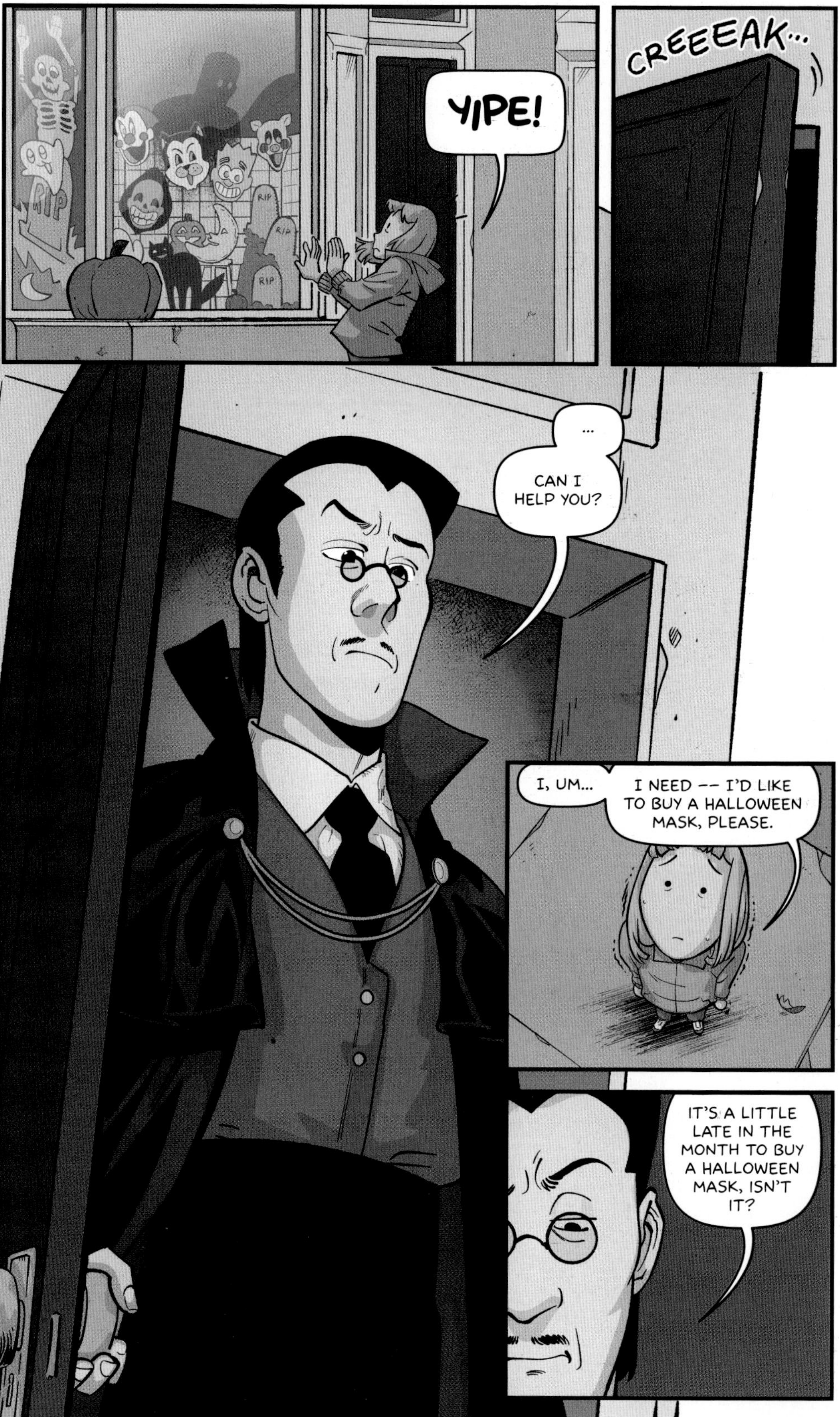
YIPE!
CREEEAK...
...
CAN I HELP YOU?
I, UM...
I NEED -- I'D LIKE TO BUY A HALLOWEEN MASK, PLEASE.
IT'S A LITTLE LATE IN THE MONTH TO BUY A HALLOWEEN MASK, ISN'T IT?

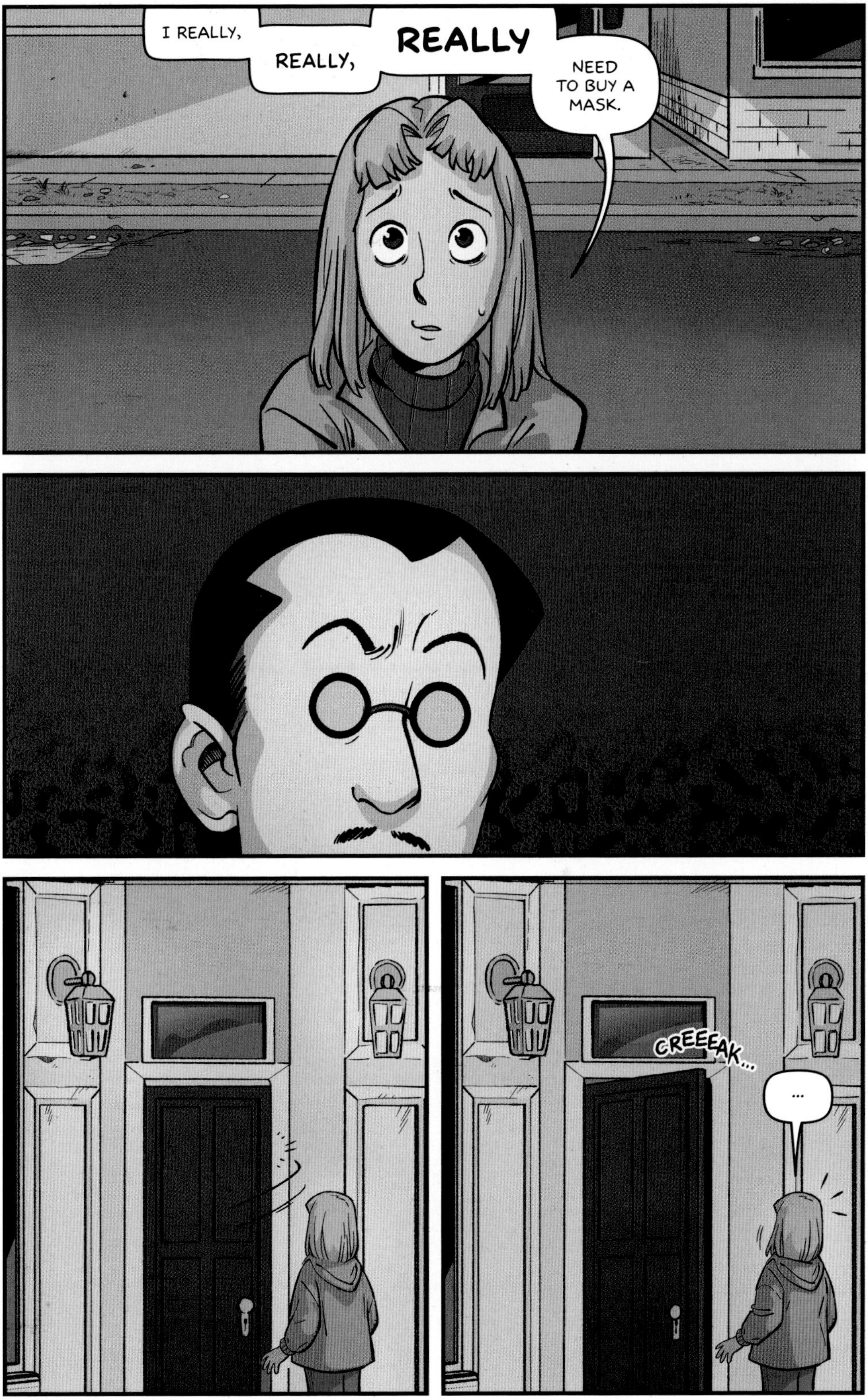
I REALLY,
REALLY,
REALLY
NEED TO BUY A MASK.
CREEEAK...
...

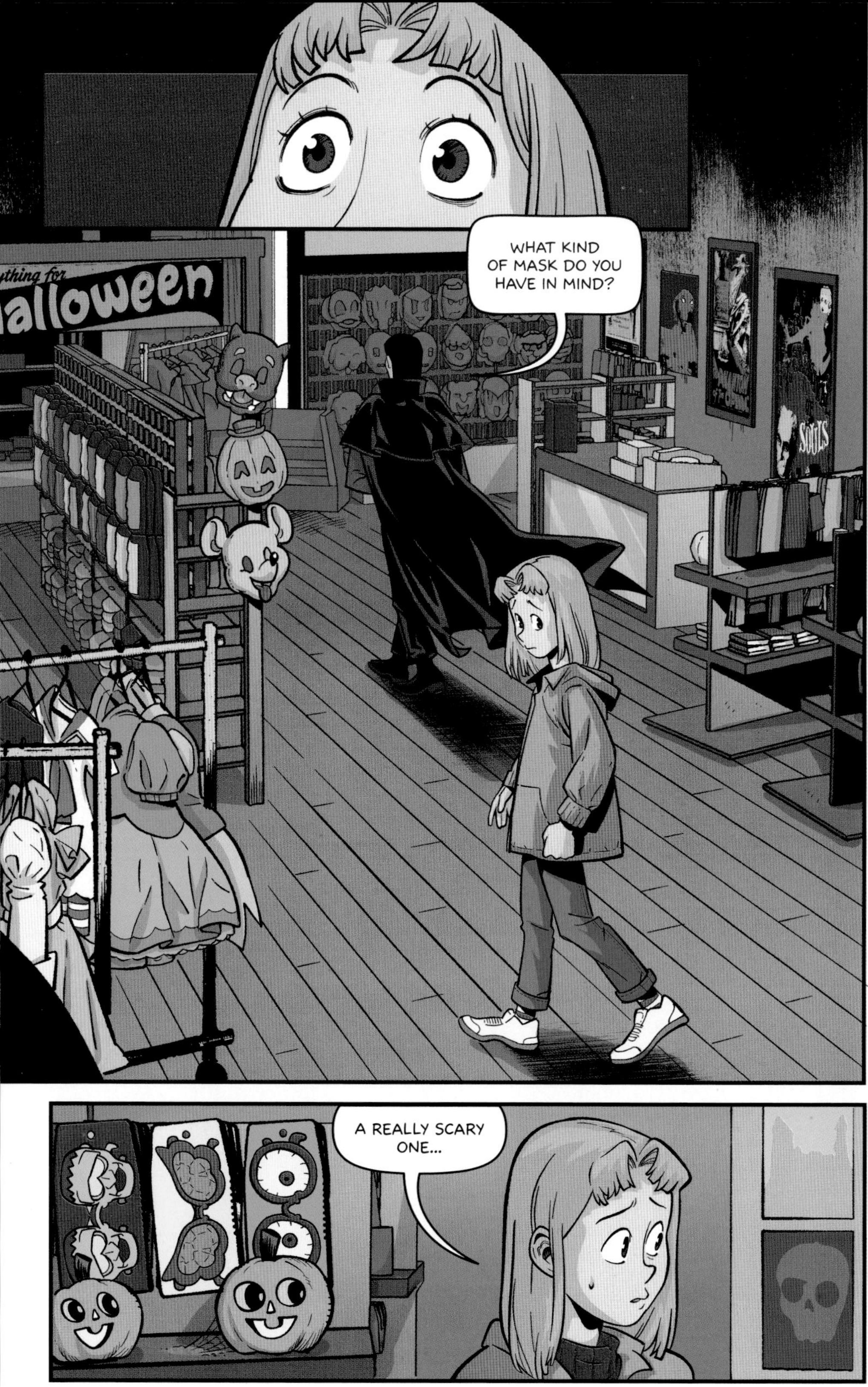
WHAT KIND OF MASK DO YOU HAVE IN MIND?
A REALLY SCARY ONE...

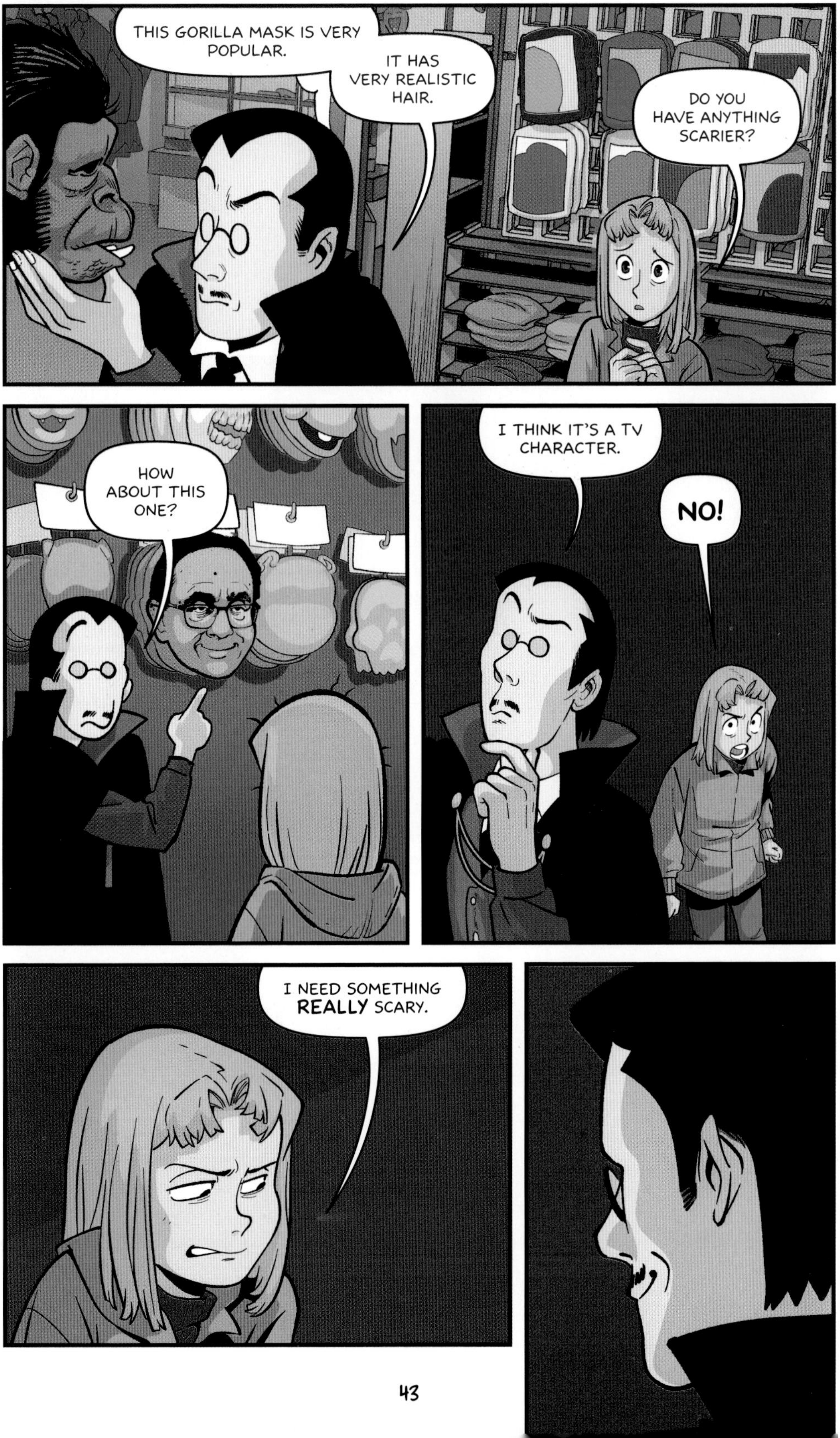
THIS GORILLA MASK IS VERY POPULAR.
IT HAS VERY REALISTIC HAIR.
DO YOU HAVE ANYTHING SCARIER?
HOW ABOUT THIS ONE?
I THINK IT'S A TV CHARACTER.
NO!
I NEED SOMETHING **REALLY** SCARY.

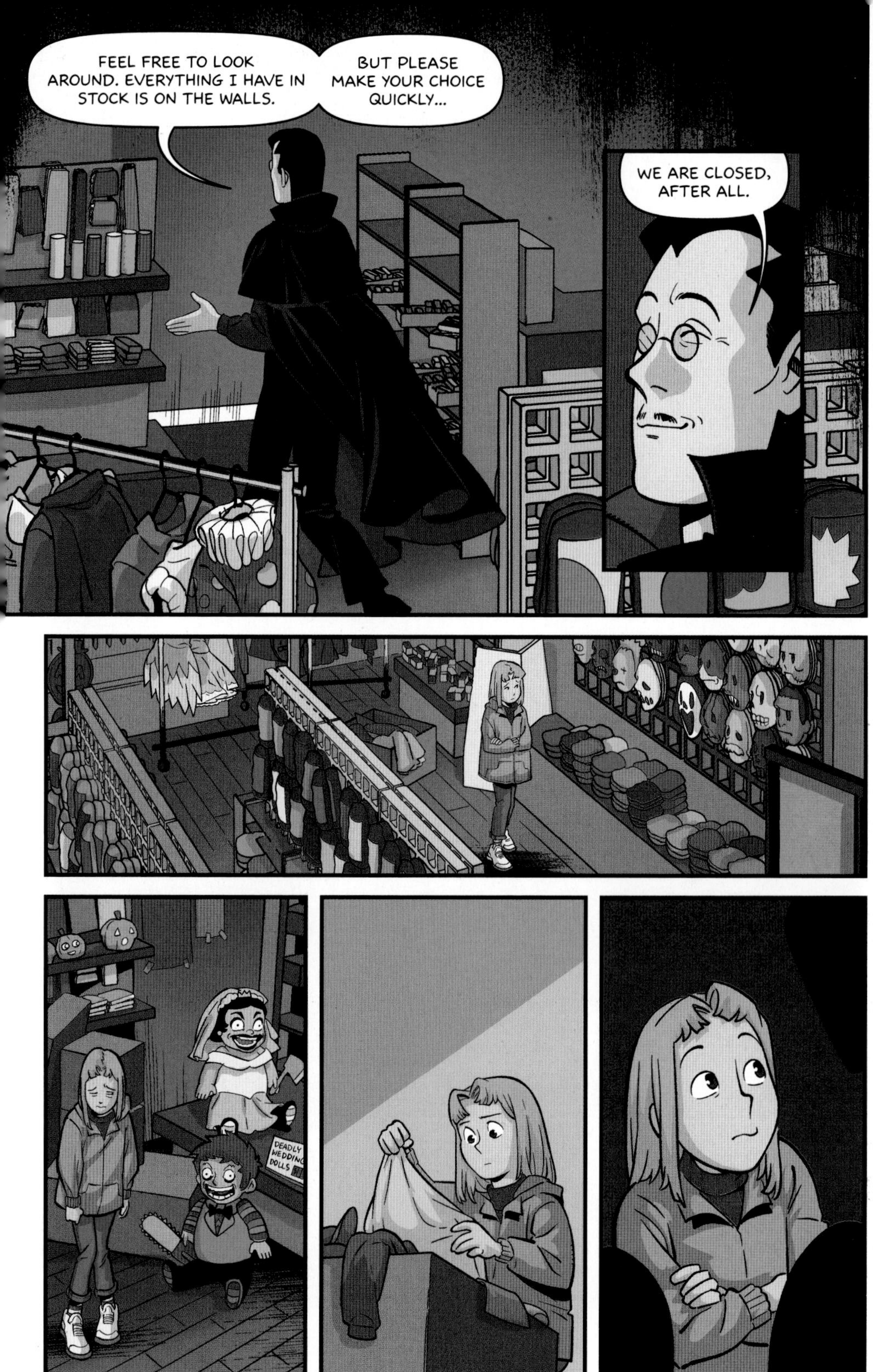
FEEL FREE TO LOOK AROUND. EVERYTHING I HAVE IN STOCK IS ON THE WALLS.
BUT PLEASE MAKE YOUR CHOICE QUICKLY...
WE ARE CLOSED, AFTER ALL.
DEADLY WEDDING DOLLS

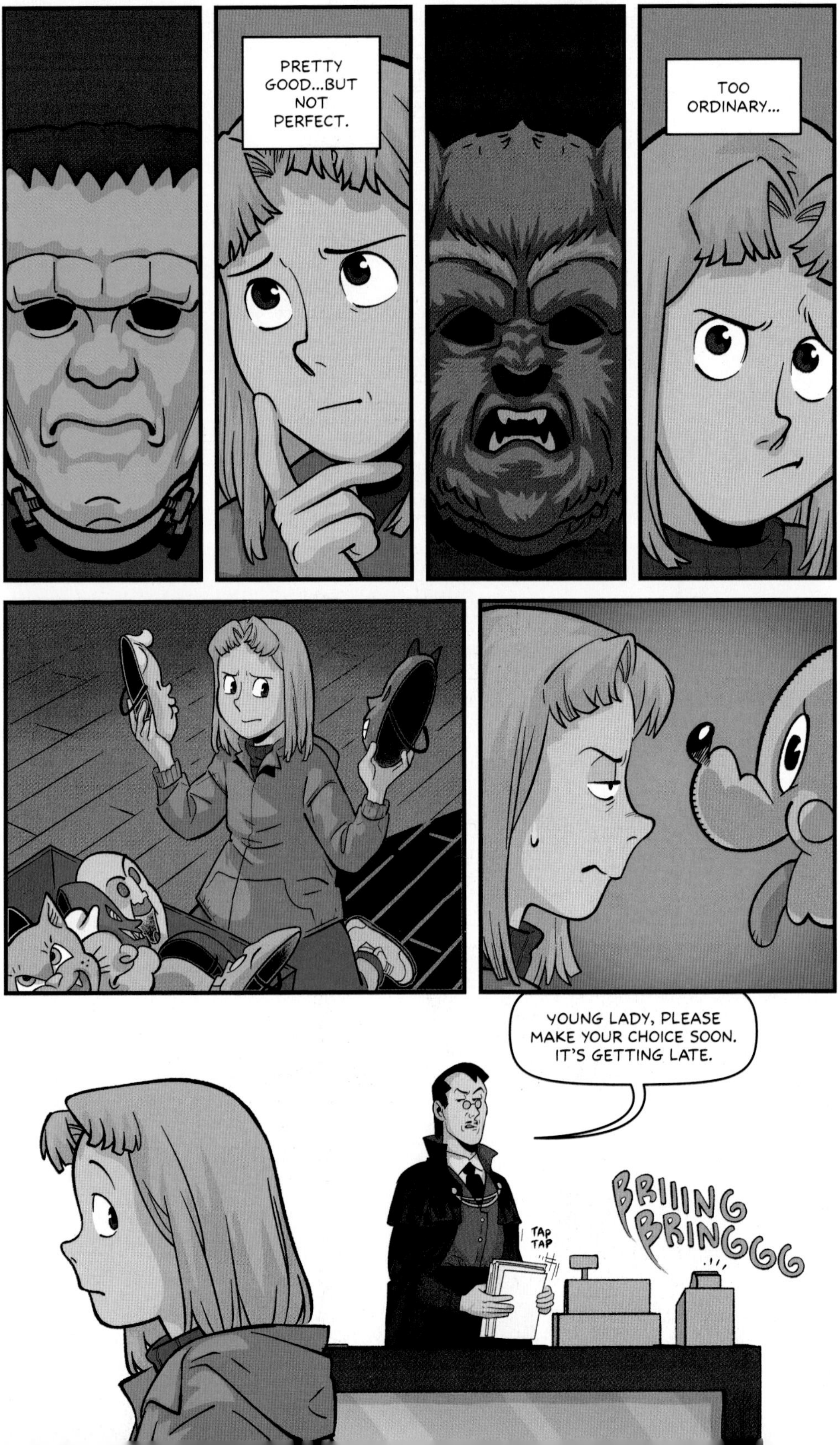
PRETTY GOOD...BUT NOT PERFECT.
TOO ORDINARY...
YOUNG LADY, PLEASE MAKE YOUR CHOICE SOON. IT'S GETTING LATE.
TAP TAP
BRIIING BRINGGG

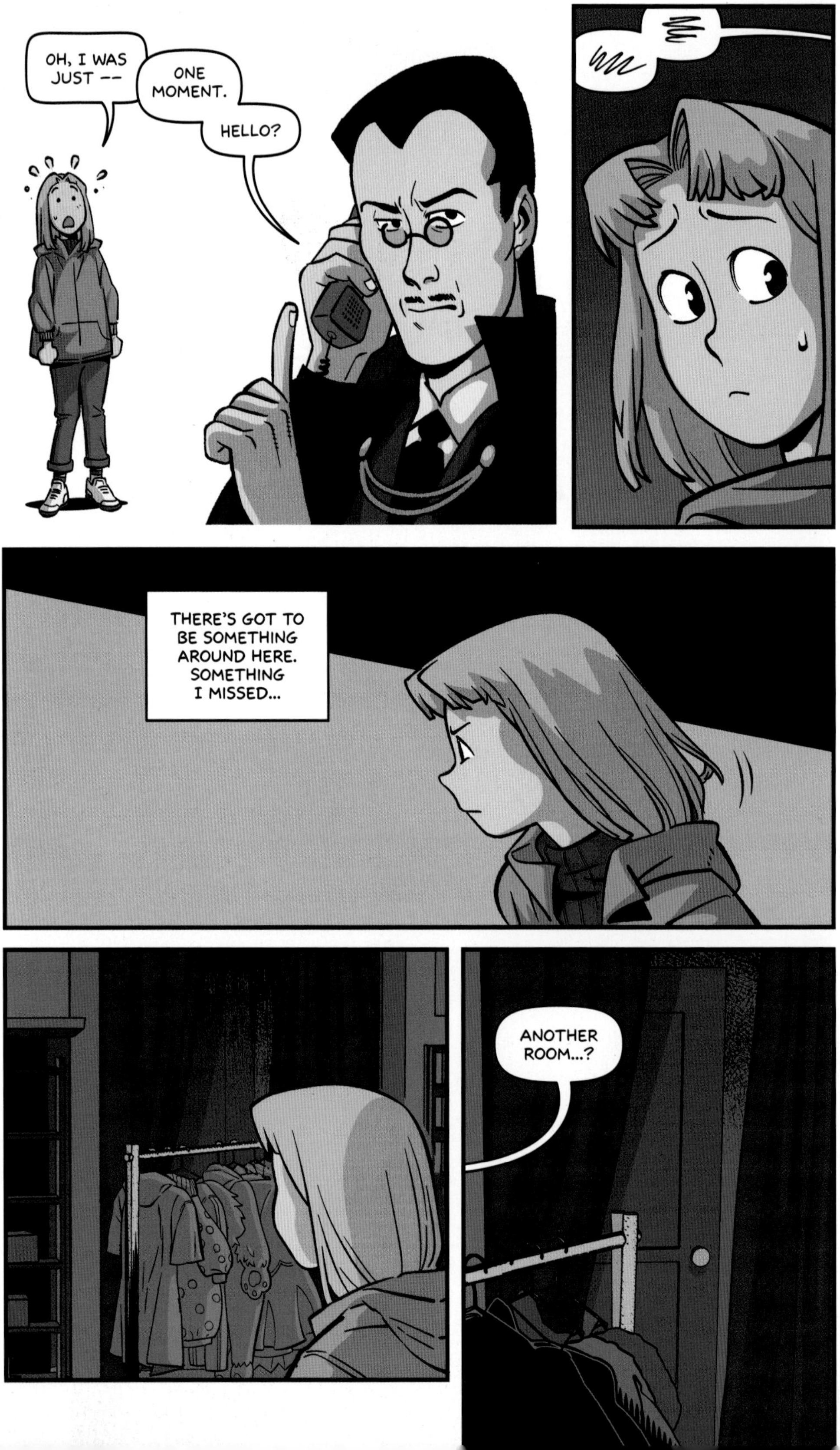
OH, I WAS JUST --
ONE MOMENT.
HELLO?
THERE'S GOT TO BE SOMETHING AROUND HERE. SOMETHING I MISSED...
ANOTHER ROOM...?

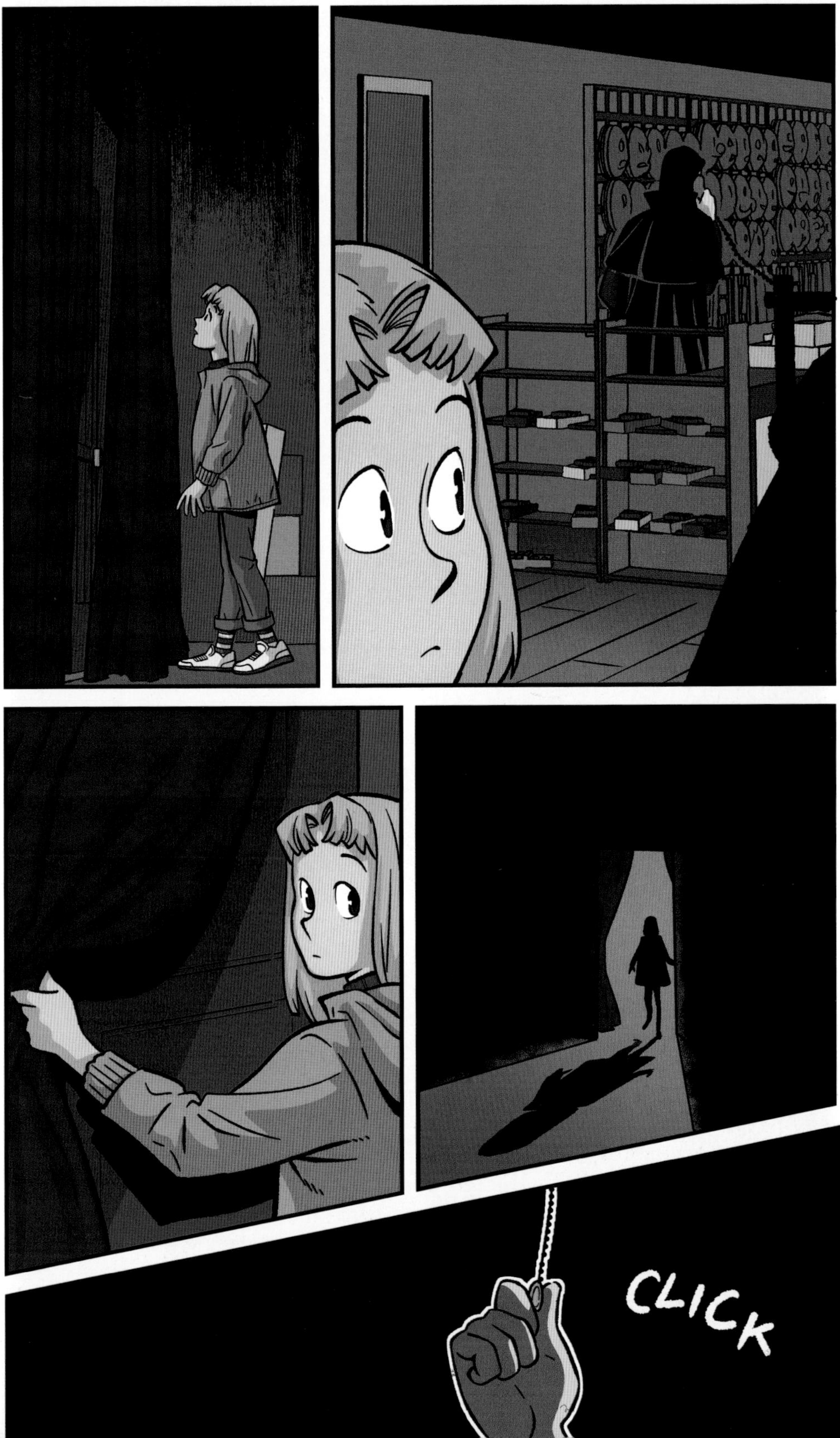
CLICK

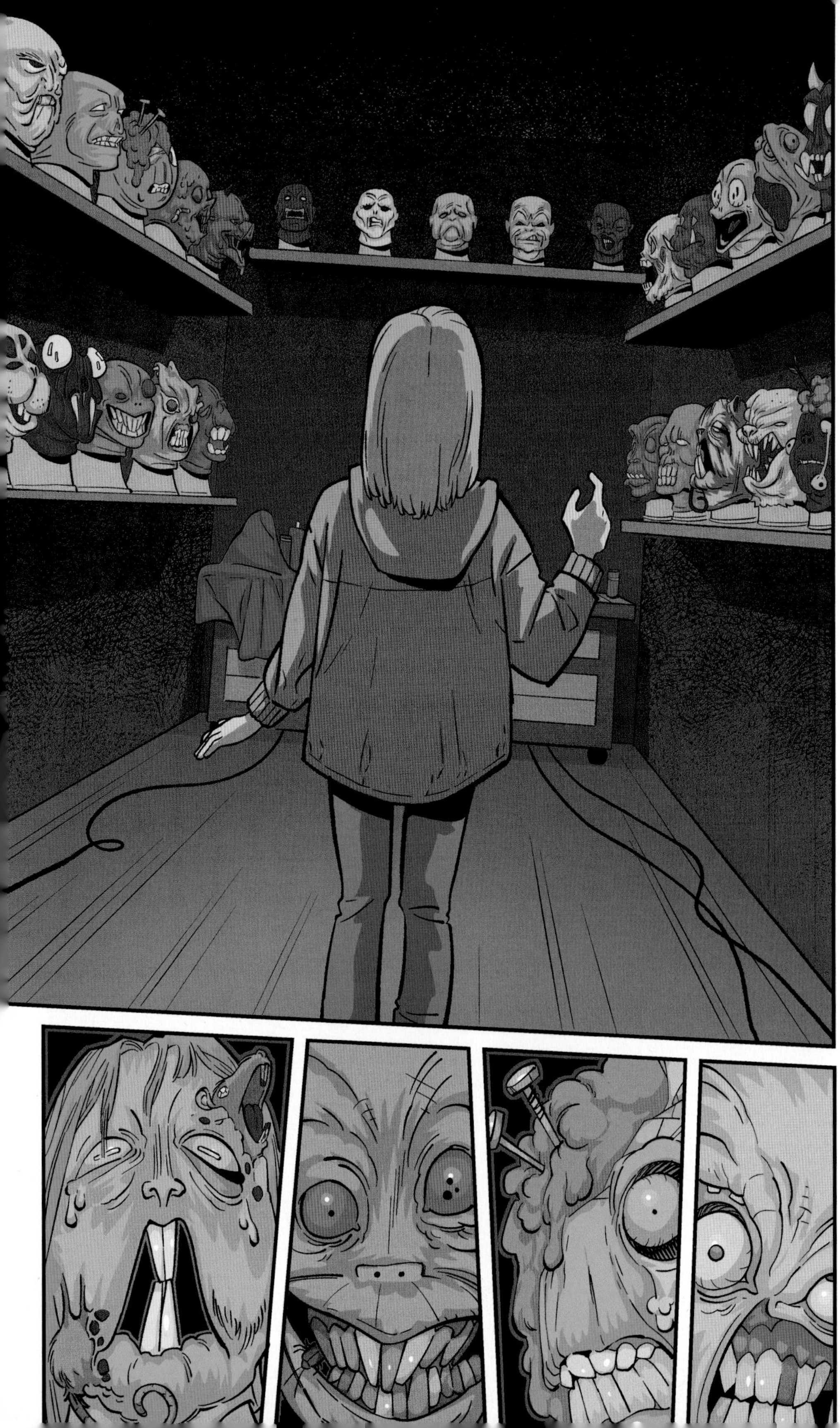

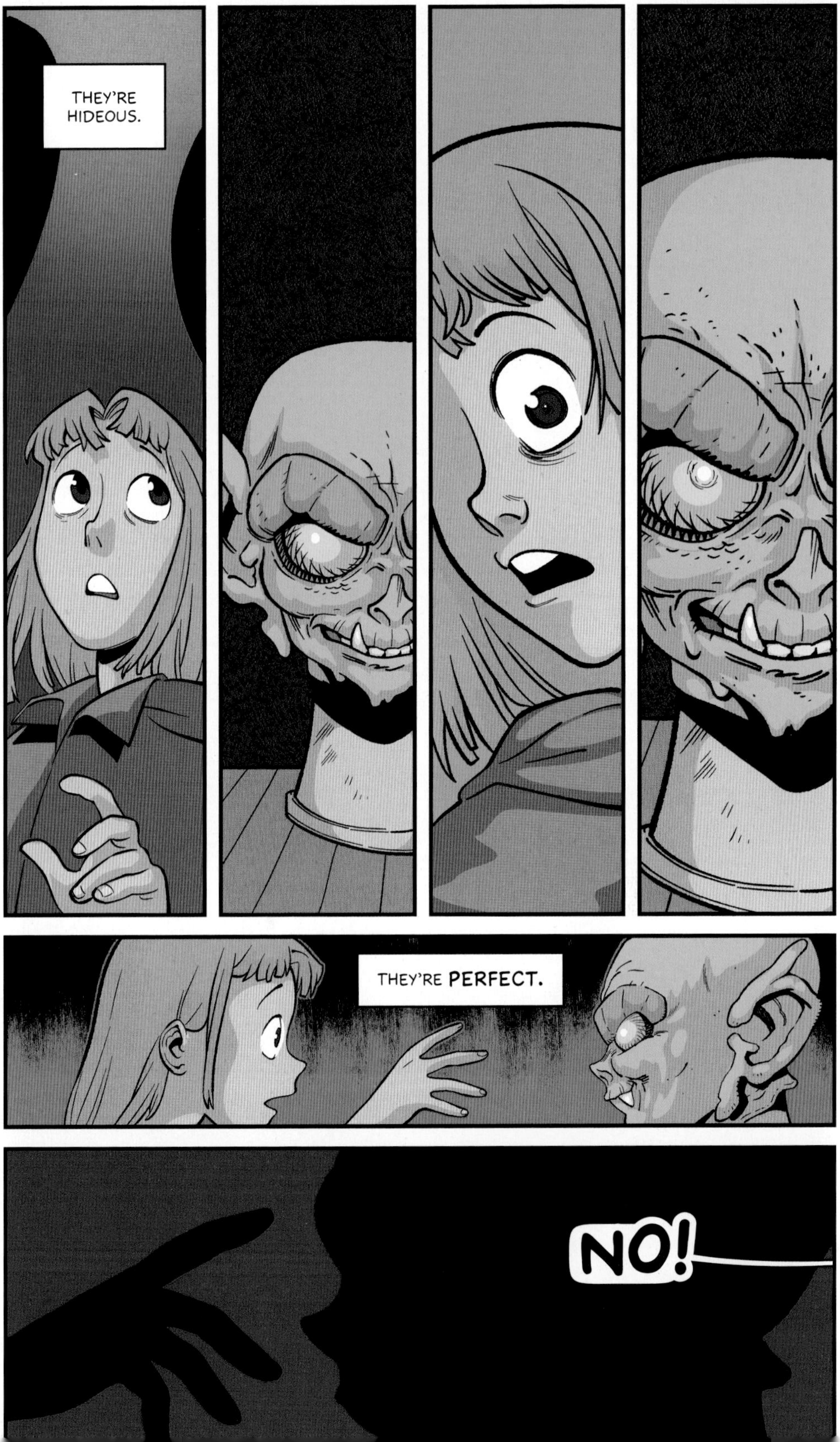
THEY'RE HIDEOUS.
THEY'RE PERFECT.
NO!

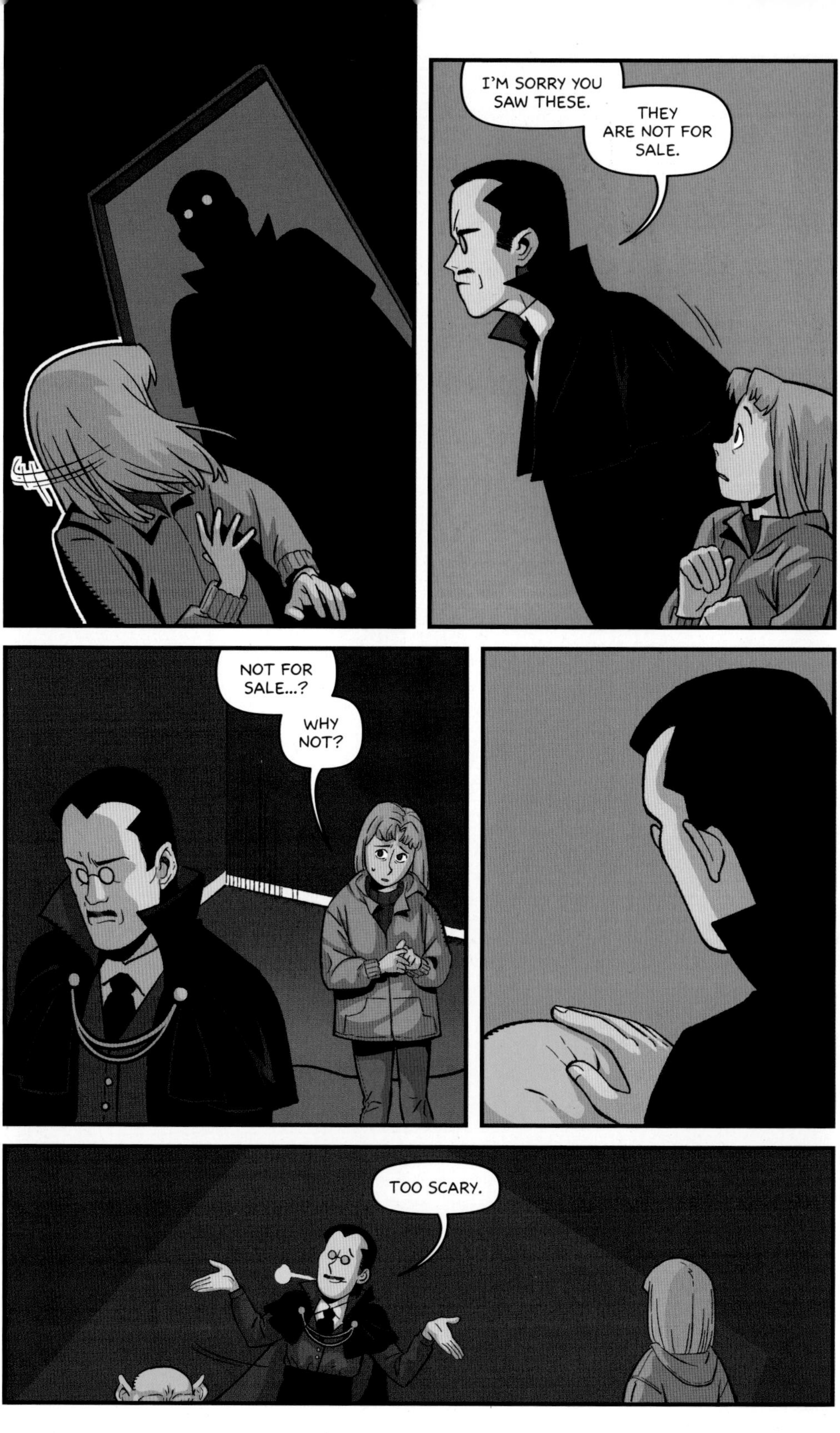
I'M SORRY YOU SAW THESE.
THEY ARE NOT FOR SALE.
NOT FOR SALE...?
WHY NOT?
TOO SCARY.

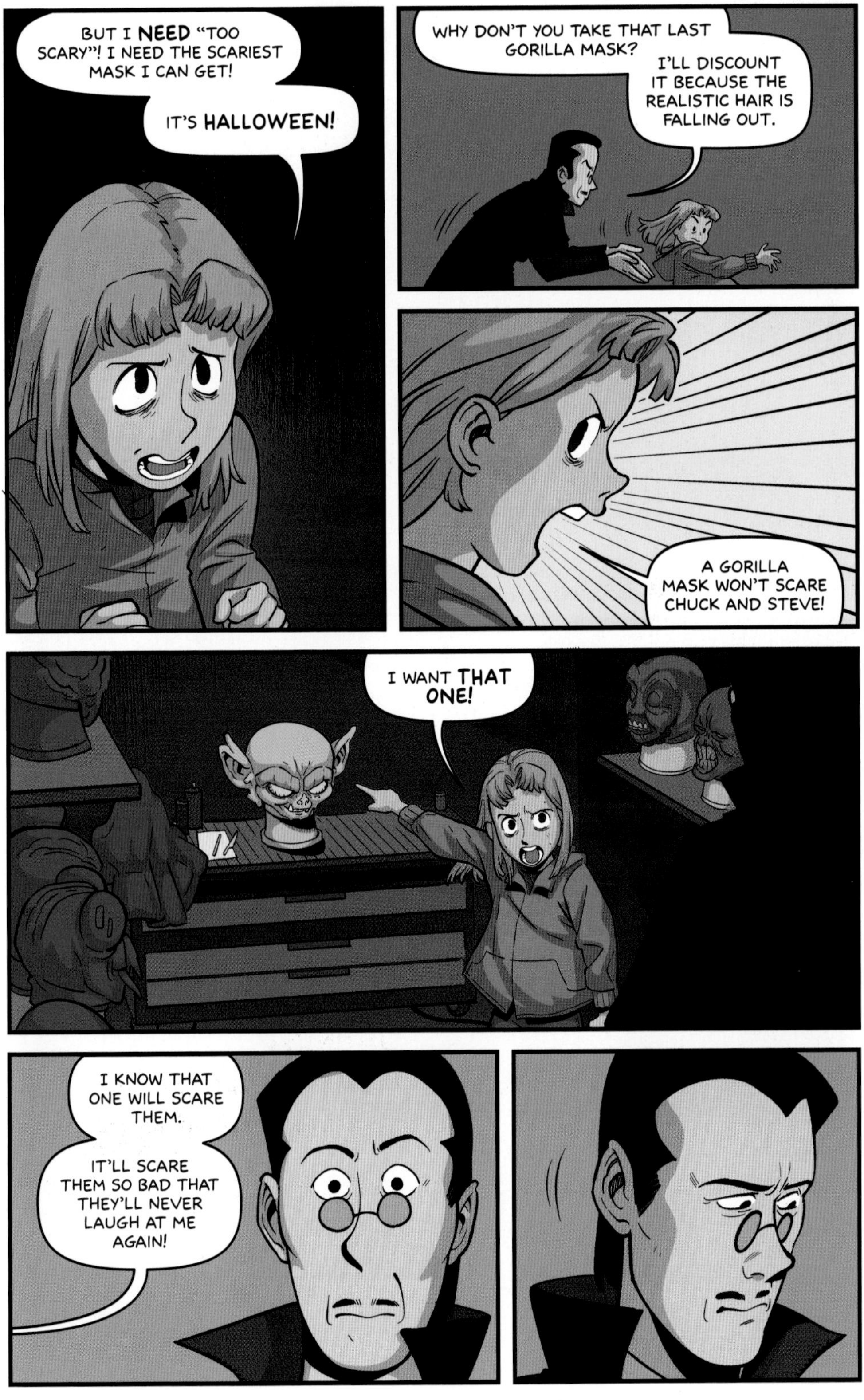
BUT I NEED "TOO SCARY"! I NEED THE SCARIEST MASK I CAN GET!
IT'S HALLOWEEN!
WHY DON'T YOU TAKE THAT LAST GORILLA MASK?
I'LL DISCOUNT IT BECAUSE THE REALISTIC HAIR IS FALLING OUT.
A GORILLA MASK WON'T SCARE CHUCK AND STEVE!
I WANT THAT ONE!
I KNOW THAT ONE WILL SCARE THEM.
IT'LL SCARE THEM SO BAD THAT THEY'LL NEVER LAUGH AT ME AGAIN!

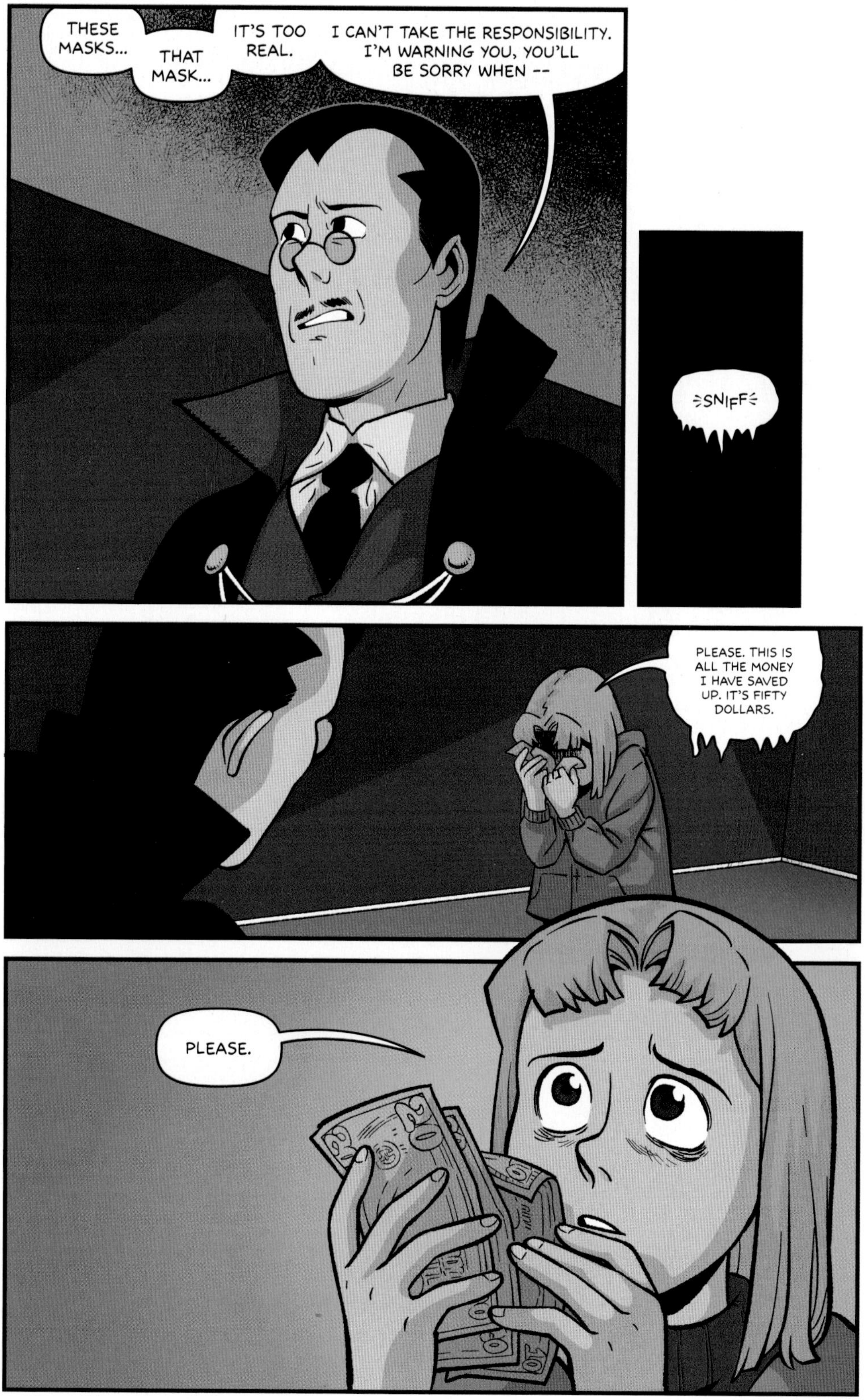
THESE MASKS...
THAT MASK...
IT'S TOO REAL.
I CAN'T TAKE THE RESPONSIBILITY. I'M WARNING YOU, YOU'LL BE SORRY WHEN --
SNIFF
PLEASE. THIS IS ALL THE MONEY I HAVE SAVED UP. IT'S FIFTY DOLLARS.
PLEASE.

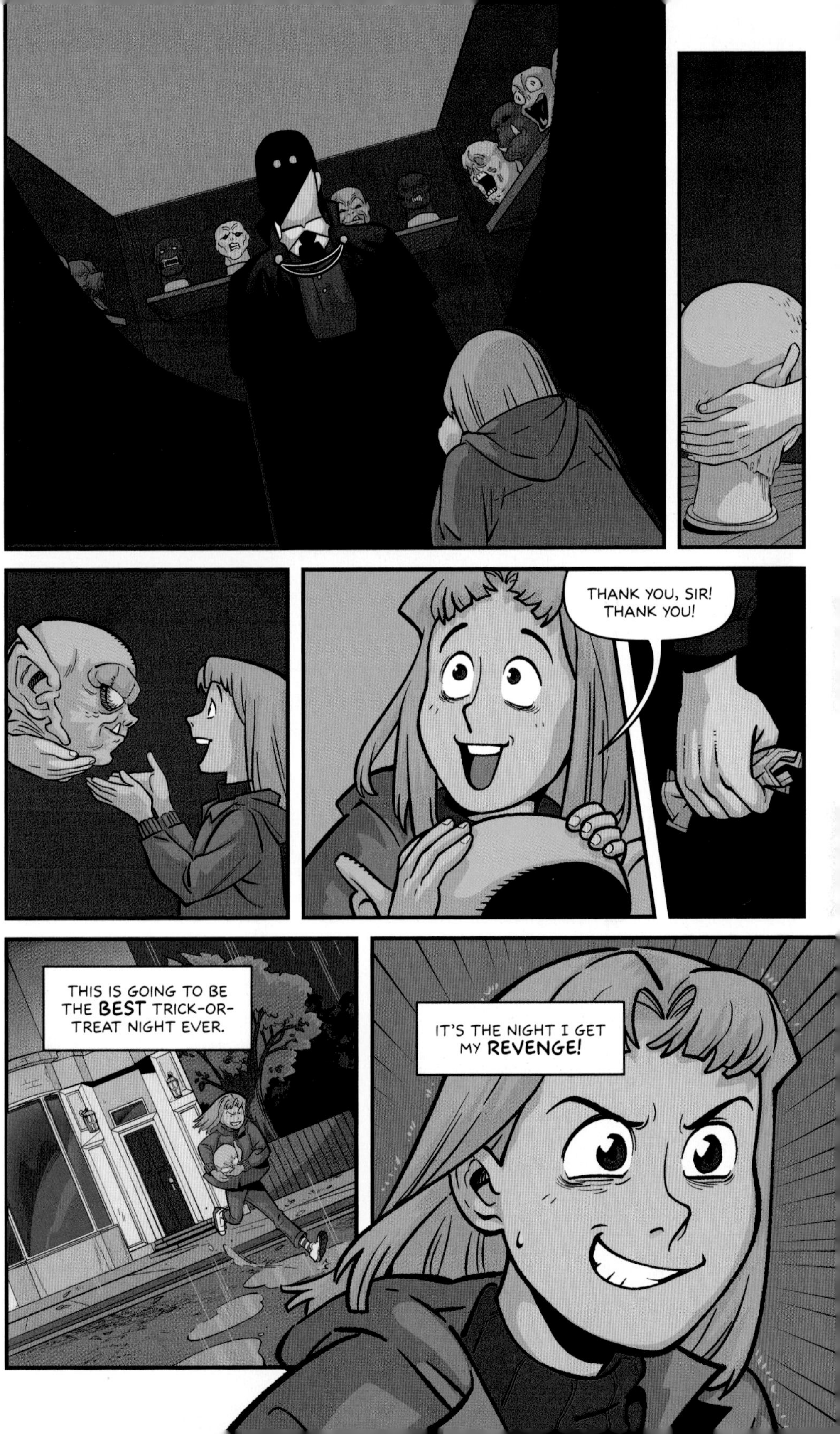
THANK YOU, SIR!
THANK YOU!
THIS IS GOING TO BE THE BEST TRICK-OR-TREAT NIGHT EVER.
IT'S THE NIGHT I GET MY REVENGE!

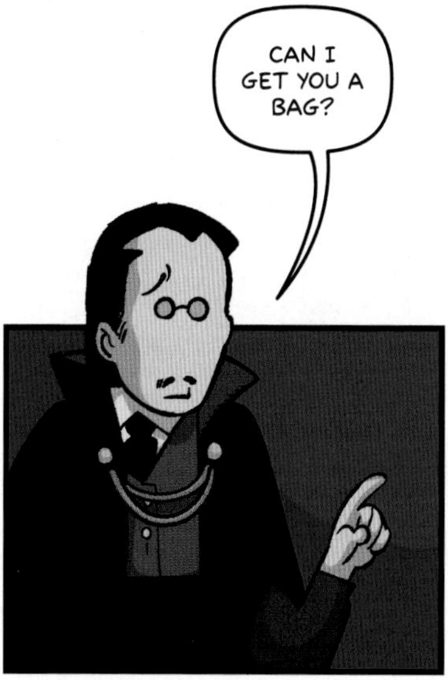
CAN I GET YOU A BAG?

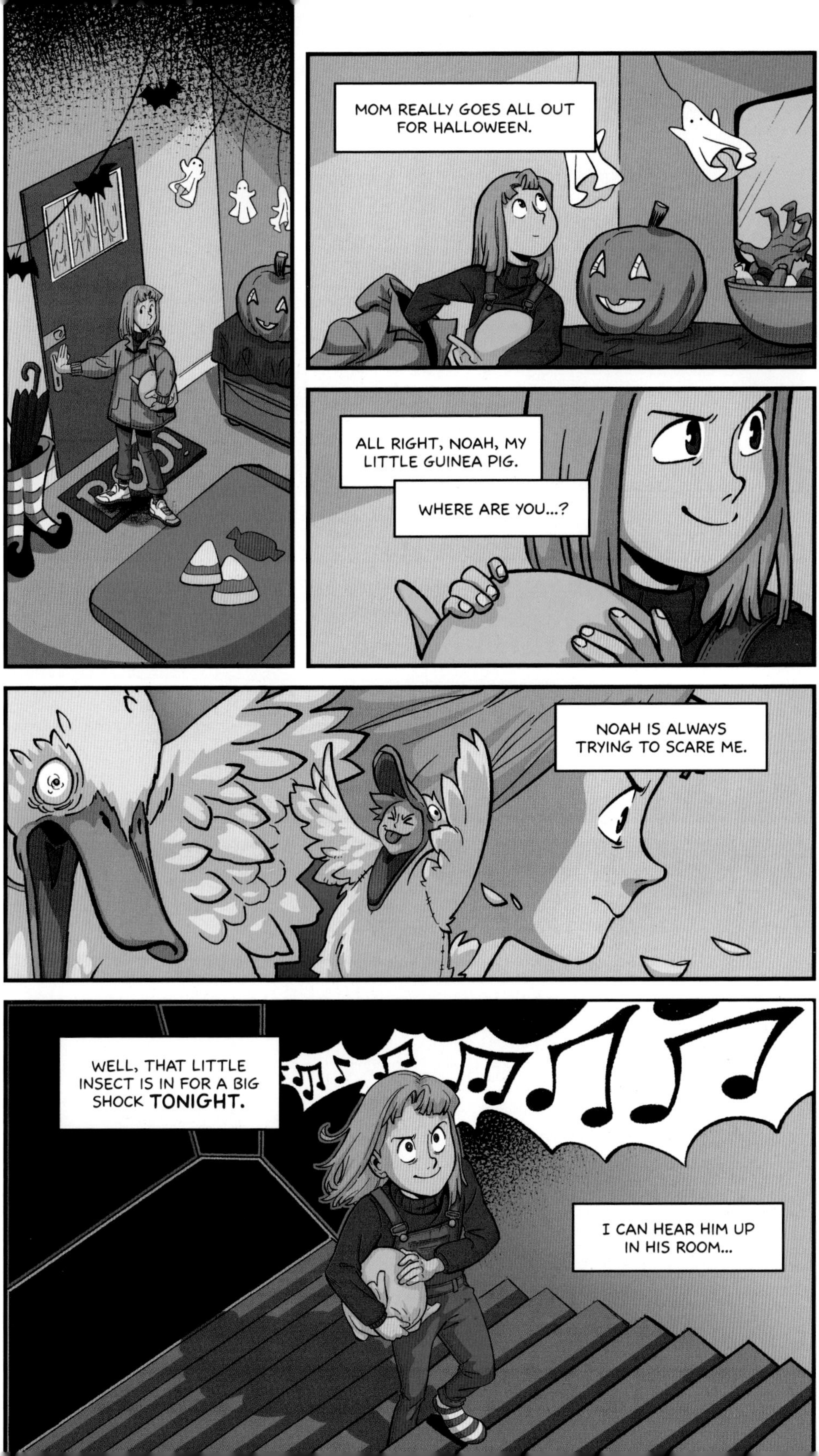
BOO!
MOM REALLY GOES ALL OUT FOR HALLOWEEN.
ALL RIGHT, NOAH, MY LITTLE GUINEA PIG.
WHERE ARE YOU...?
NOAH IS ALWAYS TRYING TO SCARE ME.
WELL, THAT LITTLE INSECT IS IN FOR A BIG SHOCK **TONIGHT.**
I CAN HEAR HIM UP IN HIS ROOM...

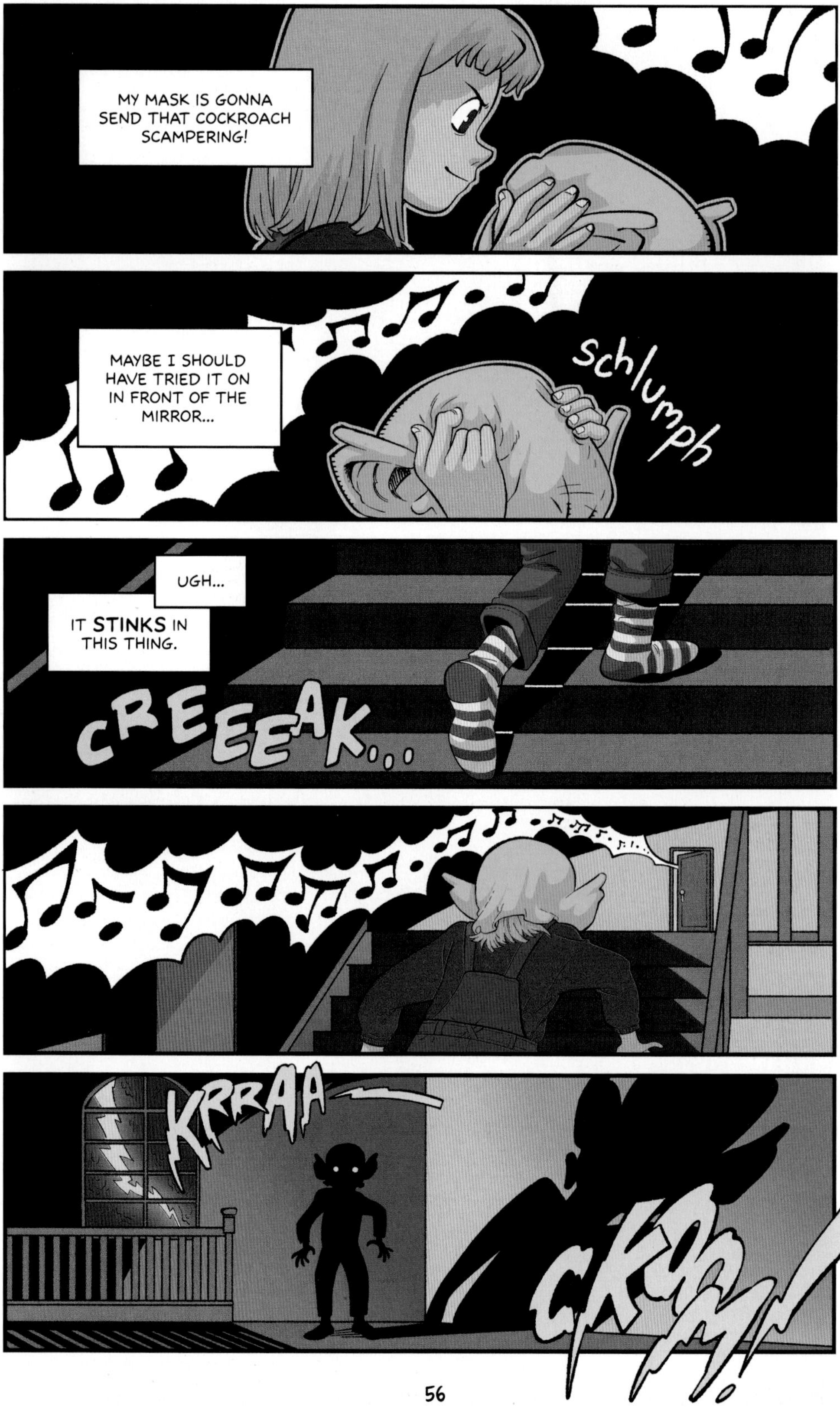

MY MASK IS GONNA SEND THAT COCKROACH SCAMPERING!
MAYBE I SHOULD HAVE TRIED IT ON IN FRONT OF THE MIRROR...
schlumph
UGH...
IT STINKS IN THIS THING.
CREEEAK...
KRRAA
CKOOM!

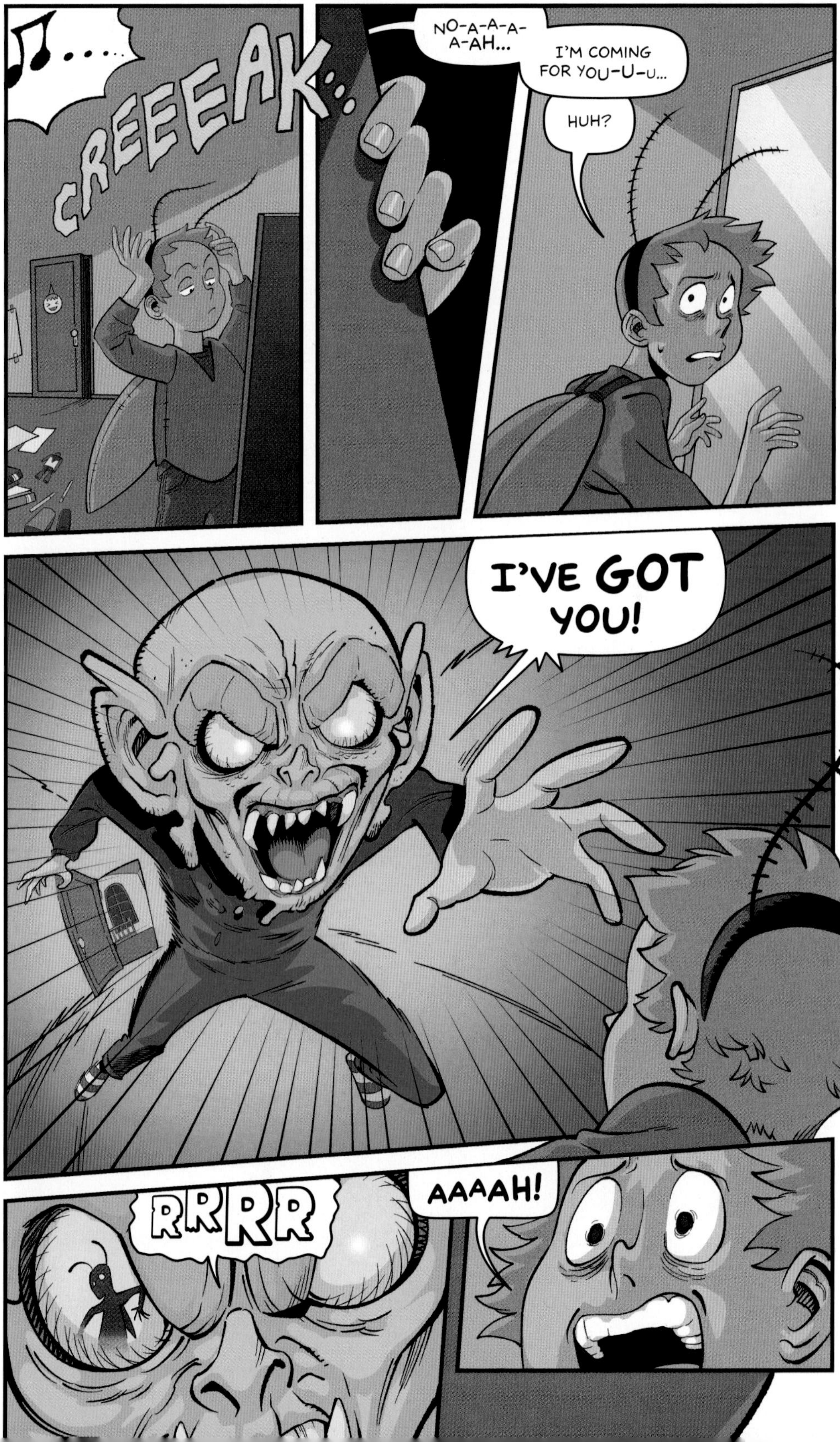
♫.....
CREEEAK...
NO-A-A-A-A-AH...
I'M COMING FOR YOU-U-U...
HUH?
I'VE GOT YOU!
RRRR
AAAAH!

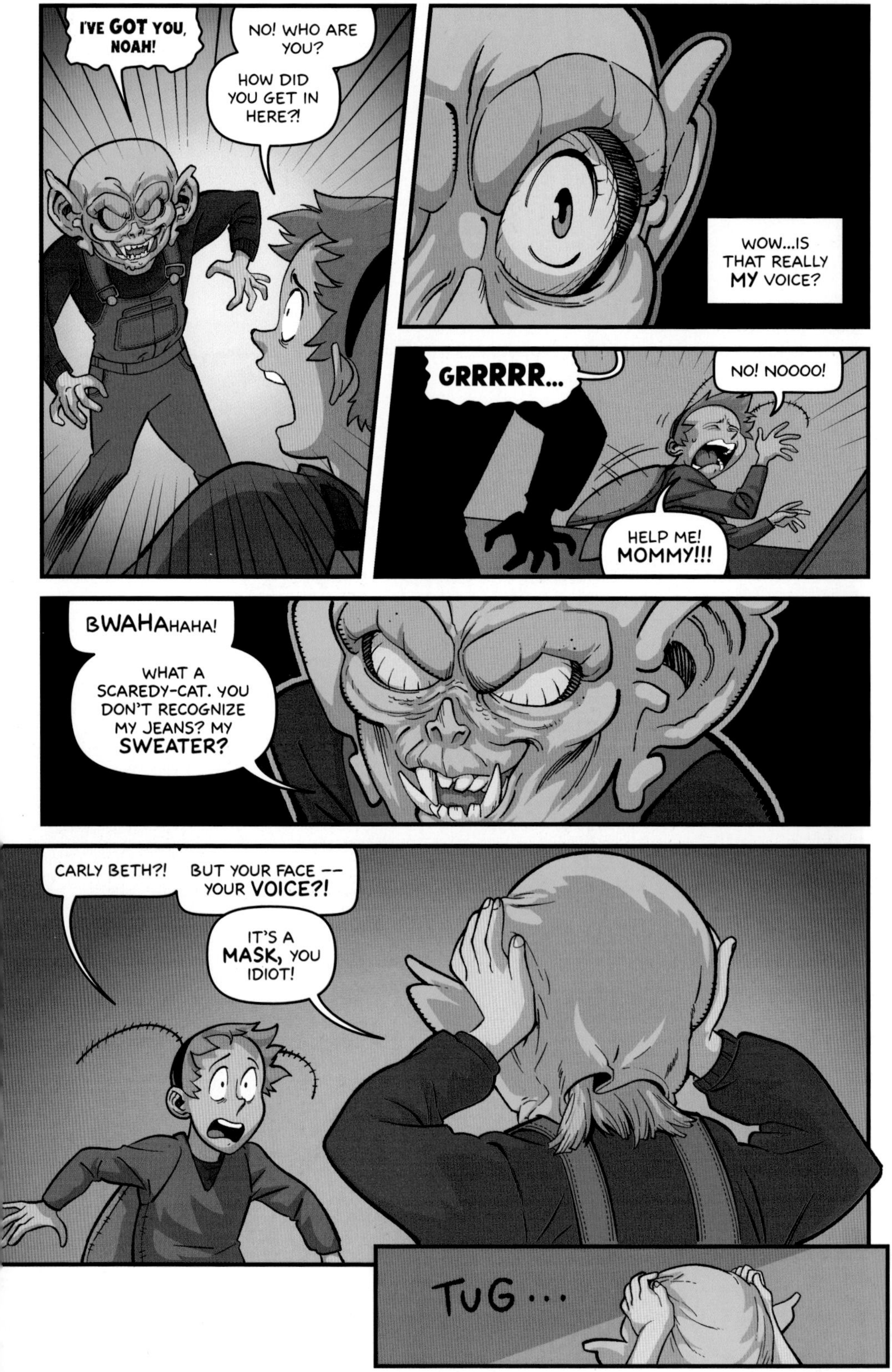

I'VE GOT YOU, NOAH!
NO! WHO ARE YOU?
HOW DID YOU GET IN HERE?!
WOW...IS THAT REALLY MY VOICE?
GRRRRR...
NO! NOOOO!
HELP ME! MOMMY!!!
BWAHAHAHA!
WHAT A SCAREDY-CAT. YOU DON'T RECOGNIZE MY JEANS? MY SWEATER?
CARLY BETH?!
BUT YOUR FACE -- YOUR VOICE?!
IT'S A MASK, YOU IDIOT!
TUG...

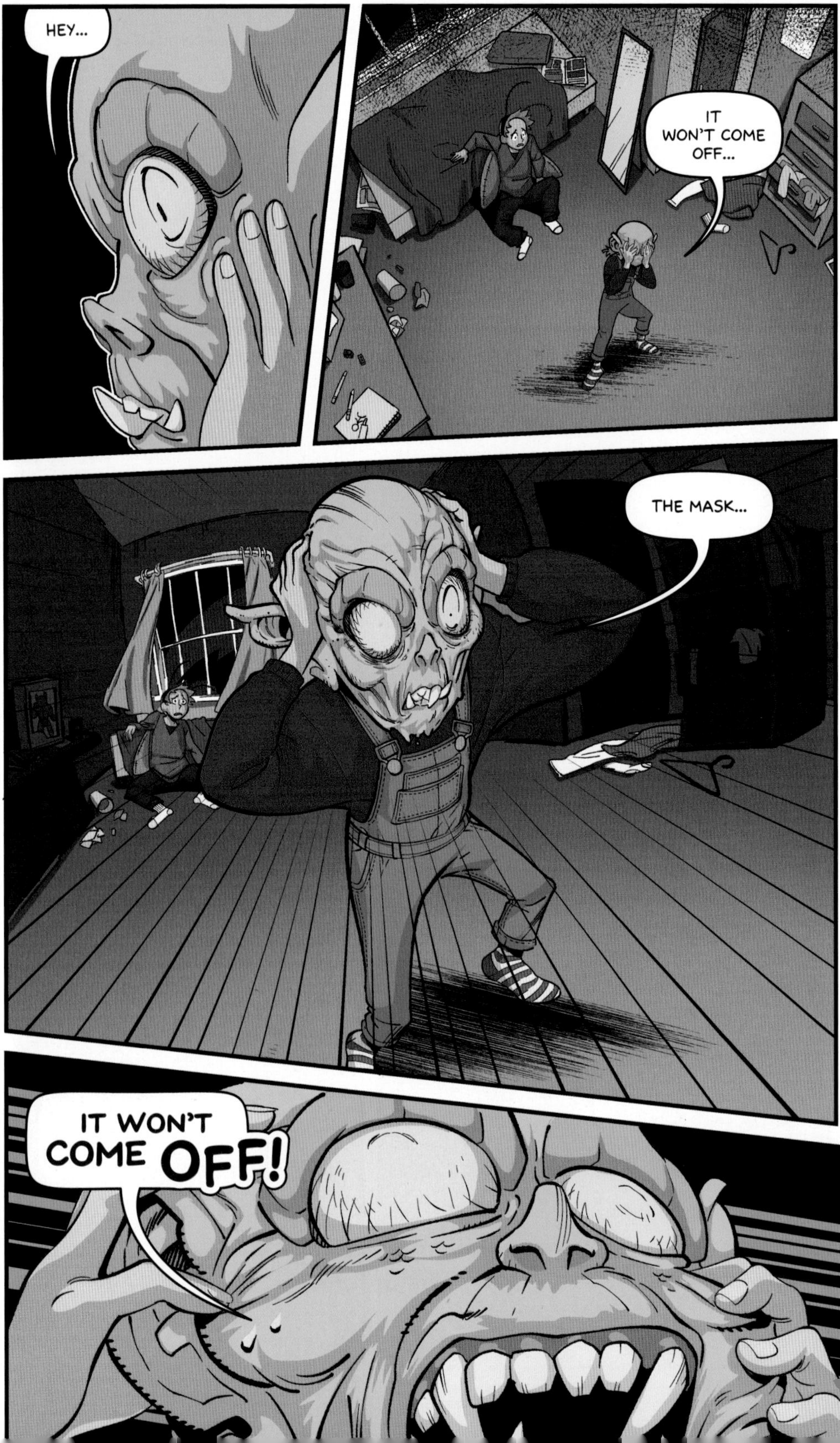
HEY...
IT WON'T COME OFF...
THE MASK...
IT WON'T COME OFF!

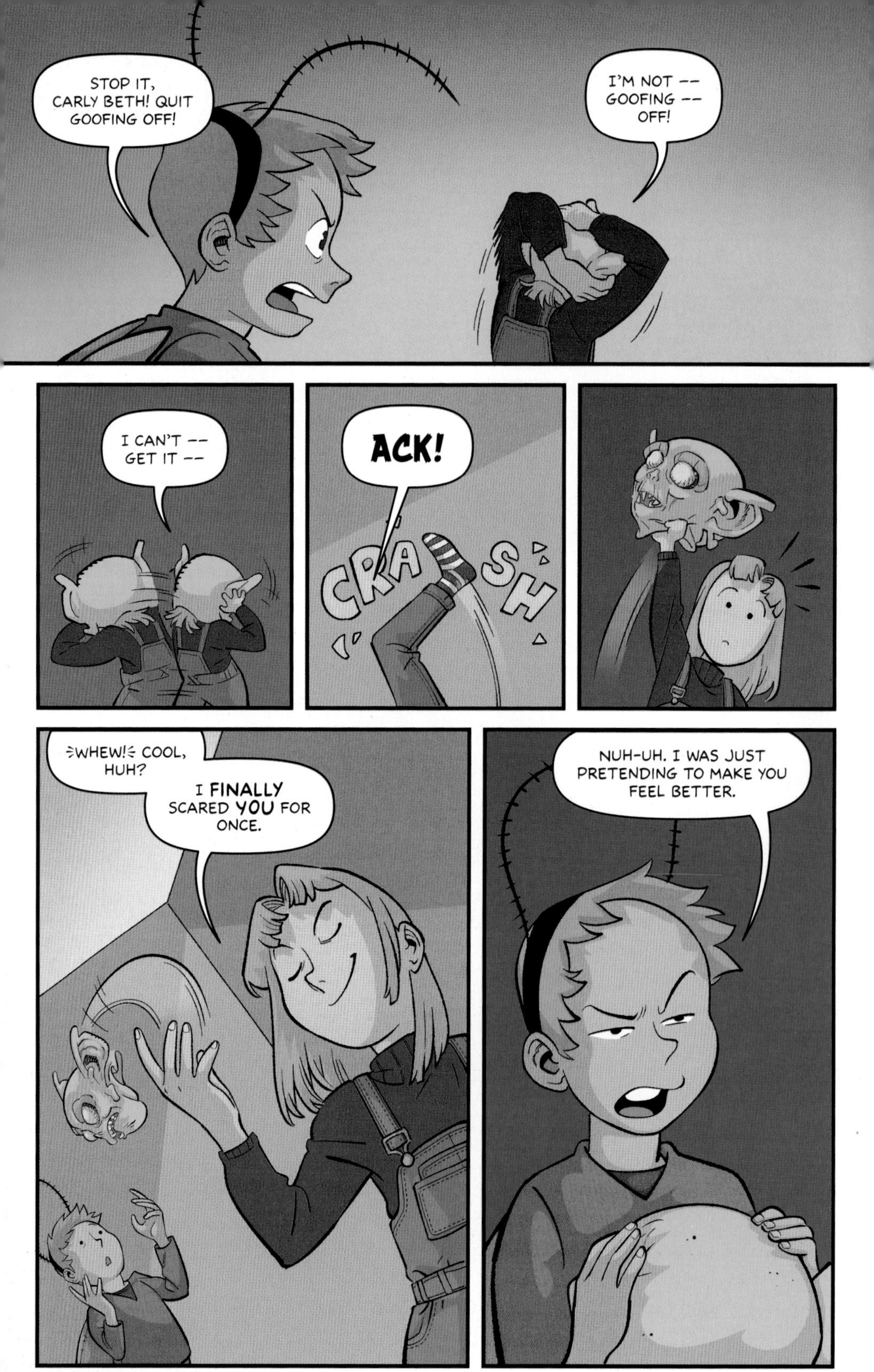
STOP IT, CARLY BETH! QUIT GOOFING OFF!
I'M NOT -- GOOFING -- OFF!
I CAN'T -- GET IT --
ACK!
CRASH
WHEW! COOL, HUH?
I FINALLY SCARED YOU FOR ONCE.
NUH-UH. I WAS JUST PRETENDING TO MAKE YOU FEEL BETTER.

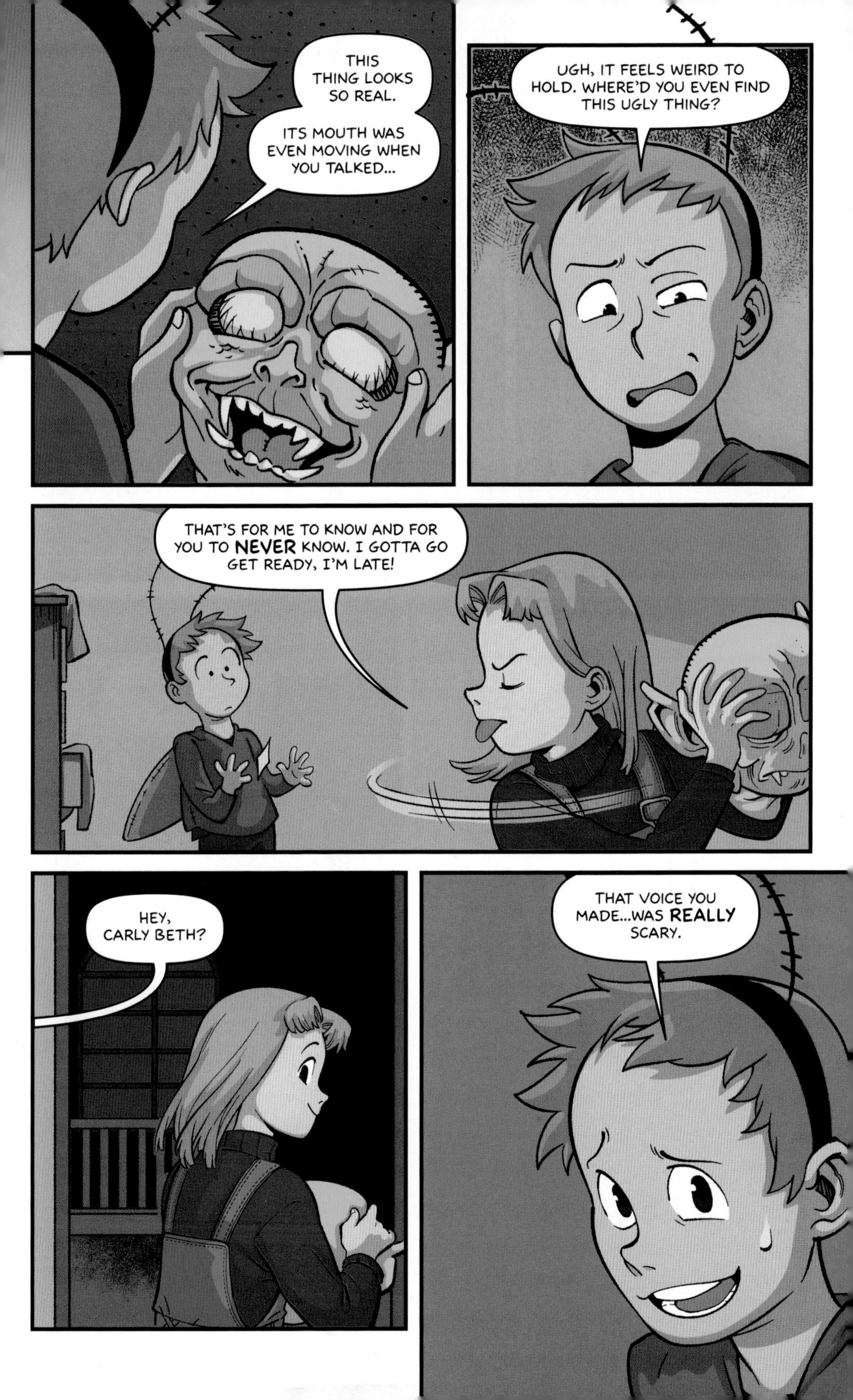
THIS THING LOOKS SO REAL.
ITS MOUTH WAS EVEN MOVING WHEN YOU TALKED...
UGH, IT FEELS WEIRD TO HOLD. WHERE'D YOU EVEN FIND THIS UGLY THING?
THAT'S FOR ME TO KNOW AND FOR YOU TO **NEVER** KNOW. I GOTTA GO GET READY, I'M LATE!
HEY, CARLY BETH?
THAT VOICE YOU MADE...WAS **REALLY** SCARY.

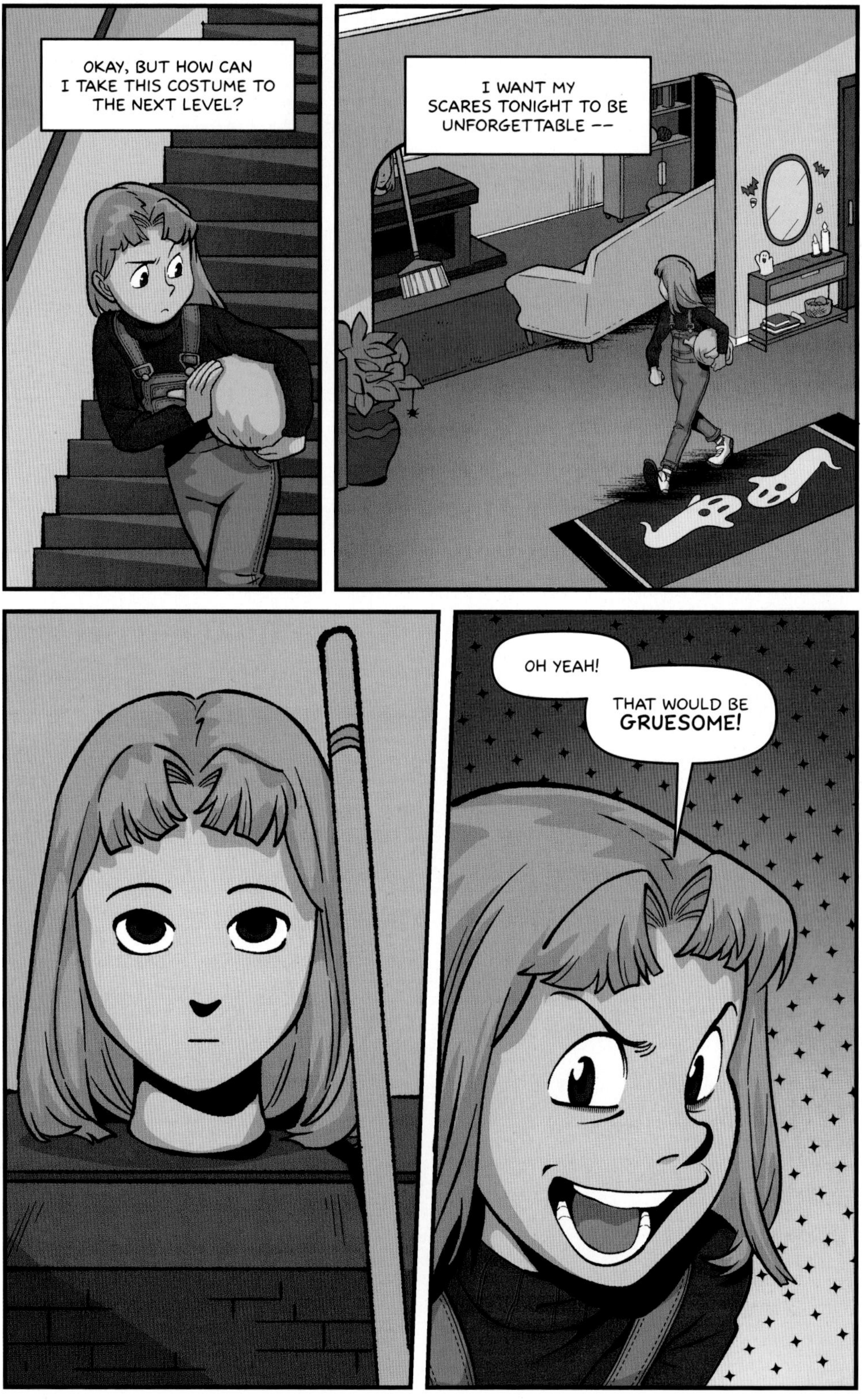
OKAY, BUT HOW CAN I TAKE THIS COSTUME TO THE NEXT LEVEL?
I WANT MY SCARES TONIGHT TO BE UNFORGETTABLE --
OH YEAH!
THAT WOULD BE GRUESOME!

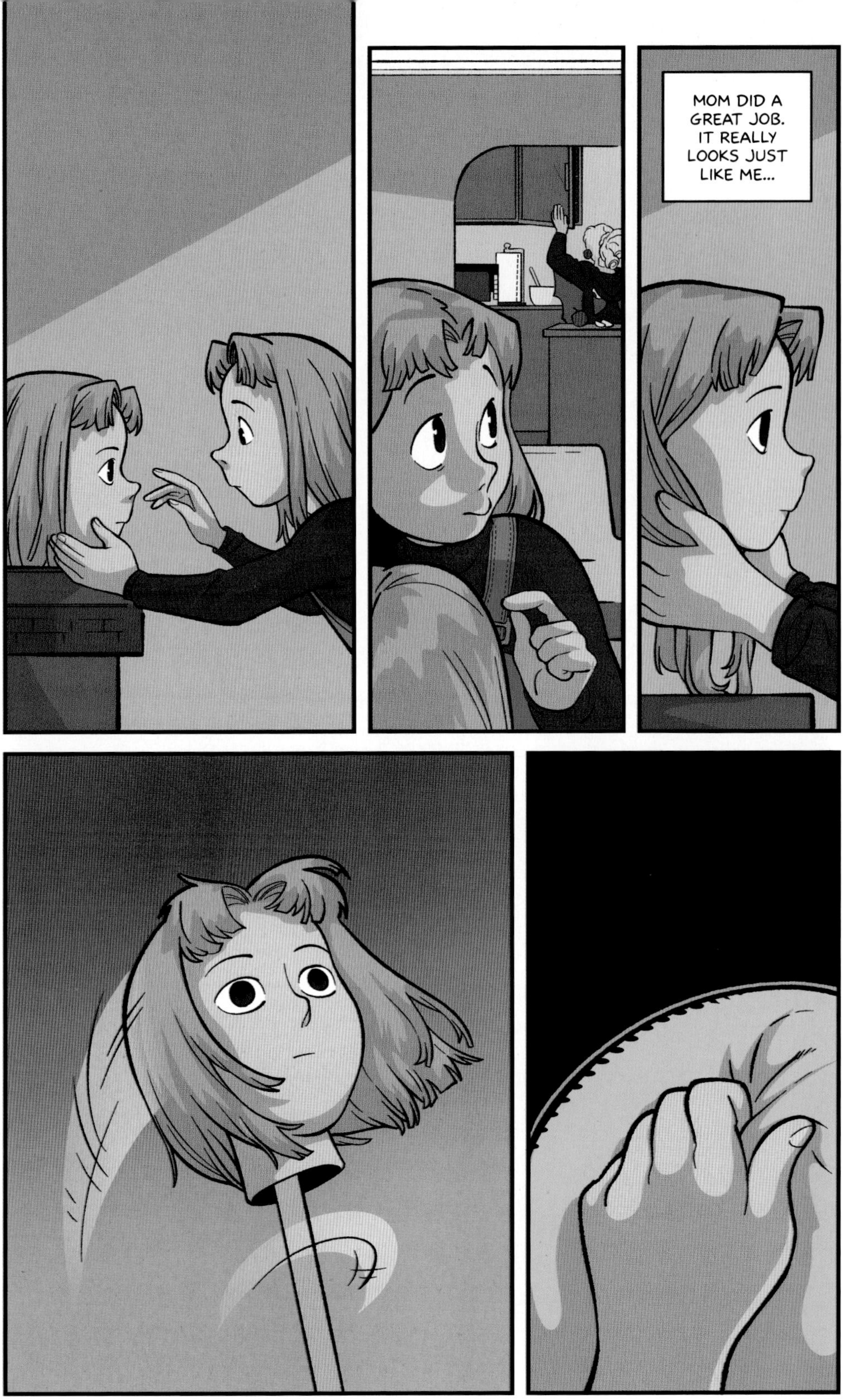
MOM DID A GREAT JOB. IT REALLY LOOKS JUST LIKE ME...

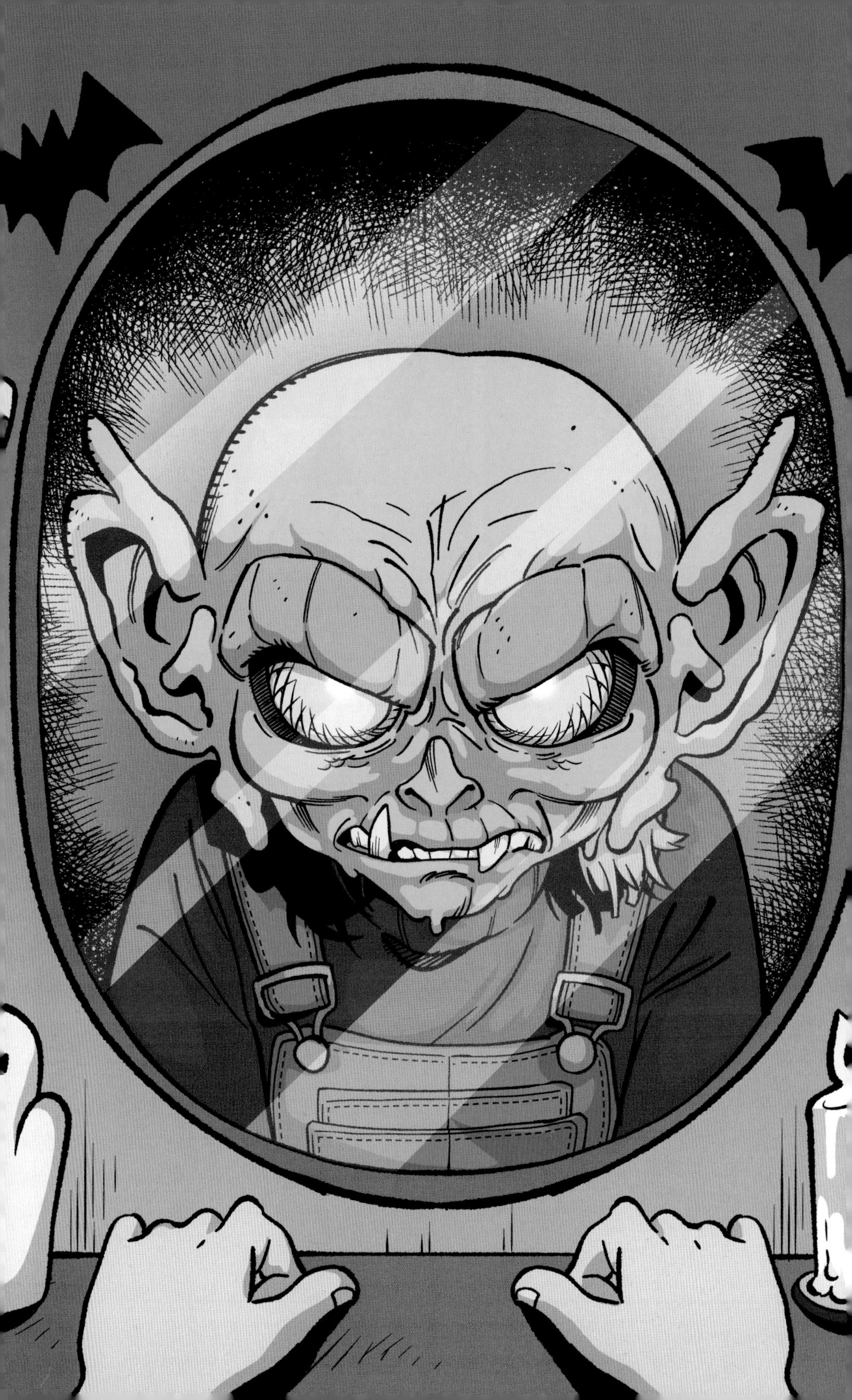

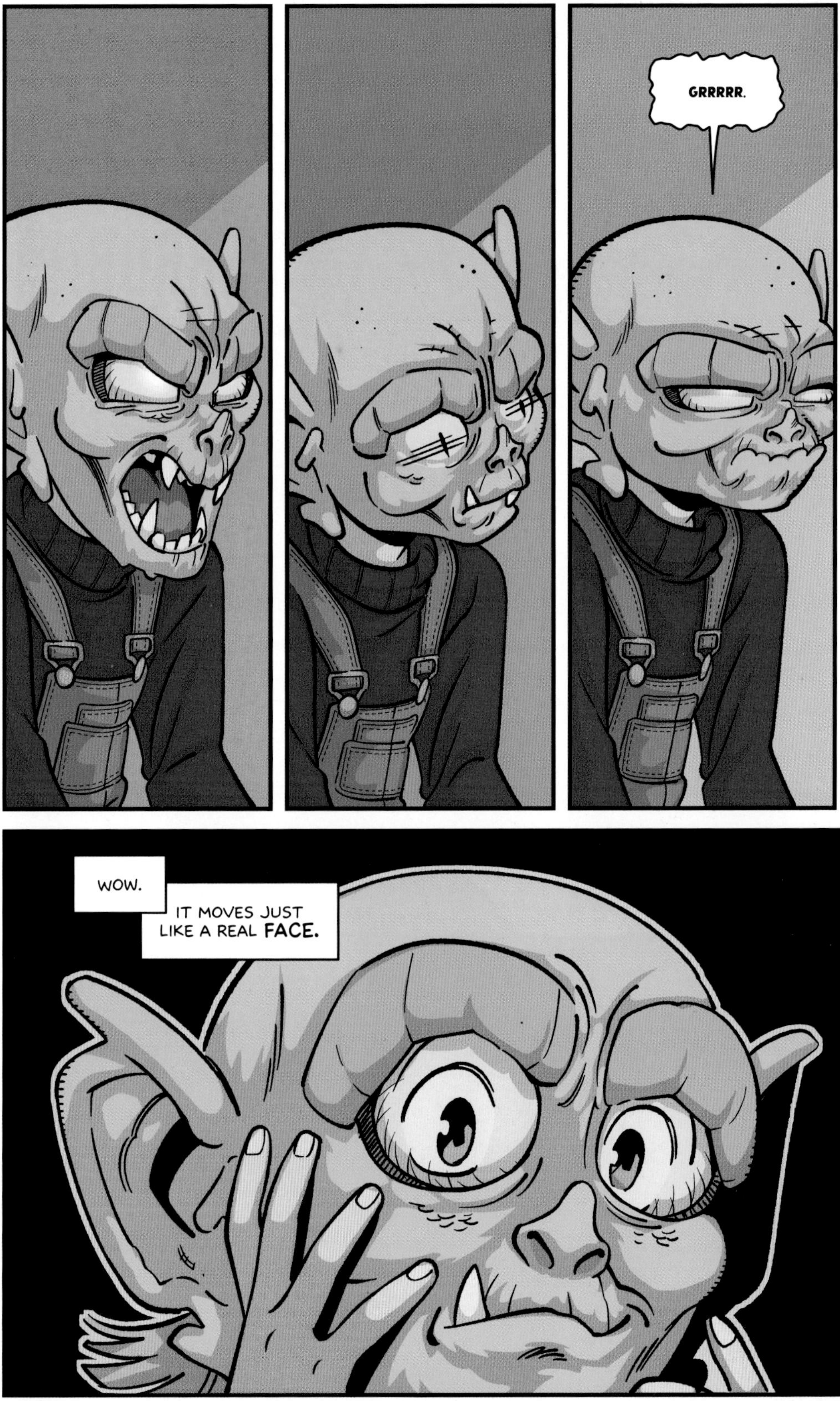
GRRRRR.
WOW.
IT MOVES JUST LIKE A REAL FACE.

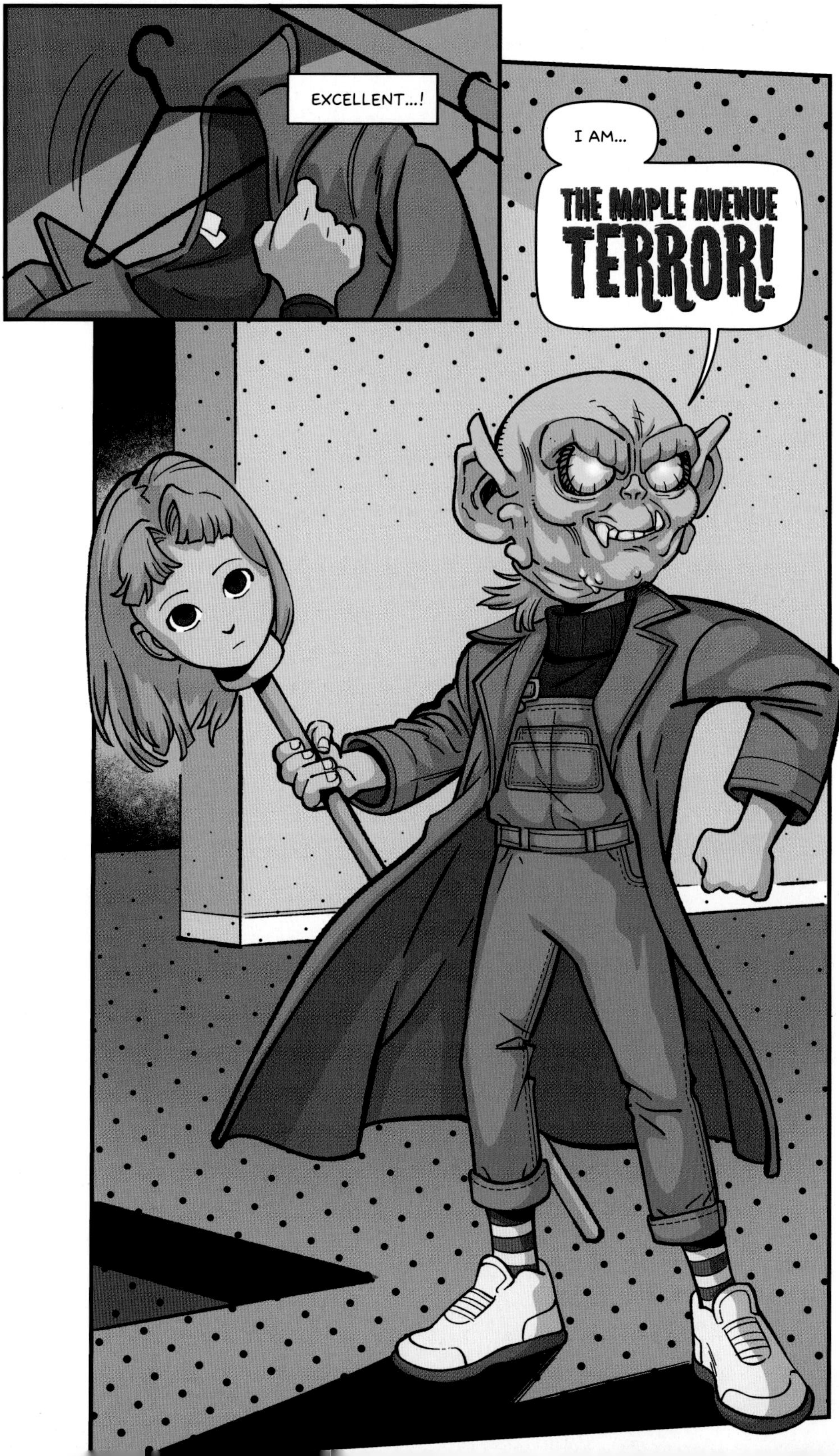
EXCELLENT...!
I AM...
THE MAPLE AVENUE TERROR!

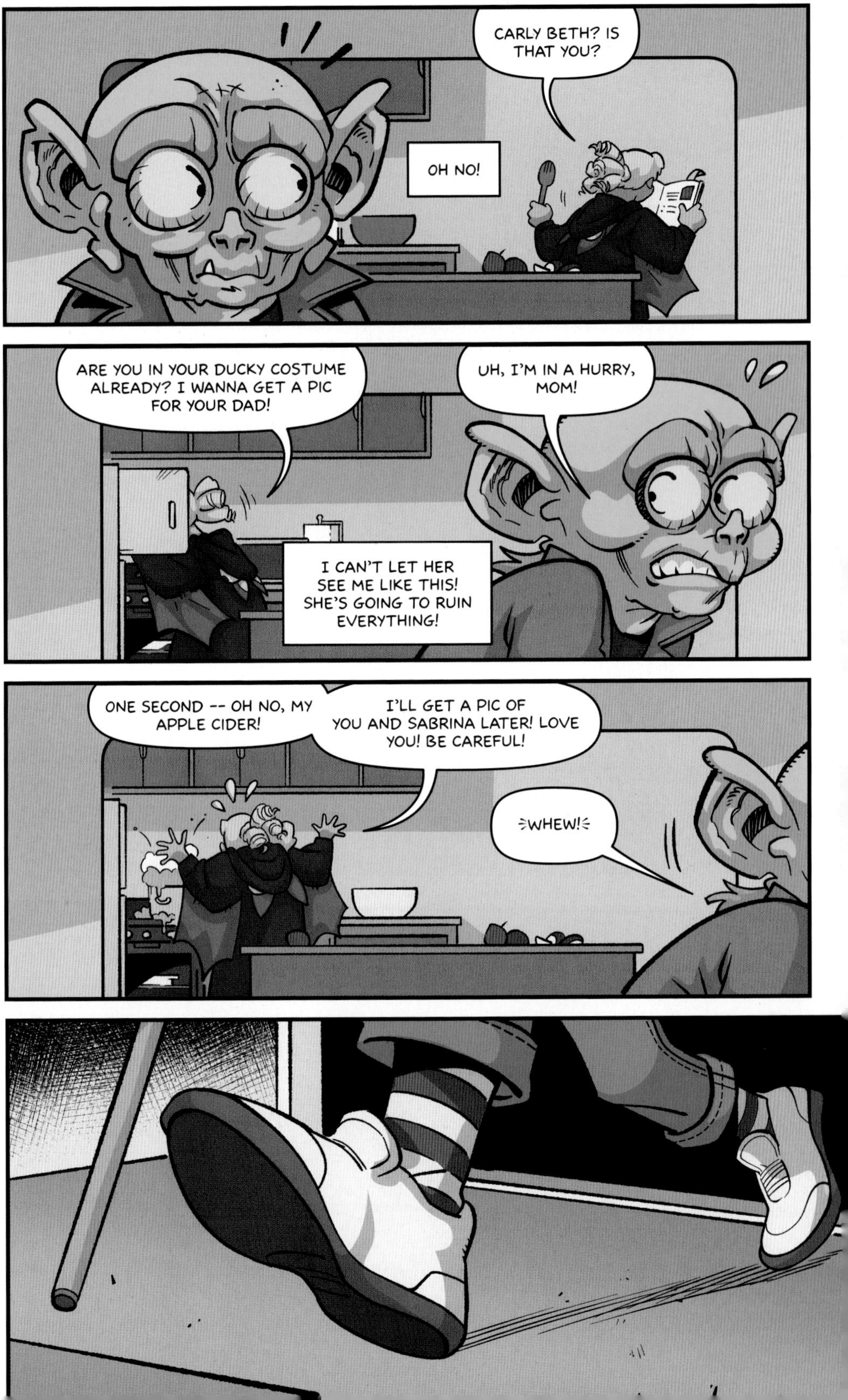
CARLY BETH? IS THAT YOU?
OH NO!
ARE YOU IN YOUR DUCKY COSTUME ALREADY? I WANNA GET A PIC FOR YOUR DAD!
UH, I'M IN A HURRY, MOM!
I CAN'T LET HER SEE ME LIKE THIS! SHE'S GOING TO RUIN EVERYTHING!
ONE SECOND -- OH NO, MY APPLE CIDER!
I'LL GET A PIC OF YOU AND SABRINA LATER! LOVE YOU! BE CAREFUL!
WHEW!

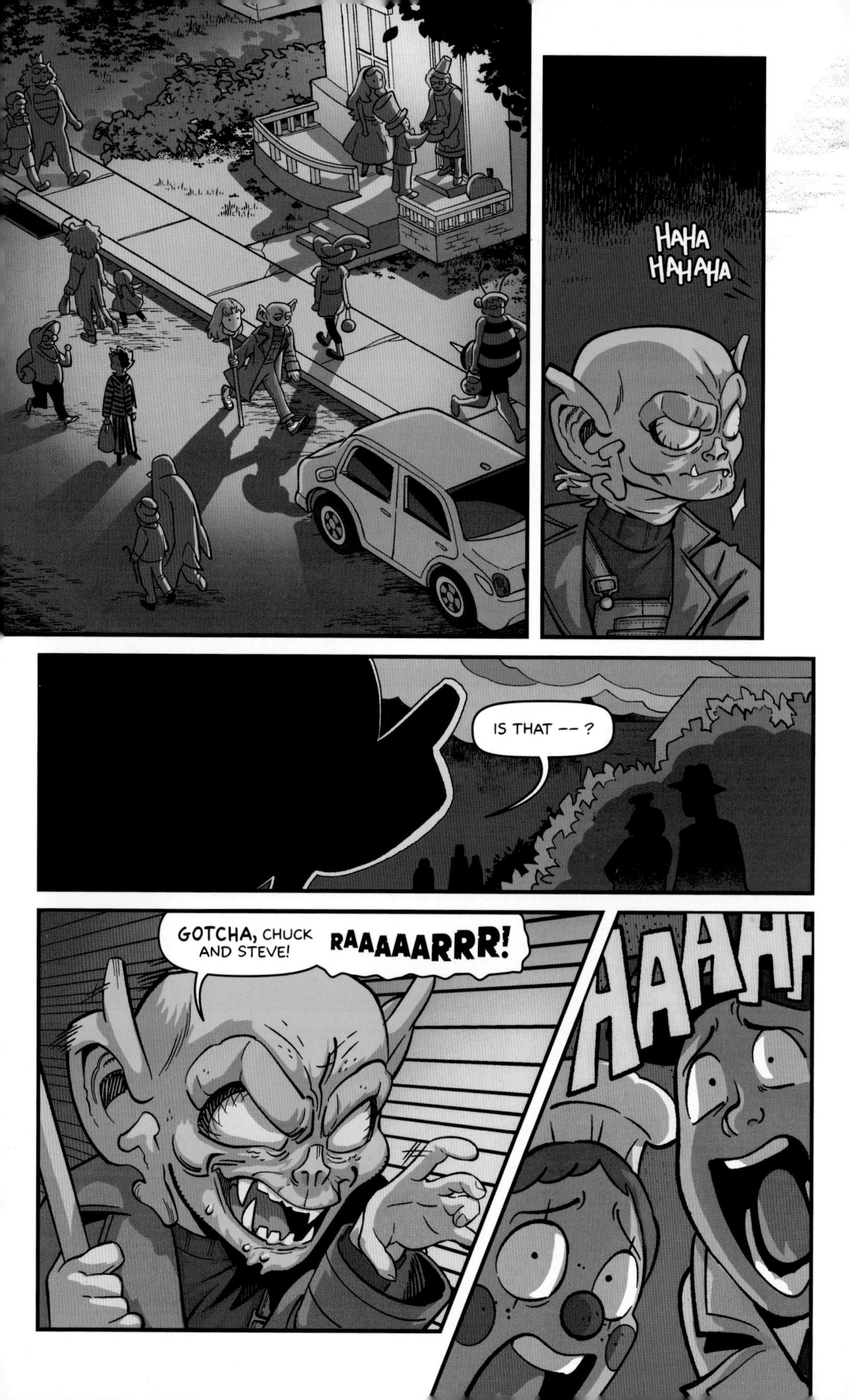
HAHA
HAHAHA
IS THAT -- ?
GOTCHA, CHUCK AND STEVE!
RAAAAARRR!
AAAH

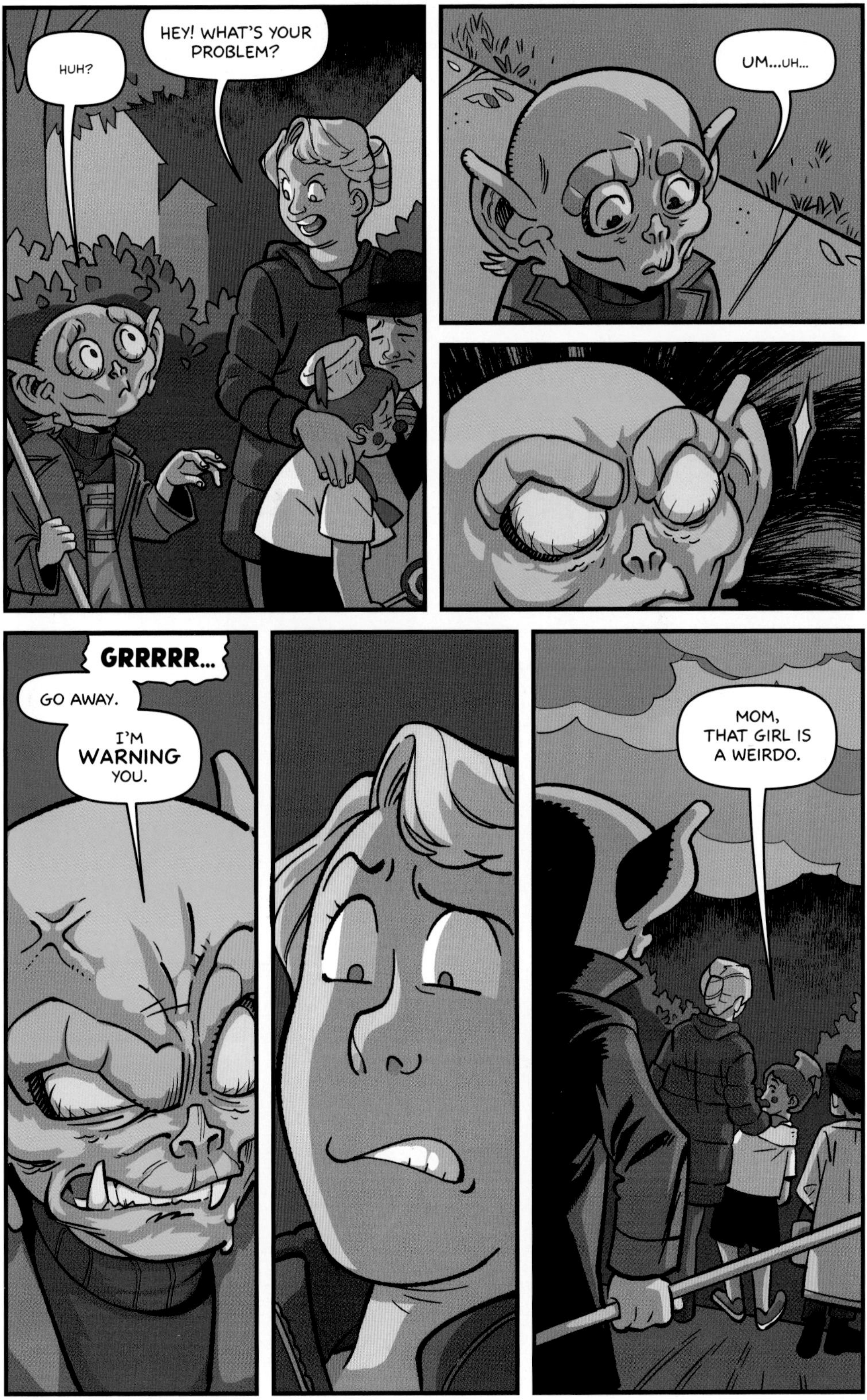
HEY! WHAT'S YOUR PROBLEM?
HUH?
UM...UH...
GRRRRR...
GO AWAY.
I'M WARNING YOU.
MOM, THAT GIRL IS A WEIRDO.

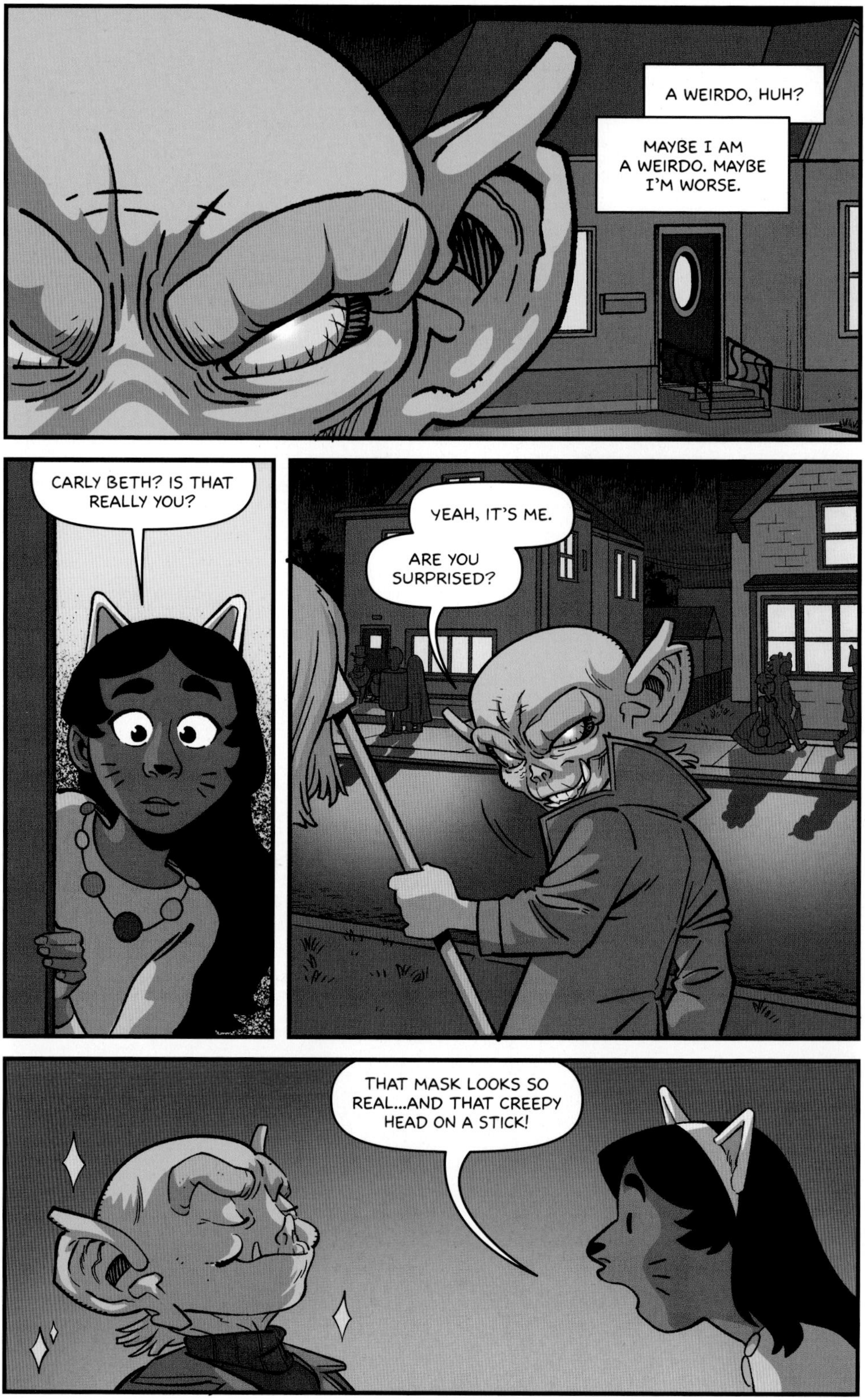
A WEIRDO, HUH?
MAYBE I AM A WEIRDO. MAYBE I'M WORSE.
CARLY BETH? IS THAT REALLY YOU?
YEAH, IT'S ME.
ARE YOU SURPRISED?
THAT MASK LOOKS SO REAL...AND THAT CREEPY HEAD ON A STICK!

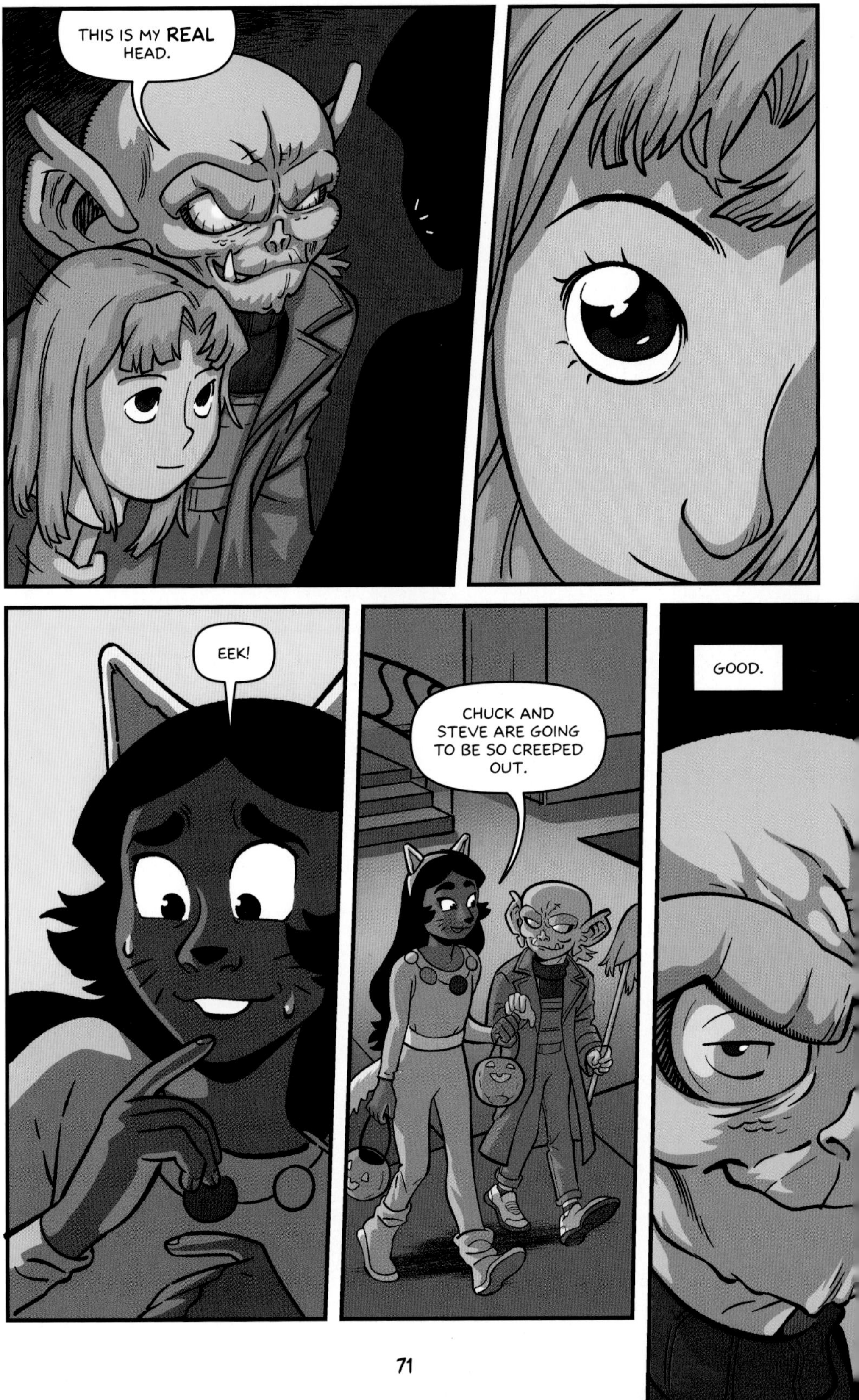
THIS IS MY **REAL** HEAD.
EEK!
CHUCK AND STEVE ARE GOING TO BE SO CREEPED OUT.
GOOD.

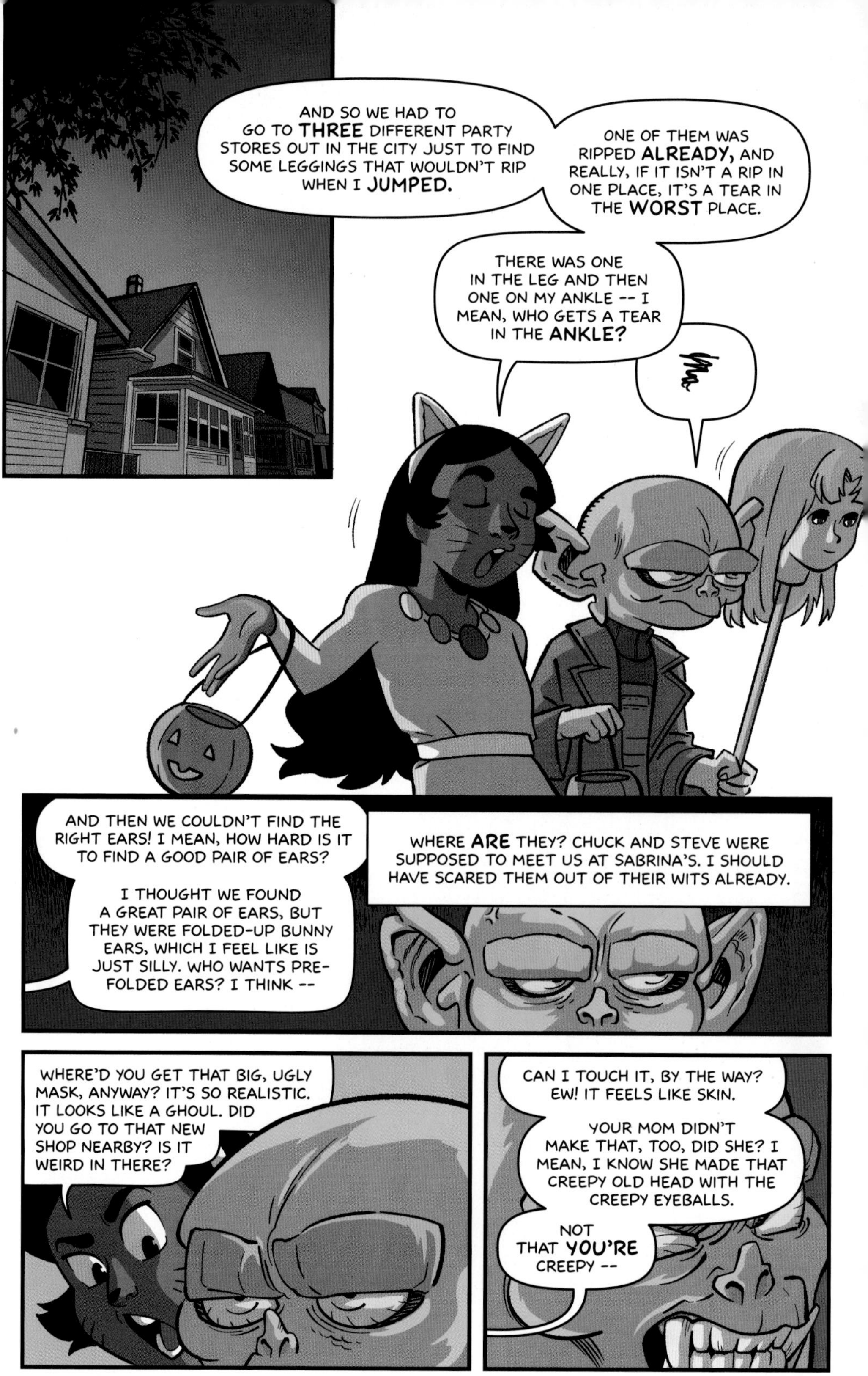
AND SO WE HAD TO GO TO THREE DIFFERENT PARTY STORES OUT IN THE CITY JUST TO FIND SOME LEGGINGS THAT WOULDN'T RIP WHEN I JUMPED.
ONE OF THEM WAS RIPPED ALREADY, AND REALLY, IF IT ISN'T A RIP IN ONE PLACE, IT'S A TEAR IN THE WORST PLACE.
THERE WAS ONE IN THE LEG AND THEN ONE ON MY ANKLE -- I MEAN, WHO GETS A TEAR IN THE ANKLE?
AND THEN WE COULDN'T FIND THE RIGHT EARS! I MEAN, HOW HARD IS IT TO FIND A GOOD PAIR OF EARS?
I THOUGHT WE FOUND A GREAT PAIR OF EARS, BUT THEY WERE FOLDED-UP BUNNY EARS, WHICH I FEEL LIKE IS JUST SILLY. WHO WANTS PRE-FOLDED EARS? I THINK --
WHERE ARE THEY? CHUCK AND STEVE WERE SUPPOSED TO MEET US AT SABRINA'S. I SHOULD HAVE SCARED THEM OUT OF THEIR WITS ALREADY.
WHERE'D YOU GET THAT BIG, UGLY MASK, ANYWAY? IT'S SO REALISTIC. IT LOOKS LIKE A GHOUL. DID YOU GO TO THAT NEW SHOP NEARBY? IS IT WEIRD IN THERE?
CAN I TOUCH IT, BY THE WAY? EW! IT FEELS LIKE SKIN.
YOUR MOM DIDN'T MAKE THAT, TOO, DID SHE? I MEAN, I KNOW SHE MADE THAT CREEPY OLD HEAD WITH THE CREEPY EYEBALLS.
NOT THAT YOU'RE CREEPY --

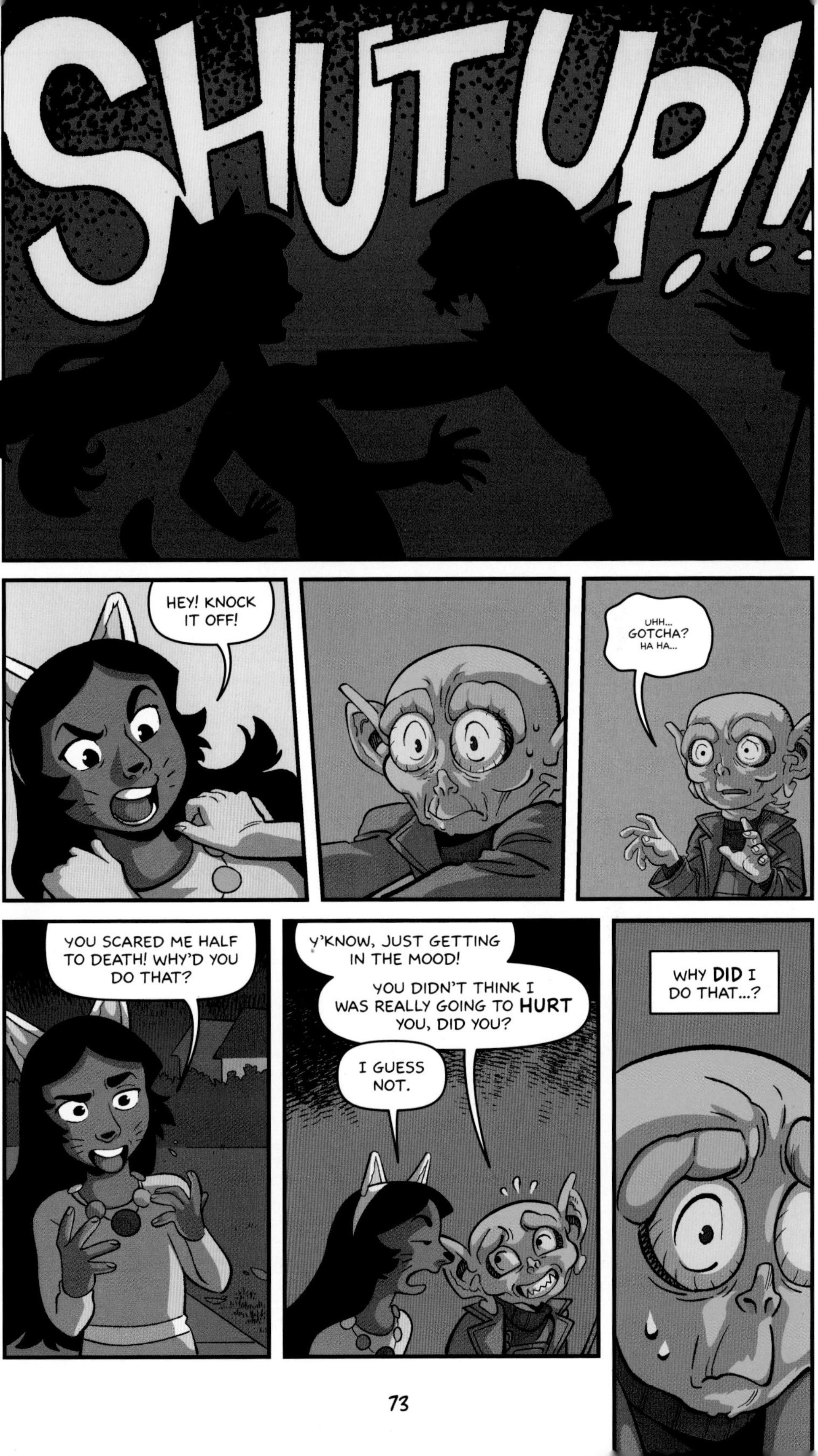
SHUT UP!!
HEY! KNOCK IT OFF!
UHH... GOTCHA? HA HA...
YOU SCARED ME HALF TO DEATH! WHY'D YOU DO THAT?
Y'KNOW, JUST GETTING IN THE MOOD!
YOU DIDN'T THINK I WAS REALLY GOING TO HURT YOU, DID YOU?
I GUESS NOT.
WHY DID I DO THAT...?

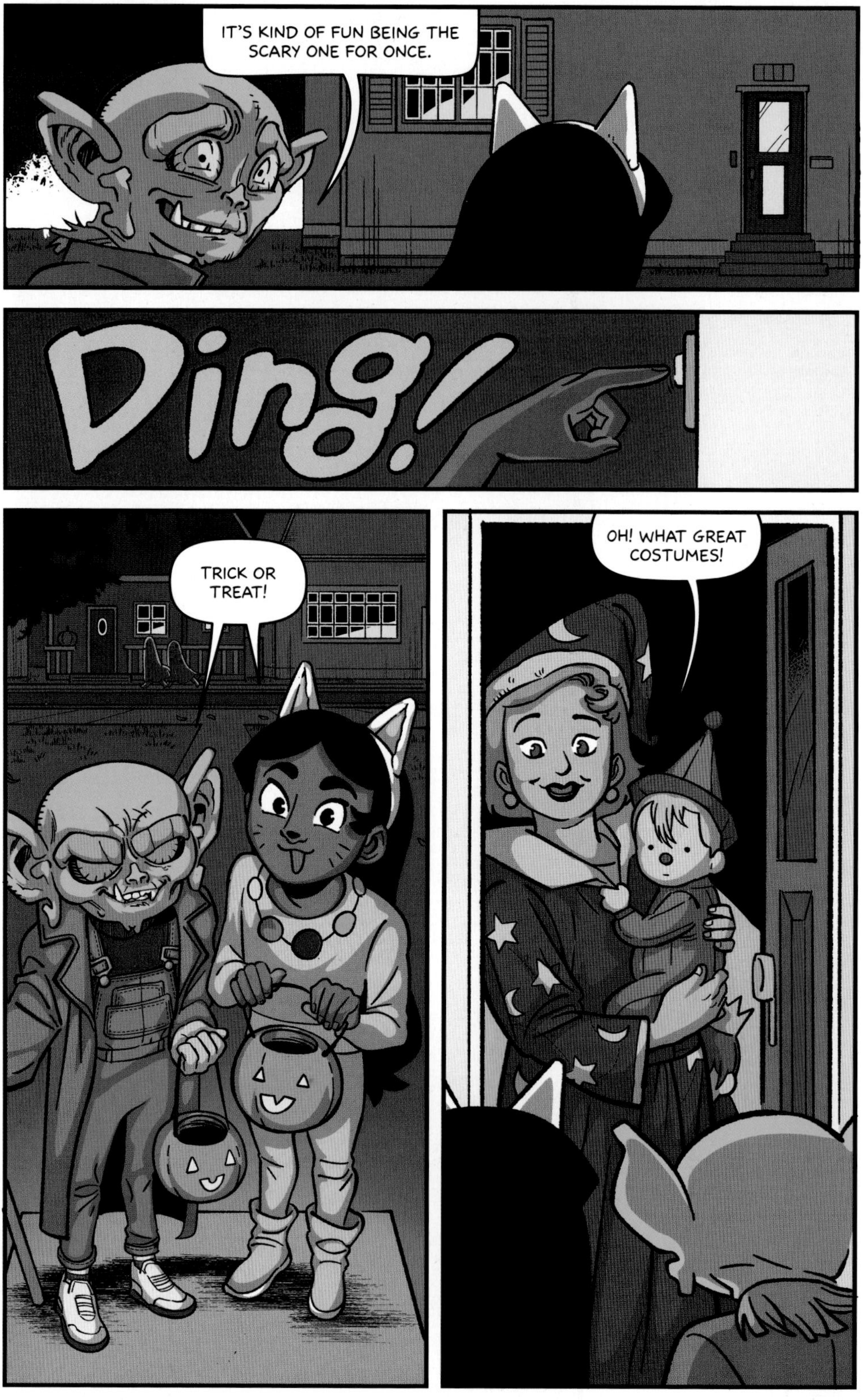
IT'S KIND OF FUN BEING THE SCARY ONE FOR ONCE.
Ding!
TRICK OR TREAT!
OH! WHAT GREAT COSTUMES!

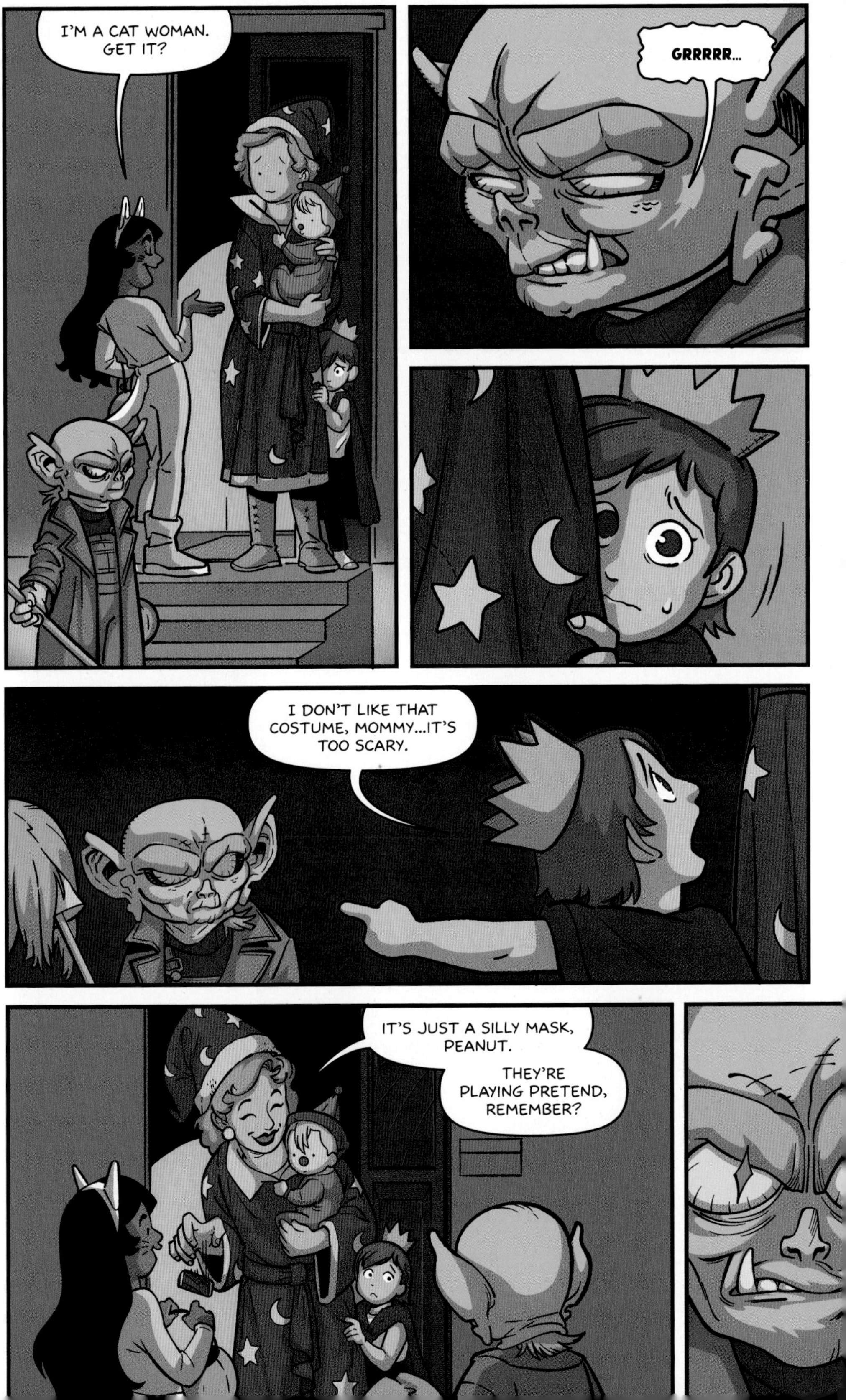
I'M A CAT WOMAN. GET IT?
GRRRRR...
I DON'T LIKE THAT COSTUME, MOMMY...IT'S TOO SCARY.
IT'S JUST A SILLY MASK, PEANUT.
THEY'RE PLAYING PRETEND, REMEMBER?

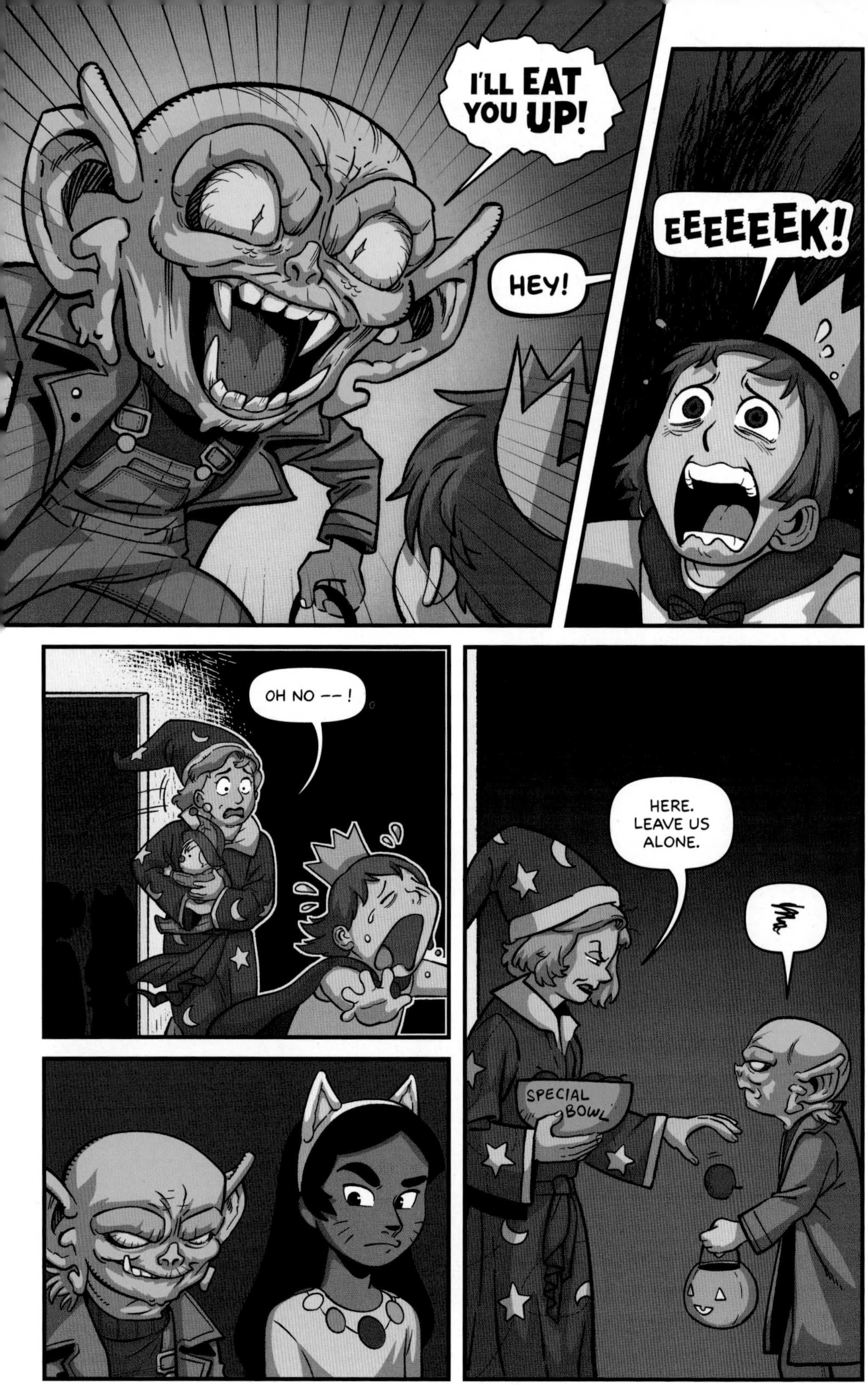
I'LL EAT YOU UP!
HEY!
EEEEEEK!
OH NO -- !
HERE. LEAVE US ALONE.
SPECIAL BOWL

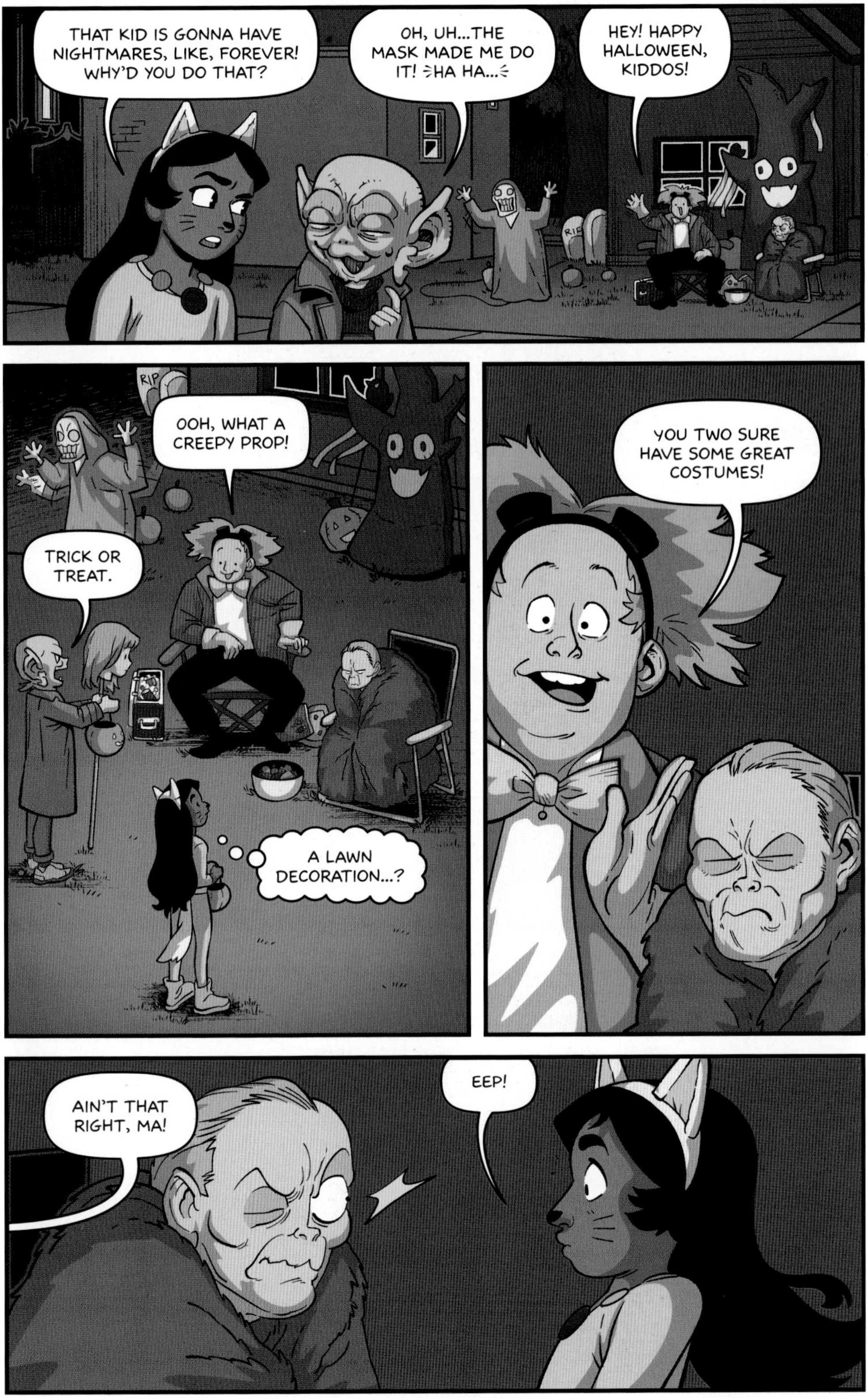
THAT KID IS GONNA HAVE NIGHTMARES, LIKE, FOREVER! WHY'D YOU DO THAT?
OH, UH...THE MASK MADE ME DO IT! ⋺HA HA...⋲
HEY! HAPPY HALLOWEEN, KIDDOS!
OOH, WHAT A CREEPY PROP!
TRICK OR TREAT.
A LAWN DECORATION...?
YOU TWO SURE HAVE SOME GREAT COSTUMES!
AIN'T THAT RIGHT, MA!
EEP!

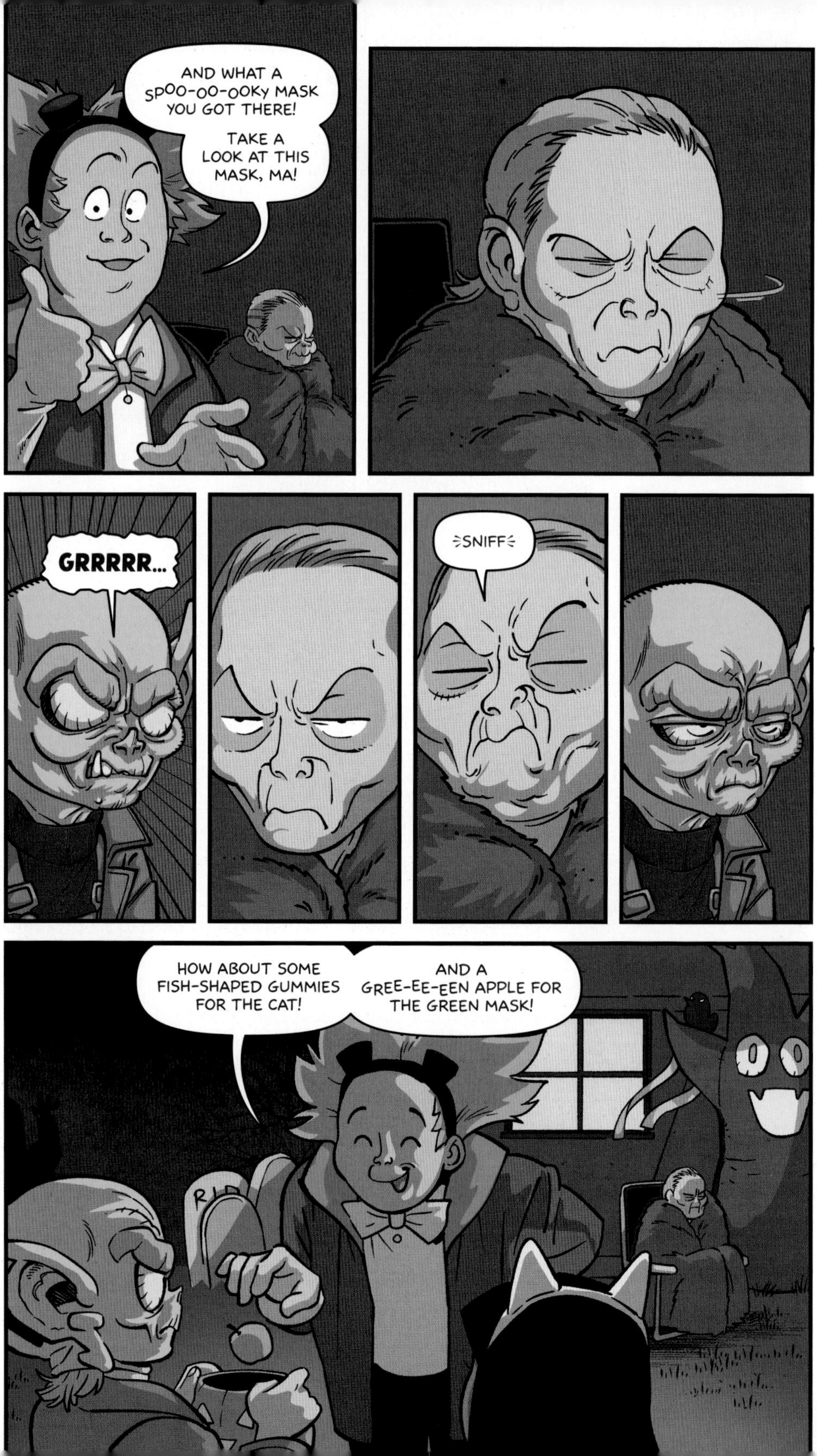
AND WHAT A SPOO-OO-OOKY MASK YOU GOT THERE!
TAKE A LOOK AT THIS MASK, MA!
GRRRRR...
SNIFF
HOW ABOUT SOME FISH-SHAPED GUMMIES FOR THE CAT!
AND A GREE-EE-EEN APPLE FOR THE GREEN MASK!
RIP

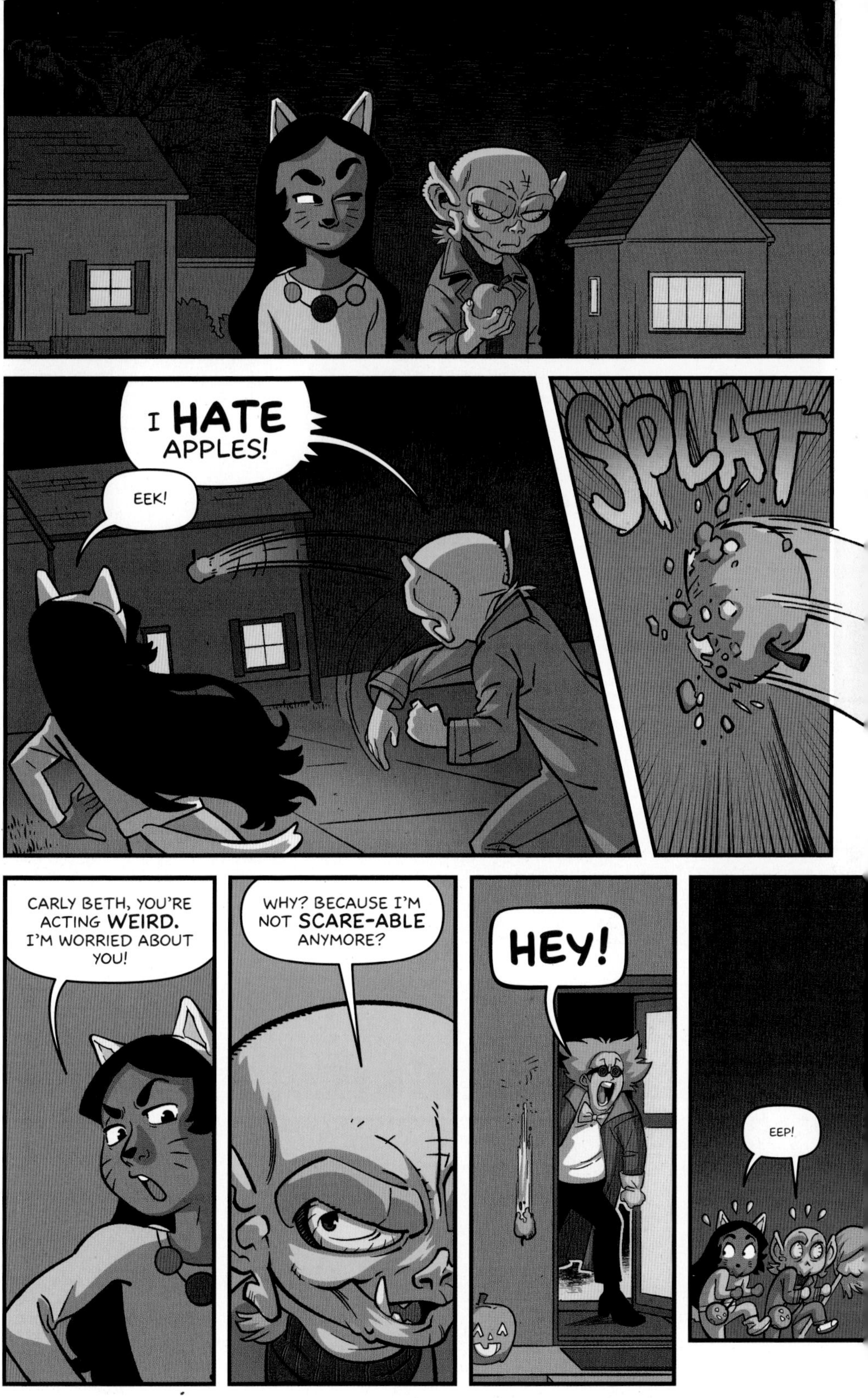
I HATE APPLES!
EEK!
SPLAT
CARLY BETH, YOU'RE ACTING WEIRD. I'M WORRIED ABOUT YOU!
WHY? BECAUSE I'M NOT SCARE-ABLE ANYMORE?
HEY!
EEP!

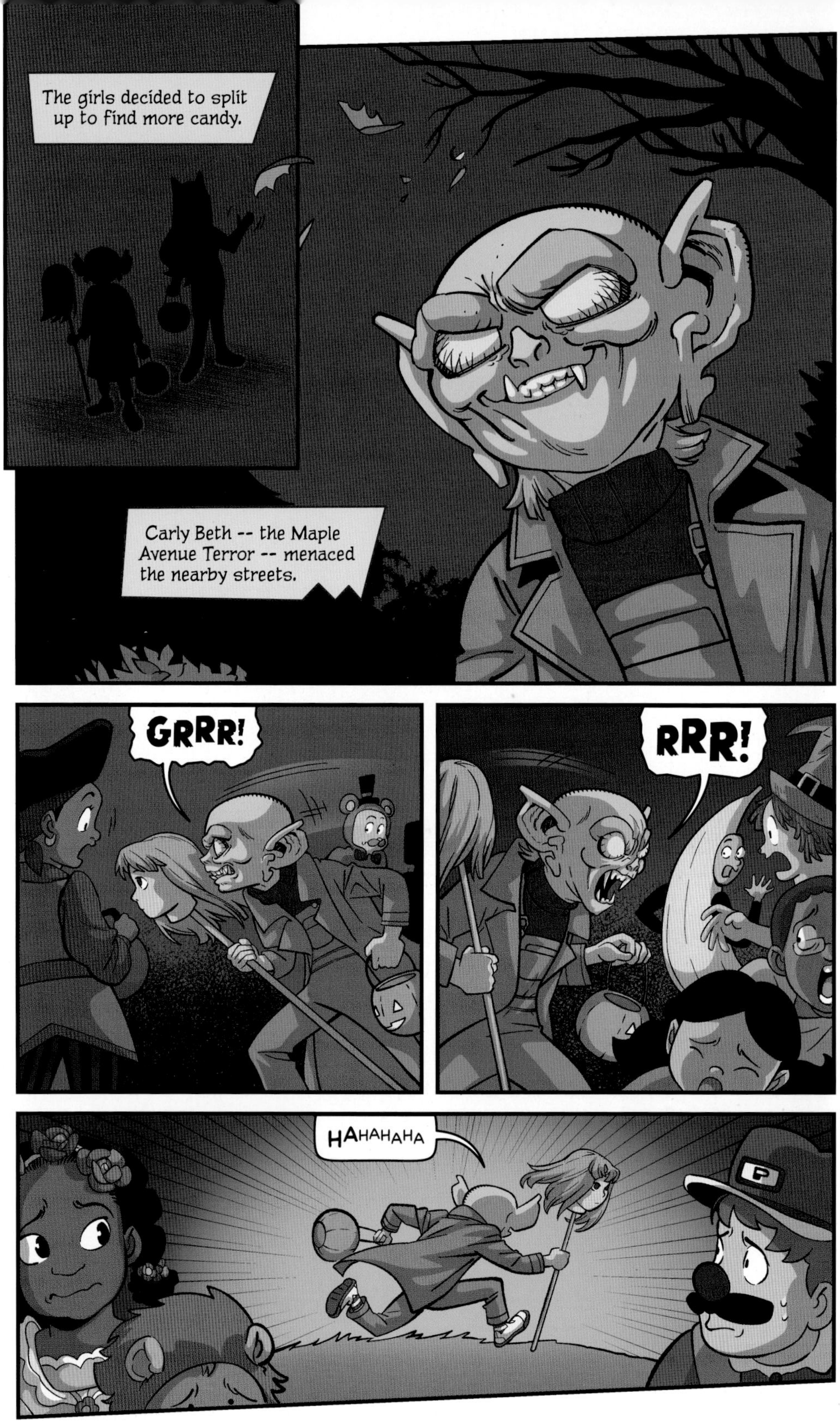
The girls decided to split up to find more candy.
Carly Beth -- the Maple Avenue Terror -- menaced the nearby streets.
GRRR!
RRR!
HAHAHAHA

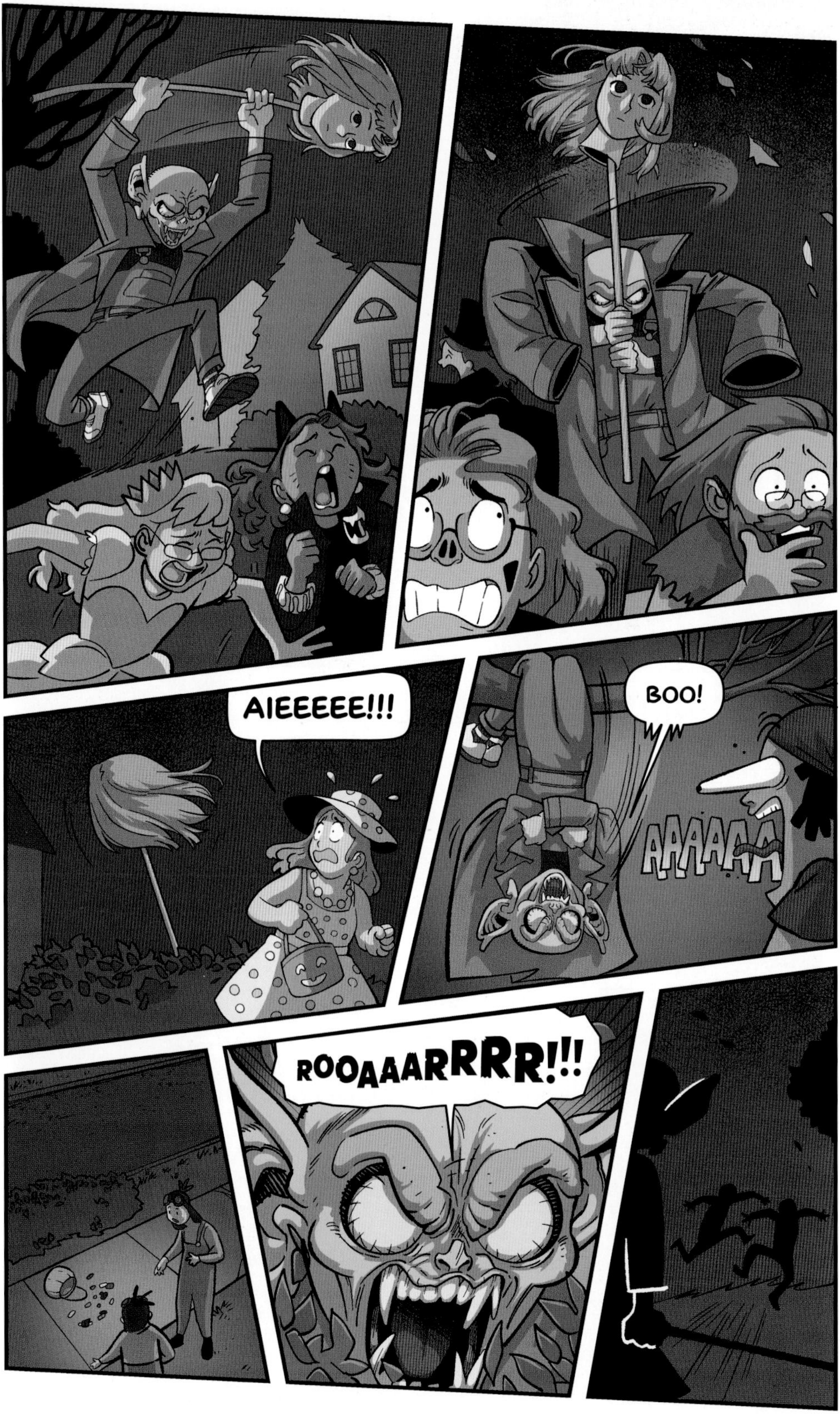
AIEEEEE!!!
BOO!
AAAAAA
ROOAAARRRR!!!

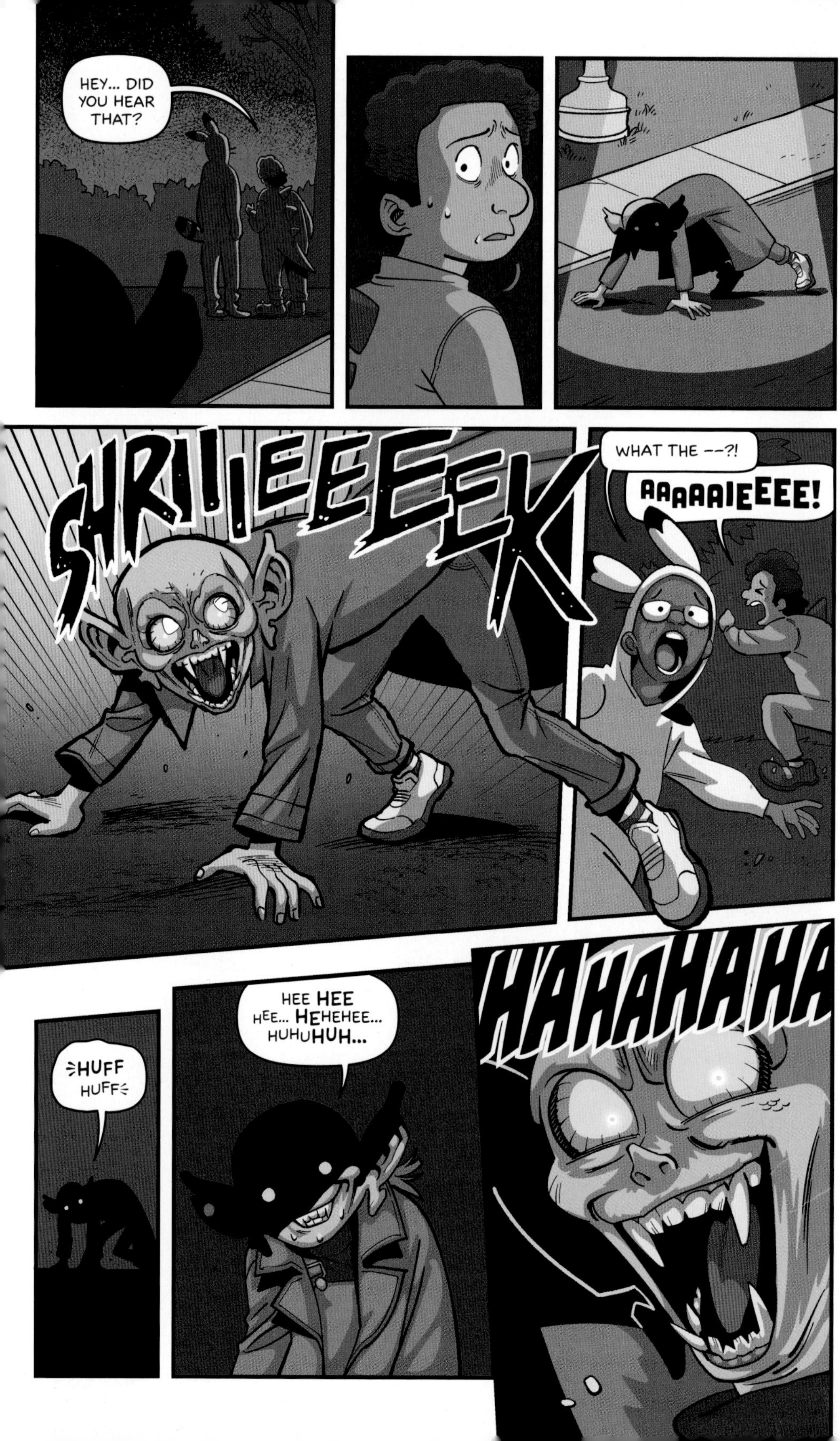
HEY... DID YOU HEAR THAT?
SHRIIIEEEEEK
WHAT THE --?!
AAAAAIEEEE!
HUFF HUFF
HEE HEE HEE... HEHEHEE... HUHUHUH...
HAHAHAHAHA

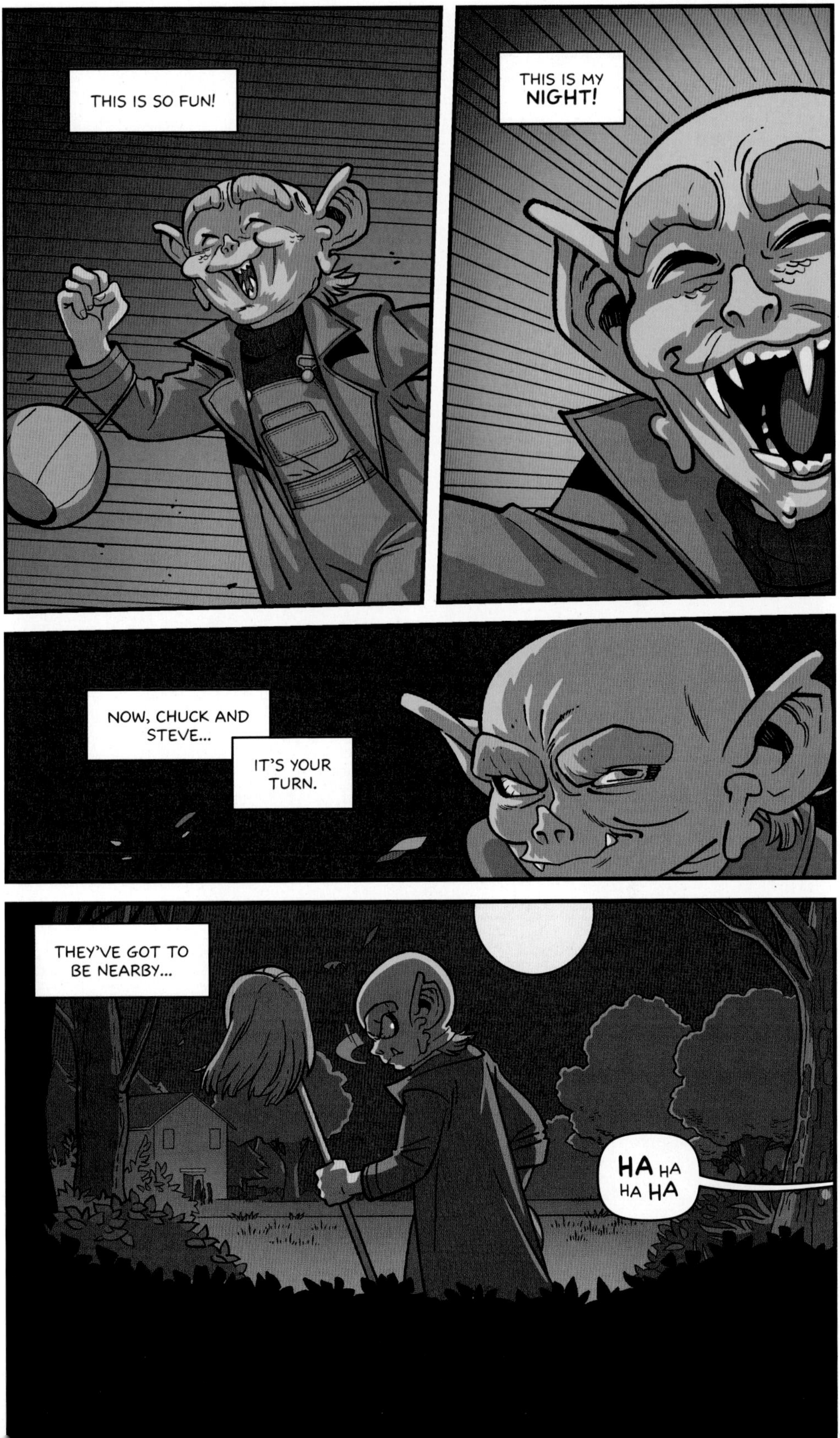
THIS IS SO FUN!
THIS IS MY NIGHT!
NOW, CHUCK AND STEVE...
IT'S YOUR TURN.
THEY'VE GOT TO BE NEARBY...
HA HA HA HA

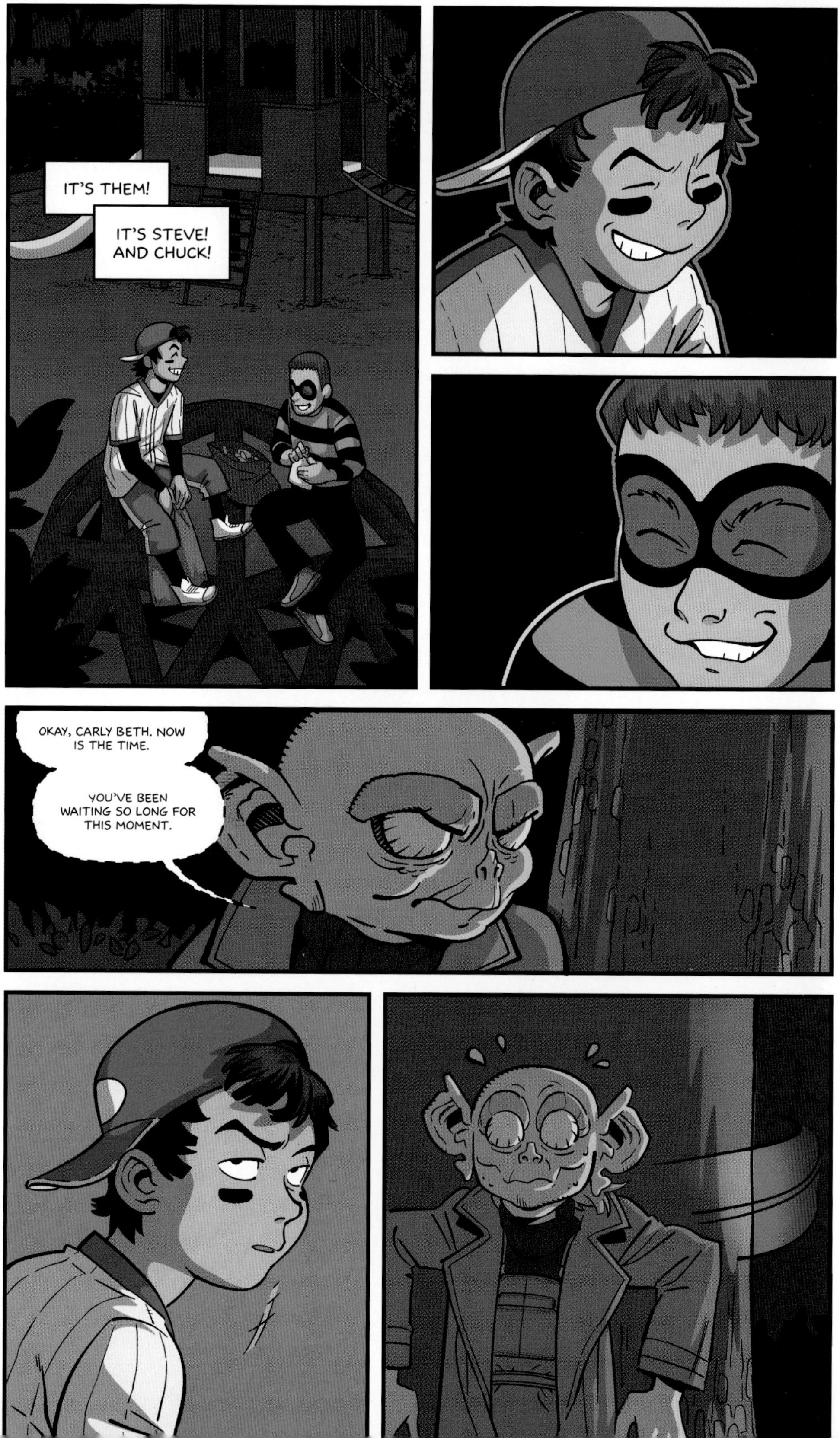
IT'S THEM!
IT'S STEVE! AND CHUCK!
OKAY, CARLY BETH. NOW IS THE TIME.
YOU'VE BEEN WAITING SO LONG FOR THIS MOMENT.

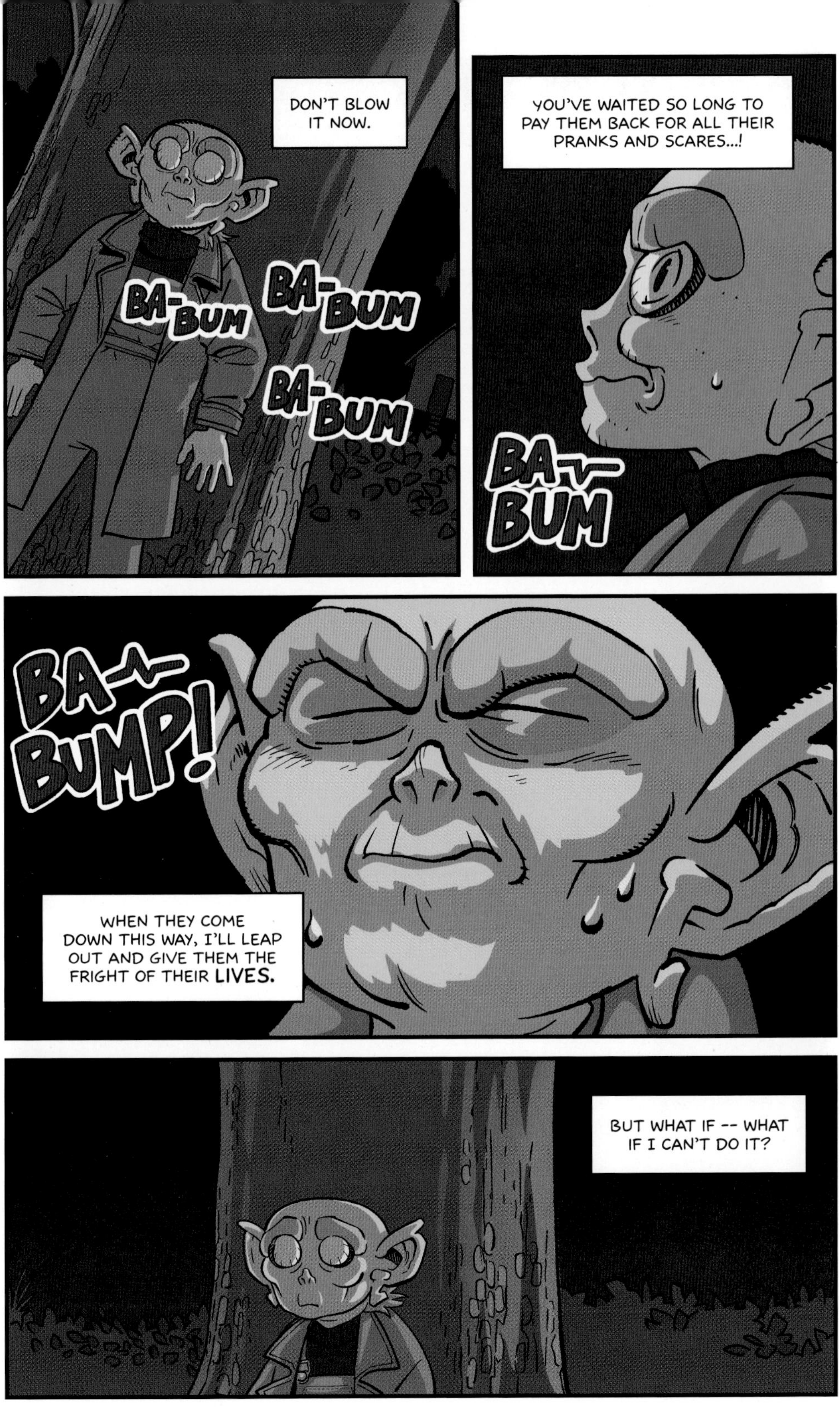
DON'T BLOW IT NOW.
BA-BUM
BA-BUM
BA-BUM
YOU'VE WAITED SO LONG TO PAY THEM BACK FOR ALL THEIR PRANKS AND SCARES...!
BA-BUM
BA-BUMP!
WHEN THEY COME DOWN THIS WAY, I'LL LEAP OUT AND GIVE THEM THE FRIGHT OF THEIR LIVES.
BUT WHAT IF -- WHAT IF I CAN'T DO IT?

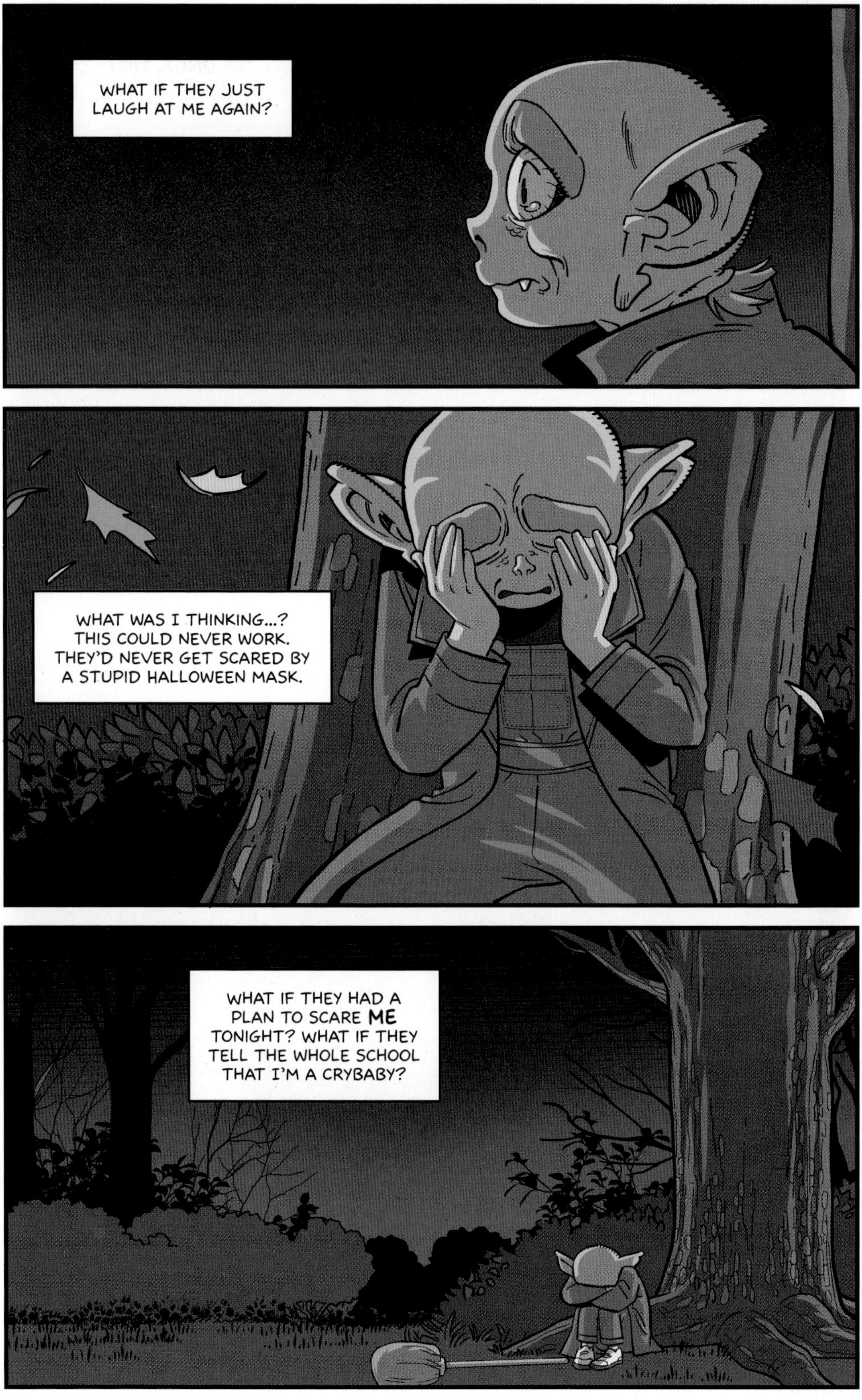
WHAT IF THEY JUST LAUGH AT ME AGAIN?
WHAT WAS I THINKING...? THIS COULD NEVER WORK. THEY'D NEVER GET SCARED BY A STUPID HALLOWEEN MASK.
WHAT IF THEY HAD A PLAN TO SCARE ME TONIGHT? WHAT IF THEY TELL THE WHOLE SCHOOL THAT I'M A CRYBABY?

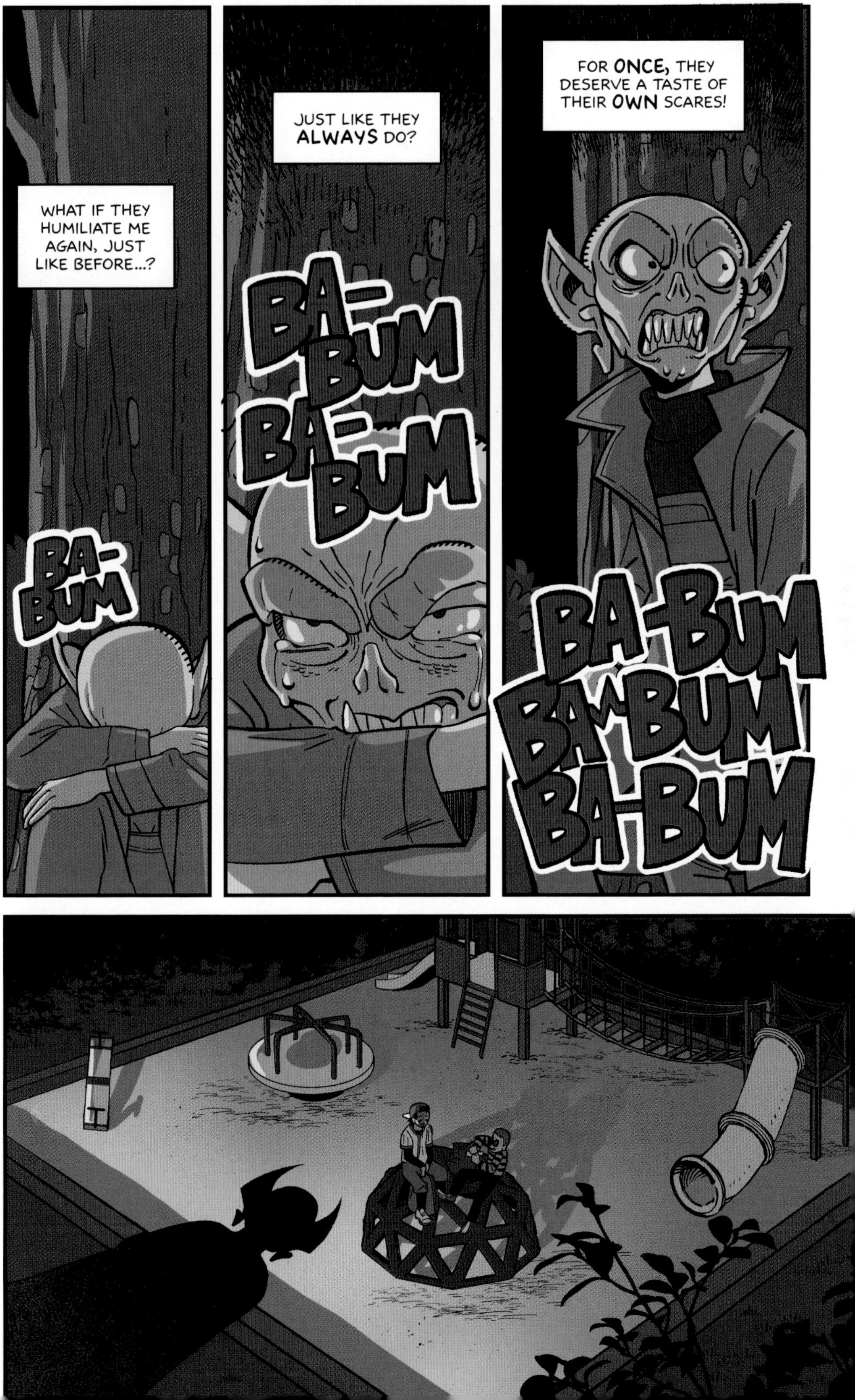
WHAT IF THEY HUMILIATE ME AGAIN, JUST LIKE BEFORE...?
BA-BUM
JUST LIKE THEY ALWAYS DO?
BA-BUM BA-BUM
FOR ONCE, THEY DESERVE A TASTE OF THEIR OWN SCARES!
BA-BUM BA-BUM BA-BUM

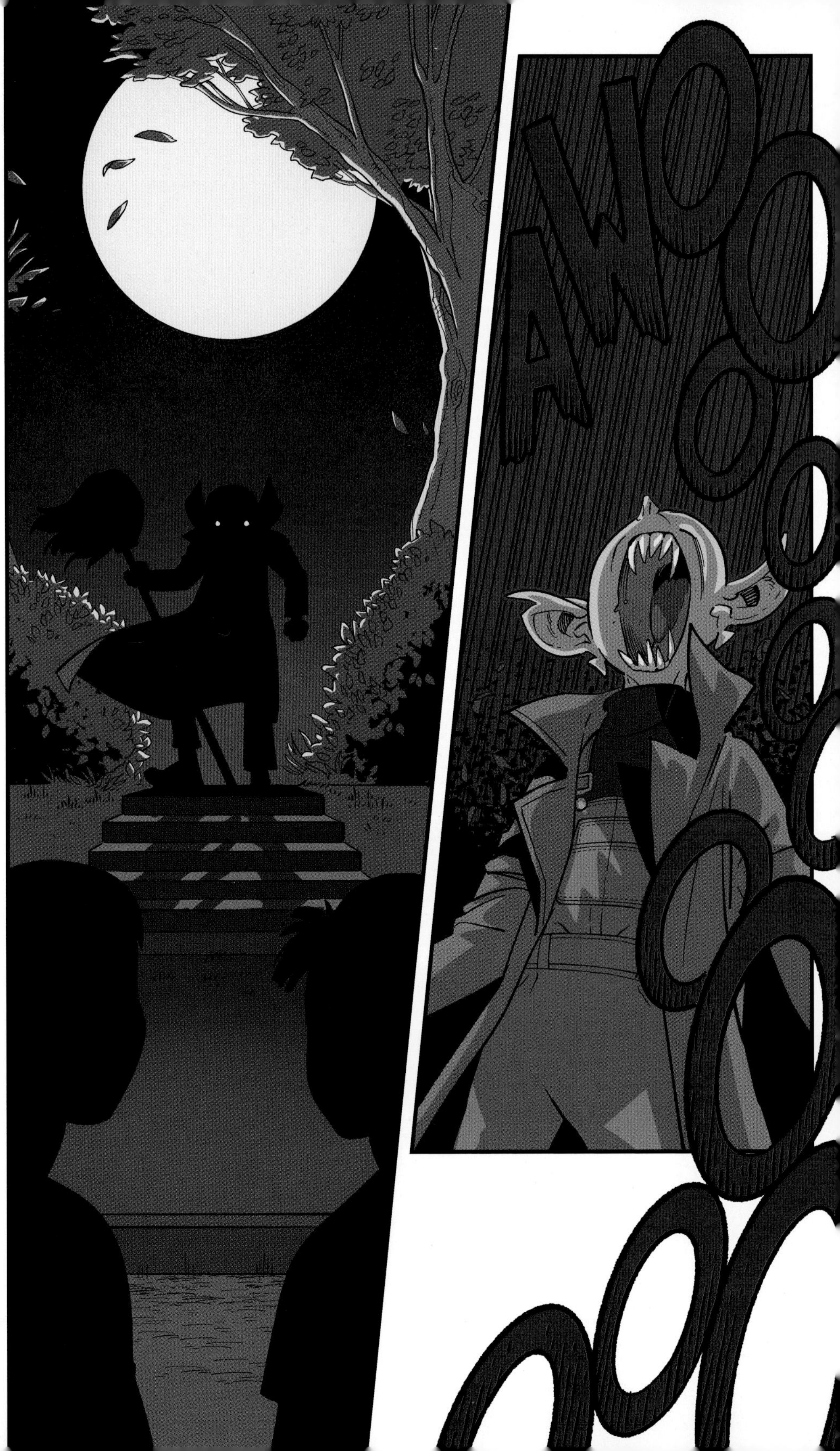
AWOOOOOOOOOOOOOO

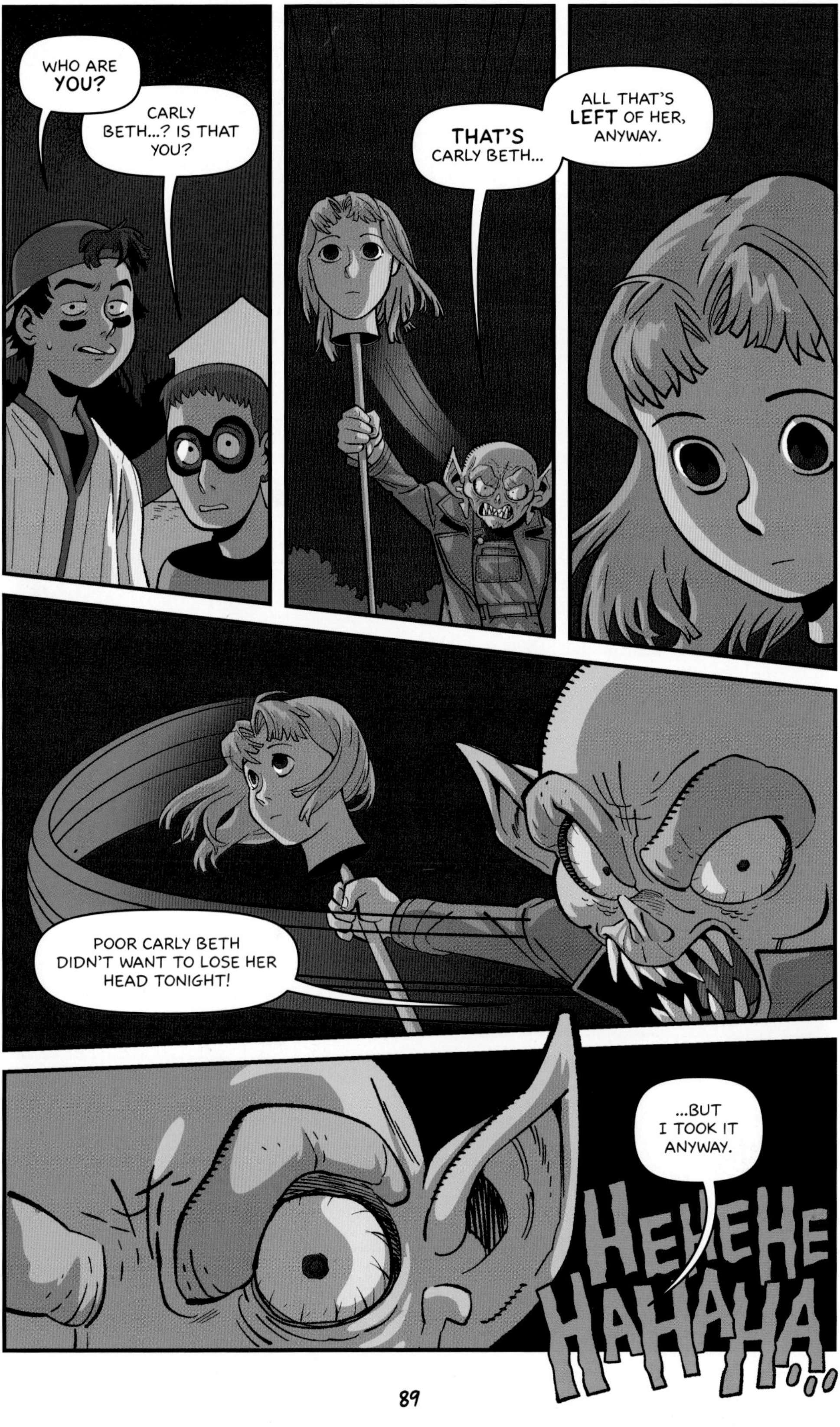
WHO ARE YOU?
CARLY BETH...? IS THAT YOU?
THAT'S CARLY BETH...
ALL THAT'S LEFT OF HER, ANYWAY.
POOR CARLY BETH DIDN'T WANT TO LOSE HER HEAD TONIGHT!
...BUT I TOOK IT ANYWAY.
HEHEHE HAHAHA...

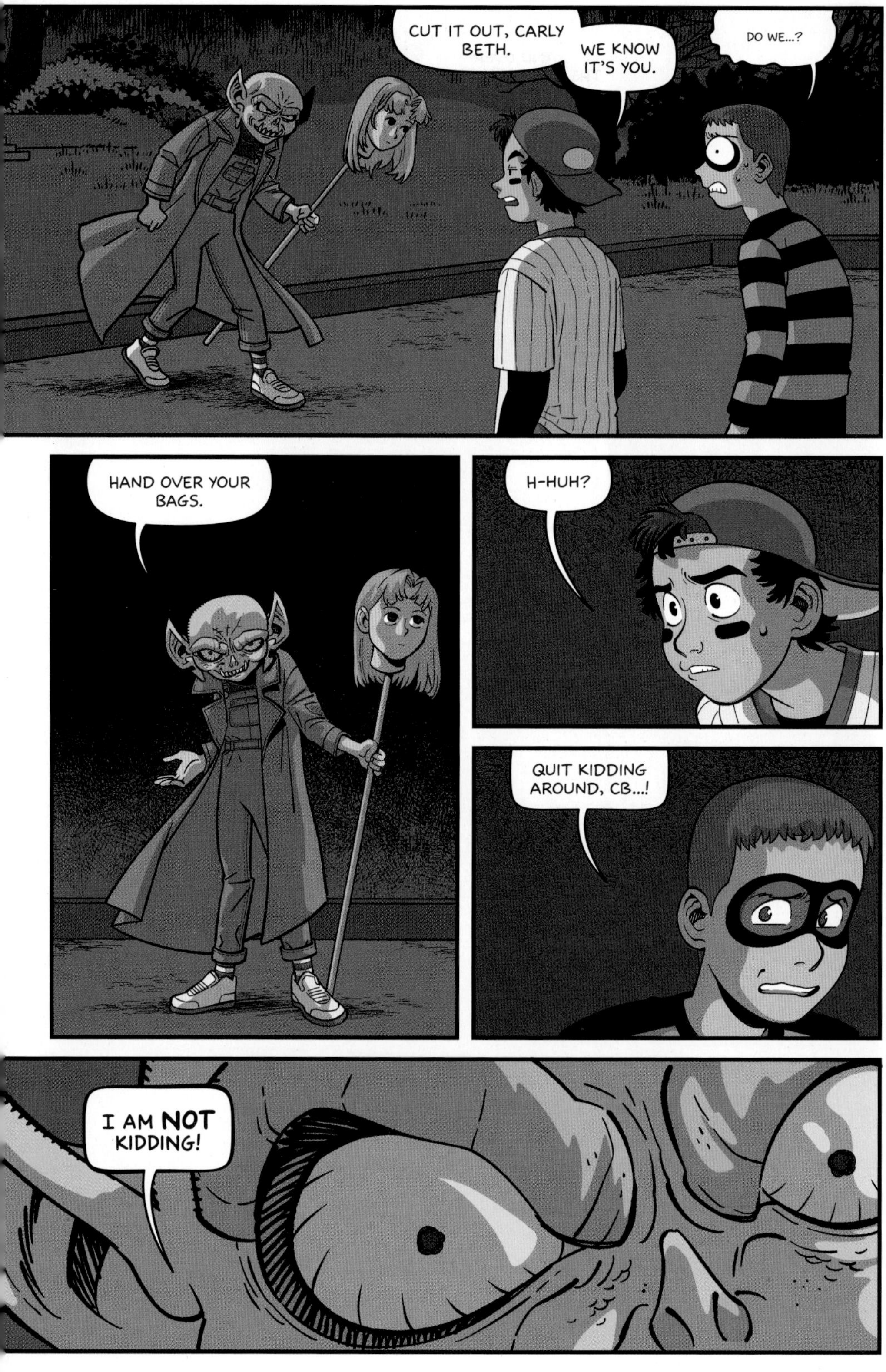
CUT IT OUT, CARLY BETH.
WE KNOW IT'S YOU.
DO WE...?
HAND OVER YOUR BAGS.
H-HUH?
QUIT KIDDING AROUND, CB...!
I AM **NOT** KIDDING!

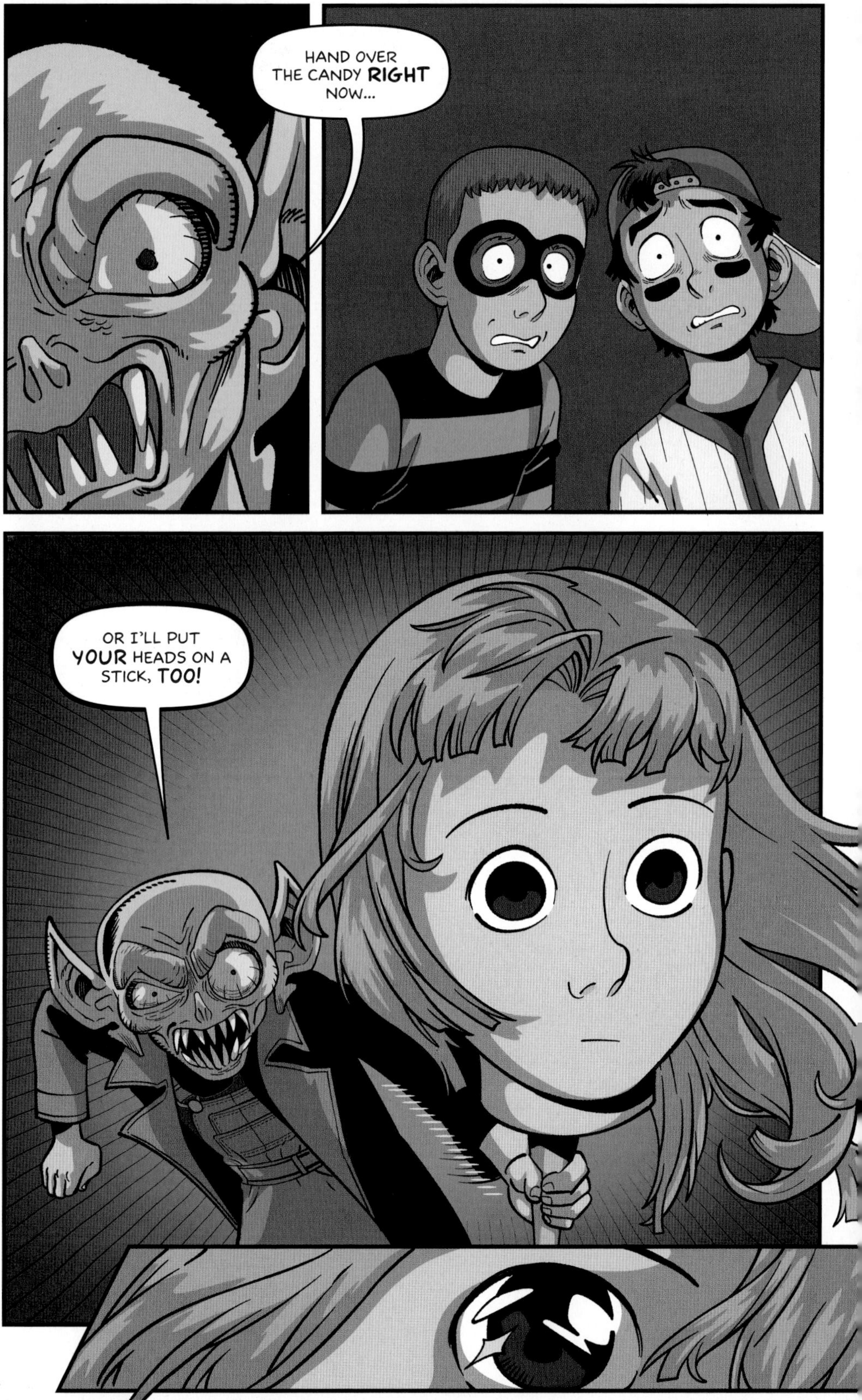
HAND OVER THE CANDY **RIGHT** NOW...
OR I'LL PUT **YOUR** HEADS ON A STICK, **TOO!**

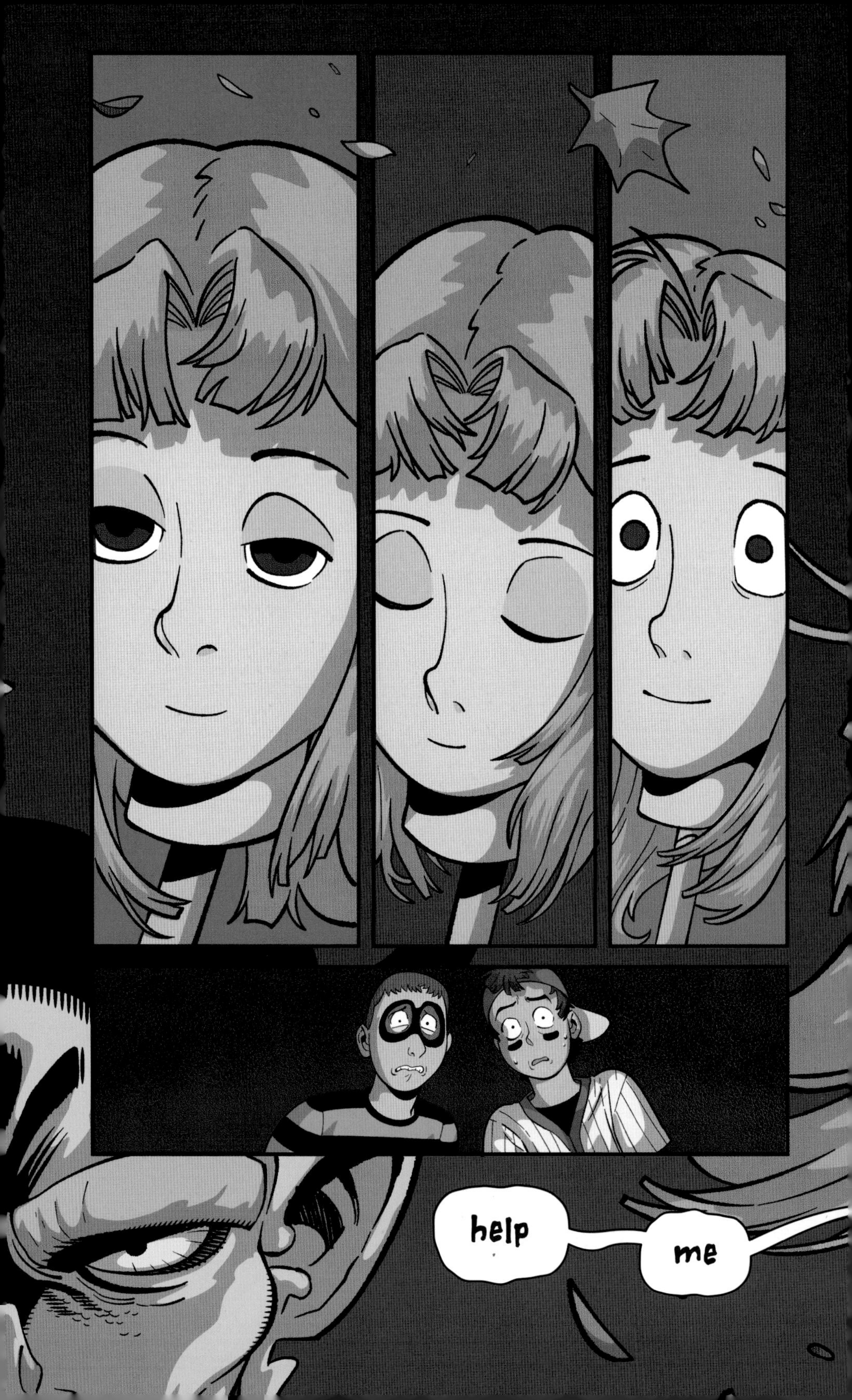
help
me

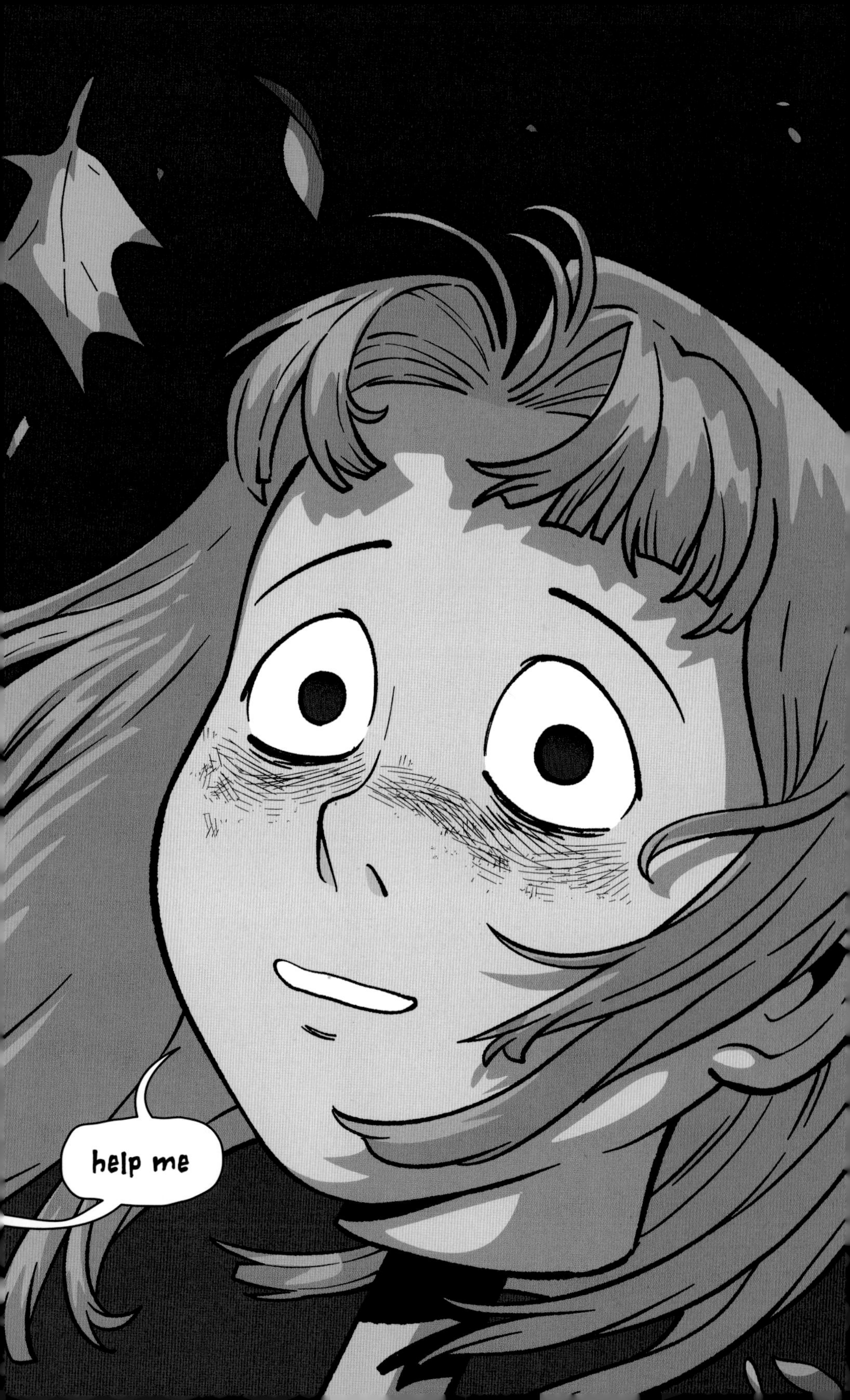
help me

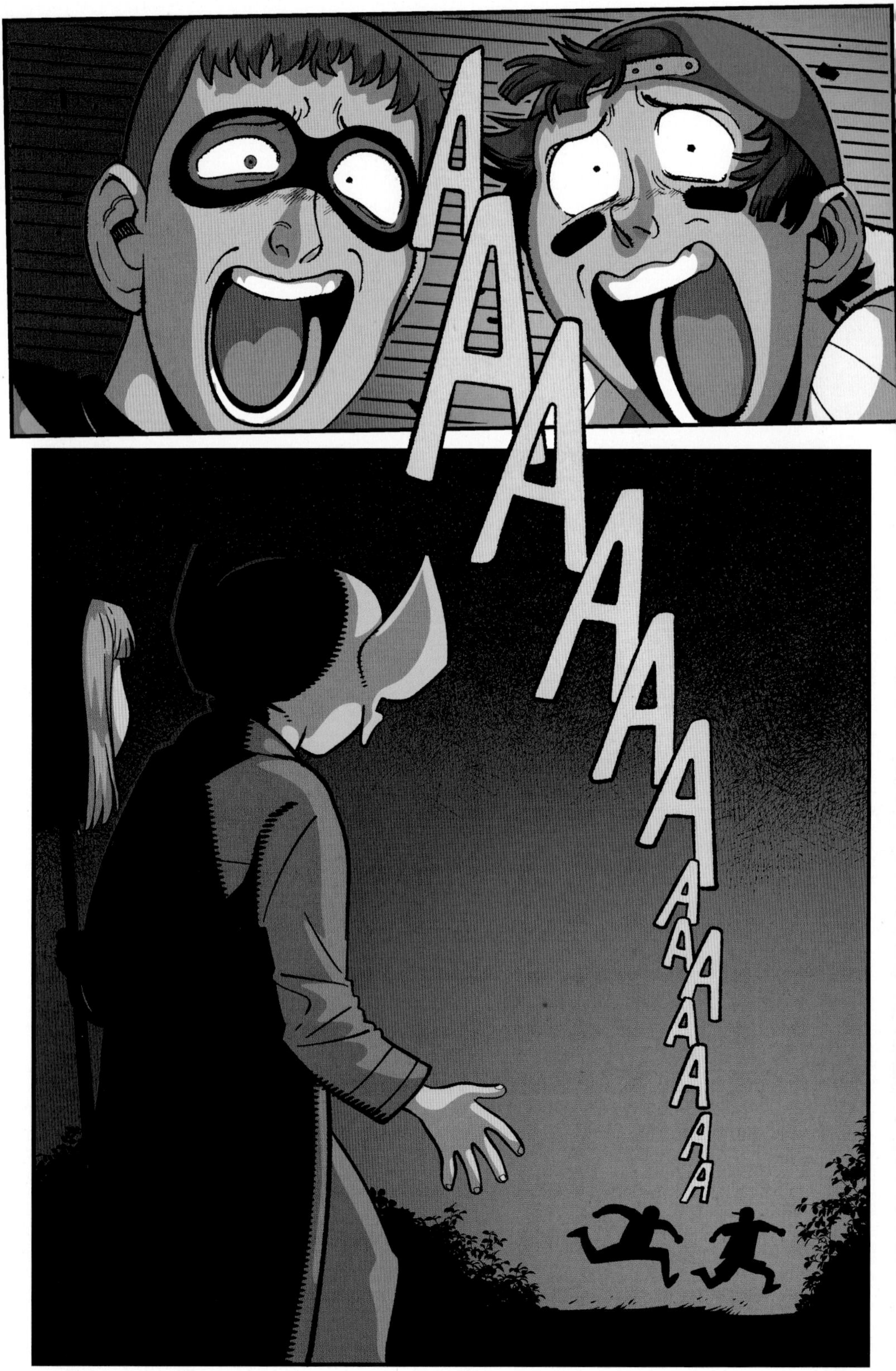
AAAAAAAAAAAAAAAAA

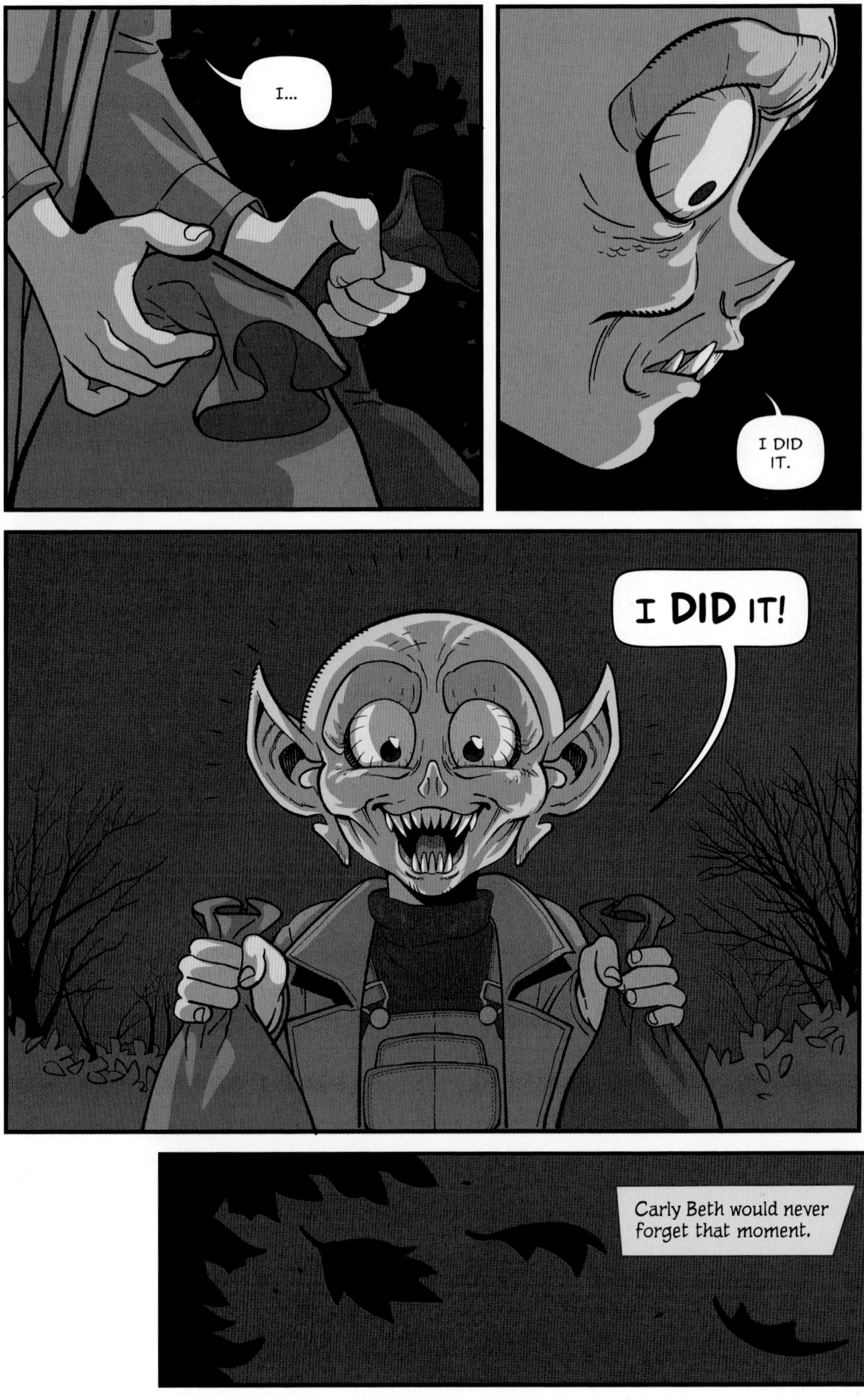

I...
I DID IT.
I DID IT!
Carly Beth would never forget that moment.

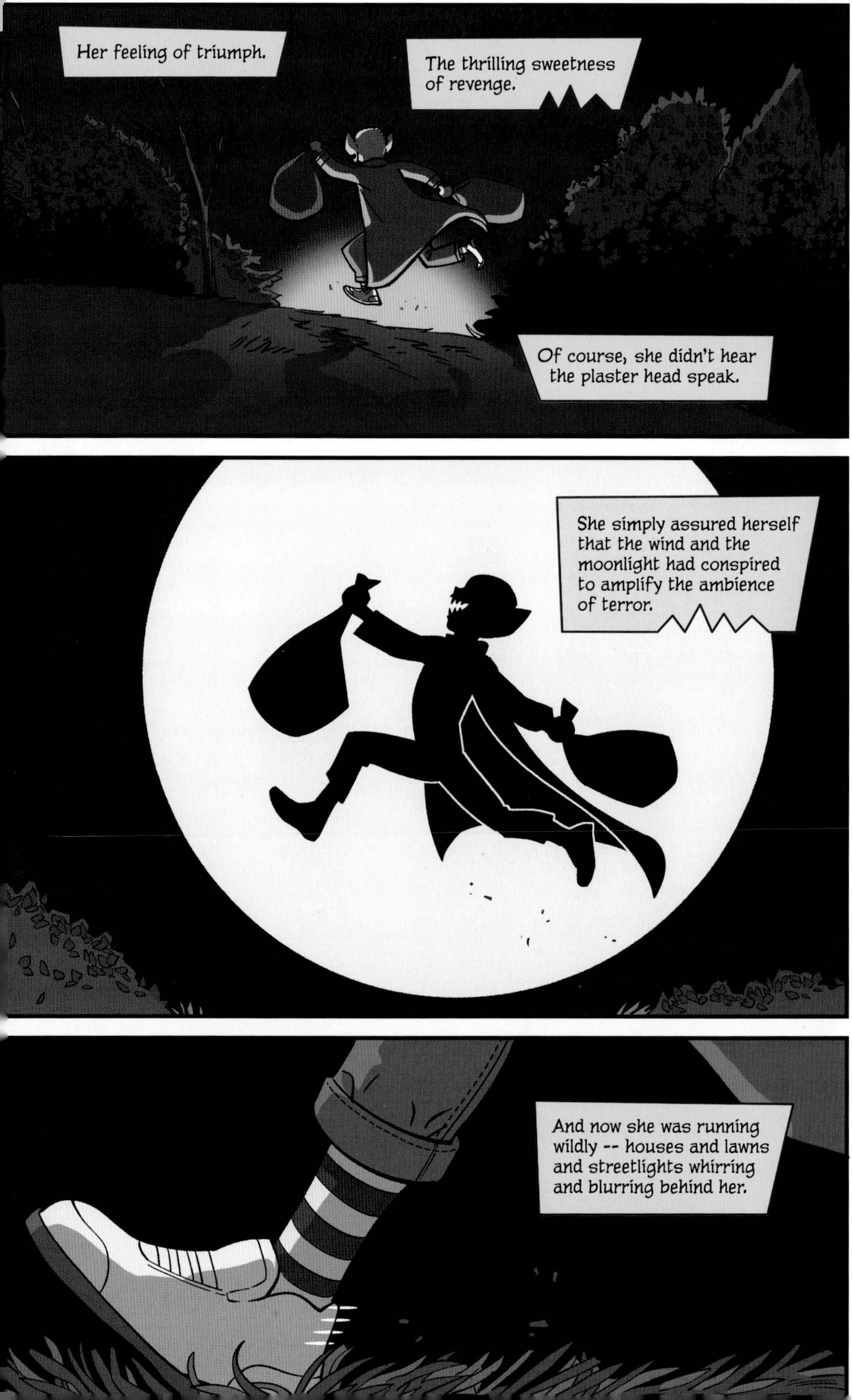
Her feeling of triumph.
The thrilling sweetness of revenge.
Of course, she didn't hear the plaster head speak.
She simply assured herself that the wind and the moonlight had conspired to amplify the ambience of terror.
And now she was running wildly -- houses and lawns and streetlights whirring and blurring behind her.

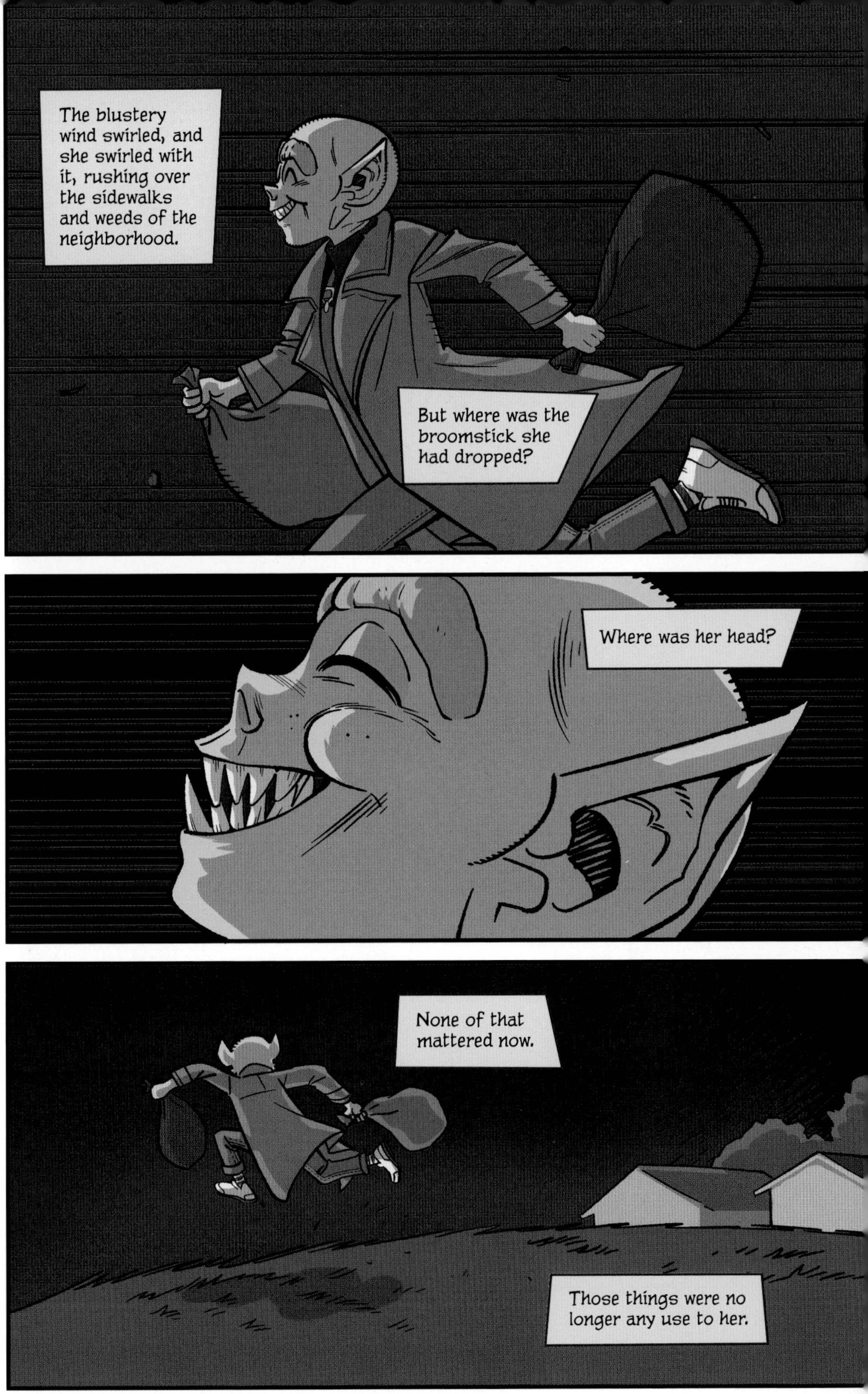
The blustery wind swirled, and she swirled with it, rushing over the sidewalks and weeds of the neighborhood.
But where was the broomstick she had dropped?
Where was her head?
None of that mattered now.
Those things were no longer any use to her.

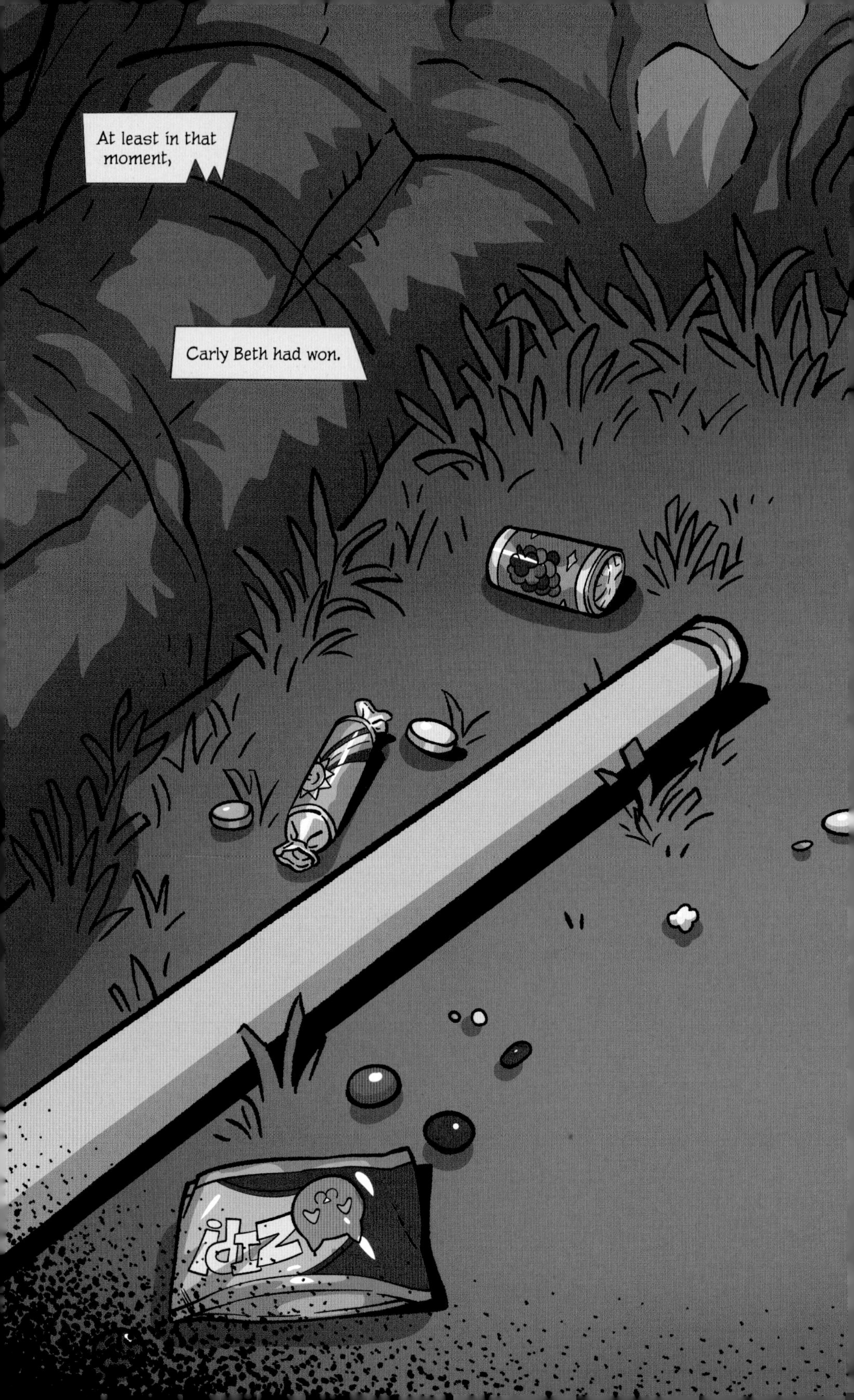
At least in that moment,
Carly Beth had won.

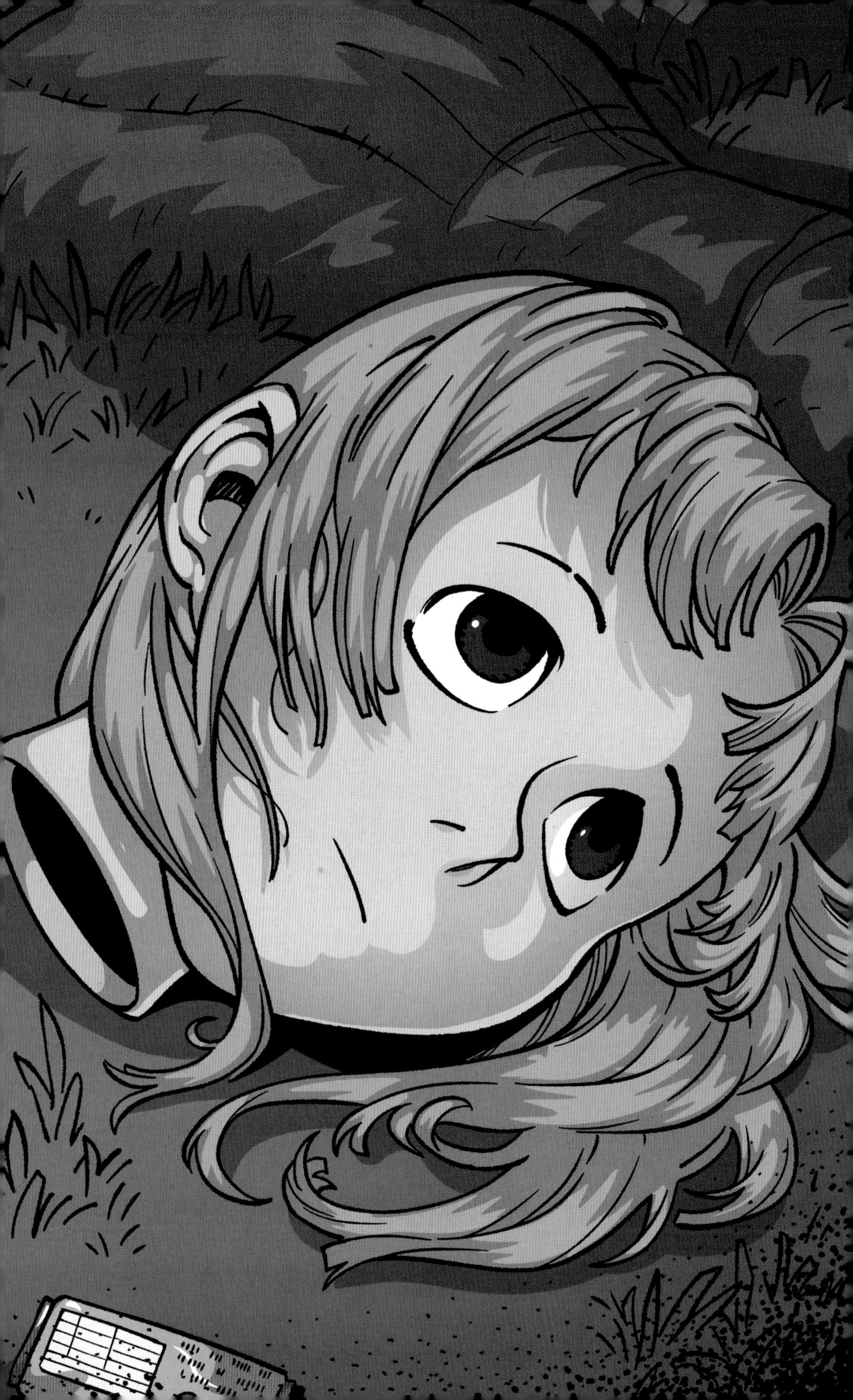

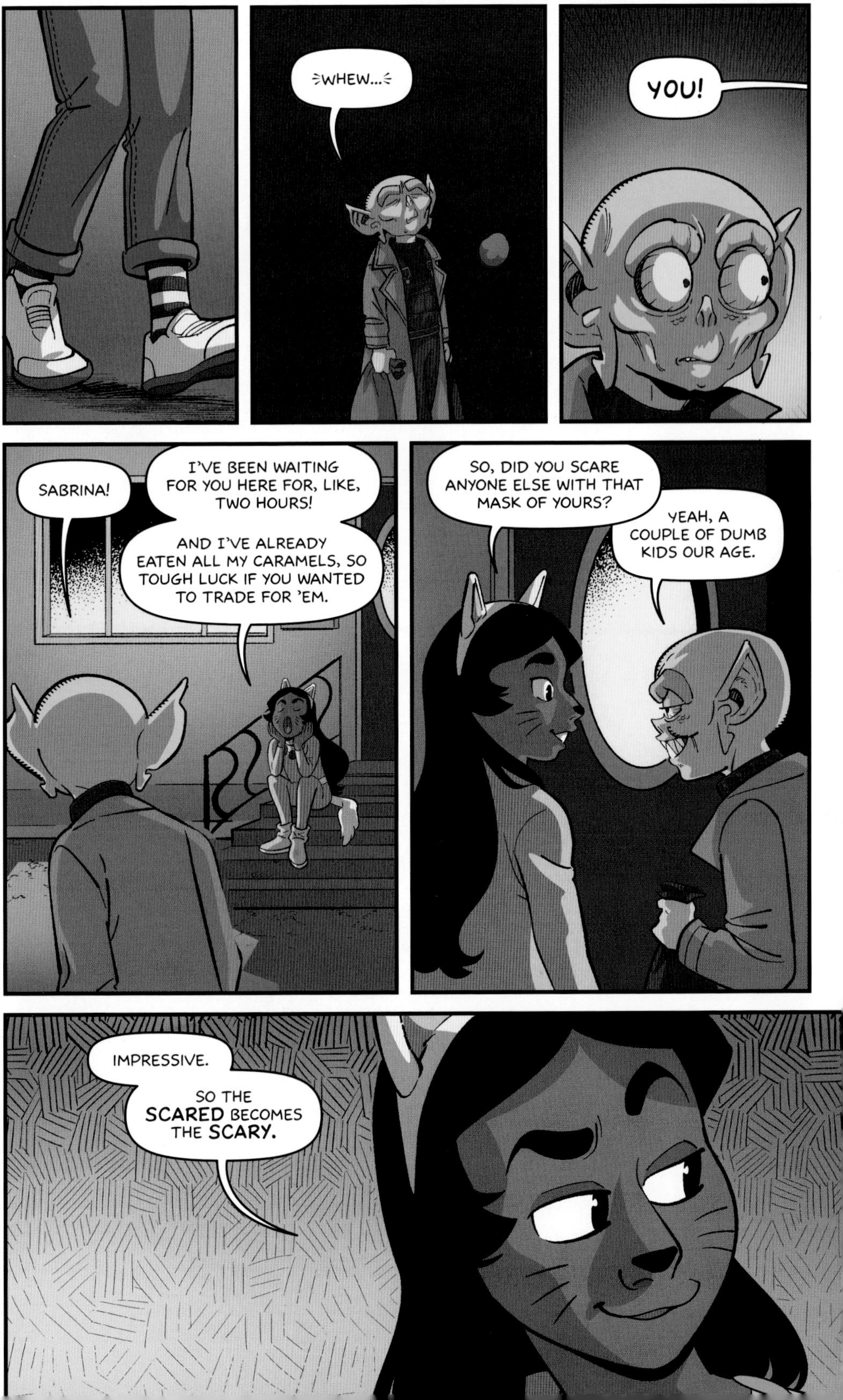

WHEW...
YOU!
SABRINA!
I'VE BEEN WAITING FOR YOU HERE FOR, LIKE, TWO HOURS!
AND I'VE ALREADY EATEN ALL MY CARAMELS, SO TOUGH LUCK IF YOU WANTED TO TRADE FOR 'EM.
SO, DID YOU SCARE ANYONE ELSE WITH THAT MASK OF YOURS?
YEAH, A COUPLE OF DUMB KIDS OUR AGE.
IMPRESSIVE.
SO THE SCARED BECOMES THE SCARY.

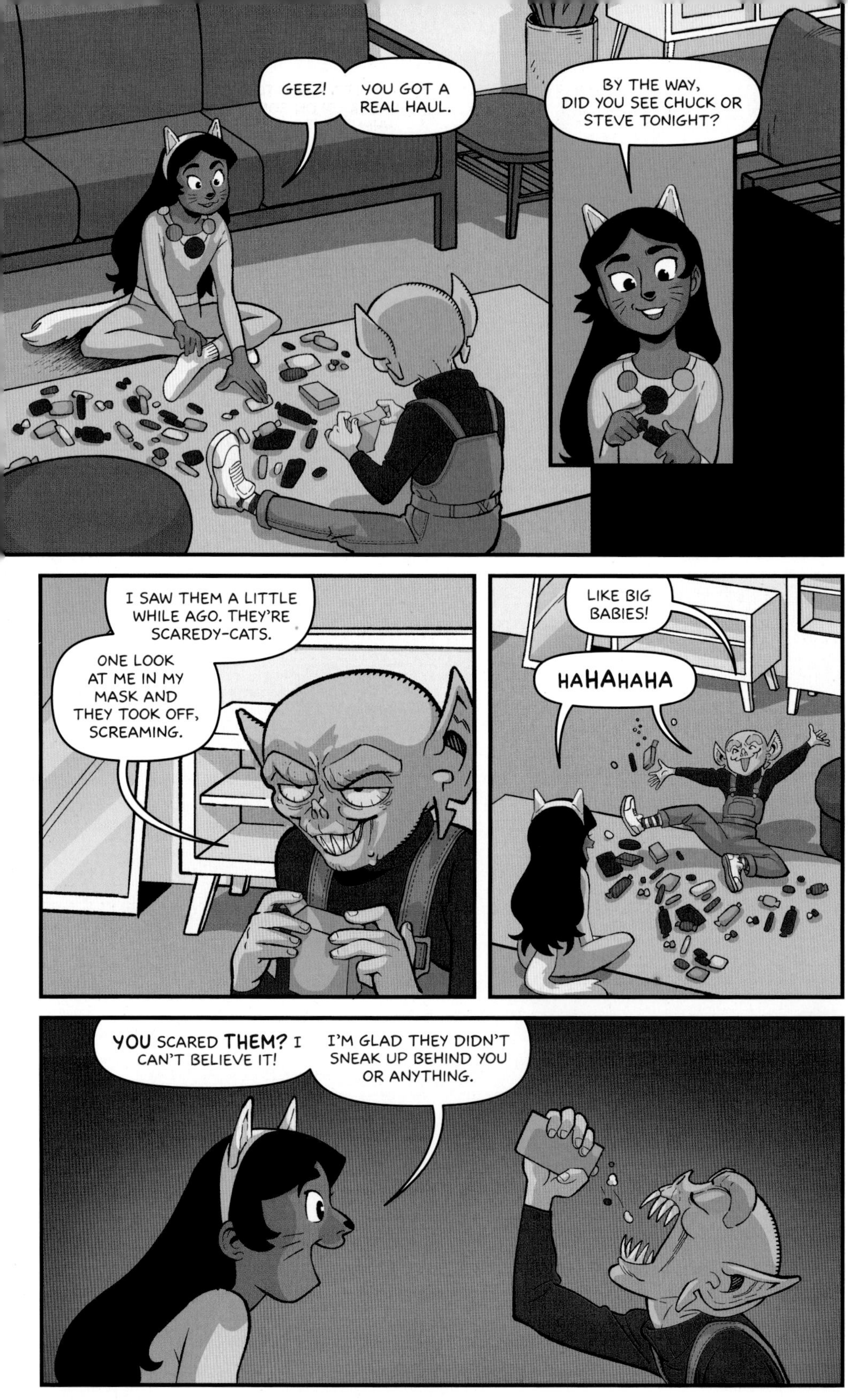
GEEZ!
YOU GOT A REAL HAUL.
BY THE WAY, DID YOU SEE CHUCK OR STEVE TONIGHT?
I SAW THEM A LITTLE WHILE AGO. THEY'RE SCAREDY-CATS.
ONE LOOK AT ME IN MY MASK AND THEY TOOK OFF, SCREAMING.
LIKE BIG BABIES!
HAHAHAHA
YOU SCARED THEM? I CAN'T BELIEVE IT!
I'M GLAD THEY DIDN'T SNEAK UP BEHIND YOU OR ANYTHING.

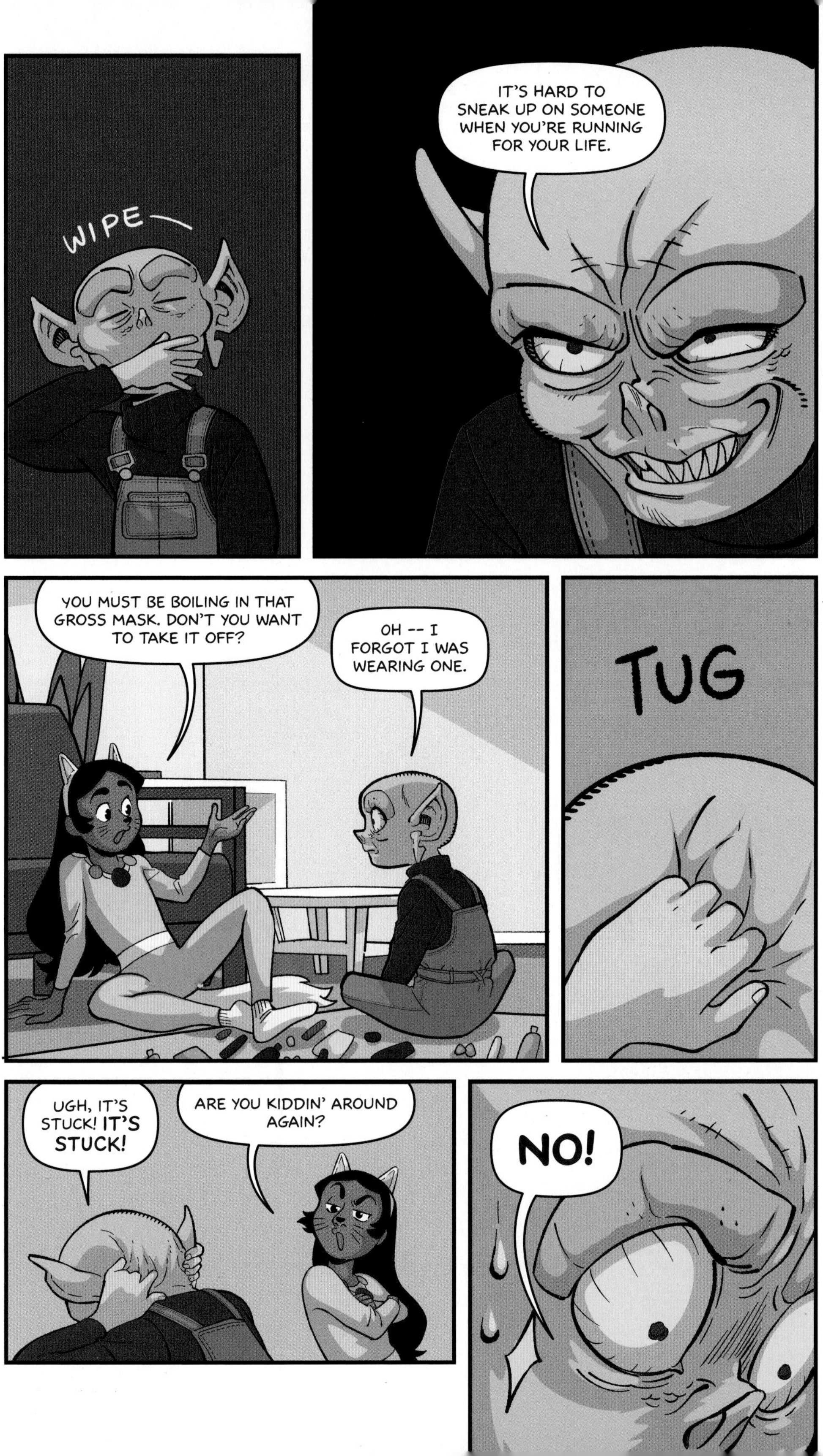
WIPE
IT'S HARD TO SNEAK UP ON SOMEONE WHEN YOU'RE RUNNING FOR YOUR LIFE.
YOU MUST BE BOILING IN THAT GROSS MASK. DON'T YOU WANT TO TAKE IT OFF?
OH -- I FORGOT I WAS WEARING ONE.
TUG
UGH, IT'S STUCK! IT'S STUCK!
ARE YOU KIDDIN' AROUND AGAIN?
NO!

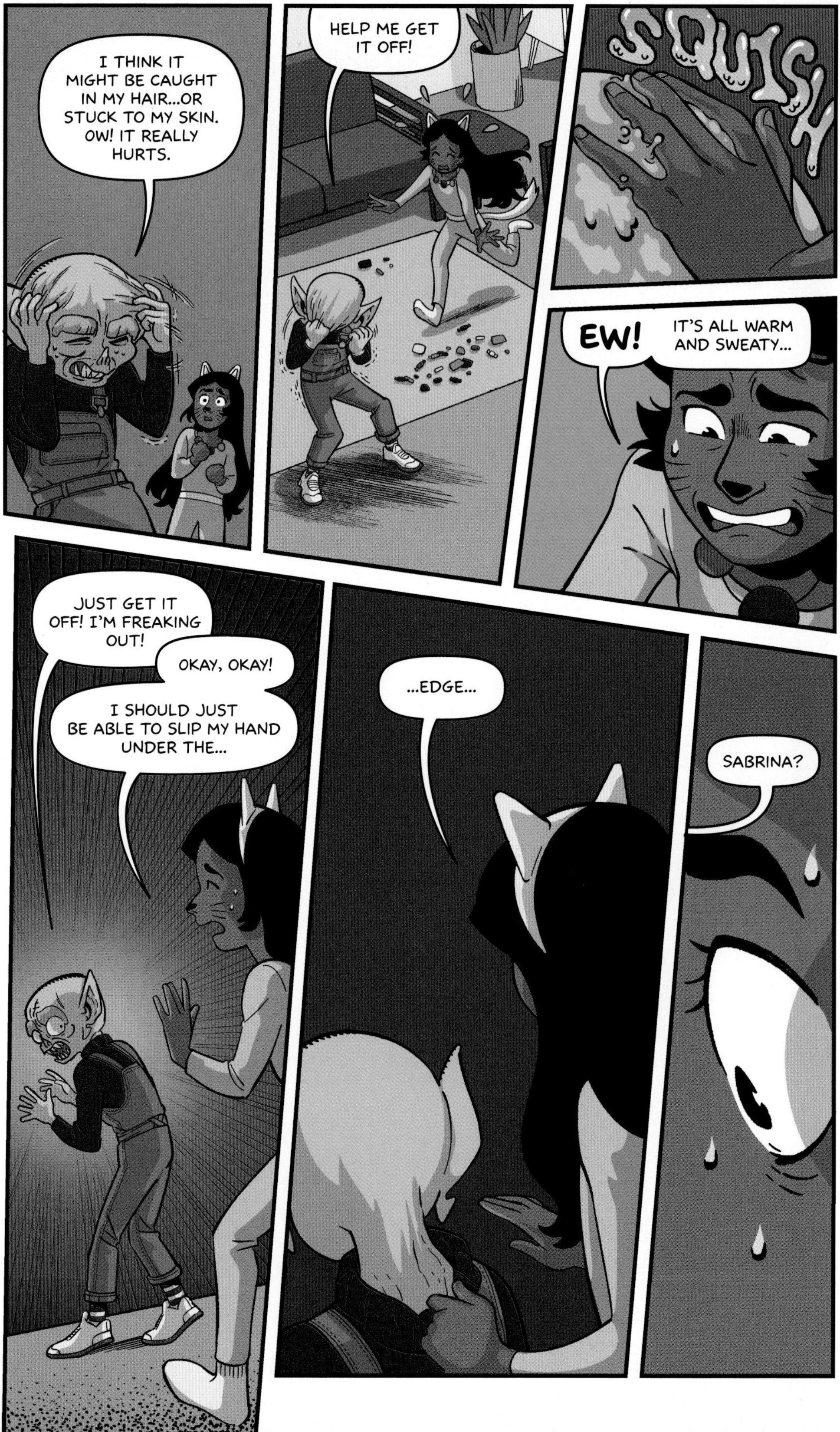
I THINK IT MIGHT BE CAUGHT IN MY HAIR...OR STUCK TO MY SKIN. OW! IT REALLY HURTS.
HELP ME GET IT OFF!
SQUISH
EW!
IT'S ALL WARM AND SWEATY...
JUST GET IT OFF! I'M FREAKING OUT!
OKAY, OKAY!
I SHOULD JUST BE ABLE TO SLIP MY HAND UNDER THE...
...EDGE...
SABRINA?

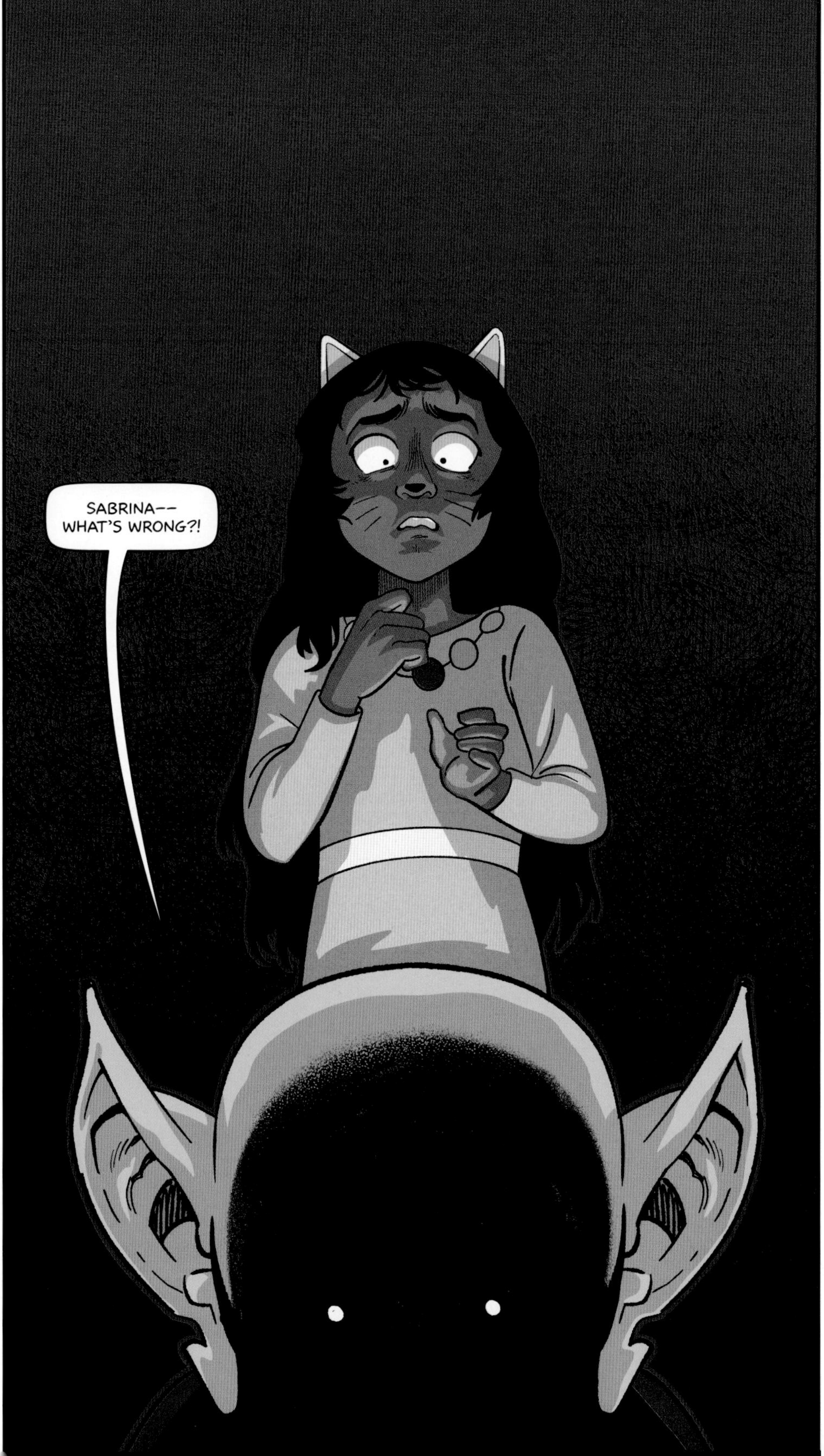
SABRINA--
WHAT'S WRONG?!

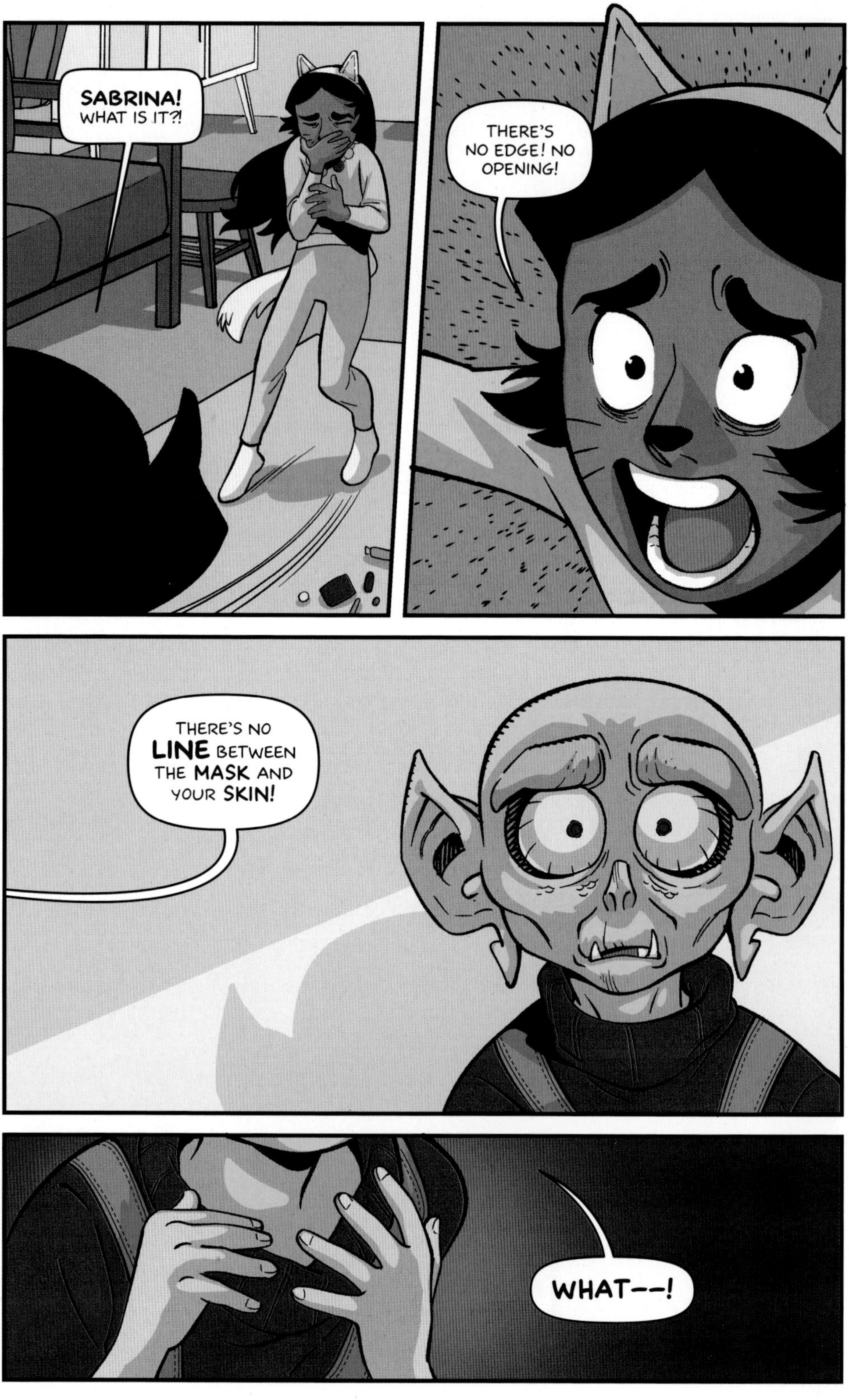
SABRINA! WHAT IS IT?!
THERE'S NO EDGE! NO OPENING!
THERE'S NO LINE BETWEEN THE MASK AND YOUR SKIN!
WHAT--!

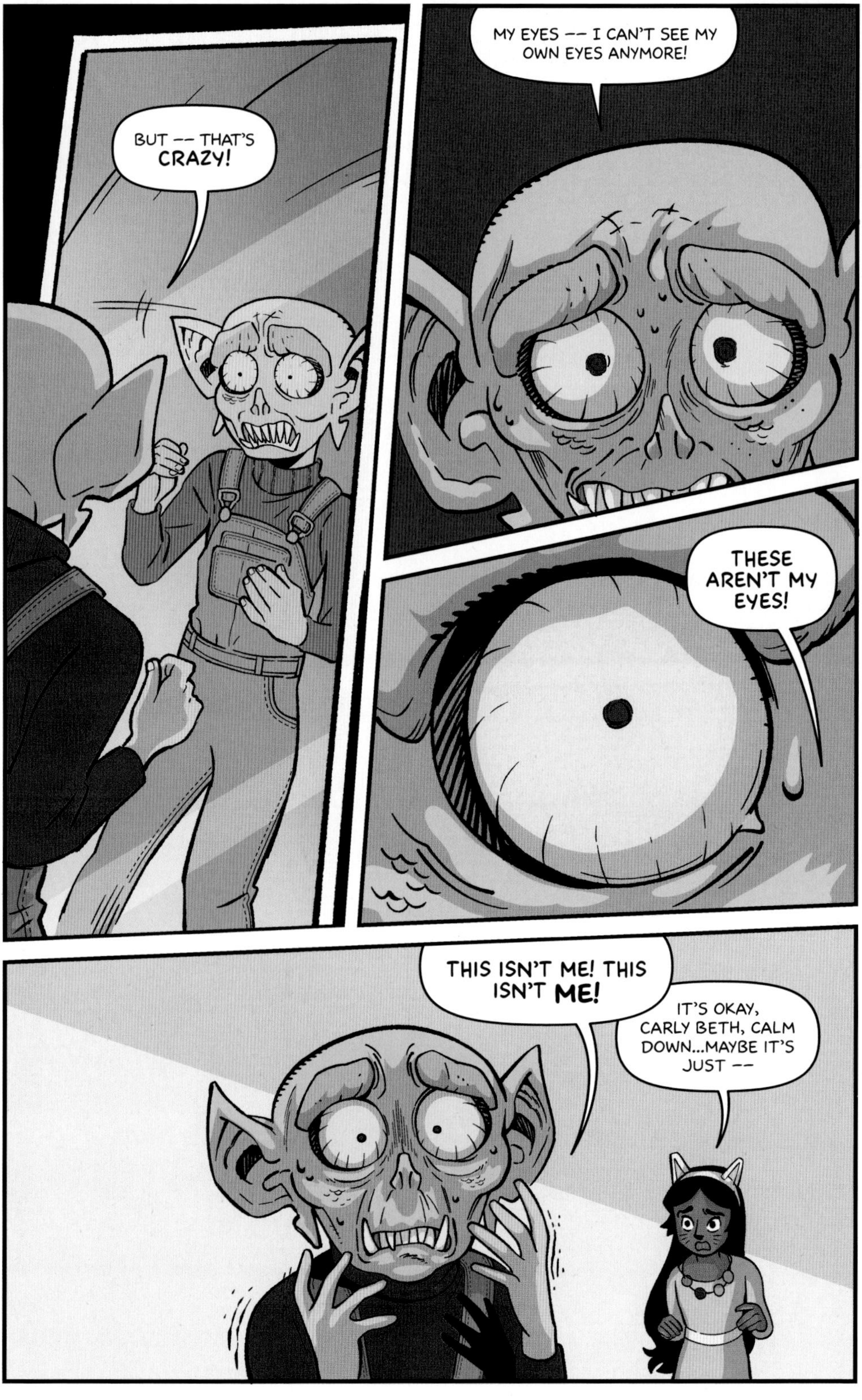

BUT -- THAT'S CRAZY!
MY EYES -- I CAN'T SEE MY OWN EYES ANYMORE!
THESE AREN'T MY EYES!
THIS ISN'T ME! THIS ISN'T ME!
IT'S OKAY, CARLY BETH, CALM DOWN...MAYBE IT'S JUST --

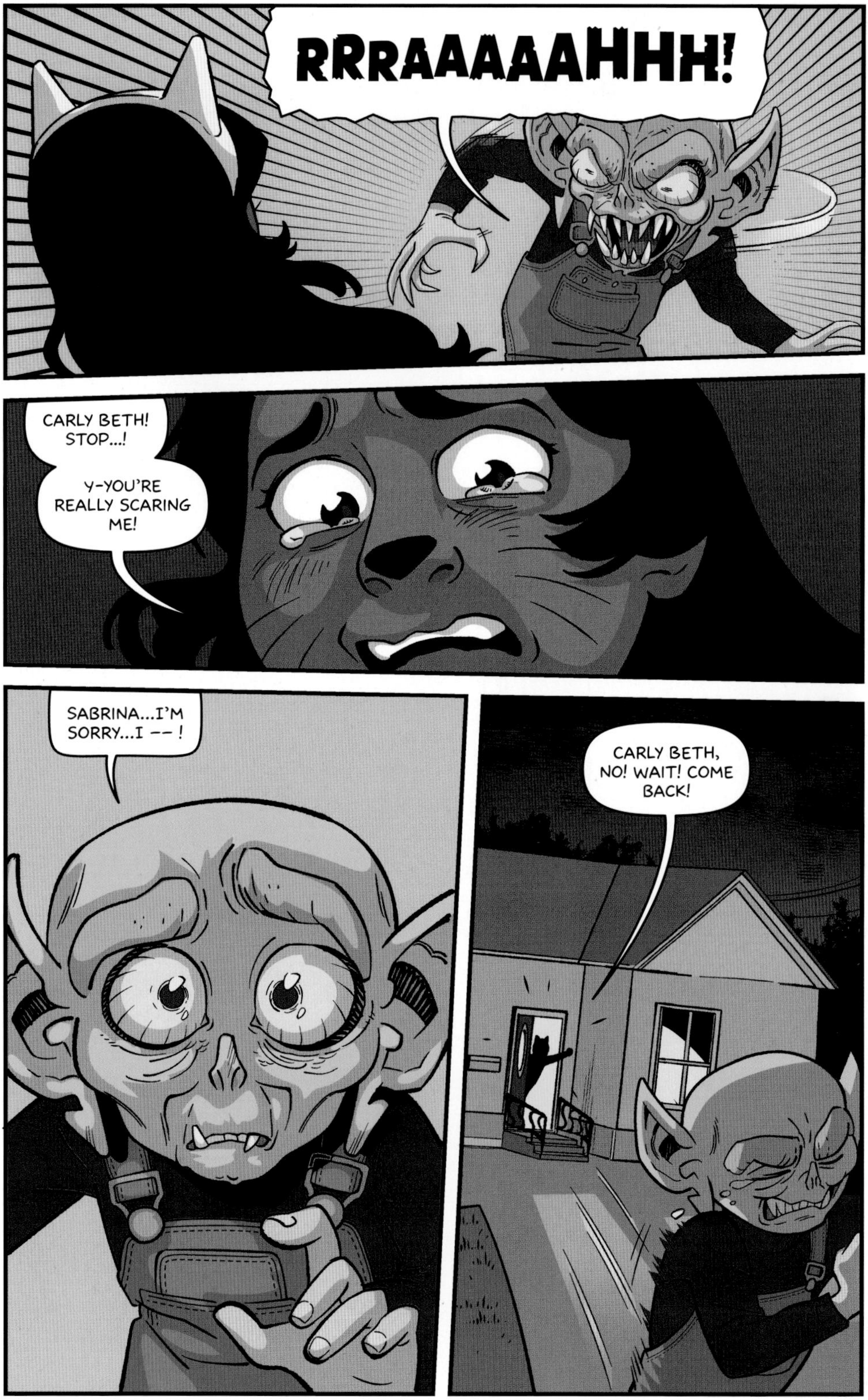
RRRAAAAAAHHH!
CARLY BETH! STOP...!
Y-YOU'RE REALLY SCARING ME!
SABRINA...I'M SORRY...I -- !
CARLY BETH, NO! WAIT! COME BACK!

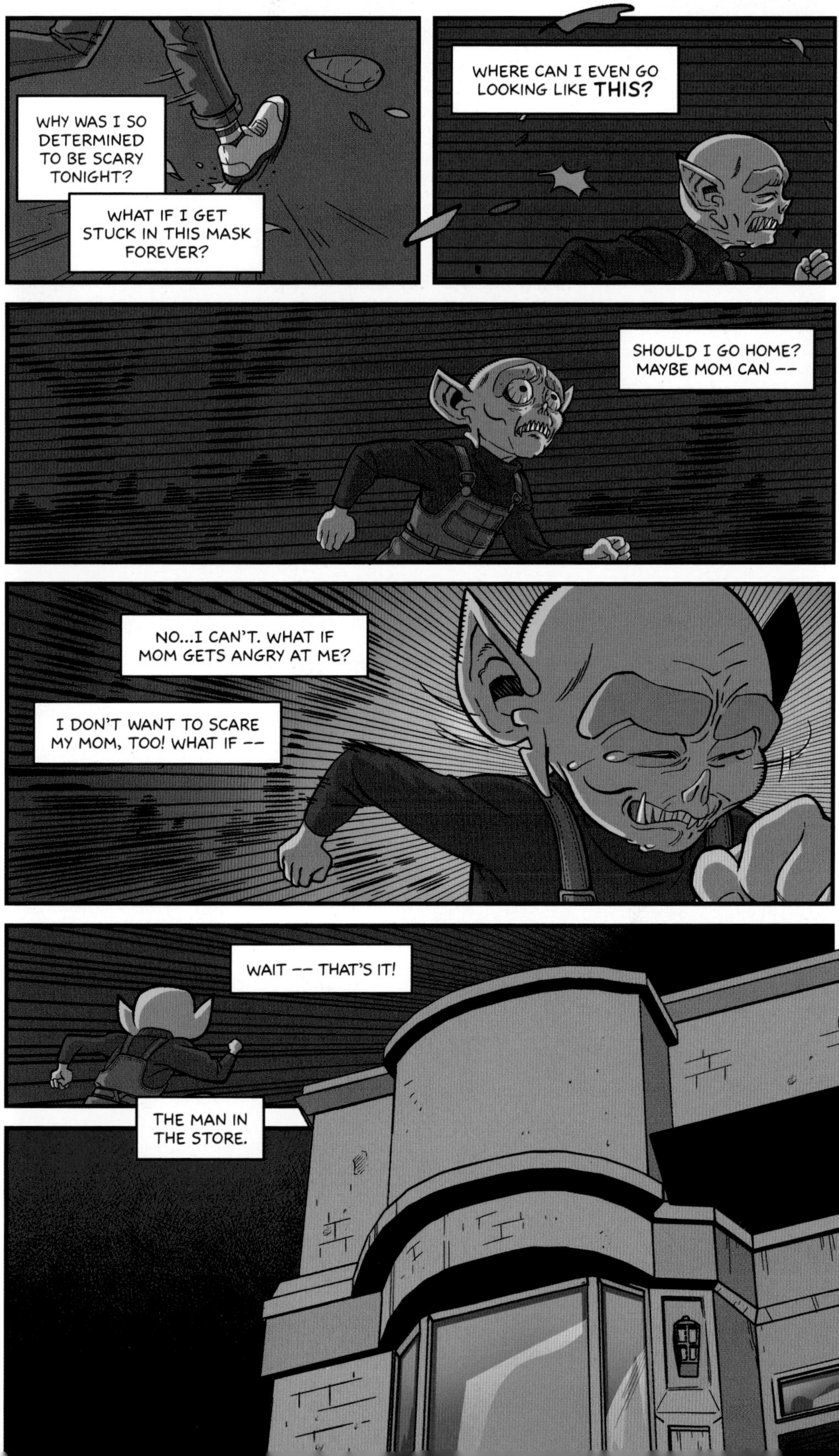
WHY WAS I SO DETERMINED TO BE SCARY TONIGHT?
WHAT IF I GET STUCK IN THIS MASK FOREVER?
WHERE CAN I EVEN GO LOOKING LIKE THIS?
SHOULD I GO HOME? MAYBE MOM CAN --
NO...I CAN'T. WHAT IF MOM GETS ANGRY AT ME?
I DON'T WANT TO SCARE MY MOM, TOO! WHAT IF --
WAIT -- THAT'S IT!
THE MAN IN THE STORE.

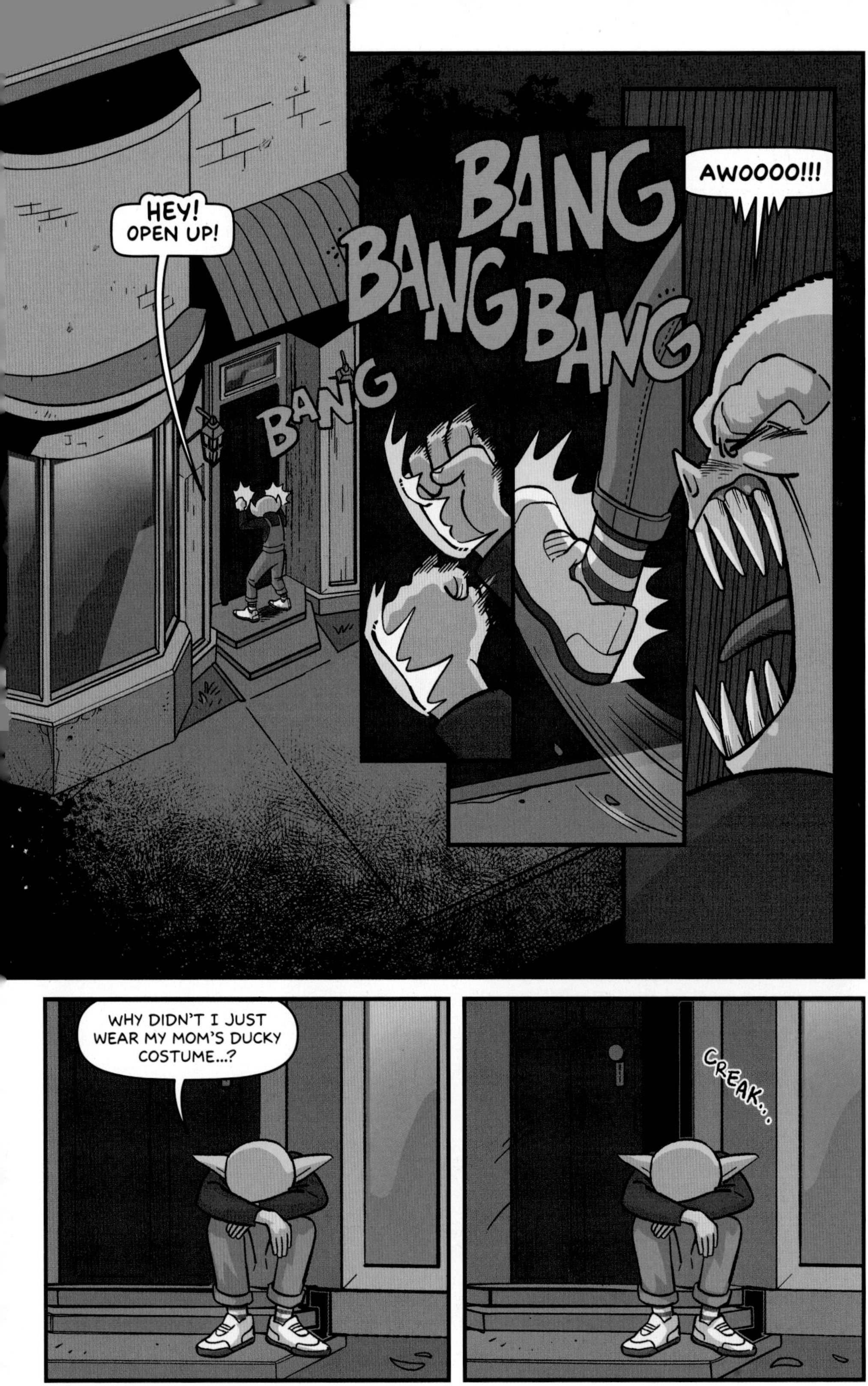
HEY! OPEN UP!
BANG
BANG
BANG
BANG
BANG
AWOOOO!!!
WHY DIDN'T I JUST WEAR MY MOM'S DUCKY COSTUME...?
CREAK...

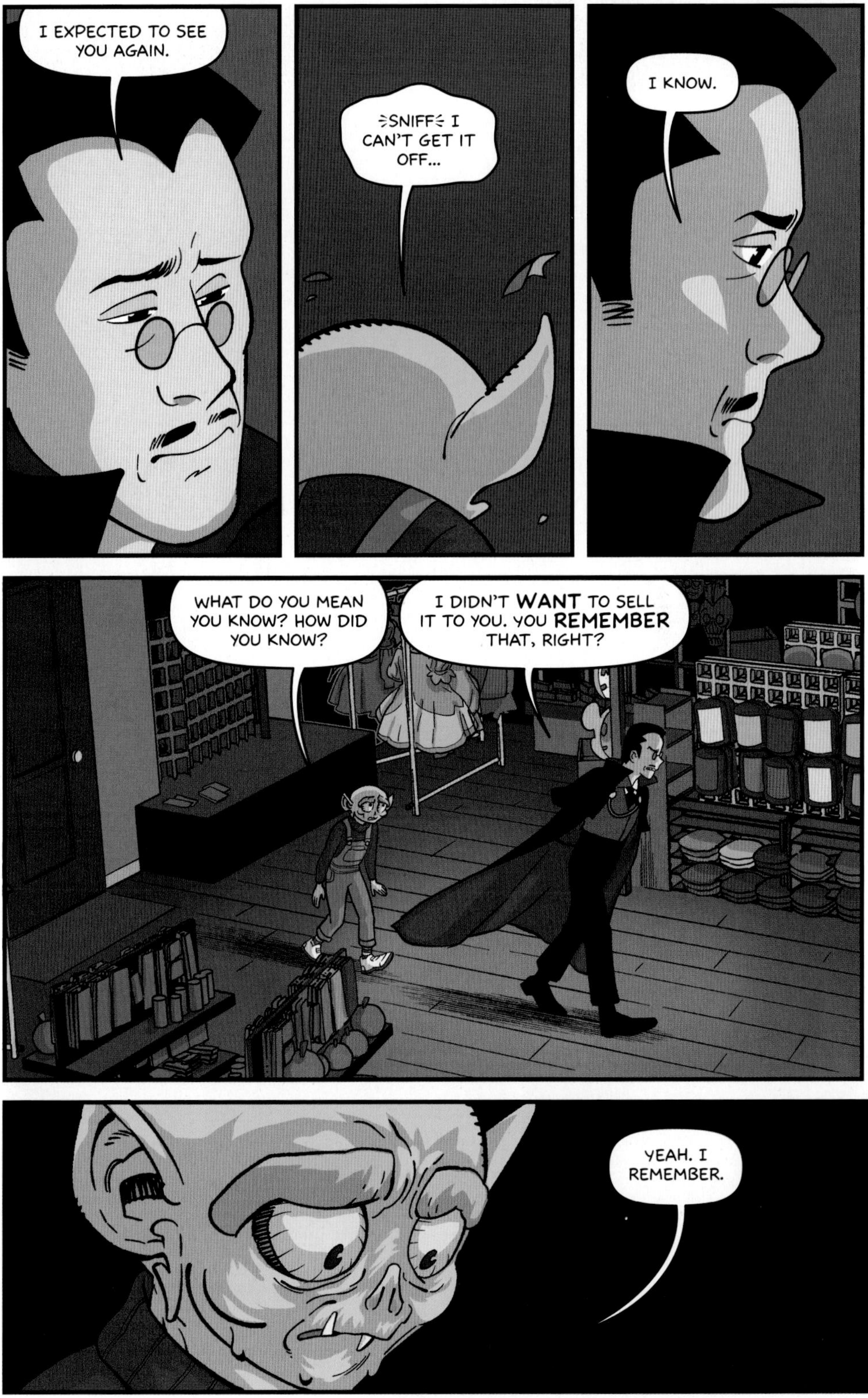
I EXPECTED TO SEE YOU AGAIN.
≶SNIFF≶ I CAN'T GET IT OFF...
I KNOW.
WHAT DO YOU MEAN YOU KNOW? HOW DID YOU KNOW?
I DIDN'T WANT TO SELL IT TO YOU. YOU REMEMBER THAT, RIGHT?
YEAH. I REMEMBER.

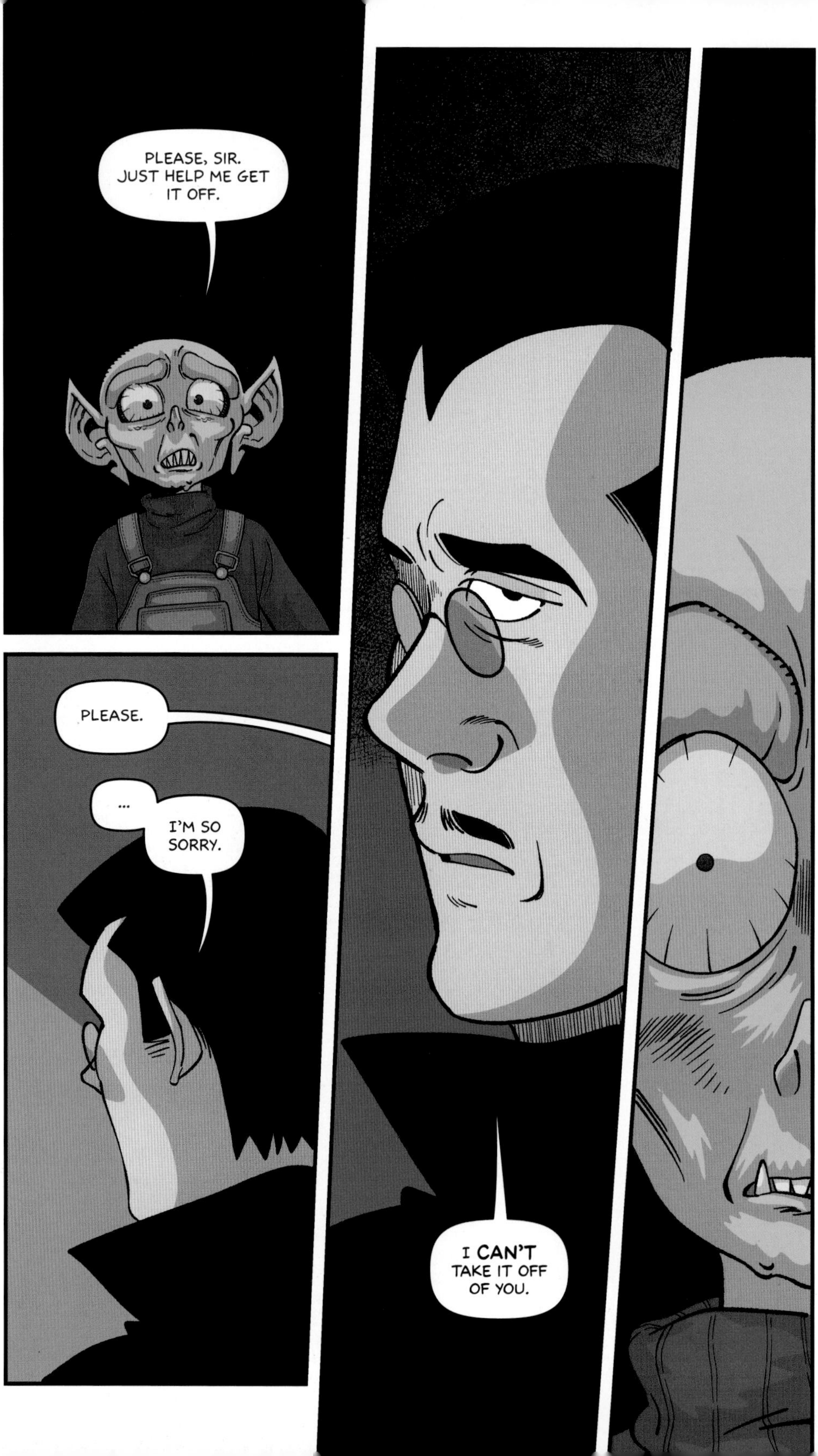
PLEASE, SIR. JUST HELP ME GET IT OFF.
PLEASE.
...
I'M SO SORRY.
I **CAN'T** TAKE IT OFF OF YOU.

WHAT DO YOU MEAN YOU CAN'T TAKE IT OFF OF ME?!
WHY NOT?!
THAT "MASK" YOU'RE WEARING --
IT ISN'T A MASK.
WH--?
IT'S A REAL FACE.

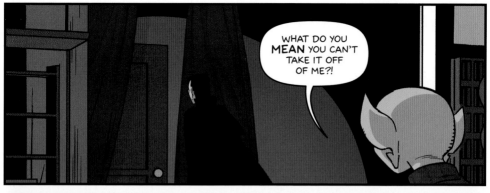

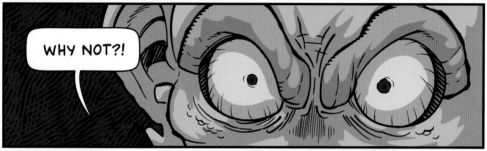

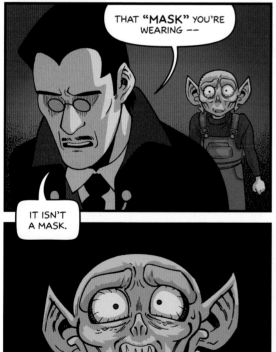

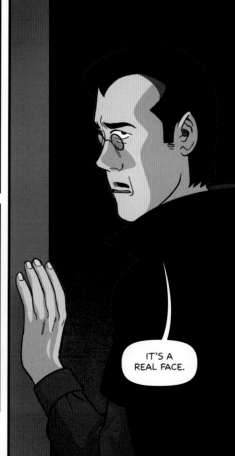

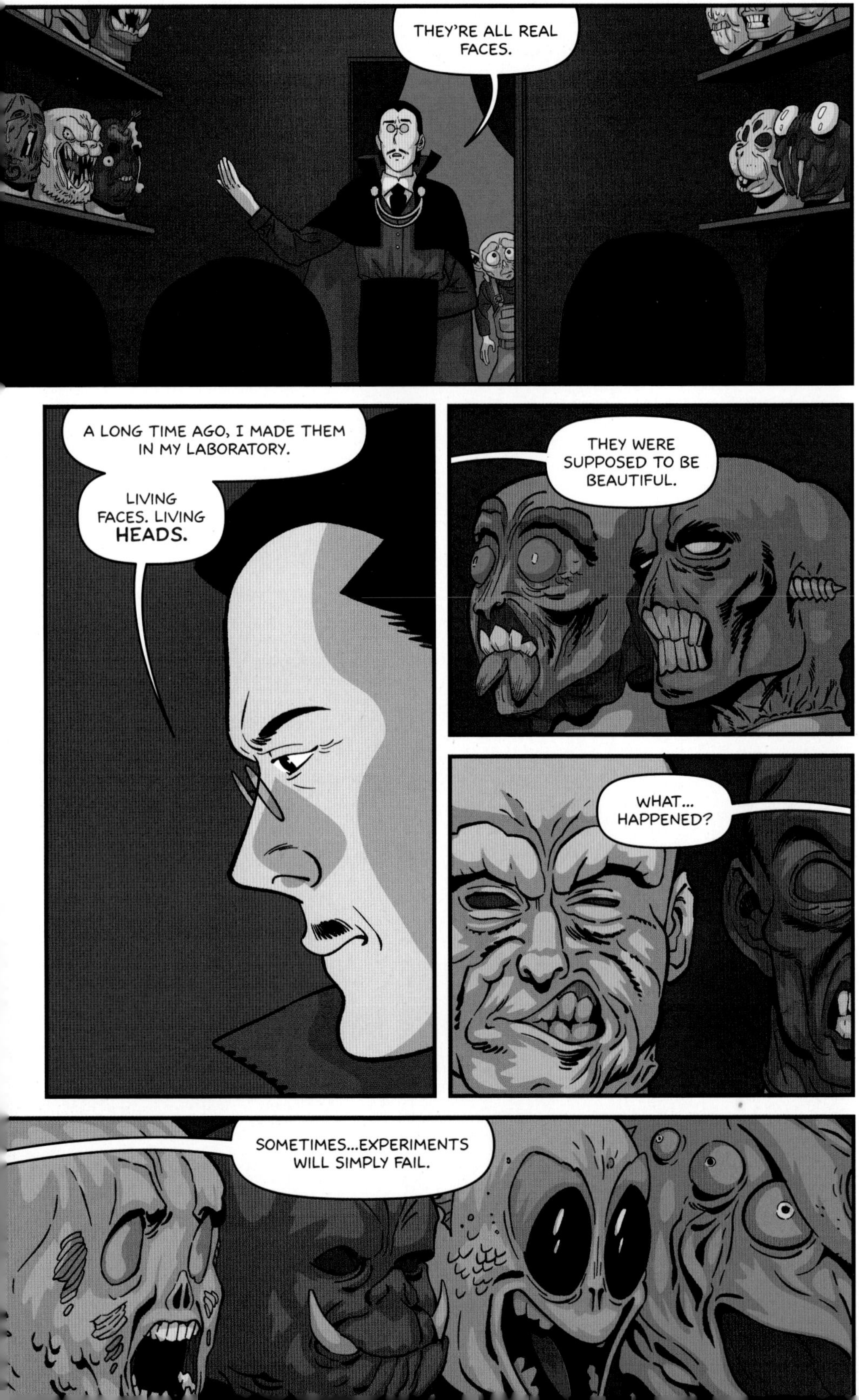
THEY'RE ALL REAL FACES.
A LONG TIME AGO, I MADE THEM IN MY LABORATORY.
LIVING FACES. LIVING HEADS.
THEY WERE SUPPOSED TO BE BEAUTIFUL.
WHAT... HAPPENED?
SOMETIMES...EXPERIMENTS WILL SIMPLY FAIL.

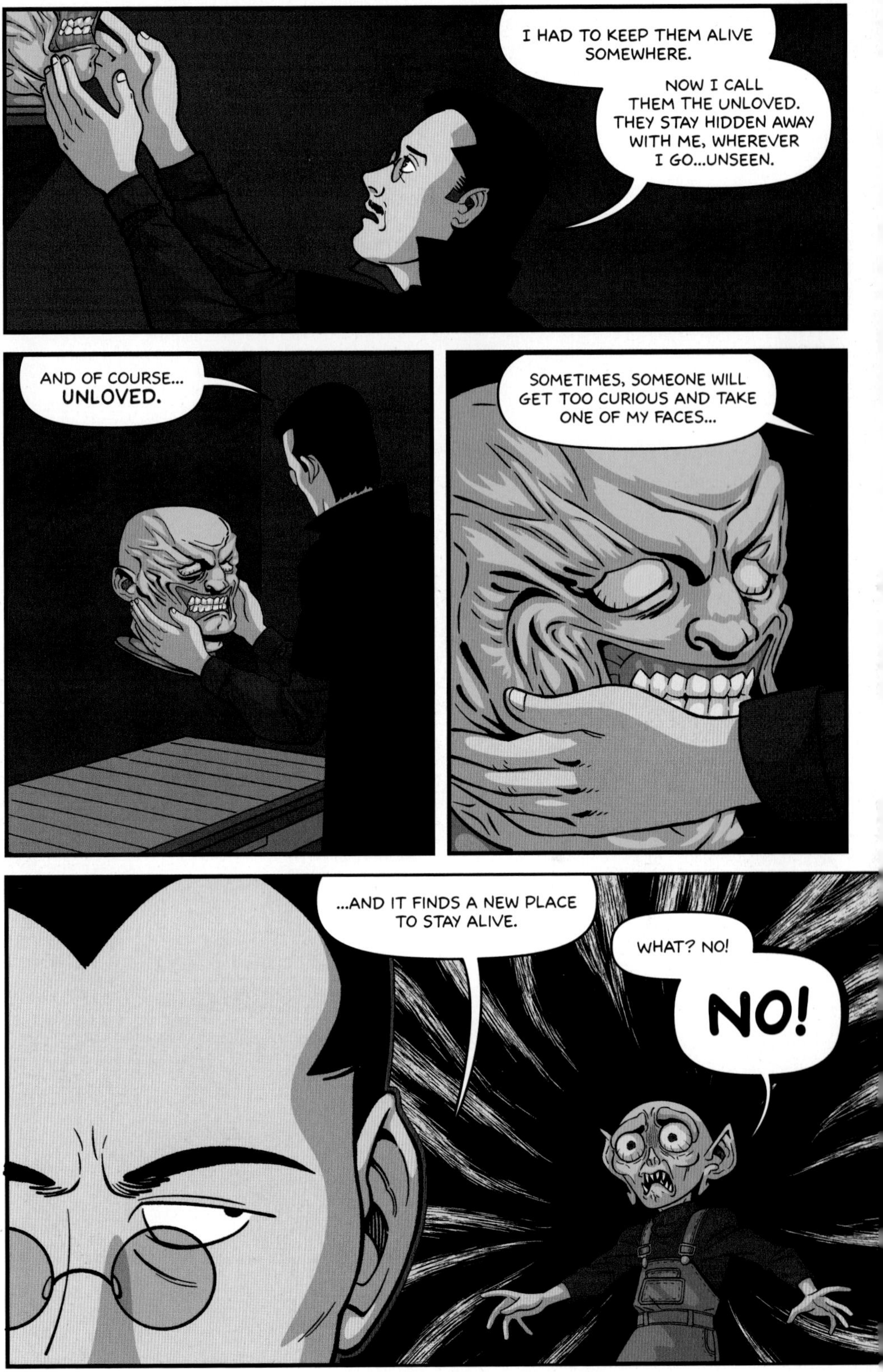
I HAD TO KEEP THEM ALIVE SOMEWHERE.
NOW I CALL THEM THE UNLOVED. THEY STAY HIDDEN AWAY WITH ME, WHEREVER I GO...UNSEEN.
AND OF COURSE... **UNLOVED.**
SOMETIMES, SOMEONE WILL GET TOO CURIOUS AND TAKE ONE OF MY FACES...
...AND IT FINDS A NEW PLACE TO STAY ALIVE.
WHAT? NO!
NO!

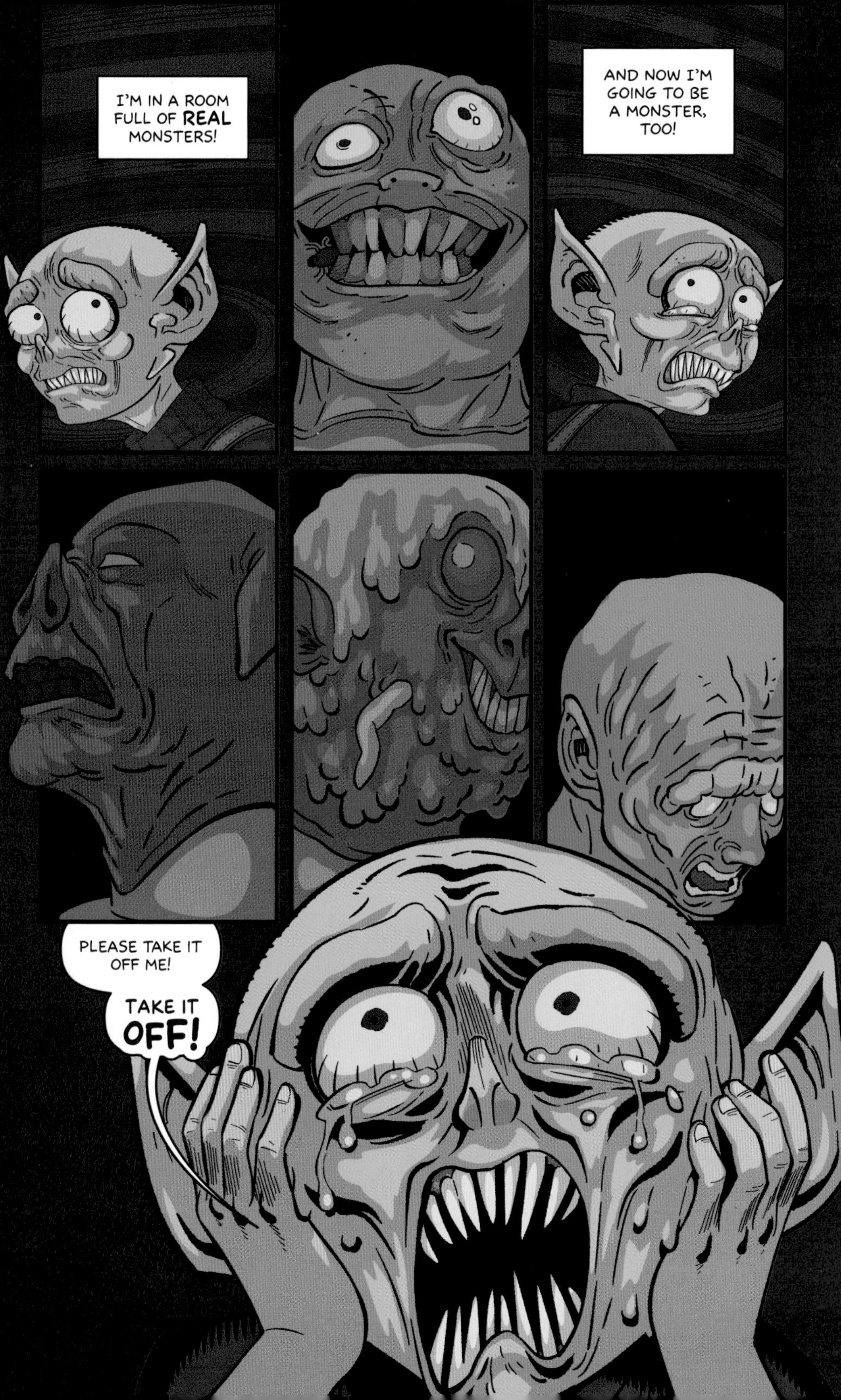
I'M IN A ROOM FULL OF **REAL** MONSTERS!
AND NOW I'M GOING TO BE A MONSTER, TOO!
PLEASE TAKE IT OFF ME!
TAKE IT **OFF!**

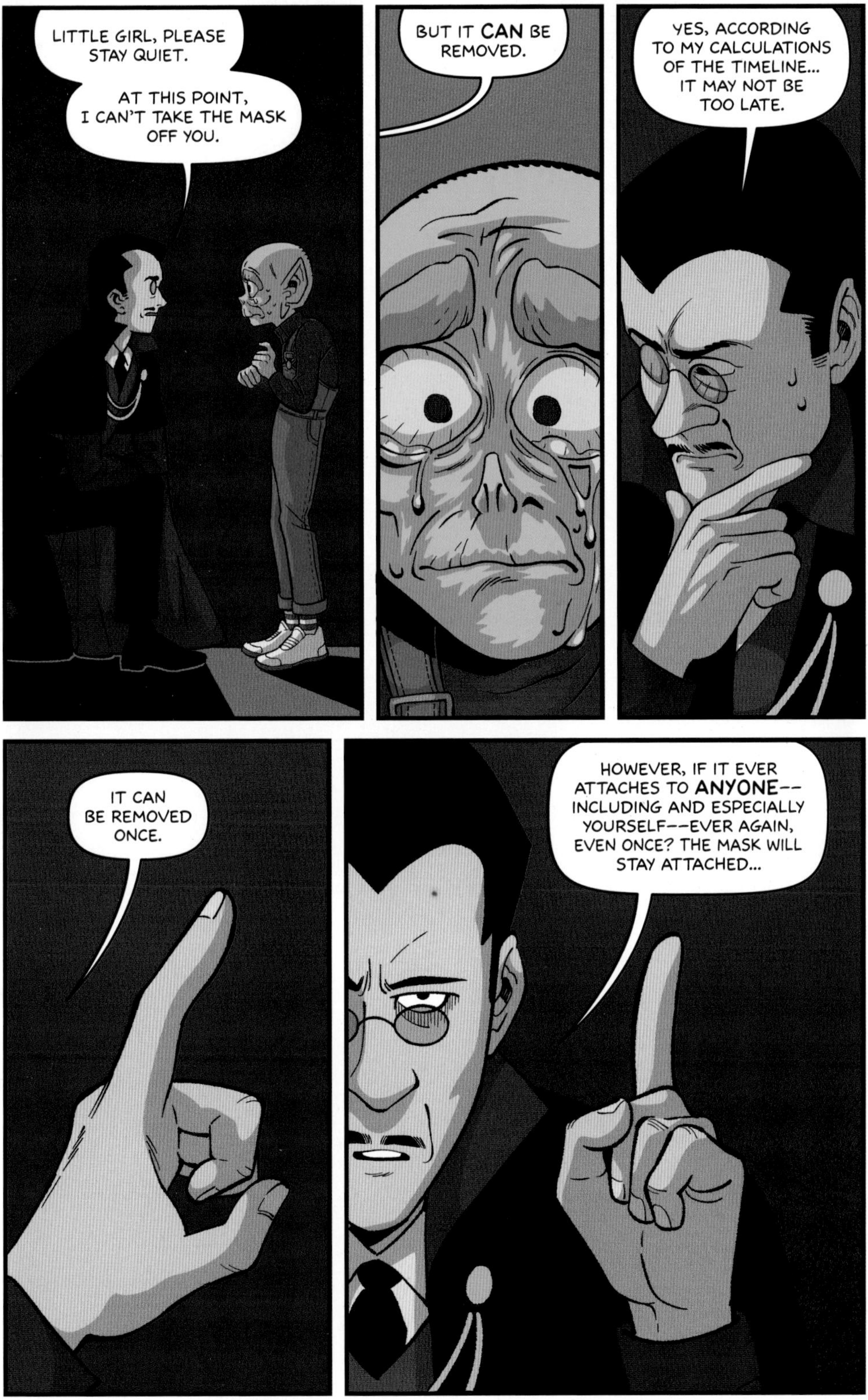
LITTLE GIRL, PLEASE STAY QUIET.
AT THIS POINT, I CAN'T TAKE THE MASK OFF YOU.
BUT IT **CAN** BE REMOVED.
YES, ACCORDING TO MY CALCULATIONS OF THE TIMELINE... IT MAY NOT BE TOO LATE.
IT CAN BE REMOVED ONCE.
HOWEVER, IF IT EVER ATTACHES TO **ANYONE**--INCLUDING AND ESPECIALLY YOURSELF--EVER AGAIN, EVEN ONCE? THE MASK WILL STAY ATTACHED...

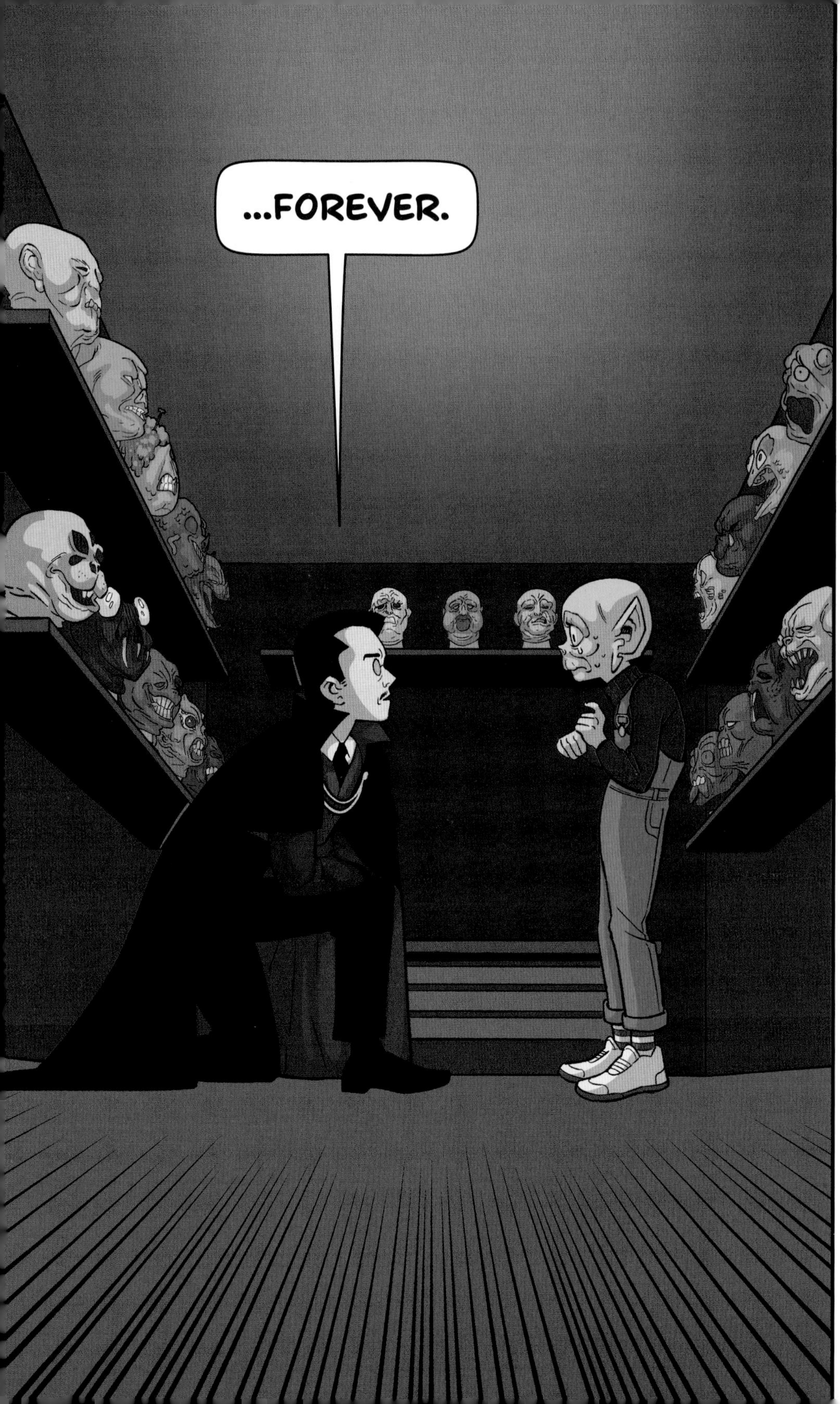
...FOREVER.

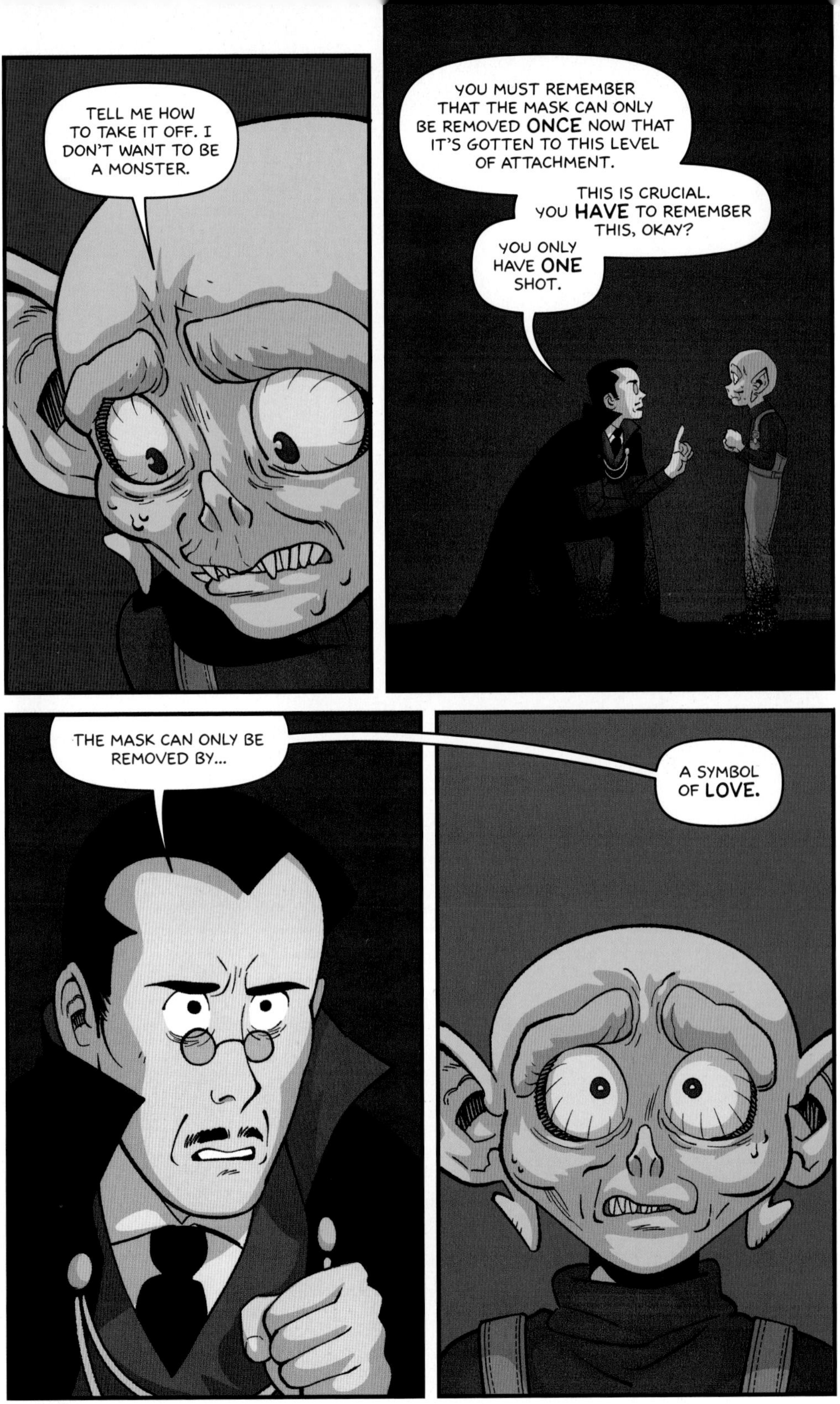
TELL ME HOW TO TAKE IT OFF. I DON'T WANT TO BE A MONSTER.
YOU MUST REMEMBER THAT THE MASK CAN ONLY BE REMOVED **ONCE** NOW THAT IT'S GOTTEN TO THIS LEVEL OF ATTACHMENT.
THIS IS CRUCIAL. YOU **HAVE** TO REMEMBER THIS, OKAY?
YOU ONLY HAVE **ONE** SHOT.
THE MASK CAN ONLY BE REMOVED BY...
A SYMBOL OF **LOVE.**

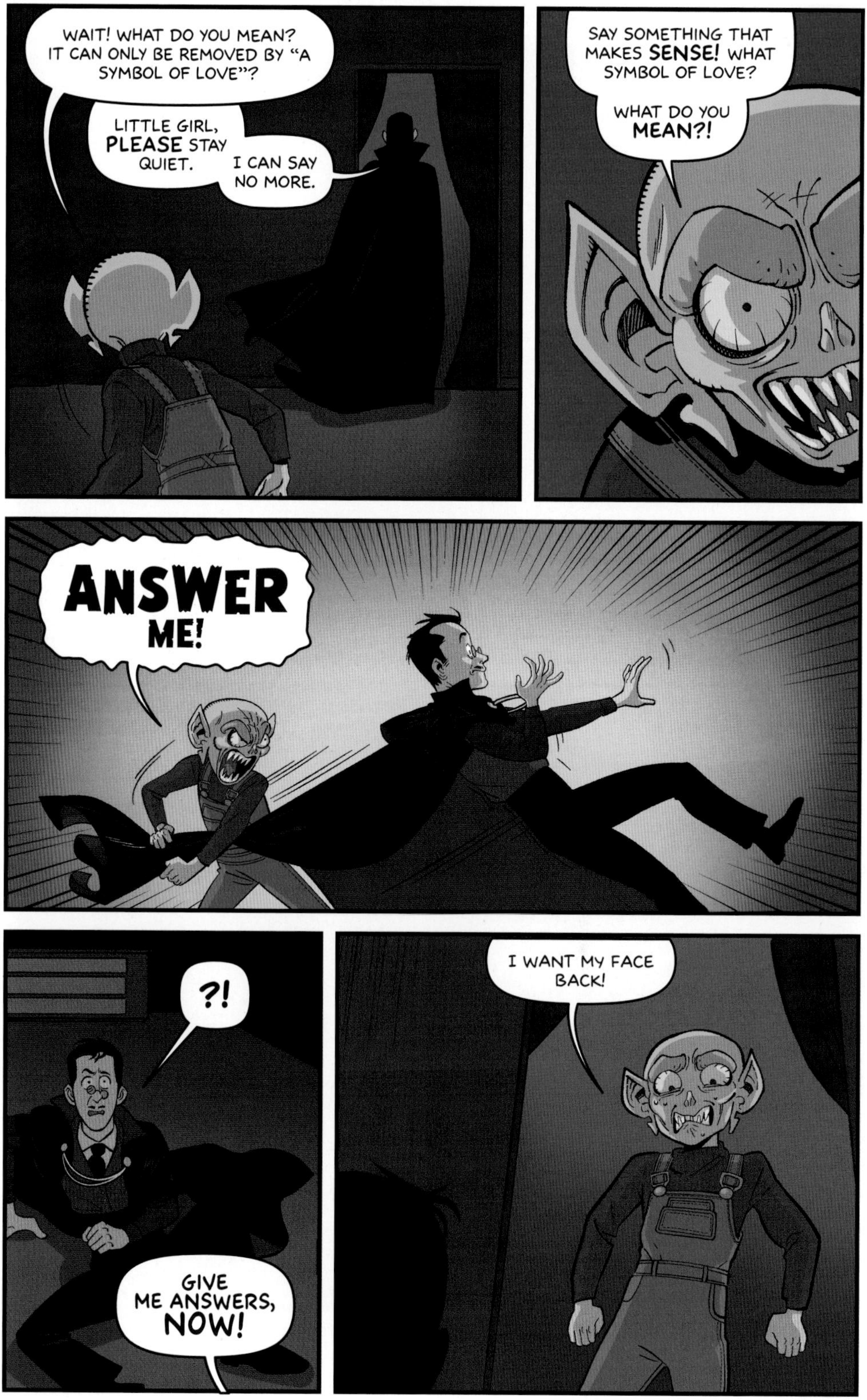
WAIT! WHAT DO YOU MEAN? IT CAN ONLY BE REMOVED BY "A SYMBOL OF LOVE"?
LITTLE GIRL, PLEASE STAY QUIET.
I CAN SAY NO MORE.
SAY SOMETHING THAT MAKES SENSE! WHAT SYMBOL OF LOVE?
WHAT DO YOU MEAN?!
ANSWER ME!
?!
GIVE ME ANSWERS, NOW!
I WANT MY FACE BACK!

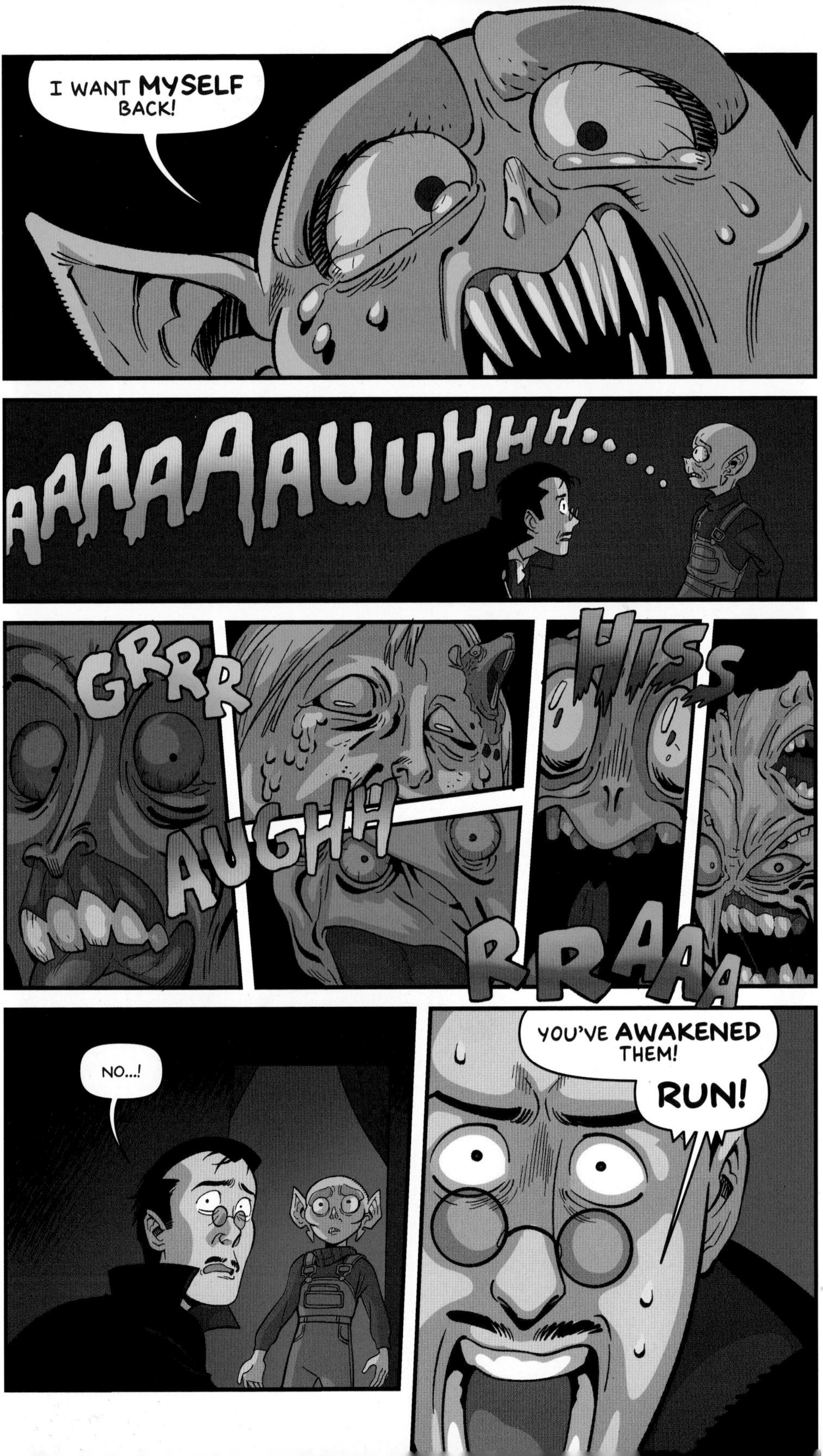
I WANT MYSELF BACK!
AAAAAAUUHHH...
GRRR
AUGHH
HISS
RRAAA
NO...!
YOU'VE AWAKENED THEM!
RUN!

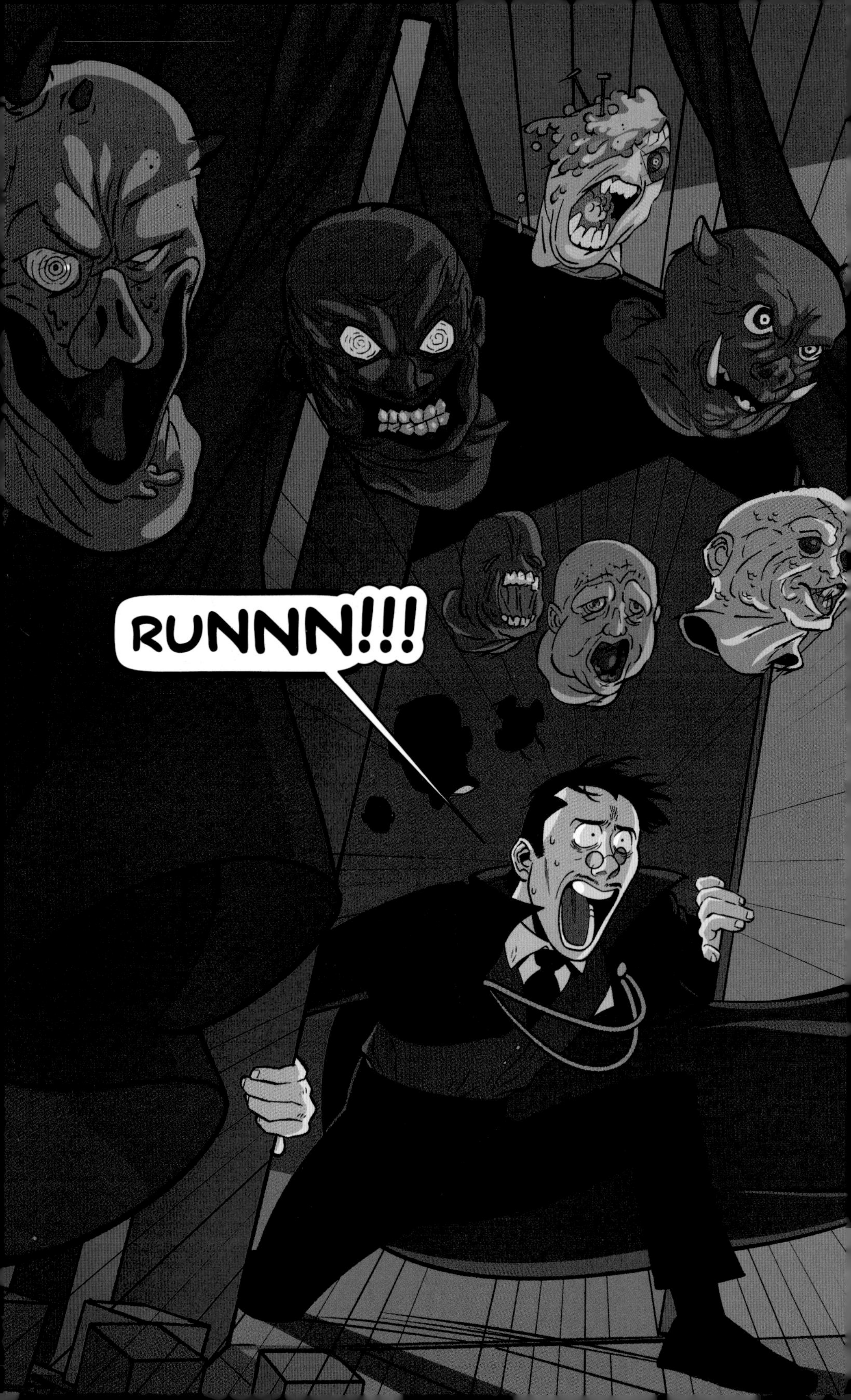
RUNNN!!!

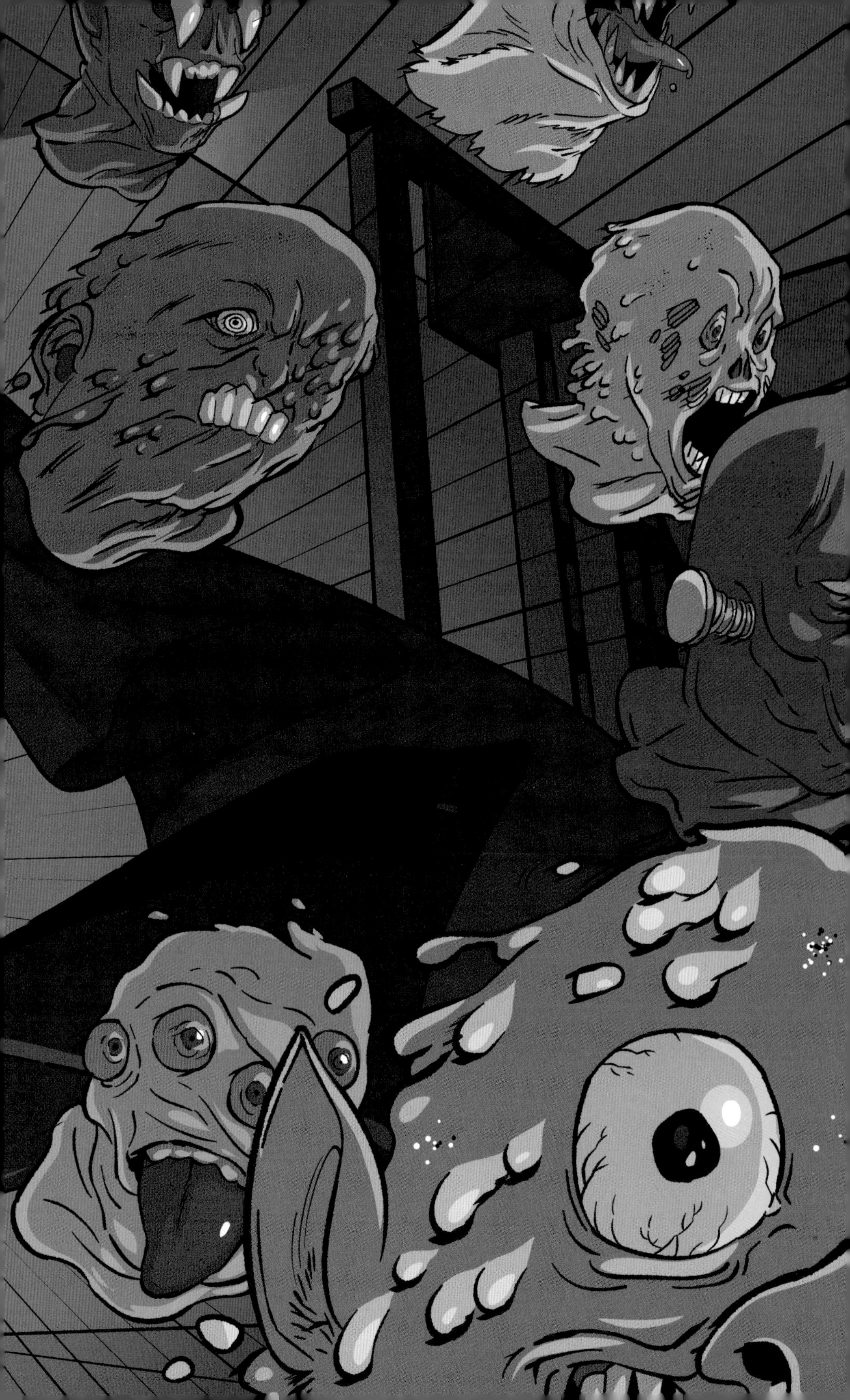

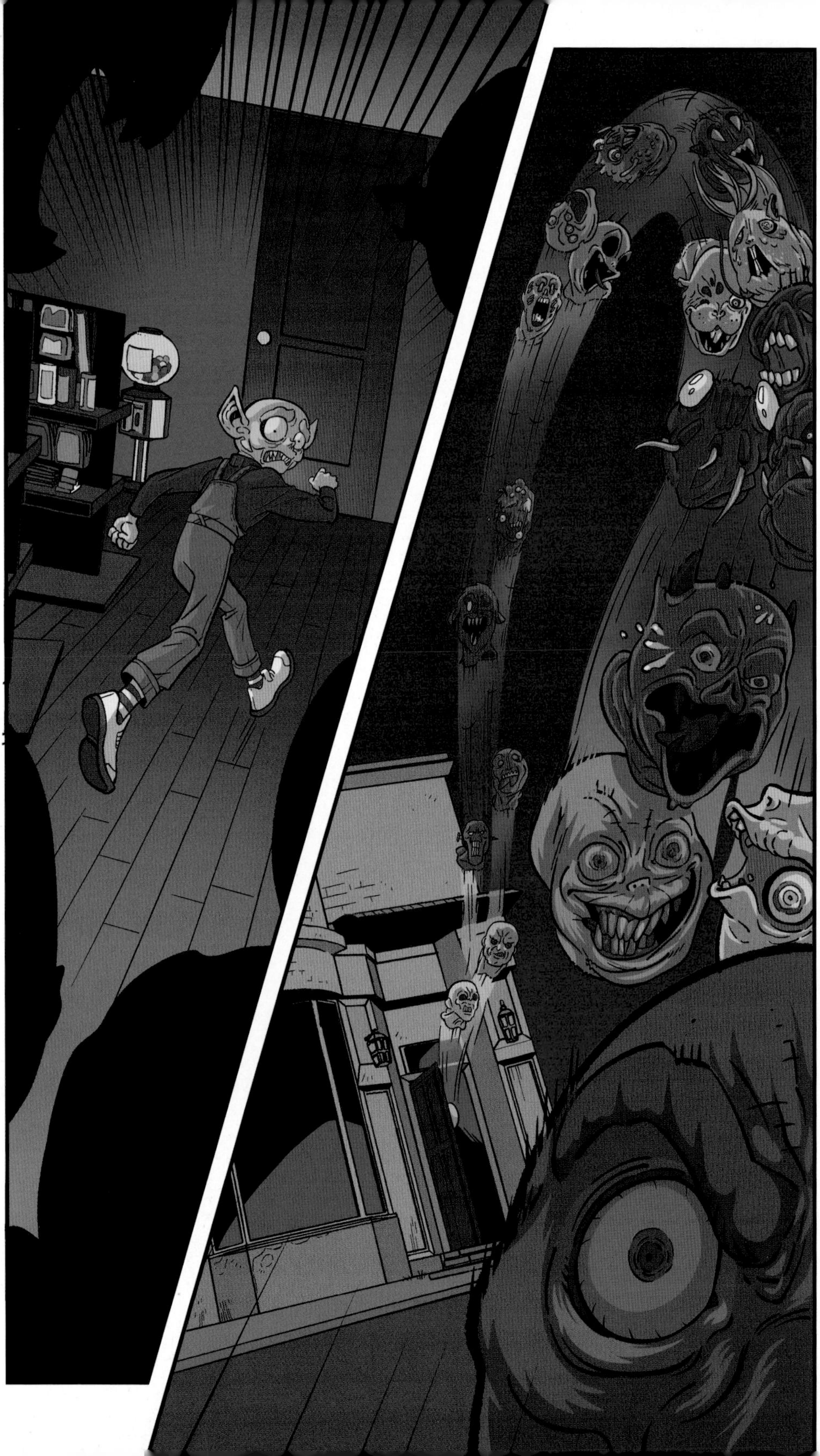

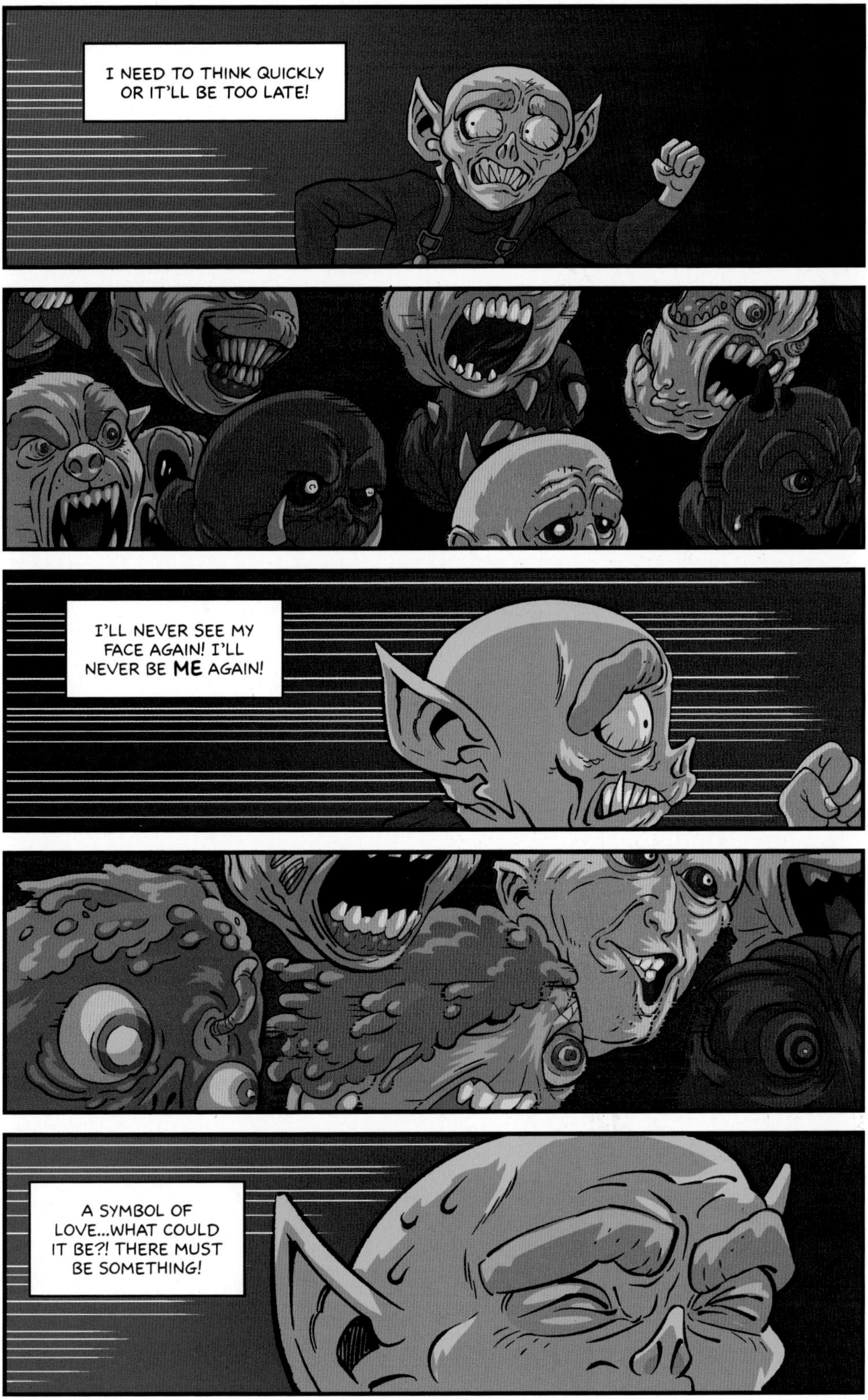
I NEED TO THINK QUICKLY OR IT'LL BE TOO LATE!
I'LL NEVER SEE MY FACE AGAIN! I'LL NEVER BE **ME** AGAIN!
A SYMBOL OF LOVE...WHAT COULD IT BE?! THERE MUST BE SOMETHING!

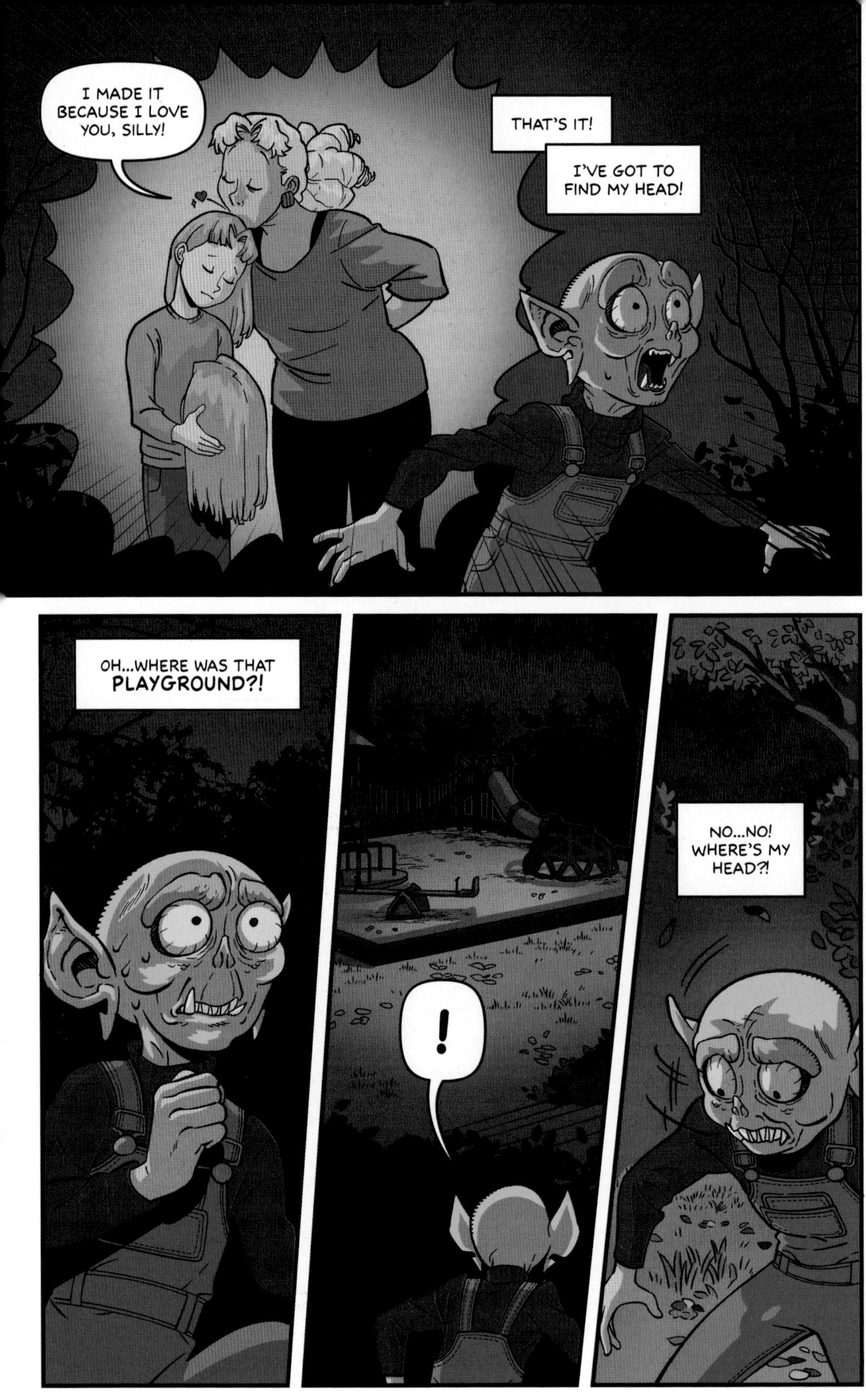
I MADE IT BECAUSE I LOVE YOU, SILLY!
THAT'S IT!
I'VE GOT TO FIND MY HEAD!
OH...WHERE WAS THAT PLAYGROUND?!
!
NO...NO! WHERE'S MY HEAD?!

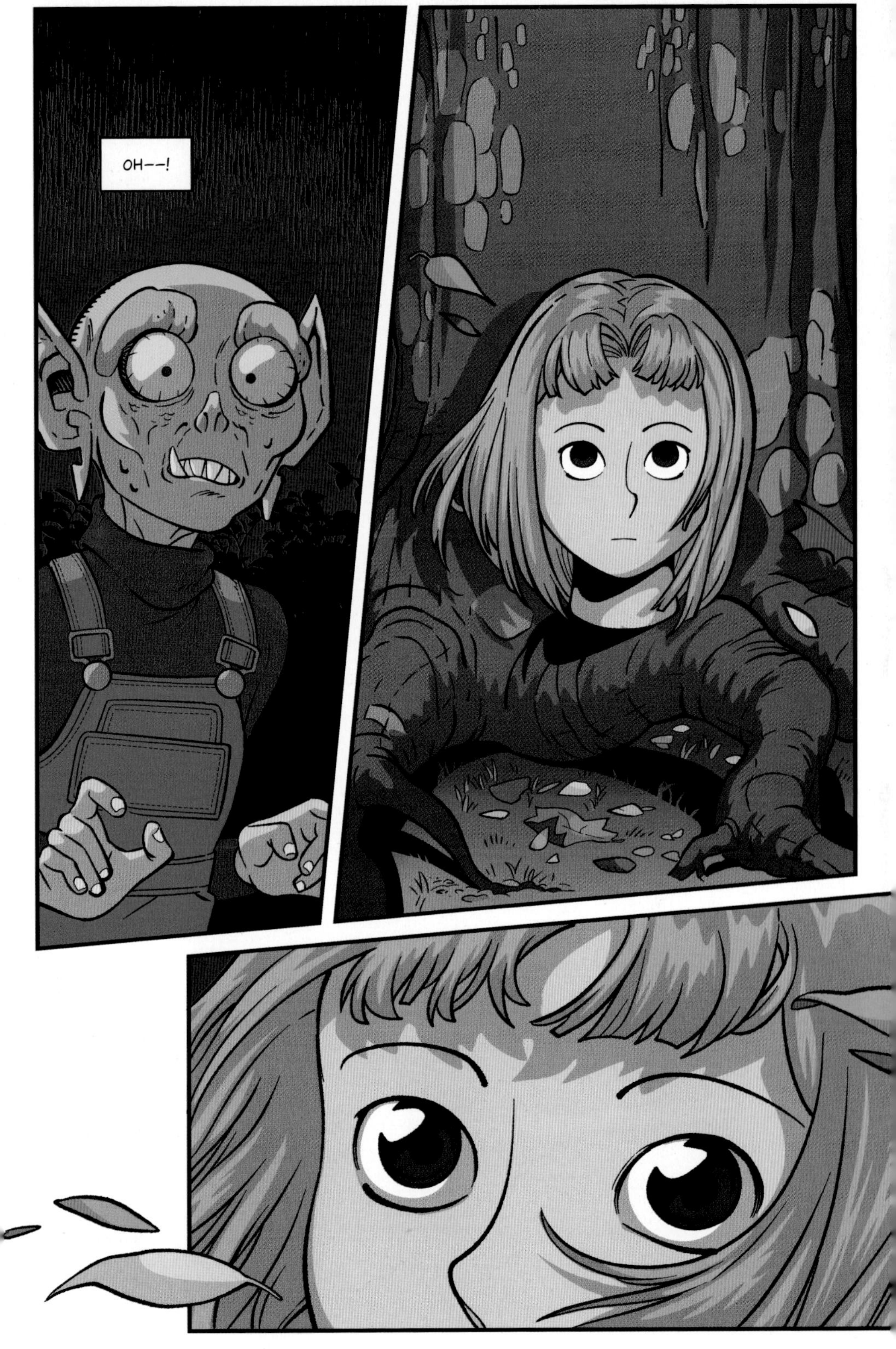
OH--!

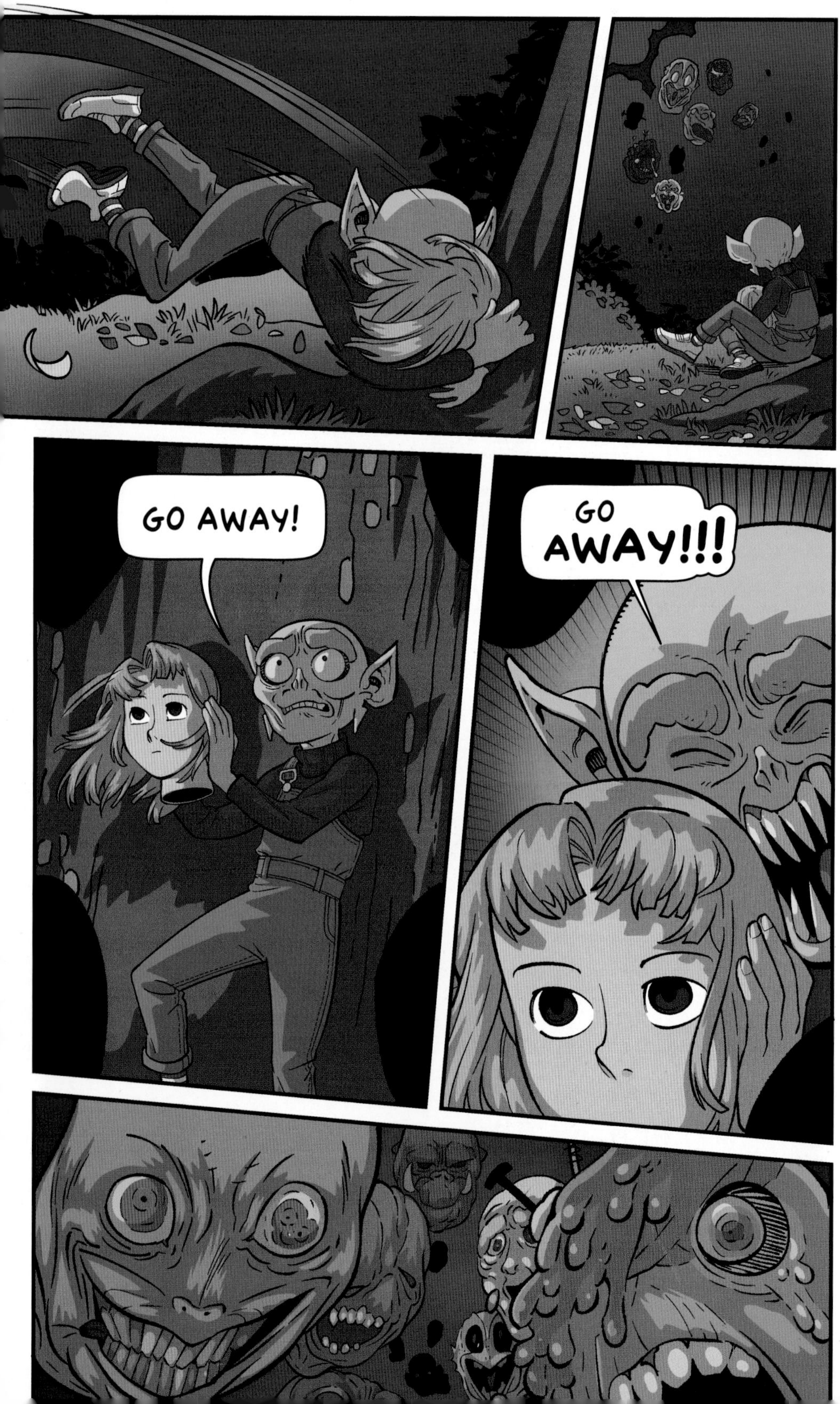
GO AWAY!
GO AWAY!!!

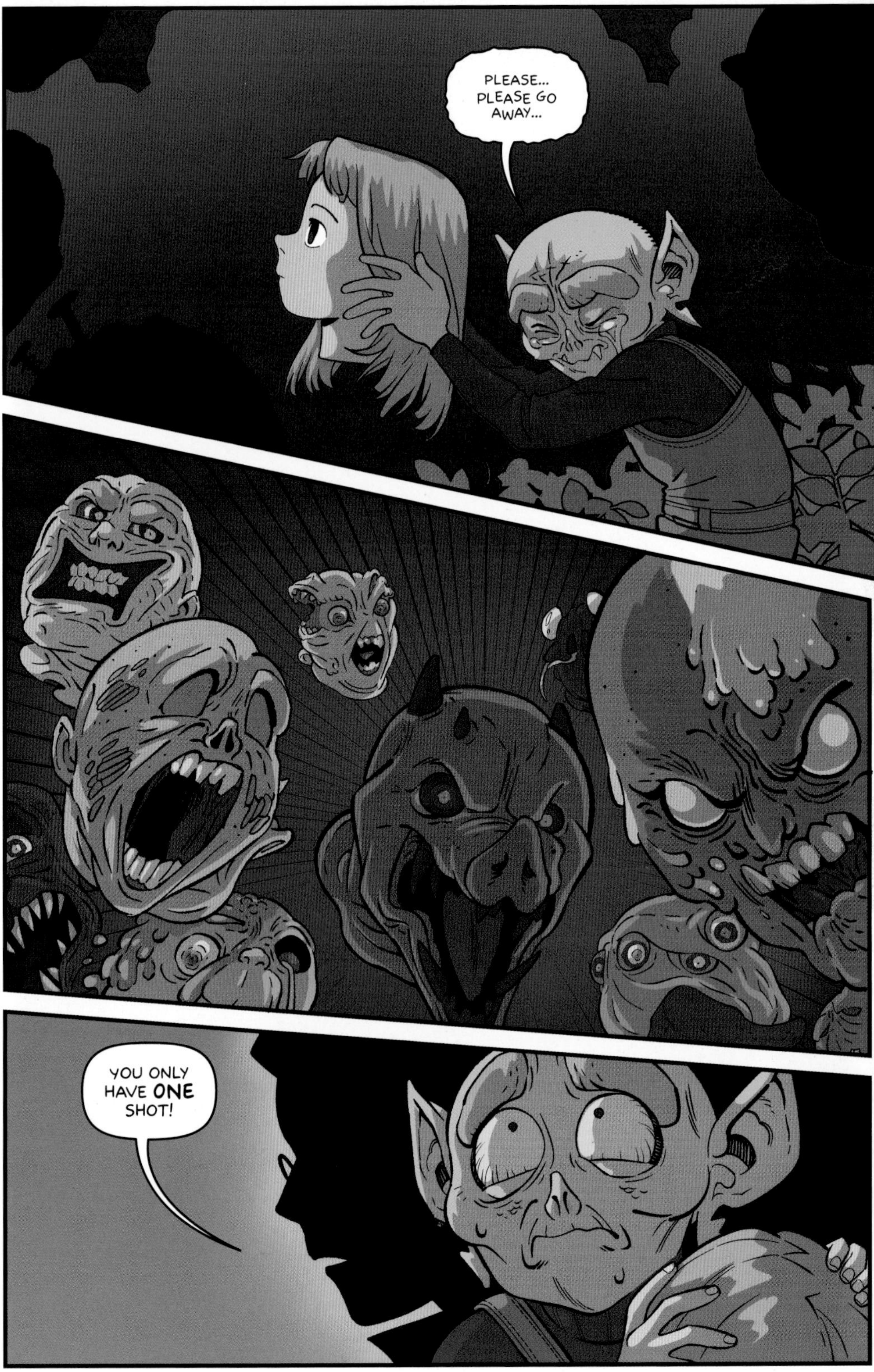
PLEASE... PLEASE GO AWAY...
YOU ONLY HAVE **ONE** SHOT!

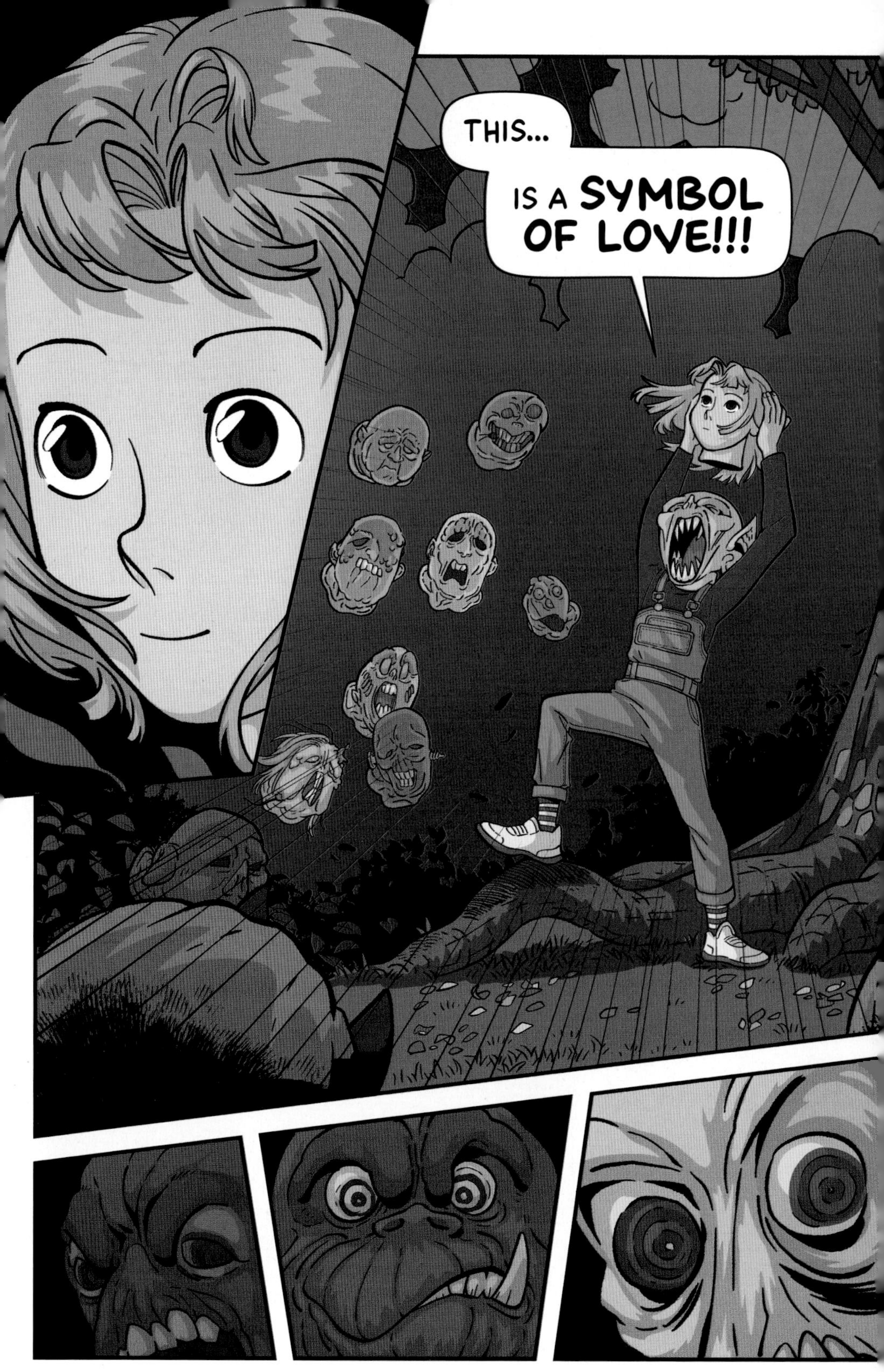
THIS...
IS A SYMBOL OF LOVE!!!

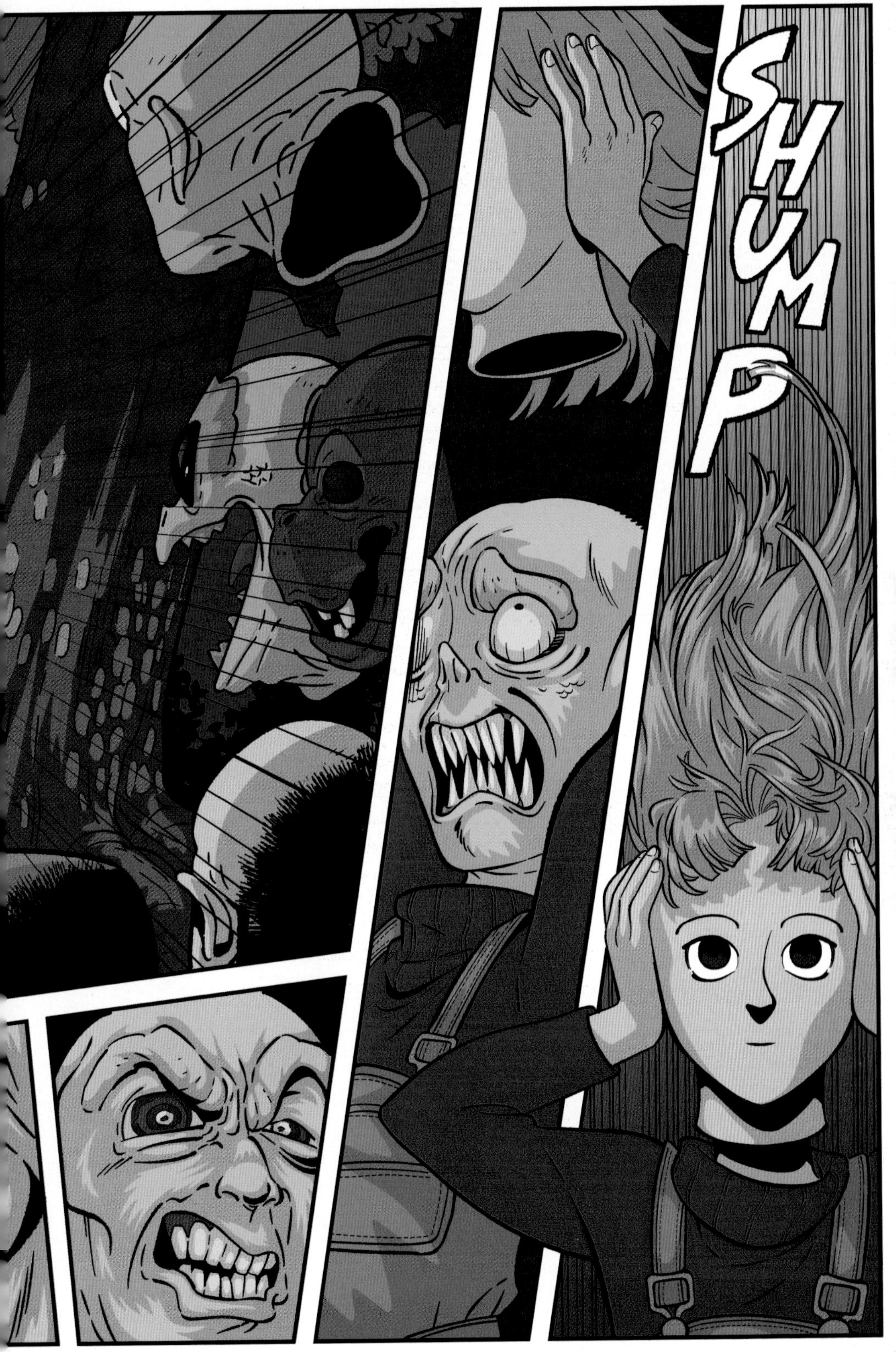
SHUMP

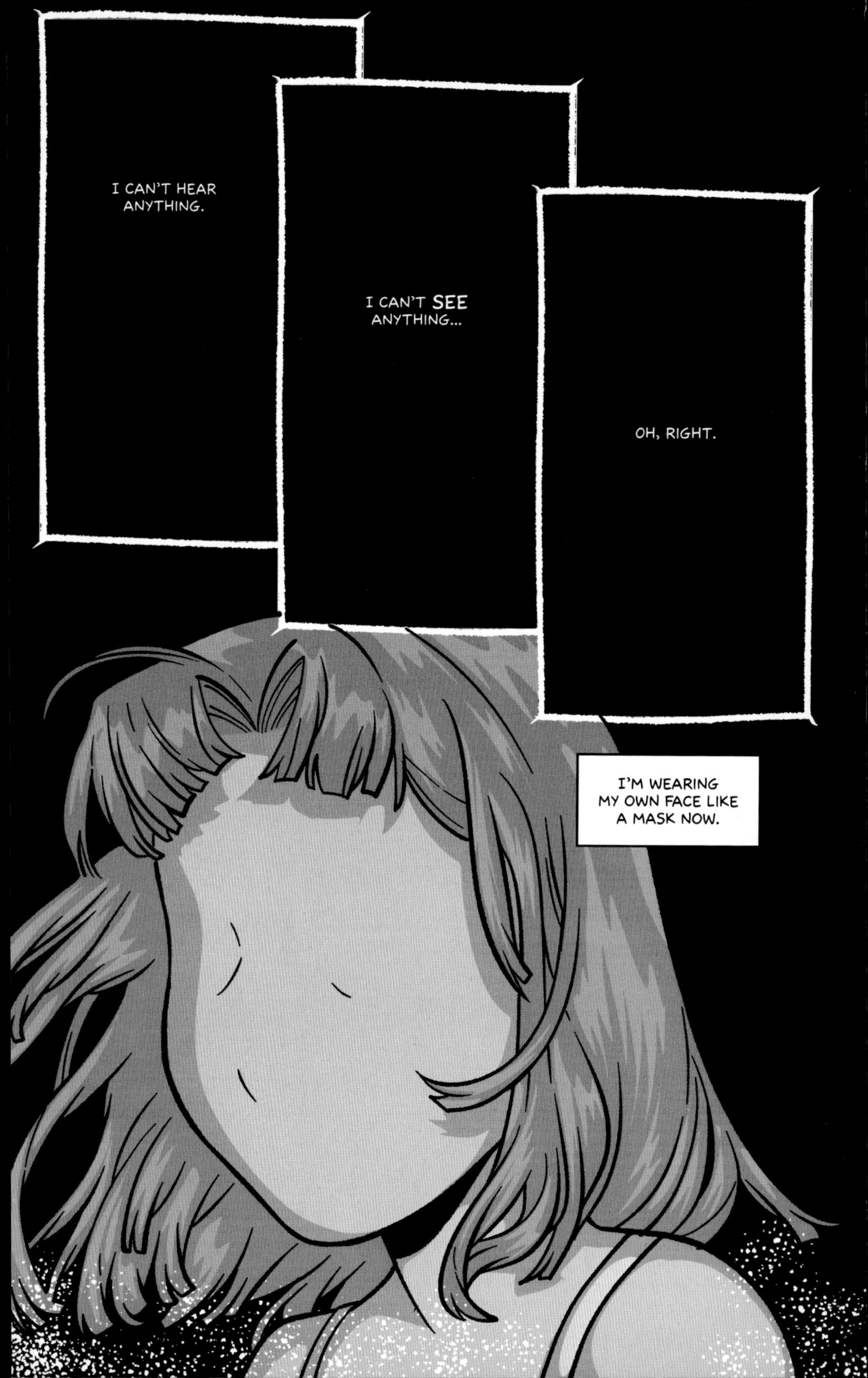
I CAN'T HEAR ANYTHING.
I CAN'T SEE ANYTHING...
OH, RIGHT.
I'M WEARING MY OWN FACE LIKE A MASK NOW.

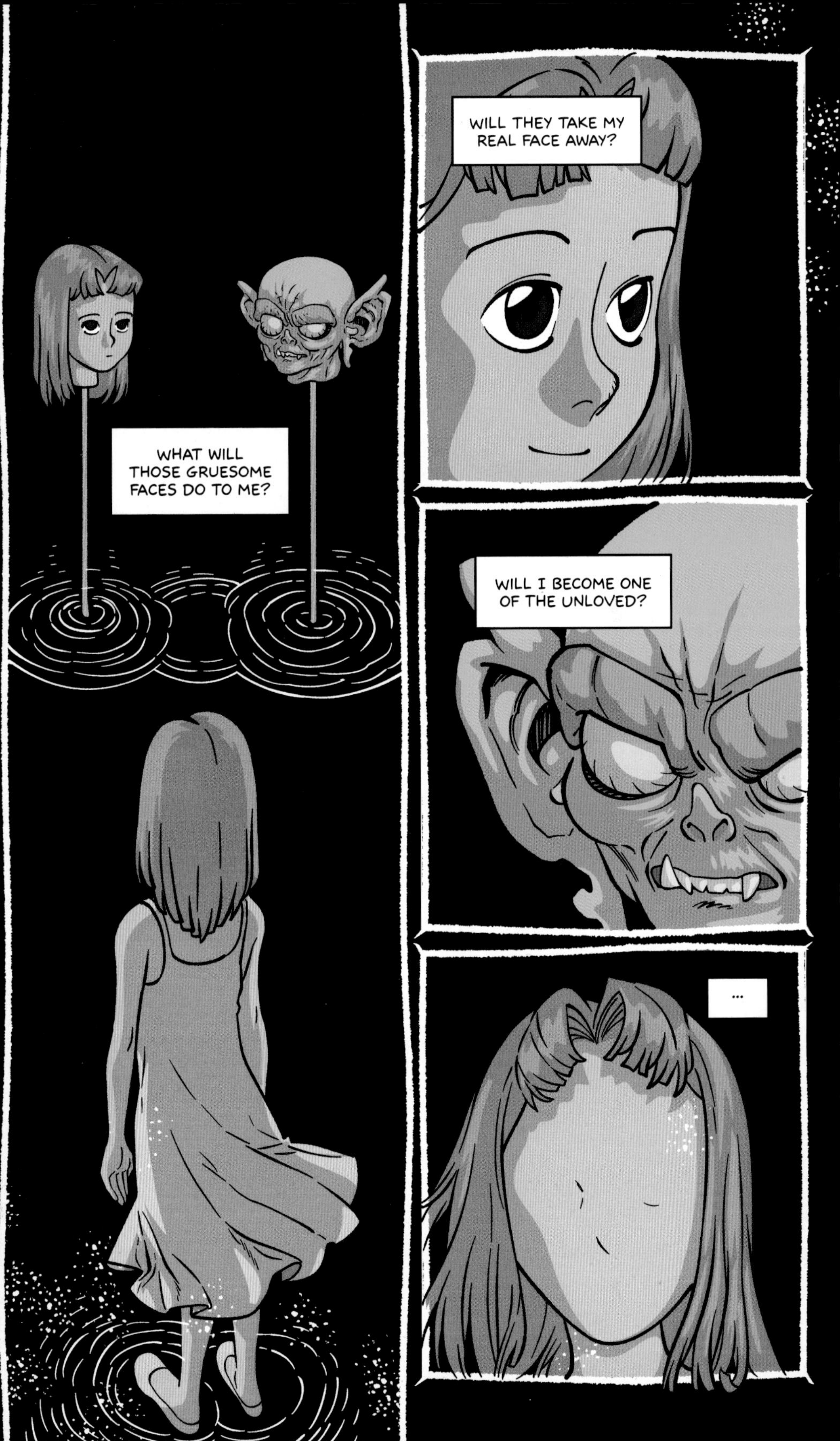
WHAT WILL THOSE GRUESOME FACES DO TO ME?
WILL THEY TAKE MY REAL FACE AWAY?
WILL I BECOME ONE OF THE UNLOVED?
...

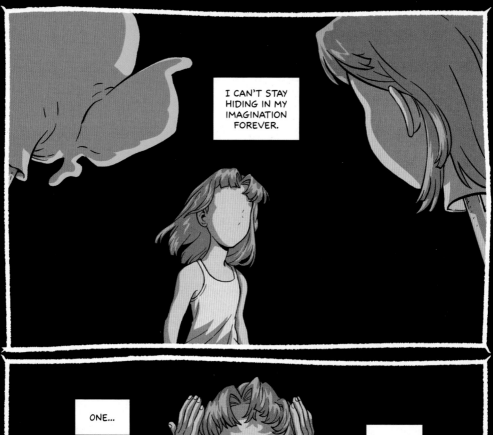

I CAN'T STAY HIDING IN MY IMAGINATION FOREVER.

ONE...

TWO...!

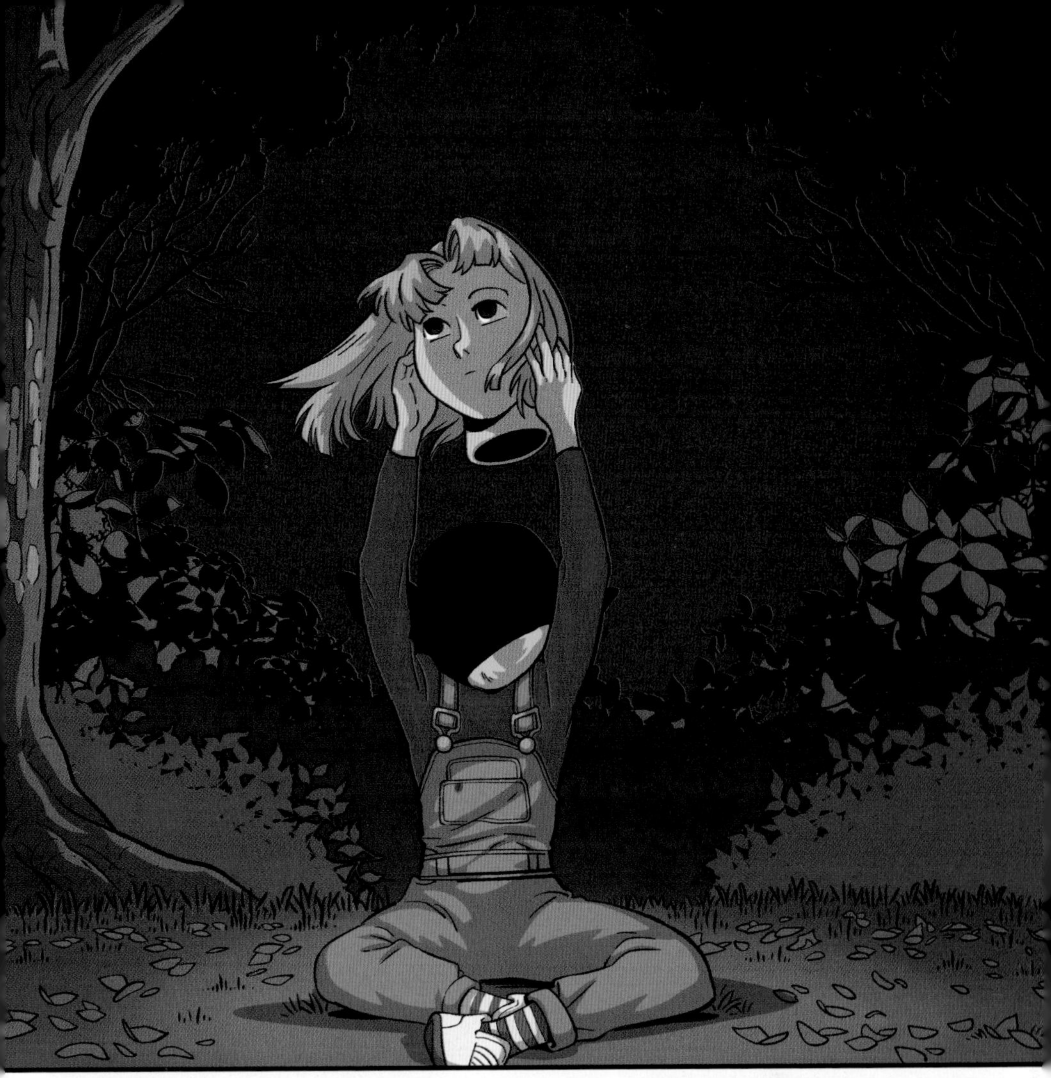

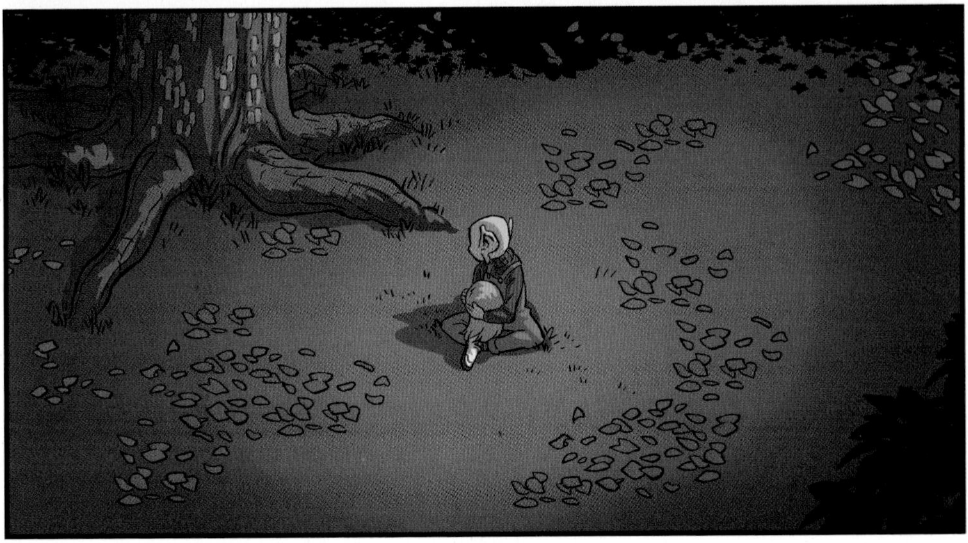

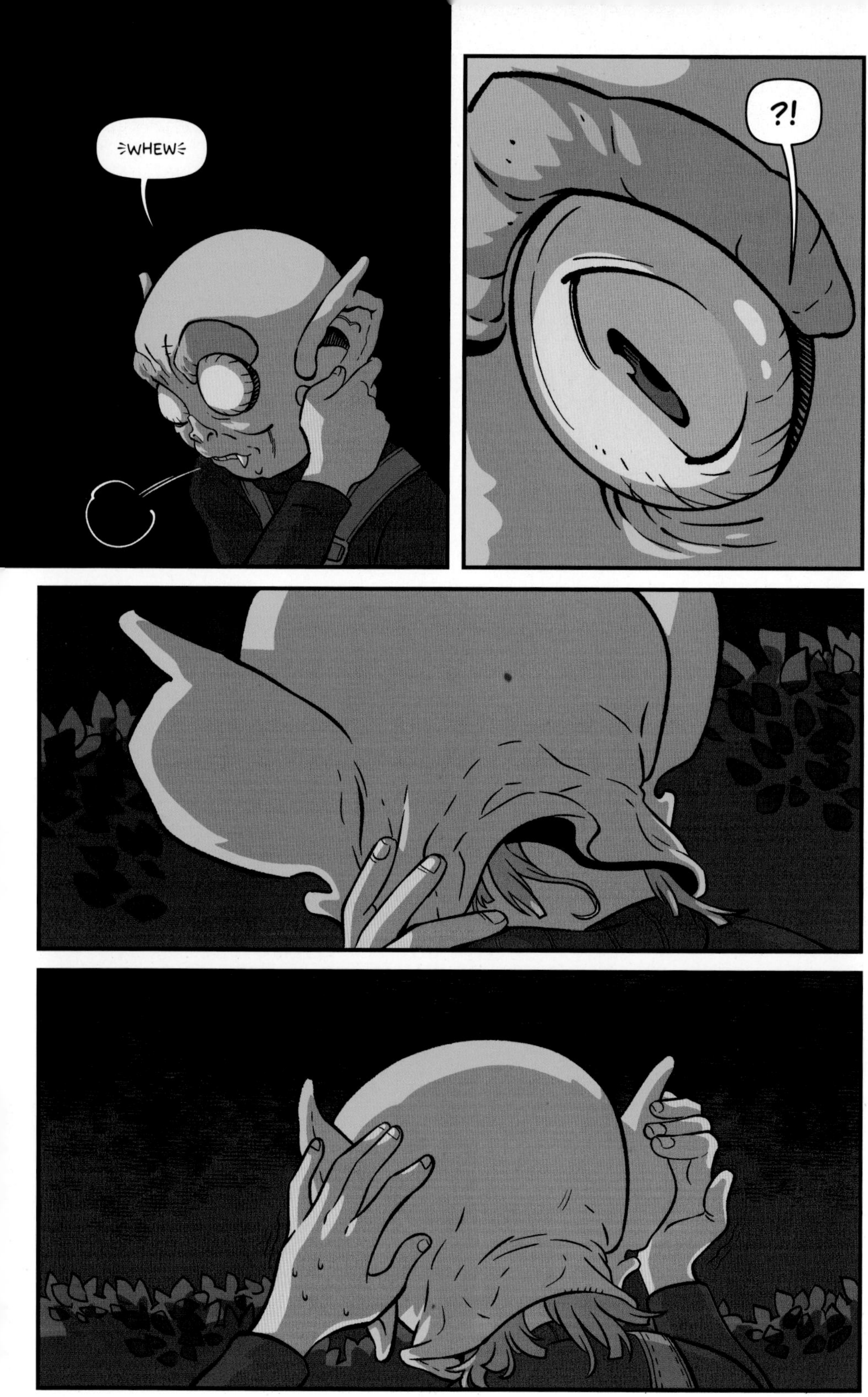
WHEW
?!

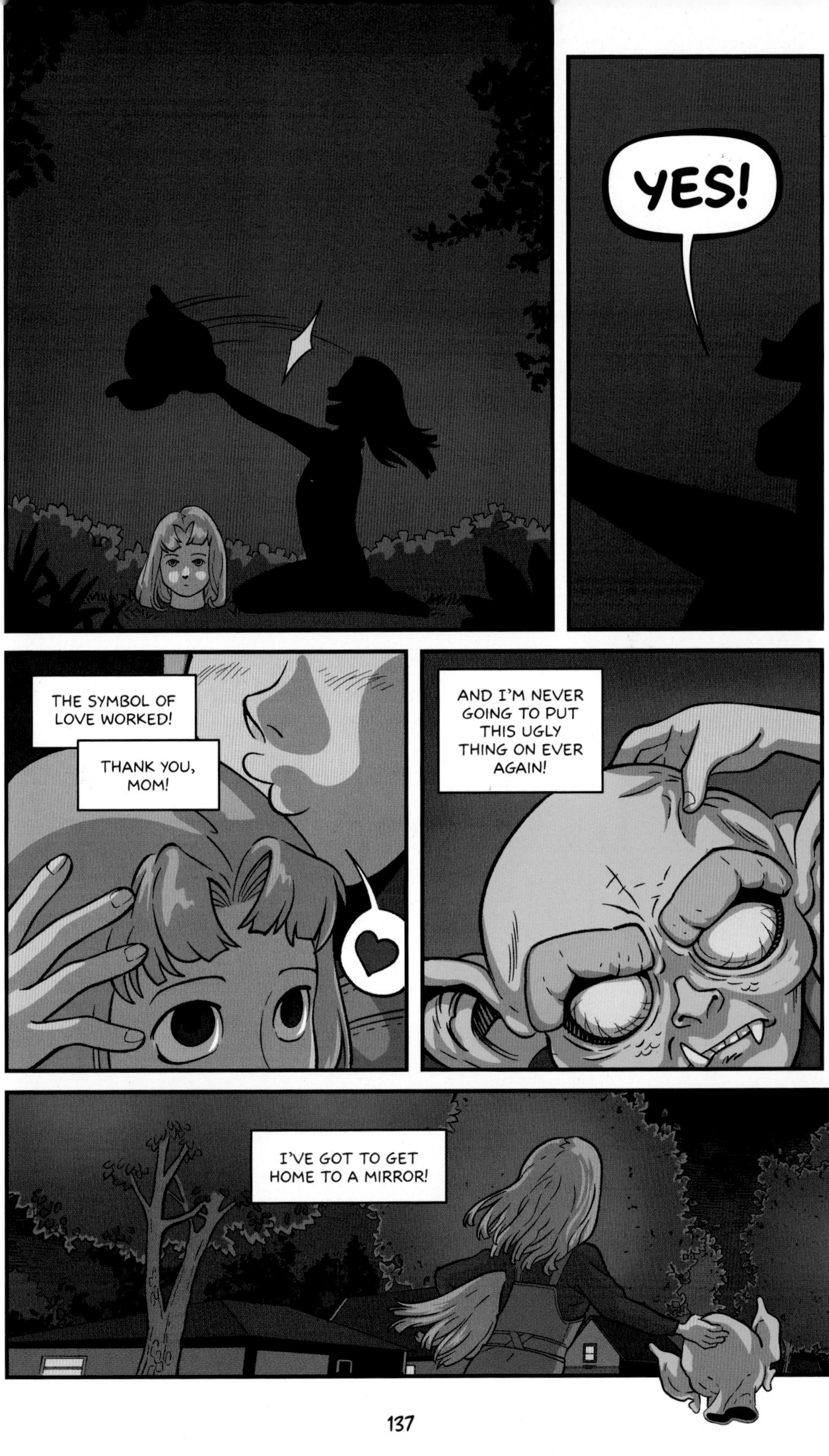
YES!
THE SYMBOL OF LOVE WORKED!
THANK YOU, MOM!
AND I'M NEVER GOING TO PUT THIS UGLY THING ON EVER AGAIN!
I'VE GOT TO GET HOME TO A MIRROR!

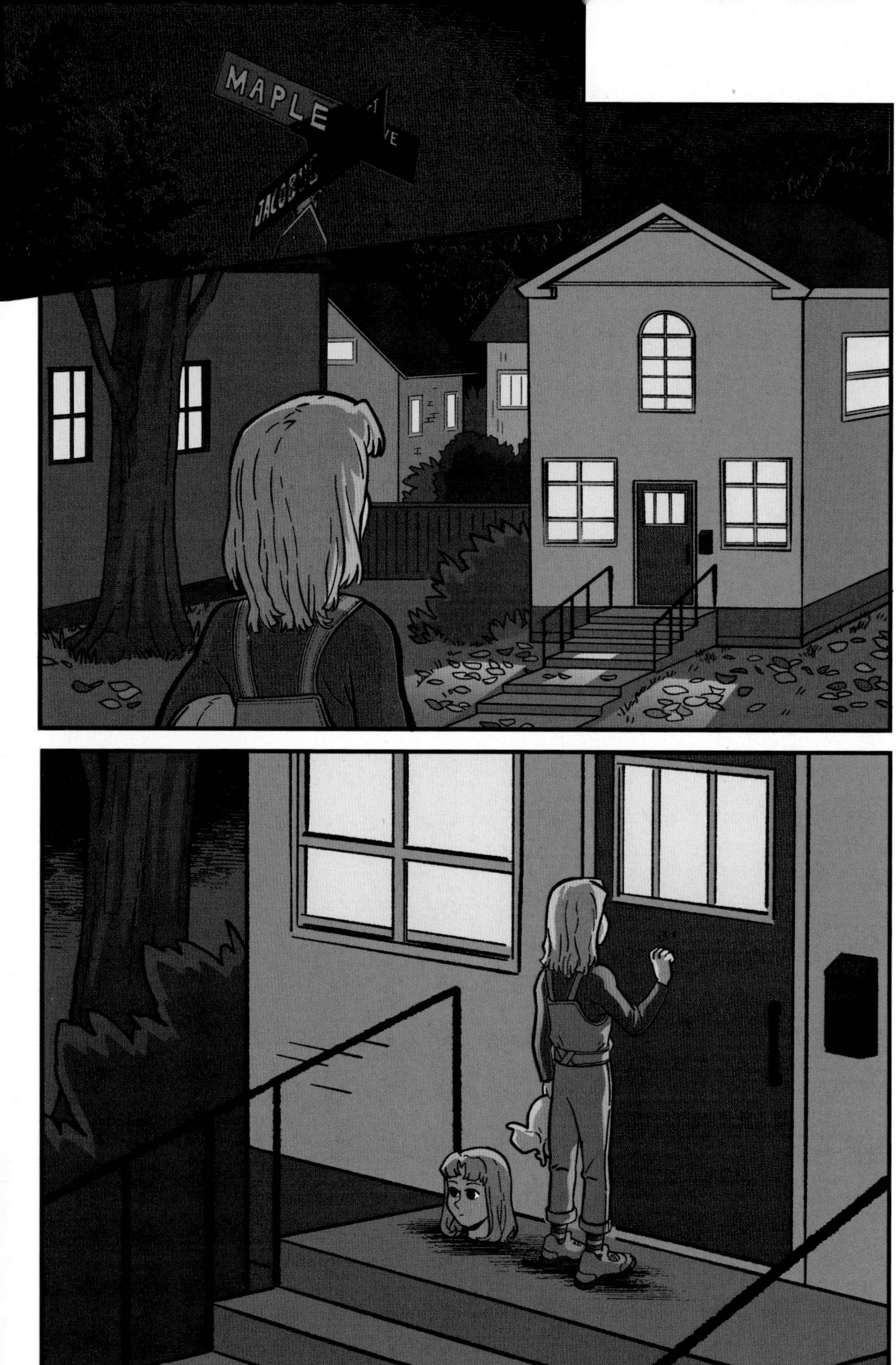
MAPLE

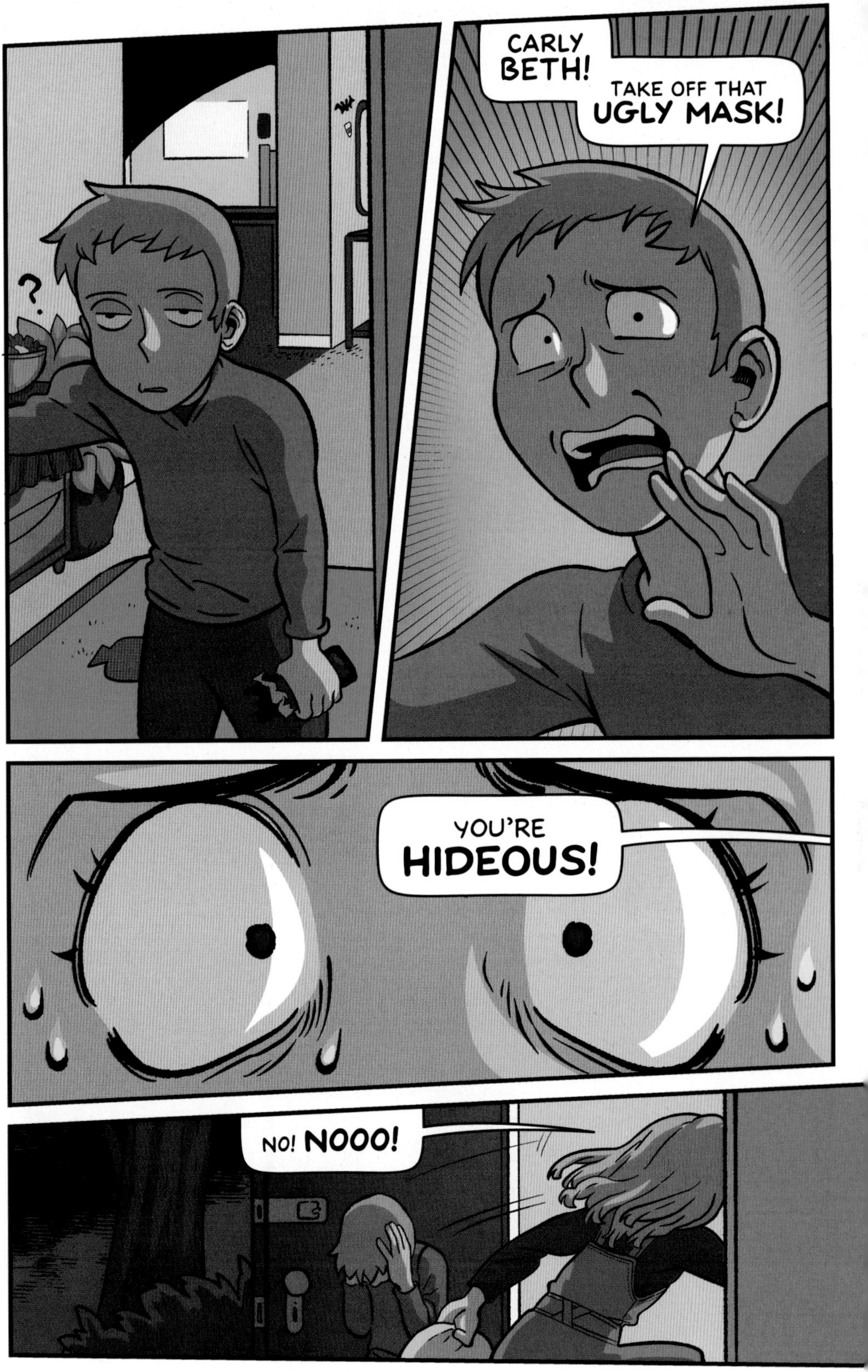
?
CARLY BETH!
TAKE OFF THAT UGLY MASK!
YOU'RE HIDEOUS!
NO! NOOO!

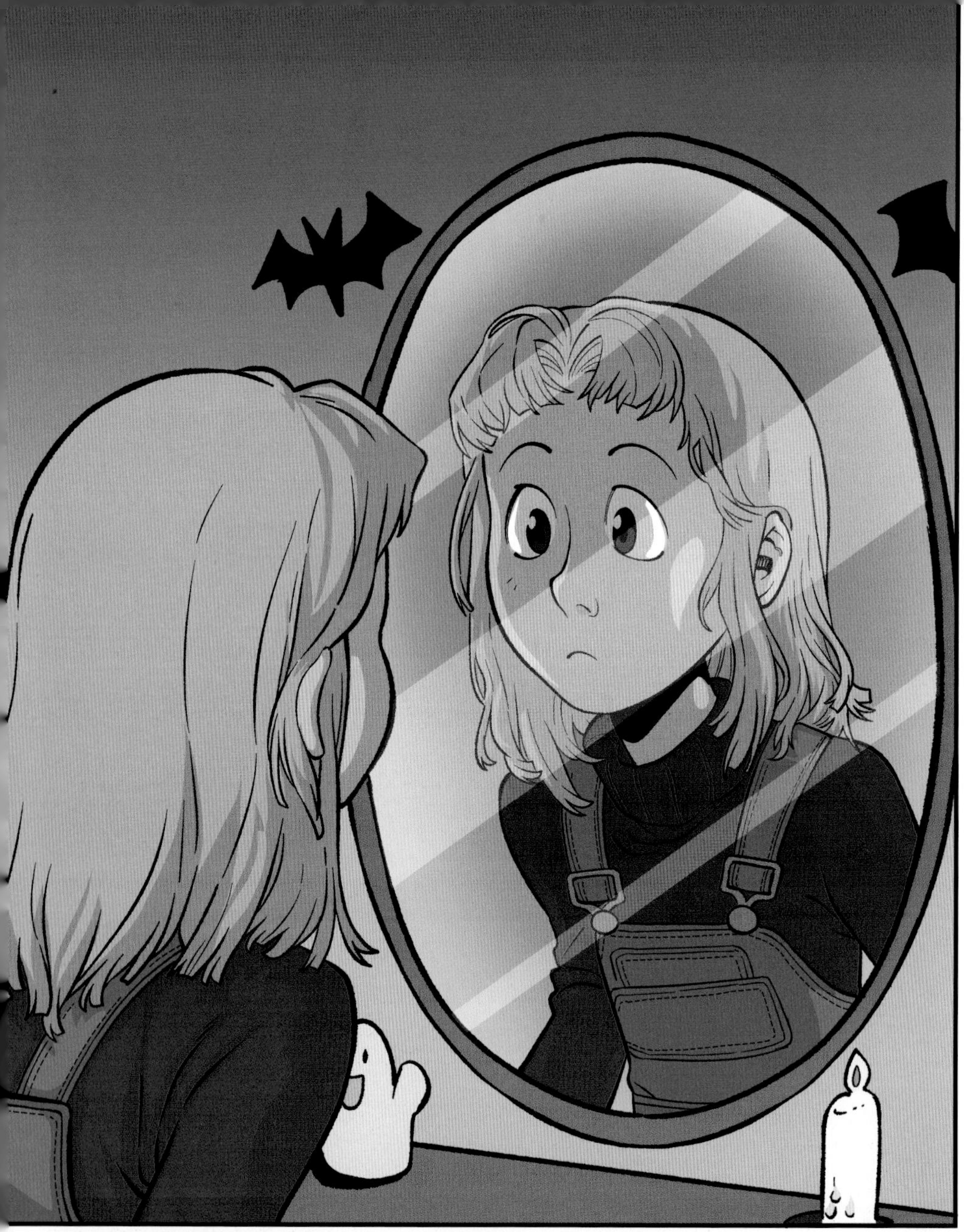

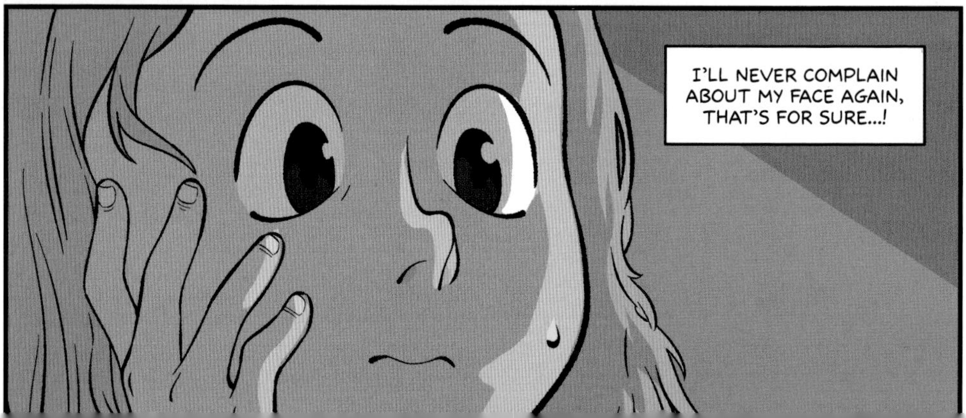
I'LL NEVER COMPLAIN ABOUT MY FACE AGAIN, THAT'S FOR SURE...!

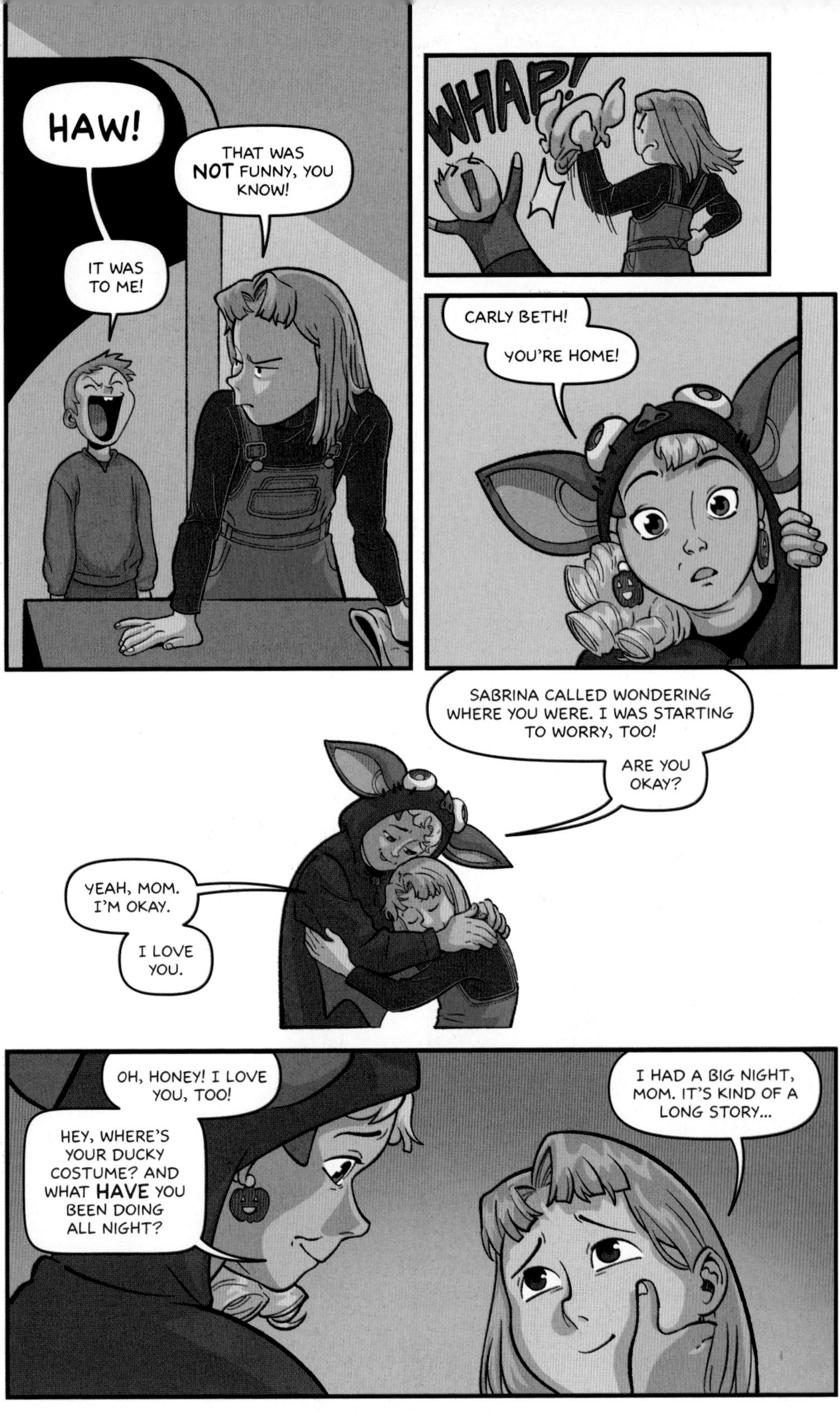
HAW!
IT WAS TO ME!
THAT WAS NOT FUNNY, YOU KNOW!
WHAP!
CARLY BETH!
YOU'RE HOME!
SABRINA CALLED WONDERING WHERE YOU WERE. I WAS STARTING TO WORRY, TOO!
ARE YOU OKAY?
YEAH, MOM. I'M OKAY.
I LOVE YOU.
OH, HONEY! I LOVE YOU, TOO!
HEY, WHERE'S YOUR DUCKY COSTUME? AND WHAT HAVE YOU BEEN DOING ALL NIGHT?
I HAD A BIG NIGHT, MOM. IT'S KIND OF A LONG STORY...

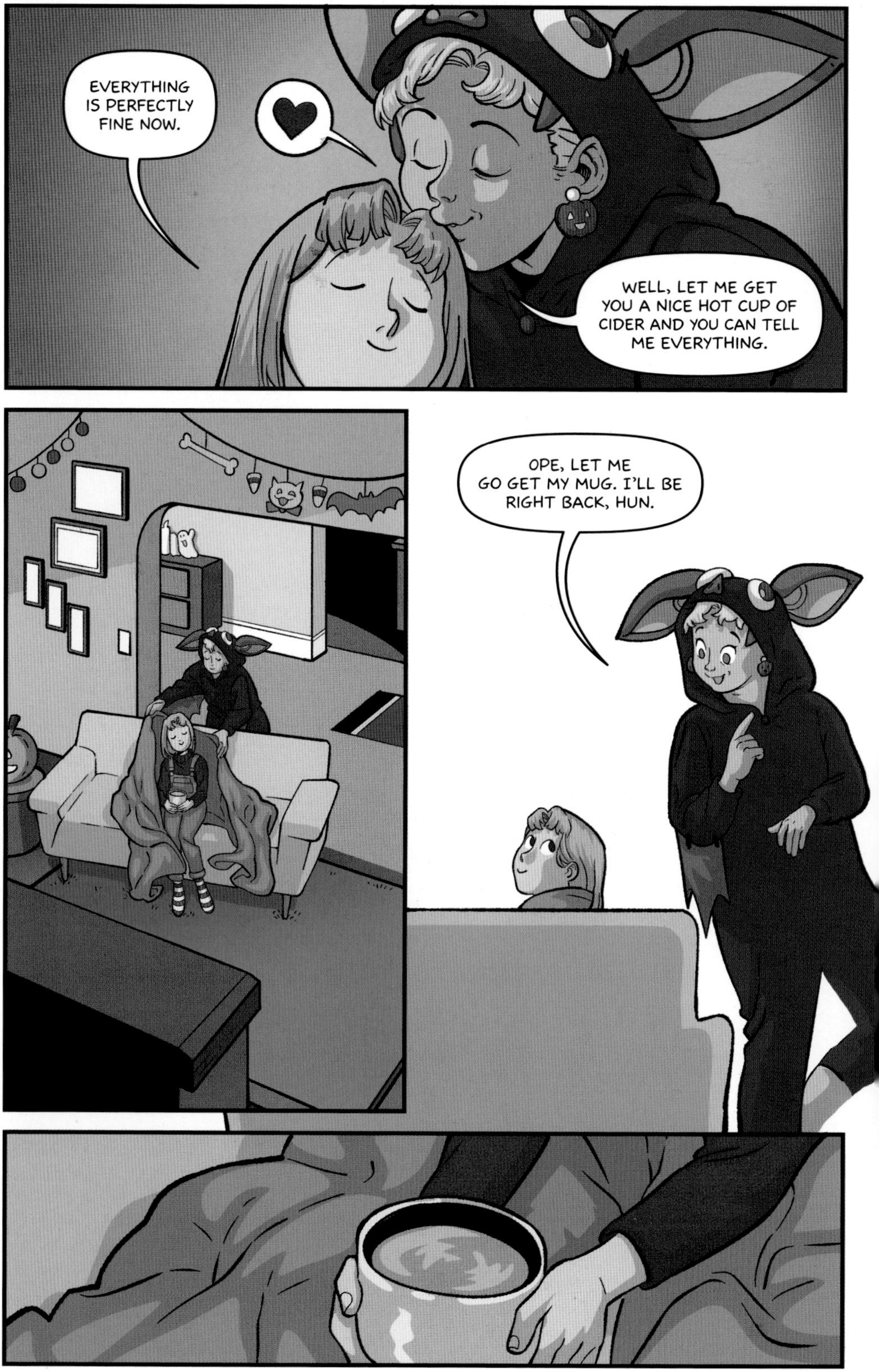
EVERYTHING IS PERFECTLY FINE NOW.
WELL, LET ME GET YOU A NICE HOT CUP OF CIDER AND YOU CAN TELL ME EVERYTHING.
OPE, LET ME GO GET MY MUG. I'LL BE RIGHT BACK, HUN.

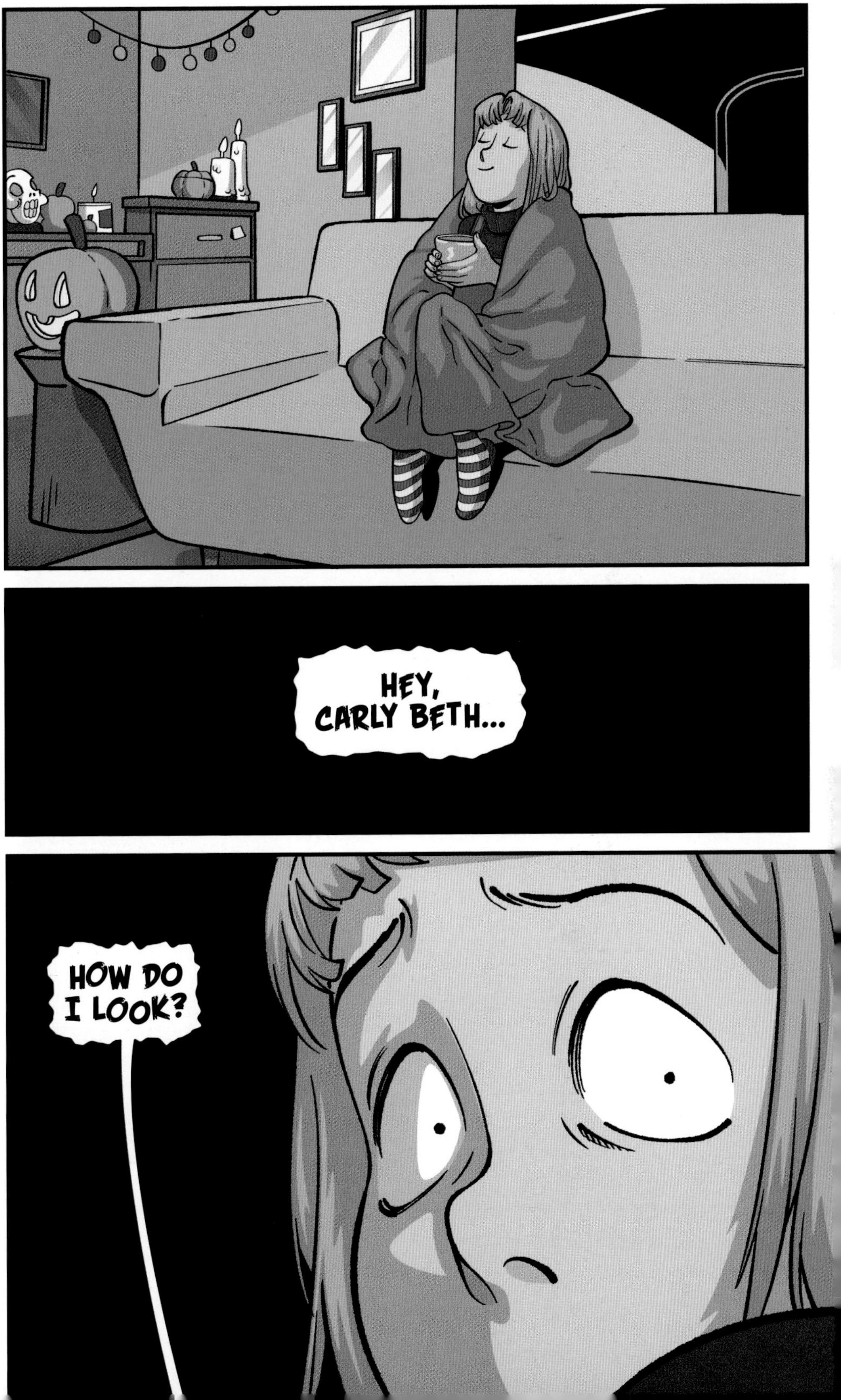
HEY, CARLY BETH...
HOW DO I LOOK?

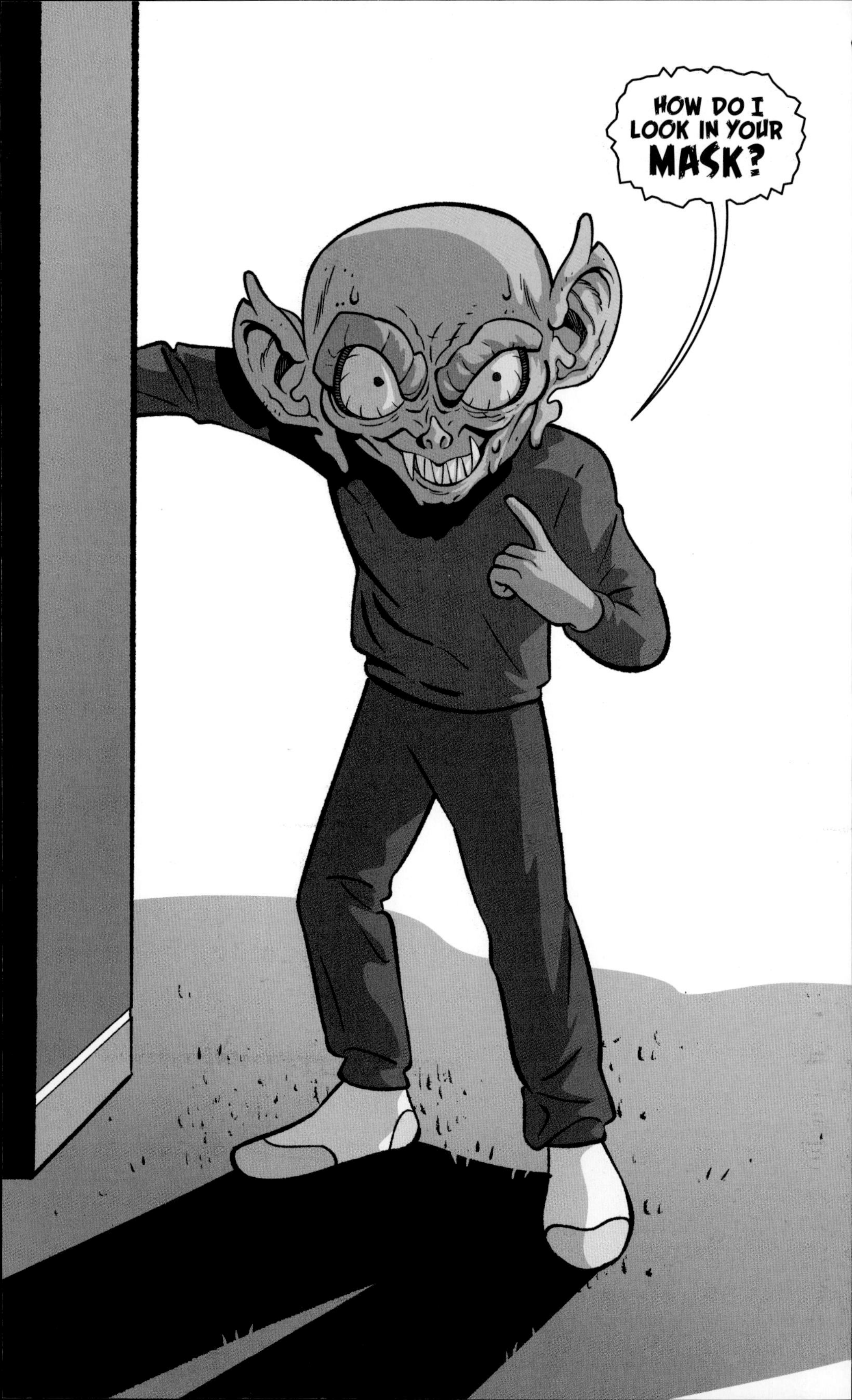
HOW DO I LOOK IN YOUR MASK?

Goosebumps

BONUS COMICS

IF YOU DON'T LAUGH, YOU'LL SCREAM!

ALTERNATE ENDING

THAT MASK WILL STAY ON... FOREVER!!!
NOOOOOO
GET IT OFF GET IT OFF G—
PO
P!
OH, THAT WAS EASY, ACTUALLY. SEE YA.
???
?

I CAN SAY NO MORE...

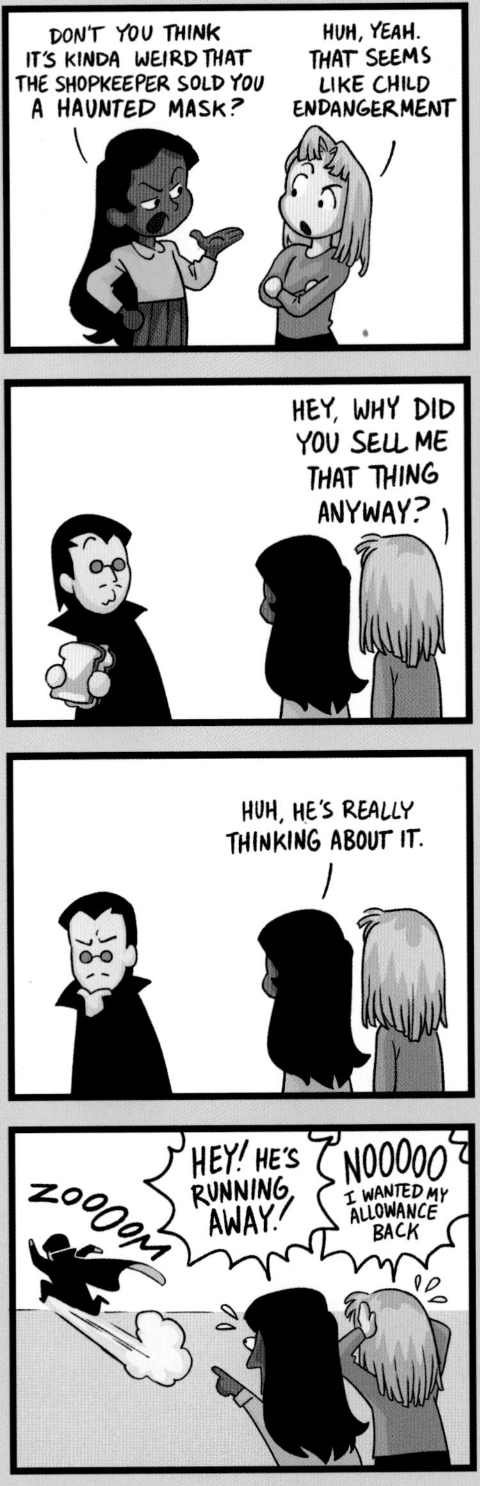

DON'T YOU THINK IT'S KINDA WEIRD THAT THE SHOPKEEPER SOLD YOU A HAUNTED MASK?
HUH, YEAH. THAT SEEMS LIKE CHILD ENDANGERMENT
HEY, WHY DID YOU SELL ME THAT THING ANYWAY?
HUH, HE'S REALLY THINKING ABOUT IT.
ZOOOOM
HEY! HE'S RUNNING AWAY!
NOOOOO I WANTED MY ALLOWANCE BACK

READER, BE CHILL

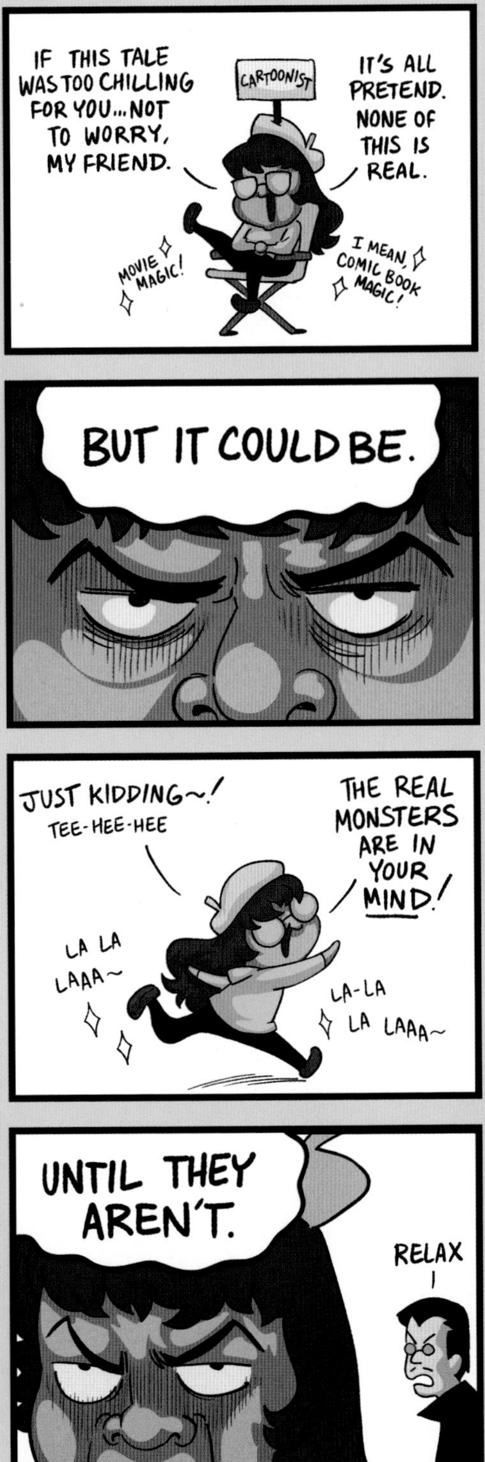

IF THIS TALE WAS TOO CHILLING FOR YOU... NOT TO WORRY, MY FRIEND.
CARTOONIST
IT'S ALL PRETEND. NONE OF THIS IS REAL.
MOVIE MAGIC!
I MEAN, COMIC BOOK MAGIC!
BUT IT COULD BE.
JUST KIDDING~! TEE-HEE-HEE
THE REAL MONSTERS ARE IN YOUR MIND!
LA LA LAAA~
LA-LA LA LAAA~
UNTIL THEY AREN'T.
RELAX

THE HAUNTED MASK:
FROM CHAPTER BOOK TO GRAPHIC NOVEL

When I was a kid, I liked to take scenes from my favorite books and draw them like comic pages. This was my first adventure into the world of ADAPTATION. What's an adaptation, you ask? The graphic novel you are holding in your hands is an example! Creating an adaptation means transforming an existing piece of media (like a novel) into another kind of media (like a graphic novel or movie).

As the cartoonist behind this book, I got to take the original material and create a whole new way to tell the story!

When developing the visual world of the Goosebumps graphic novels, a lot of work goes into keeping things consistent, and making everything feel real.

I go through multiple iterations of each character and location until I land upon the look that I want, with help from my team. Our editor, designer, color artist, and letterer all work together to make the book shine!

DEVELOPING THE CHARACTERS

I like to think about certain things like: "What would this character wear? How would they stand? How would parts of their design express or conceal aspects of their personality?" Sometimes, I refer to other official Goosebumps adaptations for inspiration.

When I've settled on looks for the characters, I draw their designs on a model sheet so I can remember their proportions and design throughout the long process of drawing the book. Sometimes things will change while I'm drawing the pages! When this happens, I make sure to keep a note of the tweaks.

Here's something I always make sure to keep handy: a drawing of everyone screaming in terror, of course!

The character designs changed a lot from the beginning of the book's development!

USING 3D MODELING

I use a computer program called Blender to create 3D models of different locations in the comic. I can use these models almost like movie sets, to keep my drawings consistent. I take images of the models and open them in my drawing program to plan the comic panels and add details.

I also use software to create 3D models of my characters' heads. It's useful to have 3D versions of characters' heads to refer to so I can draw them appropriately from every angle. The mask's ears had a tricky geometry. Referring to the model helped me make sure the mask always looked just right.

Speaking of which, did you notice that the mask's ears have a peculiar shape? You may recognize that the shape is quite similar to the iconic "G" in the original Goosebumps logo.

COVER ART

Our team had a lot of different ideas about how to approach creating the book cover. I started with some small thumbnail sketches to help us figure out what we were feeling. Some were simple, and some were more elaborate. There was a variety of moods and compositions, but our team narrowed it down to a few final ideas!

Ultimately, we settled on the version you have now. It was pretty tricky to finalize the mask's expression!

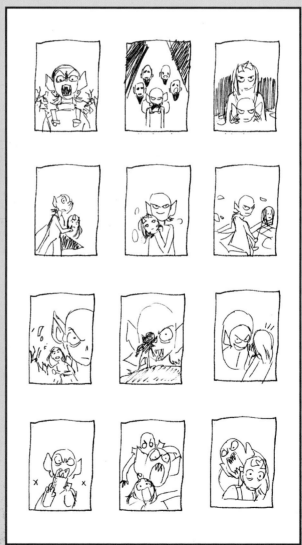

FIND CURLY

Curly is a skeleton with attitude! This handsome bag of bones is one of the most recognizable of the 1990s' Goosebumps mascots. Initially brought to life by iconic Goosebumps illustrator Tim Jacobus, Curly is a beloved icon of horror— or, at least, that's what he's telling me to write here. I gave him my phone number and he won't leave me alone.

Can you spot where we've hidden an appearance of CURLY THE SKELETON?

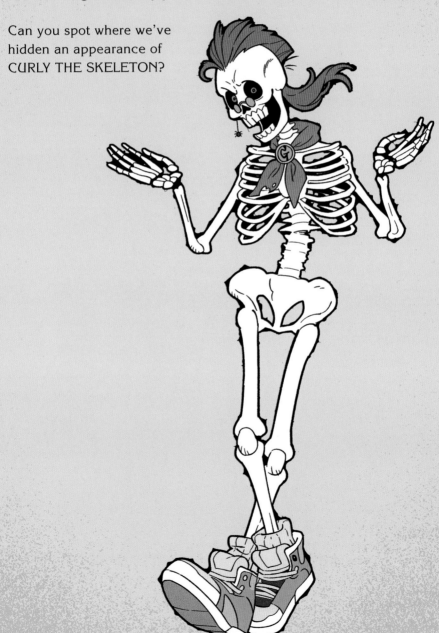

Goosebumps

GET THE ORIGINAL BOOKS—
BEFORE THEY GET YOU!

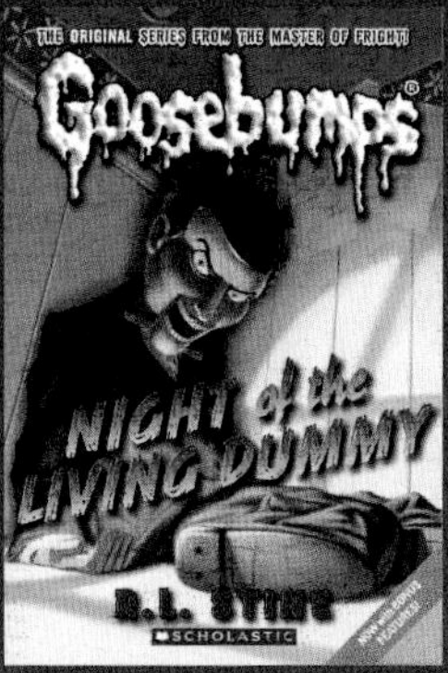
THE ORIGINAL SERIES FROM THE MASTER OF FRIGHT!
Goosebumps®
NIGHT of the LIVING DUMMY
R.L. STINE
SCHOLASTIC

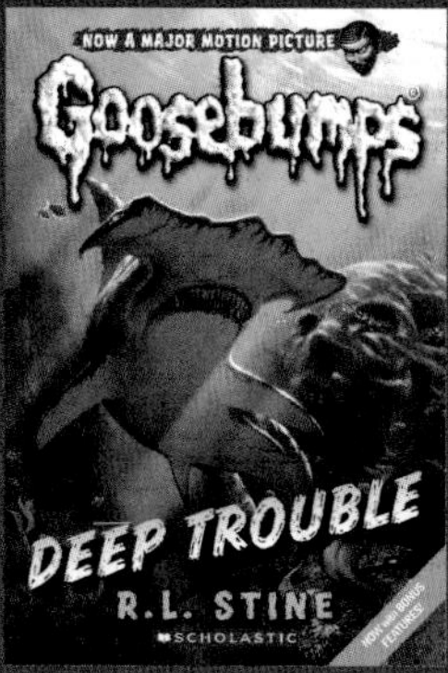
NOW A MAJOR MOTION PICTURE
Goosebumps®
DEEP TROUBLE
R.L. STINE
SCHOLASTIC

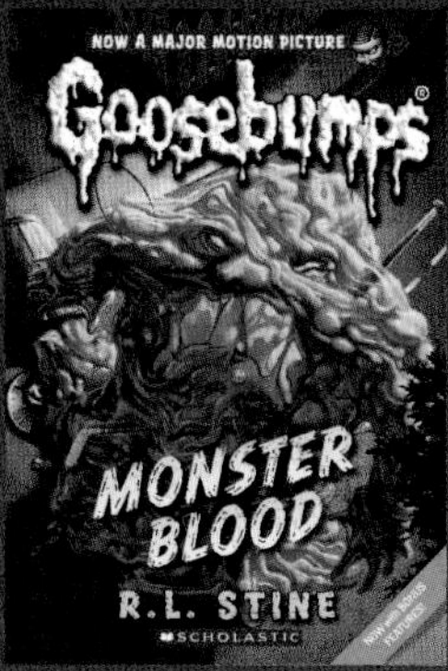
NOW A MAJOR MOTION PICTURE
Goosebumps®
MONSTER BLOOD
R.L. STINE
SCHOLASTIC

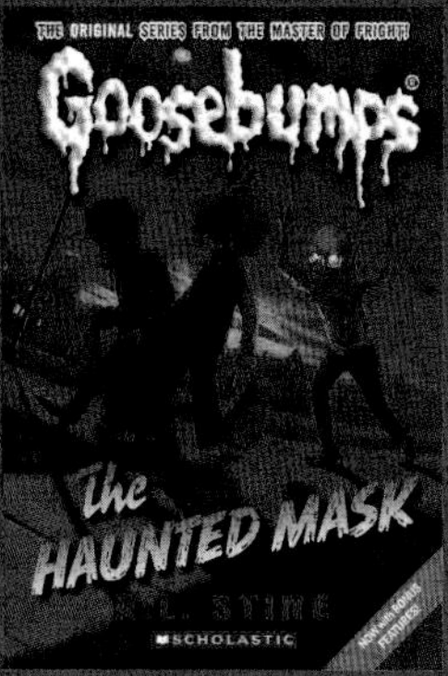
THE ORIGINAL SERIES FROM THE MASTER OF FRIGHT!
Goosebumps®
The HAUNTED MASK
SCHOLASTIC

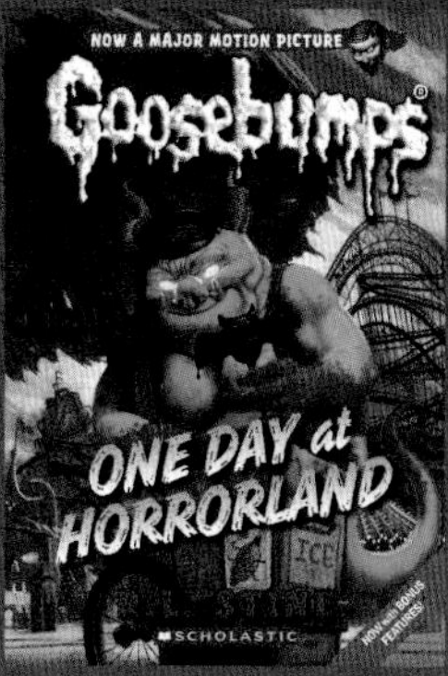
NOW A MAJOR MOTION PICTURE
Goosebumps®
ONE DAY at HORRORLAND
SCHOLASTIC

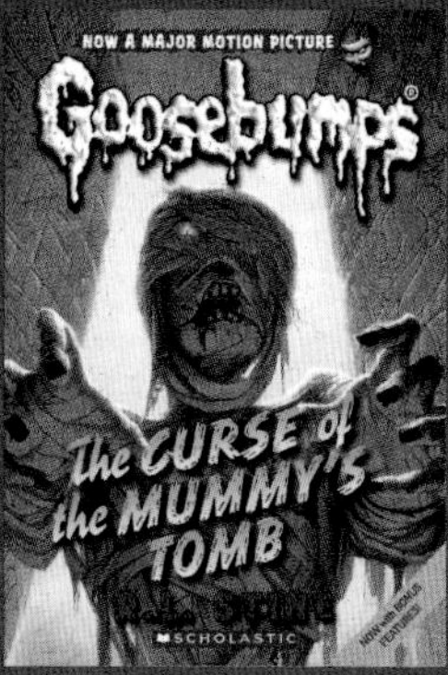
NOW A MAJOR MOTION PICTURE
Goosebumps®
The CURSE of the MUMMY'S TOMB
SCHOLASTIC

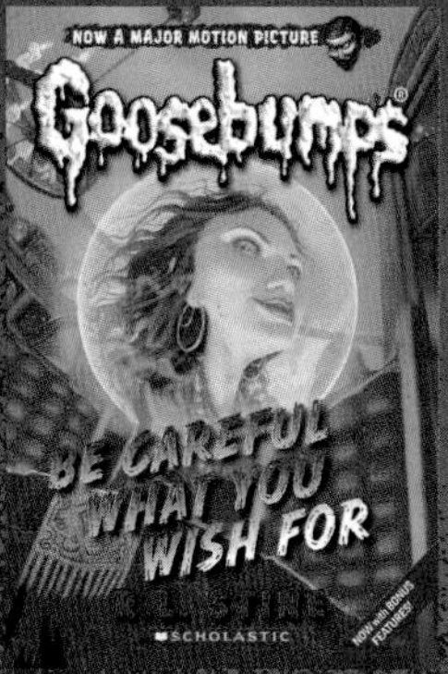
NOW A MAJOR MOTION PICTURE
Goosebumps®
BE CAREFUL WHAT YOU WISH FOR
SCHOLASTIC

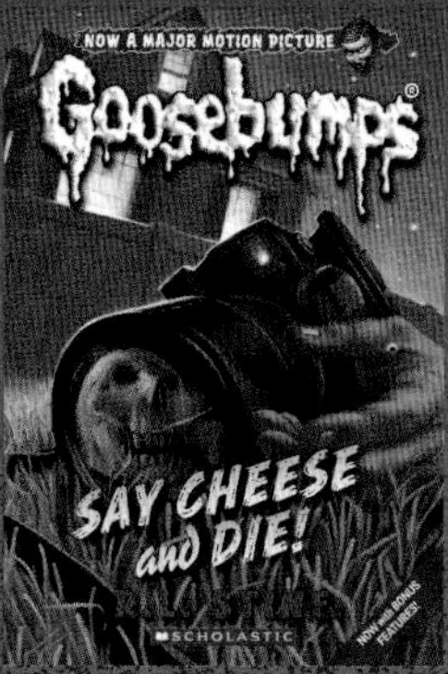
NOW A MAJOR MOTION PICTURE
Goosebumps®
SAY CHEESE and DIE!
SCHOLASTIC

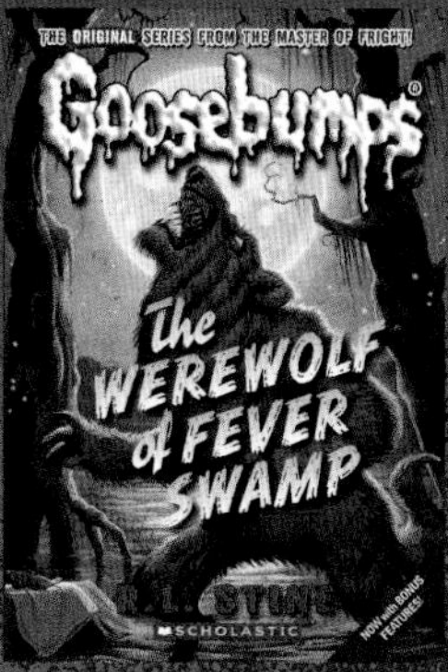
THE ORIGINAL SERIES FROM THE MASTER OF FRIGHT!
Goosebumps®
The WEREWOLF of FEVER SWAMP
SCHOLASTIC

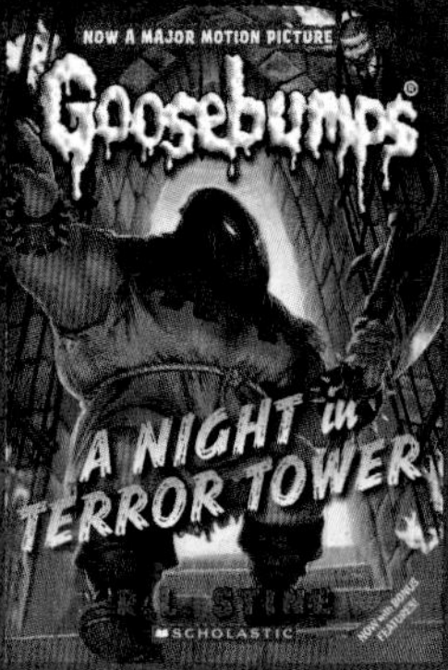
NOW A MAJOR MOTION PICTURE
Goosebumps
A NIGHT in TERROR TOWER
R.L. STINE
SCHOLASTIC

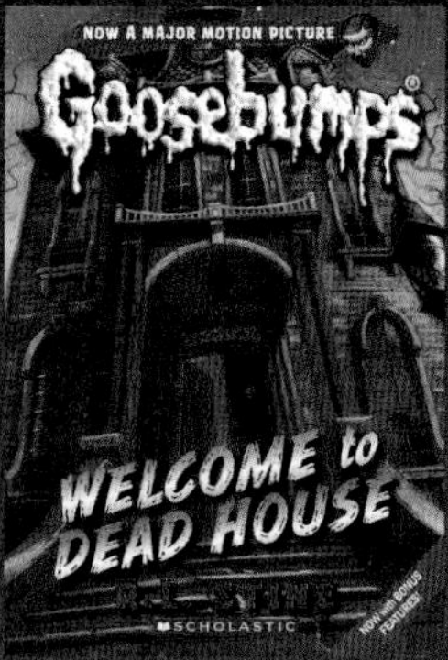
NOW A MAJOR MOTION PICTURE
Goosebumps
WELCOME to DEAD HOUSE
R.L. STINE
SCHOLASTIC

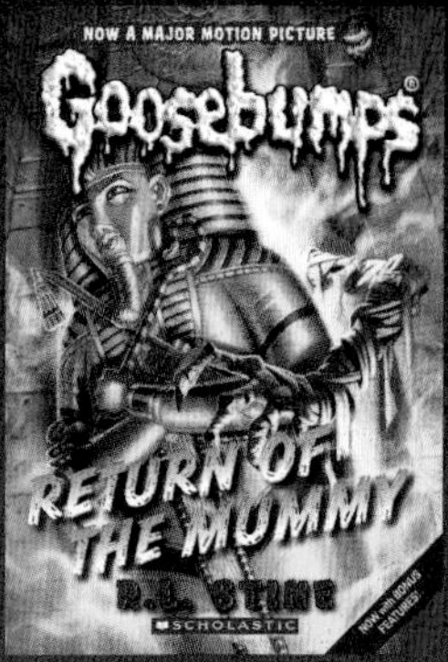
NOW A MAJOR MOTION PICTURE
Goosebumps
RETURN OF THE MUMMY
R.L. STINE
SCHOLASTIC

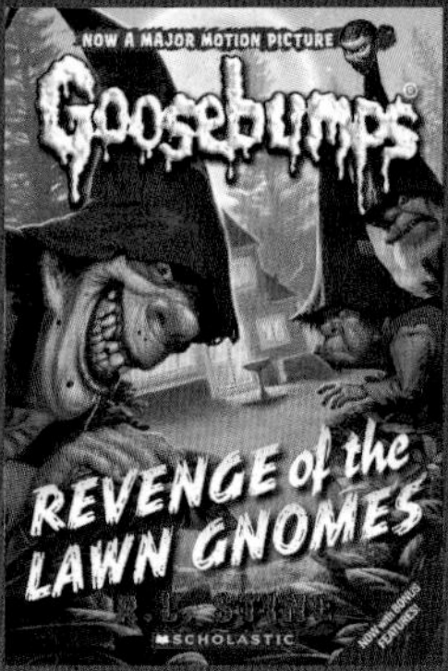
NOW A MAJOR MOTION PICTURE
Goosebumps
REVENGE of the LAWN GNOMES
R.L. STINE
SCHOLASTIC

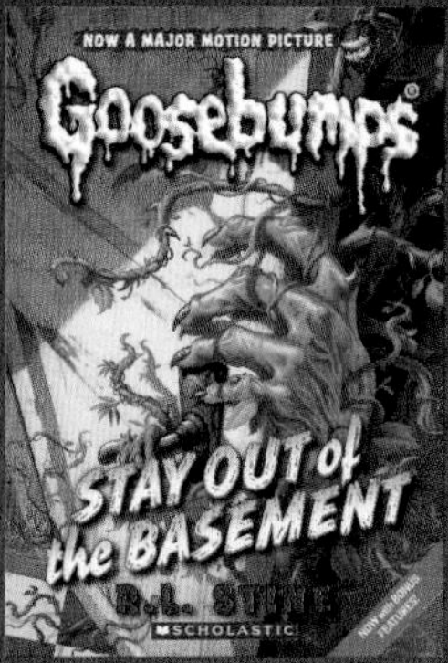
NOW A MAJOR MOTION PICTURE
Goosebumps
STAY OUT of the BASEMENT
R.L. STINE
SCHOLASTIC

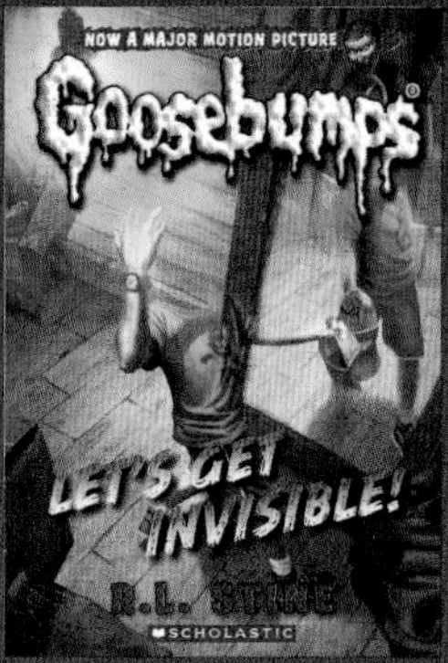
NOW A MAJOR MOTION PICTURE
Goosebumps
LET'S GET INVISIBLE!
R.L. STINE
SCHOLASTIC

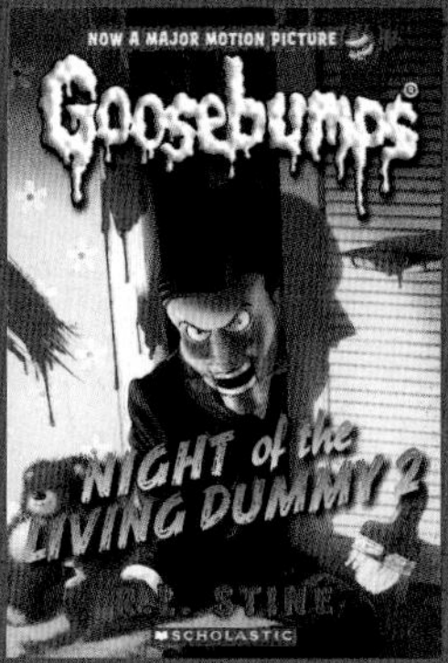
NOW A MAJOR MOTION PICTURE
Goosebumps
NIGHT of the LIVING DUMMY 2
R.L. STINE
SCHOLASTIC

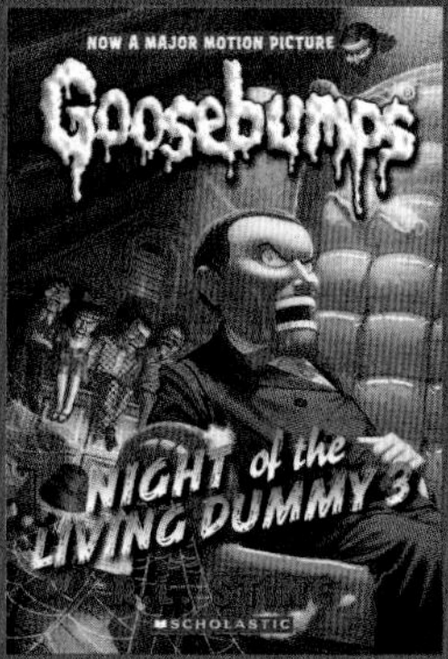
NOW A MAJOR MOTION PICTURE
Goosebumps
NIGHT of the LIVING DUMMY 3
SCHOLASTIC

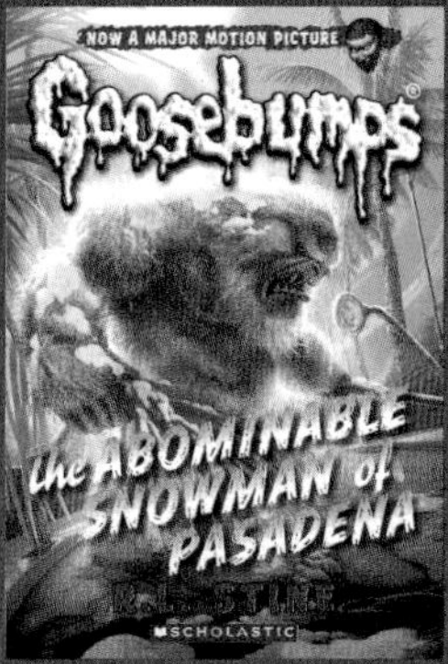
NOW A MAJOR MOTION PICTURE
Goosebumps
the ABOMINABLE SNOWMAN of PASADENA
R.L. STINE
SCHOLASTIC

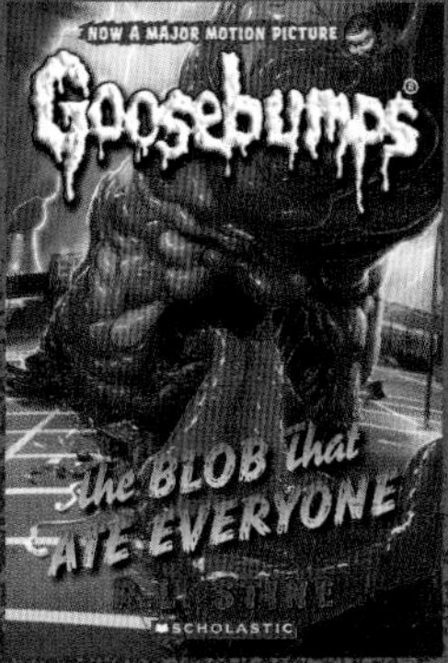
NOW A MAJOR MOTION PICTURE
Goosebumps
the BLOB that ATE EVERYONE
SCHOLASTIC

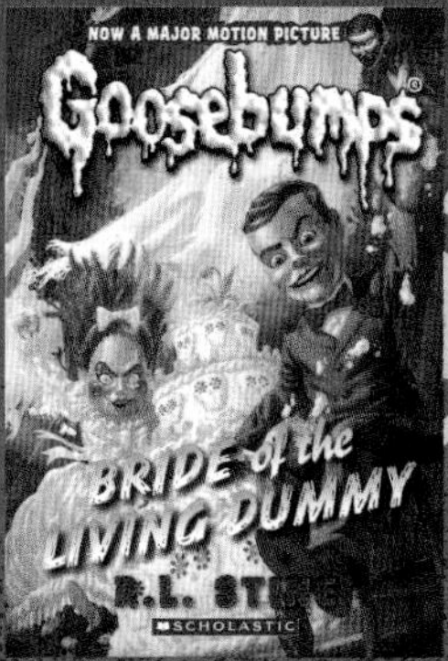
NOW A MAJOR MOTION PICTURE
Goosebumps
BRIDE of the LIVING DUMMY
SCHOLASTIC

All 62 original Goosebumps books available as ebooks!

GOOSEBUMPS SLAPPYWORLD

SLAPPY BIRTHDAY TO YOU
R.L. STINE

ATTACK OF THE JACK!
R.L. STINE

I AM SLAPPY'S EVIL TWIN
R.L. STINE

PLEASE DO NOT FEED THE WEIRDO
R.L. STINE

ESCAPE FROM SHUDDER MANSION
R.L. STINE

THE GHOST OF SLAPPY
R.L. STINE

IT'S ALIVE! IT'S ALIVE!
R.L. STINE

THE DUMMY MEETS THE MUMMY!
R.L. STINE

REVENGE OF THE INVISIBLE BOY
R.L. STINE

DIARY OF A DUMMY
R.L. STINE

THEY CALL ME THE NIGHT HOWLER!
R.L. STINE

MY FRIEND SLAPPY
R.L. STINE

MONSTER BLOOD IS BACK
R.L. STINE

FIFTH-GRADE ZOMBIES
R.L. STINE

JUDY AND THE BEAST
R.L. STINE

SLAPPY IN DREAMLAND
R.L. STINE

HAUNTING WITH THE STARS
R.L. STINE

NIGHT OF THE SQUAWKER
R.L. STINE

FRIIIGHT NIGHT
R.L. STINE

THIS IS SLAPPY'S WORLD—
YOU ONLY SCREAM IN IT!

Goosebumps
HOUSE OF SHIVERS

THE ONLY THING TO FEAR... IS EVERYTHING.

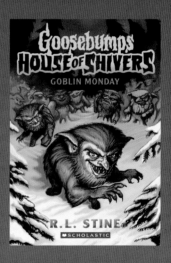

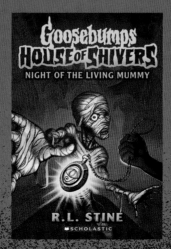

R.L. STINE says he gets to scare people all over the world. So far, his books have sold more than 400 million copies, making him one of the most popular children's authors in history. The Goosebumps series has more than 150 titles and has inspired a TV series and two motion pictures. R.L. Stine himself is a character in the movies! He has also written the teen series Fear Street, which has been adapted into three Netflix movies, as well as other scary book series. His newest picture book for little kids, illustrated by Marc Brown, is titled *Why Did the Monster Cross the Road?* R.L. Stine lives in New York City with his wife, Jane, a former editor and publisher. You can learn more about him at rlstine.com.

MADDI GONZALEZ is a cartoonist from the Rio Grande Valley, Texas. Her Ignatz Award–nominated comic art has a strong focus on humor and horror. Her favorite Goosebumps books are a tie between *The Headless Ghost* and *Stay Out of the Basement*.